THE BINDING MARK

SOPHIE WILLIAMSON

Storm
PUBLISHING

Ebook ISBN: 978-1-80508-267-5
Paperback ISBN: 978-1-80508-269-9

Cover design: Eileen Carey
Cover images: Shutterstock

Published by Storm Publishing.
For further information, visit:
www.stormpublishing.co

Sticking with a theme, this one's for all the wider family

PROLOGUE

Sadie Sadler,

We've been aware of your presence in our city for some time now, but you've kept yourself in the shadows, denying your power and fighting to live a normal life. After this summer, I suspect that's going to change.
We've heard the basics of the things that happened in Mannith. We always like to keep a close eye on our provincial cousins and old allies. And now, we find ourselves in need of someone with your unique combination of magical strength and legal prowess. There are all sorts of ways in which I could make good use of a practitioner lawyer, but above all, I need you to help me prove that vampires can't always get away with murder.
I'll admit that my motivation is revenge and that they're a dangerous group to cross, considering most of our powers don't work on them. But if it helps, bloodsuckers are all reactionary bastards. Perhaps you'd like an opportunity to teach some stuck-up rich guys who regard people as livestock a lesson in human rights?

*Meet me on Hampstead Heath at midnight, and we can discuss
the terms of your membership.*

Yours,

Lavinia Morven
Matriarch of the London Coven

PART 1

ONE

SADIE

Some people say London is the most magical city in the world, but I'm something of an expert, and it's never felt like that to me. Too many people and buildings. Too much weight of history. Dirt, pollution, homelessness and poverty behind the glamourous façade. A material, atomised, rootless kind of place. Great cocktail bars and pop-up restaurants though, I'll give it that.

After growing up in Mannith, a place saturated with magic and wonder, the gritty anonymity and realness of London is always half like coming up for air and half like the sun passing behind a cloud.

I've been back here for a matter of hours, but it's already been a long, emotionally draining day. Hell, it's been a long, emotionally draining summer.

For the last six years, I'd stayed away from Mannith, magic, and my family, in order to prevent Gabriel Thornber, the heir to my family's only rivals, from claiming on our twisted deal: sex and magic in return for sparing the life of my brother, Brendan.

But then a few months ago, my family finally persuaded me

to come back, in order to defend Brendan, who was on trial for the murder of Gabriel's father.

And what a summer it proved to be.

I started using magic again and realised just how powerful I really am.

I learnt that my own family rely on human sacrifices to keep the Dome intact and that my brother was planning a full-blown massacre in order to expand it—revelations that have put my usually close relationship with them all under strain.

And then there was Gabriel himself. He broke the lien voluntarily and he stole my heart. He claimed that his dead, demonic mother had foretold that he and I were meant to be together. And so he manipulated everything he could, in order to make me his. Ironically, I could have forgiven him pretty much all his prior misdeeds—which are numerous, to say the least—were it not for the fact he tried to play me.

I'm pretty sure I love him. I certainly lust after him. But I'm less sure I actually like him. And after the way he's behaved and the effect he has on me, I can't risk a relationship. So I left for London, and he promised he'd try to be less intense. And we both knew there was no hope of that without some time and distance between us.

When I made it back to London a few hours ago, I wanted nothing more than to curl up on the sofa, order an unhealthy takeaway, then fall into bed and attempt to sleep away the heartbreak. But there was no ignoring the letter from Lavinia:

"*Meet me on Hampstead Heath at midnight, and we can discuss the terms of your membership... Lavinia Morven, Matriarch of the London Coven.*"

So here I am, out on Hampstead Heath at midnight, beneath a full moon. It's a sprawling ancient piece of land, whose overgrown oak and beech woods, secluded ponds, and wild grassy expanses make it look, smell, and feel more like the countryside than the capital.

I'm at the tip of Parliament Hill, with the London skyline below me, surrounded by an inner and outer circle of practitioners. I've just traversed into place, and now the most beautiful woman I've ever seen is standing opposite me, staring like a scientist who's just found an interesting new specimen.

Against the odds, there's magic in the air.

"Sadie! Darling! I'm so glad you could make it."

The woman, presumably Lavinia Morven, notorious Matriarch of the London Coven, makes it sound like she's invited me for birthday drinks at a local pub.

I force a smile. "Nice to meet you, Lavinia. I've heard a lot about you."

"From your gorgeous father, no doubt. He's such a sweetheart."

Enemies, allies, and friends alike use a lot of words to describe my dad. "Sweetheart" is not generally the first one that springs to mind when confronted with the muscular, commanding practitioner in his early sixties.

Just like Dad's vague descriptions, Lavinia is willowy, with an English rose complexion, hair down to her chest in a hundred different shades of blonde, and huge blue eyes. And massive boobs on her otherwise slender frame, though Dad never specified that. But that description of a generically attractive woman (aside from the small detail of her diamond-shaped, practitioner pupils) doesn't do justice to all the little perfect details and the glow radiating from her.

Despite being back in London, I'd used magic to style and straighten my shoulder-length, naturally curly dark hair, brighten my pale complexion, and better shape my black dress to my curves. I'd been pleased with the result. But now, I feel dowdy in comparison.

"I gather you and Dad were friends back in the eighties and nineties," I say. "Or business associates. Something like that."

She gives a tinkling little laugh. "Something like that. Quite."

If my dad met her when he was in his twenties—by which point she was already a powerful force on the London magical scene—she must be at least as old as him. And yet, she appears to be just a couple of years older than me.

Few older female practitioners show their age. My mum is sixty and looks like a polished forty-five-year-old, as though she's used the magical equivalent of Botox and liposuction on herself. But Lavinia genuinely looks like a particularly stunning thirty-year-old.

I know that to look like that, in magical terms, is the difference between donning a temporary disguise and fundamentally altering the structure of your body. You'd have to consciously keep the spell going at all times while getting on with whatever else you were doing. Rather like body-switching, it shouldn't be possible, but considering Gabriel turned out to be capable of the former, perhaps I needed to rethink our limitations.

"It's more impressive than you think," she says. "I was born in 1930. I look great for my age, don't I? As I always tell the clients at my wellness emporium, it's so important to avoid smoking, do yoga, and take your vitamins."

I laugh, even though she's read my thoughts and is apparently over ninety. "They must be some awfully powerful multivitamins."

"Indeed. Though as I tell my more *specialist* clients, a lot of magic and a little vampire blood works wonders, too. For your hair and skin, as well as for your telepathy skills."

"Vampire blood? Really?" I wince at the idea. Most practitioners have a natural aversion to vampires. Their blood-drinking ways are an uncomfortable reminder for us that however much we witches may act human, we all ultimately share the same demonic lineage.

I've heard the theory that drinking vampire blood can shore up your powers. One of those funny old pieces of practitioner lore. But I didn't realise it was something anyone attempted nowadays, or that it actually worked. Aside from the practicalities—how would you even get a vampire to donate enough blood?—it feels wrong, unnatural. Most practitioners harbour dreams of being stronger than they naturally are but few, if any, would resort to something like that.

Lavinia laughs. "Don't look so horrified. I've been taking it for decades. There's always something rather satisfying about seducing a vampire and making him give you his blood, rather than vice versa. But more importantly, it's kept me young. And the cumulative effect over the years has taken my natural powers from strong but unremarkable to the sort of level you usually only see in top lineages where families have kept the blood from getting diluted or where recent demon ancestry is involved."

Those two alternative options would essentially describe me and Gabriel, respectively. Desperate not to pursue that line of conversation, I glance around the circle in the hope of spying a familiar or friendly face. The only person I remotely recognise is Chris, the human guy I'd been tricked into going on a date with when my family had asked Lavinia to get a message to me at the start of the summer. He tries to make eye contact and give me a welcoming smile, but I look away. That little episode is in no way forgiven.

I turn back to Lavinia and attempt to take control of the conversation. "You ordered me here, and I came. What do you want to discuss?"

"Let's take a seat." She gestures behind me to a wide swinging chair that hadn't been there before.

I sit down gingerly, but the seat's solid enough and doesn't do anything alarming like pin me in place.

"Drink?" Lavinia sits down beside me.

A silver tray holding two large and heavily garnished gin goblets appears between us. I could use a drink, but I shake my head.

The relentless magic is obviously designed to impress, but I've lived with magic my entire life and could easily replicate her conjuring tricks if I wanted to. My mum's always been scathing of people who regularly use magic just to show off or to achieve things they could do as easily by hand. Still, for all that she's acting like she's got something to prove, it's obvious she possesses some serious magical firepower.

"Ah, the old 'not accepting drinks from strangers in case it puts you in their power' routine. How quaint. Have it your way. Though the drink is entirely untampered with. And I heard you like gin and tonic, so I got you something from one of my favourite artisan distilleries."

She smiles and takes a delicate sip of her own drink.

If she's as good at telepathy as seems to be the case, she can presumably sense my discomposure, but pride demands I at least made a show of not giving a damn. I breathe in once and out once. If only I could attempt a full-blown core meditation.

"The situation is really quite straightforward. You are in London. You are a Born Practitioner—a pretty powerful one by all accounts, and certainly one from a respected family. All the female witches in London are a part of my coven."

She gestures to the view in front of us. The main city is several miles away, but from our vantage point, it seems like we could almost touch it.

"I've lived in London for years," I reply.

"I know. I sensed you the instant you entered the city, straight out of university and ready to launch your legal career."

"But you didn't bother getting in touch?"

"You'd sworn off magic. My coven had no need for a non-practicing practitioner, and I had no need to keep your activities under control."

She finishes her drink, clicks her fingers, and starts on another. All the time, the rest of the group just stand there, watching and listening.

"And now?"

"You've spent the summer using your powers in all sorts of interesting ways. Near-murders, near-resurrections, influencing the outcome of major criminal trials."

"In Mannith. That's well outside the sway of the London Coven. What I do there is my family's business."

"Absolutely. I wouldn't want darling Philip to think I was attempting to impinge on his territory. But you're back now. So, here's the deal. You join the coven. You keep working as a lawyer and using your magic in a personal capacity. But you also put both your legal prowess and your practitioner skills to use for me. You'll be paid. You'll have the companionship of your own kind. And the opportunity to develop your impressive powers still further. Perhaps even a chance to rise through the ranks of the coven, especially as I won't be around forever."

"Or what?"

"Or I'm afraid you'll need to leave London."

"What if I just went back to my old way of life? Pretending to be a regular lawyer. London without magic."

"I don't believe for a moment that you could spend a summer living the practitioner lifestyle and then begin repressing yourself again."

She's right. I'm not intending to burn through quite so much magic as I did in Mannith, but the idea of abandoning it again completely is almost intolerable.

I look around the gathering once more. Those standing in the inner circle are all female and, judging from their auras, all Born Practitioners, albeit of differing strength levels.

Compared to the practitioners I know from back home, they're much more racially diverse. To the best of my knowledge, Nikki, Gabriel's best friend and second-in-command, my brother in law, Ray, and my twin baby nieces, Ceridwen and Chioma, are the only practitioners in Mannith who aren't white, which is pretty horrifying. At the same time, the members of the coven also appear to be from much wealthier backgrounds.

They look vaguely like the sort of people I hung around with at university or who inhabit my chambers at work. I could probably have a lovely brunch, yoga class, or wine tasting session with them. But while I don't know much about joining a proper old-fashioned coven, I suspect the connection's supposed to go a bit deeper than that.

They've also all either been very lucky in the genetic lottery, or, more likely, worked a fair amount of beautification magic over the years, albeit not quite to the same jaw-dropping extent as Lavinia. Their idea of how to make yourself look when it's entirely in your gift is also different from the girls in Mannith: less Kim Kardashian, more Kate Middleton.

The outer circle, on the other hand, contains both men and women, and on the whole, they appear to be either Learnt Practitioners or entirely without magic. When I'd spoken to Chris, following our disastrous date, he'd seemed convinced that if he served Lavinia and the coven faithfully enough, they'd eventually teach him magic. Looking at the eager eyes surrounding me, I'm ninety per cent convinced she's conning them all. Servitude now for some dubious promise of magic at an unspecified future date.

"Maybe," Lavinia says, replying to my unspoken thought. "But I wouldn't take advantage of you like that. Eager, willing human acolytes are a mass commodity. True witches are a valuable resource."

"Charming. And please don't read my mind."

"Surely you know how to stop me?"

Dad taught me to block telepathy around the time he was teaching me to read. But I've not practiced it in years. In London, few people can see your thoughts. In Mannith, those who can generally wouldn't risk trying it on me.

"How long do I have to decide?"

"Have a drink, if you dare. Talk to some of my girls. Or just have a walk around the heath to clear your head. Come back to me in an hour's time."

"An hour? That's ridiculous. It's a decision that would affect every facet of my life."

I'm not inherently against joining the coven, in the abstract. In London, my life has always revolved around work. Over the last couple of years, I've had no contact with fellow practitioners, and to be quite honest, a fairly limited social circle full stop. I'd need to understand better what the coven does and what its members are like, but the idea of a readymade friendship group, a connection to my culture, and the ability to use my magic in interesting ways has a certain appeal.

But I've got two big worries. The first is fairly straightforward. Traditional covens are rigidly hierarchical—I'd essentially be putting myself in Lavinia's power. My dad has always spoken highly of her, but that's quite a commitment to make to someone I've never met before. Besides, it's very different from my usual solitary and self-contained approach to life in London. And though Mannith is also extremely hierarchical in its own way, my position as a daughter of the ruling family always gave me an awful lot of leeway.

The second issue is more fundamental and more complex: initiation would mean committing myself to a life in London and truly giving up on Mannith. As I understand it, based on things Dad's mentioned about them in passing, if you join the coven, you join for the long term. And though you can leave London for trips, it needs to be your home.

There's a bit of me that would have loved to stay in Mannith and that's longing to return. To enjoy the unique magic of the town, to be a part of my close-knit, loving family again, and above all, to be with Gabriel.

But the town's joy and wonder are built on dark magic. My brother is capable of truly awful things, and to a lesser extent, so are the wider family. And though I'm pretty sure Gabriel is the love of my life, I simply cannot risk opening myself up to him after all the ways he's manipulated me over the years.

I need to stay away. Focus on my legal career and find a nice, normal man. But I worry that one phone call from Gabriel and I'll crack. That I'll agree to visit Mannith and never leave again. Joining the coven would remove my get-out clause. Which is simultaneously the best and worst thing about Lavinia's offer.

"It's a simple choice," Lavinia says, when I don't give a further response. "Listen to your heart, don't draw up a spreadsheet."

Mannith! Gabriel! Family! My heart or intuition or whatever knows exactly what it wants. But I've always been ruled by my head. And I can at least take Lavinia up on her suggestion to talk to current members.

I start with the inner circle, picking out a petite Black woman at random. She's wearing smart heels and a tailored navy-blue dress that highlights her toned arms. Her closely cropped hair shows off long, filigree earrings. I hover awkwardly in front of her, until she seizes the initiative by looping her arm through mine and leading me off to a park bench a few minutes' walk away.

"I'm Sadie," I say, once we're seated.

"So I gather. I'm Katrina Njoku."

The name triggers a flash of recognition that makes me examine her more closely. "Aren't you a politician?"

I've read about her and been pretty impressed. Grew up in

South London, campaigns for all sorts of social justice causes, in and out of parliament, but also gets her hands dirty with volunteer work. And captains the parliamentary women's football team, if I remember rightly. Though none of the glowing bios mentioned the minor detail of her being a Born Practitioner.

"As of the last election, yes. Women helping women, and all that. Lavinia believes in making people's dreams come true. She's working on getting me onto a select committee at the moment. A touch of mesmerism here, a few magical favours there. When the time's right, we'll push for a ministerial role."

"That sounds like one vote in favour of me joining the coven."

"Best decision I ever made," she says, with a smile. "My parents were powerful practitioners, but they always repressed their magic and made me do the same. It's been amazing to let it out."

If she or anyone else secretly hated Lavinia and the coven, they probably wouldn't risk admitting it here. But Katrina sounds genuinely positive.

"Why don't you speak to Lydia next?"

I glance around, trying to work out who she means. Suddenly, a tall, pale woman with waist-length red curls materialises in front of me. She's soaking wet and completely naked. Then she shakes her head, and instantaneously, she's dry and wearing a floaty white cotton dress that reaches the floor and billows out around her bare feet, as well as a chain of flowers around her neck.

"I decided to take a quick dip in the ladies' pond," she announces. "I'd rather dive from a cliff and swim in the Atlantic, but when you're in London, you commune with nature as best you can."

I visited the pond once, though on a hot summer's day rather than an autumn night. It's designed for public swimming, but it's surrounded by trees and filled with ducks and reeds. As the name suggests, it's strictly women only—a fact that some otherwise utterly staid middle-aged women take advantage of to swim nude. Not that there appears to be anything staid about Lydia.

Katrina smiles. "I've never known anyone to spend more time in water than you. Anyway, I'll leave you two to it."

"I'm Sadie," I say again, once Katrina walks away. I'm caught off guard by her dramatic appearance.

Before Lydia can reply, another coven member strides over. "Tell us something we don't know. The infamous Sadler family's perfect little princess."

The newcomer is a tall, toned white woman with dark hair cut into a bob and an almost painfully posh voice. She's sporting scarlet lipstick on an otherwise entirely unmade up face—her skin's radiant enough that she doesn't need any. She's wearing a simple outfit of jeans, riding boots and a crisp white shirt, but the clothes all fit her perfectly and look like they cost a small fortune. A huge, magnificent Dalmatian follows at her heels.

"I wouldn't say my family are that big a deal. Not outside of Yorkshire, anyway."

"Most practitioners hide away in little groups, living as unobtrusively as they can," the woman with the Dalmatian says. "The Sadlers shamelessly control an entire town. Growing up with my family and their tiny little coven in Hampshire, I longed to live in Mannith. The London Coven's the next best thing. I'm Clarissa, by the way."

"Do you think I should join?"

"I can't even begin to understand why you don't head home and be the Queen in the North. But if that's off the table for you, then for goodness' sake work with Lavinia," Clarissa says.

"She seems a bit full-on."

Lydia—who's not managed to get a word in since Clarissa appeared—shrugs. "She takes some getting used to. But you'll never hear me say a word against her. Not since she worked the spell that made the entire world physically unable to remember my deadname or even the fact that it existed. And beyond that, she and the rest of the coven have given me friendship. Purpose. Power."

I frown. "Somehow, I wouldn't have thought she'd be very into trans rights. Looking at her inner circle, she strikes me as someone who believes all that old biological basis of magic stuff."

Lydia waves a hand. "She's pretty progressive for someone born in 1930. It's a little odd that she still believes only women should practice magic, but she's never had the slightest issue with accepting that I am a woman."

The more impassioned Lydia gets, the more what appears to be a Cornish accent comes to the fore.

"She only accepts Born Practitioners, too, doesn't she?"

"Says the girl with the purest Born Practitioner lineage going," Clarissa puts in. You know you can trace your family back to the 1300s and there are no humans anywhere on the tree, right?"

"Yeah, I know. I've seen the statues in the Witches' Church. I've read the records. It's just that I believe magic's something you do, not something you are."

Though try telling that to Brendan, since the rest of my family drained my eldest brother's power.

"Why don't you talk to one of the outer circle, if you're so concerned?" Lydia suggests.

Before I can respond, she gestures to a young woman who can't be more than nineteen. "Cara, come here."

Cara bounds over with a big smile on her face. She's stunning, all curves and golden hair and skin, like something from a 1970s holiday poster.

"Hey, Lydia, Clarissa. And it's so exciting to meet you, Sadie."

"I really don't need an introduction around here, do I?"

"Cara, please reassure Sadie that we don't actually treat the less magically gifted coven members like animals," Clarissa says.

I half expect Lydia and Clarissa to linger and make sure Cara stays on message, but they both glide back to the circle.

Cara looks at me intently. "I've made a great group of friends. I've had way more support with my dream of becoming a fashion designer than I ever did at the art school I dropped out of. And it's been amazing to see all the magic in action, and just a little bonus when I've picked up a spell or two."

"I don't want to join an organisation that treats certain people as second-class citizens, just because of an accident of birth."

"It's really not like that. I'd encourage any and all women I know to sign themselves up to be acolytes. And if you're a Born Practitioner being welcomed to the inner circle with open arms, you'd be crazy to say no."

She takes my arm and leads me back towards the circle.

Chris is frantically waving and trying to get my attention.

"Thanks for the advice," I tell Cara, then grudgingly walk over to Chris. He's just like I remember him on that farce of a date. Smiling and blandly attractive, with his mid-length, mid-brown hair, and toned but unremarkable body. He'd seemed like the most middle-of-the-road guy imaginable, until he'd revealed he was working for Lavinia. Even now, in a deserted park at midnight, surrounded by witches, it's hard to imagine him as someone interested in magic.

"Assuming that you want to persuade me to join Lavinia's little gang, the best thing you could do is keep your mouth shut." I cross my arms over my chest. "The women I've spoken to have done a good job of selling it to me, but nothing could put me off faster than speaking to you."

His cheery face collapses into a frown. "What have I done wrong? We had a lovely evening in the summer. I'm only sorry there was never a second date."

"Seriously, Chris? You acted like you were just a nice, regular guy who was interested in me. Then it turned out you worked for the coven and the whole date was just a ruse so you could get a message to me. And you waited until after we'd screwed to drop that bombshell."

He reaches out a hand to touch my arm reassuringly, but I jolt away like he's holding a snake.

"It wasn't a ruse," he says. "Lavinia found someone you'd like and who'd like you. The date was fun, the sex was great, the message I had to deliver was just a side issue."

"You lured me into bed on false pretences. And for the record, both the conversation and the sex were pleasant but dull." I wouldn't usually be so mean, but I'm still angry about the whole thing.

He folds his arms. "Lavinia gave me some of your backstory. I don't see why you can hold a grudge against me for being a little bit lacking in transparency, but you can forgive this Gabriel Thornber guy for branding you, torturing you, and killing your friends."

I glare extra hard, because he's sort of got a point. "I am not having this discussion with you," I snap.

"All I'm saying is that if you're going to join the coven—which you one hundred per cent should—maybe we should give it another try?"

I walk away without responding. Lavinia probably wouldn't like it if I unleashed Greenfire on one of her hangers-on, even a male, non-magical one.

I glance around both the inner and outer circle. I could keep on talking to people all night, and I wouldn't learn anything more. Lavinia has her prejudices and her flaws, but she supports her coven, and to some degree, her acolytes, often in life-changing ways. I am seemingly once again completely underestimating my own magical privilege.

Besides, I've got my career. I've got my sleek little apartment. And I've already made the decision to stay in London and get on with my normal life. I can't risk going back to Mannith, and I can't imagine starting over in an entirely new city. Joining the coven will allow me to keep my life in London and add a whole new dimension to it. And it'll also protect me from weakening my resolve.

I stride back to the centre of the hill, where Lavinia is waiting patiently.

"Well?"

"I'd like to join."

Lavinia stands up and throws her hands in the air. "You hear that, everyone? The lovely Sadie Sadler will be joining our coven."

She must be amplifying her voice, as even the outer circle start clapping and cheering uproariously.

"I'll just sort out the lien mark, and then we can all get on with having a delightful evening."

Every muscle in my body tenses. "You didn't say anything about a lien."

"Have you ever known your family make a deal with someone and not back it up with a lien mark?"

I shake my head violently. My whole body's cold. "I lived with a lien mark for six years. It ruined that period for me. There's no way I'd agree to another one."

"Then much as I'd love to have you in my organisation, I suggest you head back up to Mannith."

The crowd are watching me intently. Does she have all of them branded, too? The human acolytes like Cara and Chris, almost certainly. But Lydia? Katrina? Clarissa? All the rest of her pretty, poised practitioners?

I cup my hand under my chin to magically enhance my voice, appealing to them as much as to Lavinia. "Can't we just draw up a contract? Get the right lawyers involved and it can be just as binding. But a lot less barbaric."

Lavinia laughs. "I know all about your old lien. The problem was the content, the person it was with, and the fact you had no choice but to agree. If the agreement had been made on the basis of signatures on paper, it would have been no less traumatic."

That's not quite true. If Gabriel had simply drawn up a contract, at least I could have locked it away in a drawer.

"That experience clouded your understanding of liens," she continues. "Most are just contracts written on your skin. I emphatically do not want to steal your magic or make you my sex slave. I just want you to be my in-house lawyer."

I close my eyes and try to steady my breathing.

I've already made the decision to join the coven and Lavinia's technically right that there's nothing inherently awful about a lien mark. Many of my father's acolytes sport bands around their upper arms as a sign of loyalty to the Sadlers, and most of Gabriel's people have those little star and heart designs by their ear. Getting a lien is probably a standard part of the process of joining a coven, with no sinister undertones.

But it's different for me. The one Gabriel inflicted on me changed the course of my life for years. I just couldn't bear to get another. I physically couldn't make myself do it.

"I'll join the coven. I'll sign whatever bits of paper you need, and I'll do what it takes to prove my loyalty. But no lien mark."

Lavinia must see the determination in my face and understand that the words to talk me around just don't exist. She sighs.

"If you want to join the coven, you need to be marked. And if you want to stay in London as a practitioner, you need to join the coven."

I open my mouth to argue back with all the force of my legal training, but she shakes her head and continues.

"I can see it's been a long day and that this has been a shock to you. I can let my enthusiasm run away with me sometimes.

You don't have to commit to anything tonight. Stay and drink and chat—or head back to your flat, it's up to you. And then take six weeks to think things over. Stay in London with my blessing, keep in touch, and on the next new moon, let me know what you've decided."

I nod gratefully. My answer will be the same in six weeks' time. Nothing could persuade me to take the lien. Could she be convinced to accept me into the coven without it? If she can't, I'm in trouble. But I've built an entire career around being persuasive.

Tonight, I'm exhausted, and she's caught me off guard and on her territory. In a few weeks, when I'm well-rested and have had time to plan, surely we can come to a compromise. In the meantime, despite the lure of champagne and conversation, I'm going to head home, collapse into bed and think as little as possible about any of the events of the day.

TWO

BRENDAN

On the outside, I've never looked more like the Sadler family's golden child than I do tonight. I'm wearing the sharpest of dark grey suits, accessorised with some of our oldest and most powerful rubies. My dark hair's artfully slicked back, and I've shaken off the pallor and gauntness that weeks in prison bestowed on me. I mean, I'm still pale and thin, but in a way that hopefully looks sexy and mysterious, rather than like I've got days to live.

On the faces of our enemies and allies, I see nothing but the usual mix of fear, respect, and adoration. Brendan Sadler's back where he belongs.

No one but my parents and siblings know I've lost most of my once glorious power. My crime was a family crime, and my punishment was family business. They wanted to rein me in, but sure as hell didn't want to risk my reputation. The Sadlers' standing relies on a show of unity and strength—and if the news got out that Chrissie and Liam had taken a third of my magic each, we'd look fragmented and weak.

If there's ever been a time when we can't afford that, it's

tonight. Time to forge a godforsaken alliance with the person I despise most in the entire world.

We've all gathered in the main room of my parents' house. Our lackeys have pushed the sofas and coffee tables out of the way and replaced them with a circle of chairs—half for us, half for the Thornber delegation. Vague scents of Mum's home baking and Chrissie's potion-making hover in the air and it's as cosily warm as ever, but there's none of the usual music, food, and chatter I associate with this space.

Normally, we'd hold something this large and formal in the conference room at The Windmill, if it needed to be on our turf, or somewhere like Mannith Hall if we wanted neutral territory. But for the purposes of this ceremony, the use of the family home is half the point.

The core Sadler family—with one notable and predictable omission—take up one side of the room, along with a few particularly trusted and powerful acolytes. My father has the central seat on our side, obviously, with Mum to his left and me to his right. Thornber has brought along his inner circle and mustered what little family he has. It's basically just Jim Thornber, his dead father's younger brother. It must be strange to be both an only child and an orphan. Nikki Chana, his Taught Practitioner bodyguard/concubine/whatever-the-hell-she's-supposed-to-be, is playing the part of his right-hand man.

"Allow me to welcome you into my home. Allow me to invite you to join your power to mine. Your acolytes' strength to my acolytes' strength."

It's always weird to hear Dad being formal and ritualistic. It's so at odds with his usual bluff manner.

"I am honoured to accept your invitation into your home. You are welcome to mine at any time. I join my power to yours and invite you to join your power to mine. Let our acolytes' strength be as one."

Gabriel-fucking-Thornber, on the other hand, lives for this shit. He'd wander around talking like that all day, every day, given half a chance. That said, he looks surprisingly understated tonight, perhaps even a little subdued. His wavy dark-blond hair is loose around his face rather than gelled back, he's sporting a smart but unremarkable suit—not some white or pinstriped flamboyant affair—and he's kept his jewels to a bare minimum, with just one narrow, emerald-studded silver bracelet. Like all of us, he's forgone the sunglasses tonight—no need to hide the diamond-shaped pupils and colour-changing irises that are the sure mark of a practitioner when we're all witches together.

I've never wanted to attack someone so much in my life. My chest constricts at the knowledge that I'll never be able to land a magical blow on him now. If I put ego to one side, he was always more powerful than me—perhaps the only person who was. But on a good day, with the element of surprise and the right motivation, I could have taken him. Now, I'd have about as much hope as some hopeless Learnt Practitioner.

Dad and Thornber step towards each other, then shake hands. It's such a human, everyday gesture, like they're conducting a business deal—which, to be fair, is one major aspect of what they're doing. Both families own a lot of companies in Mannith. We'll have a stake in their Prohibition Casino. They'll have a share in The Windmill, our flagship pub. And so on through a long list of less emotionally resonant bars, restaurants and goodness knows what else.

The outward, physical handshake is only a part of it though. Power flows back and forth between their two palms, sealing the deal in a more binding way. I can still see the flashes of colour and the jagged flow of energy, thank God. If Sadie had taken her share of my magic like she was supposed to, it'd probably have blinded me even to the sight of it. I should be grateful for small mercies, but that impossible desire to blast the bastard clean out of existence is intensifying by the second.

My father lets go of Thornber's hand. For a glorious moment, I almost dare to hope that this is all a double bluff in which Dad's lured him into Sadler territory and is going to destroy him while his defences are down. Or as down as they ever get.

"We intend this alliance to last," my father intones, instead. "You represent the next generation and will still be at the head of the Thornber family when control of the Sadlers has passed to my son and heir."

Everyone seems oddly inclined to skip over the reason our family is led by someone in their sixties while the Thornbers are headed up by a thirty-year-old. I guess it's just not that relevant that he killed his own father and tried to frame me for the murder. Unimportant. Minor in the scheme of things. Yesterday's news. Did I mention that I hate that bastard?

"Brendan, come forward."

On the plus side, Dad apparently still considers me to be his heir, though how I'm meant to run the family with so little power is anyone's guess.

"You must forge a similar alliance between yourselves. Shake hands now. To forgive the events of this summer and all the years before, and to look ahead to the future."

I stand up from the semi-circle of chairs, my trembling legs barely able to support my weight. My sister, Chrissie, is sitting on my right. She's dressed to kill in a tight-fitting, low-cut red dress, with her long blonde hair big and bouncy, her skin tanned, and her make-up like something from a Hollywood film. Admittedly, she tends to look a bit like that when she pops out for a pint of milk, but she's really made an effort tonight. She places a reassuring hand on my arm.

My brother, Liam, seated on Chrissie's other side, is never normally seen out of his sportswear, but he's forced his muscular frame into a smart suit for the evening and made some attempt to neaten up his unruly deep brown hair. There's a bruise on his cheek from a recent boxing match. He could hide or remove it if he wished, but he obviously sees it as a statement. He gives me a comforting smile. Shane, his best friend since toddlerhood and an honorary part of the family, does likewise.

Somehow, we're still all on good, if slightly strained, terms. Both Liam and Chrissie were fairly mediocre practitioners, other than in a few narrow disciplines, but there's an extra edge to their magic since they each took that third from me. I ought to resent them for it, but they acted entirely in line with the Old Ways. I don't blame them for punishing me for unleashing Hellfire on our youngest sister, Sadie. I blame Thornber for pushing me into committing the act in the first place.

I give both siblings a grateful glance, then take a succession of slow steps forward.

Some people pride themselves on their calmness under pressure and regard cool detachment and a poker face as a key facet of both their personality and their magic. I, on the other hand, have always taken strength from the sheer force of my mood swings and temper tantrums. I'm neither proud nor ashamed to admit it. It's simply who I am, and knowing yourself is half the battle.

Today, though, I can't afford to make a scene. That's a privilege reserved for those who've got the power to pull it off.

I force my face into the most placid expression I can manage. It's unlikely to be enough to fool anyone on either side, but at least I'm showing willing.

Thornber's better at playing the game, I'll give him that. His smile is neutral, with just a hint of superciliousness, as though shaking hands with me is pleasant at best, a minor chore at worst. In reality, he must be torn between frustration at being made to bury the hatchet, and an unbearable smugness at having brokered this alliance.

After an eternity of seconds, I reach the space at the centre of the room where my father and Thornber are standing. Dad takes a few steps back, and I take his place, breathe deeply, and hold out a hand.

Gabriel-fucking-Thornber extends a hand in turn.

I drag all the magic I have left into my palm, so that he'll feel the force of it when we touch and hopefully fail to realise I'm diminished.

It seems to work. There's no hint of surprise in his eyes, and sparks fly gratifyingly from my skin, same as they always have.

My father nudges me pointedly.

I increase the pressure on Thornber's hand, half because I'm so tense, half to make a point.

"*I am honoured to accept your invitation into your home,*" I say. "*You are welcome to mine at any time. I join my power to yours and invite you to join your power to mine. Let our acolytes' strength be as one. Let us put the past behind us.*"

He replies immediately. "*I am honoured to accept your invitation into your home. You are welcome to mine at any time. I join my power to yours and invite you to join your power to mine. Let our acolytes' strength be as one. We shall put the past behind us.*"

I relax a little and the whole room relaxes in turn. But as I release my grip on Thornber's hand, he throws up a small, subtle bubble of silence around the two of us.

"I'm making this alliance with the Sadler family in good faith," he says. "But I don't consider you part of that family anymore. And I swear that within the year, I'll kill you for the way you hurt Sadie."

Instead of responding with baseless counter-threats, I slap on my most irritating smile, which tends to have a magic all of its own.

"Such a shame my little sister couldn't be here today, isn't it? The parents invited her. Practically begged her to come back to Mannith for the weekend. I guess she's just not that interested in seeing you, now you've not got her branded."

He does a good job of keeping his expression placid, but there's a slight curl to his lips and a subtle narrowing of his eyes. Only someone as practiced as I am in provoking people would notice the signs.

"Even if she doesn't want me, I'll still kill you for her sake," he snaps. "Besides, it's not purely personal. Your death would release enough magical energy to be a sufficient sacrifice all by yourself. And at least you'd die achieving your dream."

Before I can make any sense of his words, he slams his easy smile back into place and collapses the bubble of silence. It's all happened so quickly that most people in the room won't have registered it.

"Now let's seal this alliance with a drink," he says, addressing me out loud but speaking entirely for the benefit of the audience.

Let's hope it's not going to be laced with arsenic.

Once the business-focused part of the ceremony is over, we all travel to Summer Hill, where, unbelievably, we're going to give Gabriel-fucking-Thornber equal control of the Dome, the imperceptible protective barrier my family created centuries ago to protect and enchant the town. I mean, it's not as though he tried to destroy the entire thing less than a month ago.

By mutual agreement, we drive out in a flotilla of flash cars, rather than traversing. We park at the base, then walk to the summit. It's 21st September; the weather is chilly enough to justify a scarf and there are leaves in a million shades of red and brown everywhere you look. The way Mannith does seasons properly—just another side effect of the Dome's magic—is one of my favourite things about the place. There's even a faint scent of wood smoke in the air, despite the lack of any obvious recent bonfires.

Most of the family are huddled together, chatting, even

laughing, despite the utter awfulness of what we're about to do. I'm walking alone, half taking in the stark autumnal beauty of the hillside, half lost in thought. The very image of the brooding hero.

A few months ago, I'd either have been at the absolute heart of the gathering and leading the conversation, or else strolling hand in hand with Leah. My heart contracts at the thought. I've not been back out here since the night we tried to make a baby. Or rather, the night she set me up. I missed the annual Ritual, for the first time since I turned eighteen. I missed the night my siblings defended the Dome against Thornber, and Sadie tried to blow him apart—probably the first sensible thing she's done in the last six years.

"It's really not so bad, you know." Nikki, Thornber's pet Taught Practitioner, detaches herself from the cloud of acolytes around their beloved bastard of a leader and hovers by my side.

I couldn't name most of Thornber's associates—they all blur into one mass of skinny girls in tight dresses and stacked guys in tighter T-shirts. Even if Nikki wasn't second-in-command, she'd stand out due to her height, her muscles, and her South Asian ancestry—and the fact that she's human, of course. Most people on both sides are dressed formally tonight, regardless of gender. She's dressed for battle.

I raise a supercilious eyebrow at her. She's surely the last person who'd want to talk to me, and the feeling's fairly mutual. "Which bit? The memories? The isolation from my own family? Or the way we're about to betray the Sadler legacy?"

She lifts her own perfectly plucked eyebrow in return, looking as surprised as me that I've opted to share my feelings. "Not having much inherent power to call on."

Inwardly, I flinch, but I keep my body language in the same disinterested slouch I've been maintaining all evening. "I'm sure that must play on your mind. I can't say it's something that's ever concerned me."

"I doubt anyone else can tell, but my own complete and utter lack of any natural magical abilities makes me particularly attuned to other people's power. Whenever I've seen you at a distance in the past, the magic's flooded off you. Today, it's more like a gentle stream. Still more than most people have. But less than you're used to and less than most of your family."

I start walking faster, but she easily matches my pace.

"Your magic radar's obviously not all it's cracked up to be." There's no topic I'm less inclined to discuss, and—with the notable exception of her boss—no person I'm less inclined to discuss it with.

"I'm not going to mention it to Gabe. Or to anyone else. I'm the last person in the world to start shaming someone for a lack of inherent magical prowess. You people believe that the important thing is what's in the blood. But all magic can be learnt."

I breathe out audibly. What she's saying is technically true. But the thought of dutifully learning spells and painstakingly casting them is too painful to contemplate.

"I don't know why I'm even having this conversation," she continues. "It's like commiserating with a former billionaire about how they're now merely a millionaire. Besides, I might as well be trying to cheer up a cartoon villain. The things you planned to do with the Dome. The way you tried to kill your own sister. All the moves you've made against my people over the years."

"Yes, I'm basically the living embodiment of everything that's wrong with the world, while your great leader is just a saint amongst men." I aim for relatively light-hearted sarcasm, but there's real venom in my tone.

"Gabe's my best friend. But as I once told Sadie, that doesn't mean I'm blind to his faults. Quite the opposite."

"And I'm sure Sadie listened and took all your warnings on board," I reply.

I can't begin to understand how my sister, who's undoubtedly the smartest member of the family, can be quite so oblivious to the indisputable fact that Gabriel-fucking-Thornber is a fundamentally awful person, especially after the way he's treated her in the past.

"I didn't believe in all that old fashioned 'fated couple' stuff, but I do now. There's this weird sort of energy in the air when they're together."

Chrissie said something similar. She believes she and her husband, Ray, were fated to be together, because of some dream his sister had. And then she extrapolates from their healthy, happy and slightly staid marriage the idea that Sadie should merrily become Mrs Thornber, because his literally demonic mother once had a vision.

There'd never been anything like that with me and Leah. I'd vaguely known her since childhood, in the way that everyone in Mannith is a friend of a friend if you dig hard enough. We'd hooked up after a drunken night at Wildflower, one of the clubs in town under my family's control. A one-night stand that had quickly turned into something more. I'd been fairly sure I loved her and wanted to spend the rest of my life with her, but there'd been no mystical trappings around the relationship.

"If you want to try to regain some of your old magical strength, I can teach you how to do it the hard way," Nikki says, running a hand over her pixie cut. "It's not something those blessed with power from birth can really understand."

It's unclear whether she intends this as mockery or a genuine offer of help, but either way, the thought of being taught magic by some jumped-up Learnt Practitioner is simultaneously too hilarious and too mortifying for me to formulate a response. I stare at the grass beneath our feet as though it's the most fascinating thing I've ever seen.

Before I can attempt to mumble something noncommittal and get the hell away from her, two other women who form part of the Thornber delegation backtrack down the hill.

One throws an arm around Nikki, who gives her a quick kiss in return. The other one is looking at me with that sense of awe and fascination I'm usually all too accustomed to—though not usually from those loyal to the Thornbers.

"Gabriel wants to talk to you, baby," the first woman says.

"Okay, Rachel, coming." Nikki loops an arm through her girlfriend's and speeds up her pace. "Brendan, we'll finish this conversation some other time. I've put my number in your phone."

Using some sort of electro-telepathy, presumably. I'm grudgingly impressed. I'd have thought that would be beyond her sort of magic.

The other woman lingers. Thornber loyalist or not, she's my type, with her long white-blonde hair, slender frame, and big, faraway eyes. Not a million miles away from Leah. I'm not in the mood for anything serious at this point in time, but it's tempting to turn on the charm. Losing most of my magic's not affected what my rather more aggressively masculine-looking brother always mockingly refers to as my pretty-boy good looks. Nor has it dimmed my way with words and ability to flirt. And if all else fails, there's always my status as the Sadler heir to fall back on.

I relax my smile into something less ironic and more seductive, making determined eye contact. She steps a little closer, slinking into my personal space.

Then I freeze, and try to think with my head, rather than my heart or any other part of my anatomy. She could be a spy for Thornber. If he could get my own fiancée to act against me—a girl from a good Sadler loyalist family—what hope have I got when it comes to a member of his own organisation?

Even if she's not officially spying for him, she'd be bound to talk to him and accidentally or deliberately let things slip. Not that I'd be stupid enough to tell her anything sensitive, but

Thornber seems like someone who could easily use a collection of inconsequential facts against you.

And now his best friend and second-in-command knows the one secret I actually care about. I push the thought aside. Maybe I'm still the gullible idiot that let Leah play me, but somehow, I believe Nikki when she claims she won't tell him. My understanding of their dynamic is that she's the honest, straight to the point counterbalance to his guile and scheming.

"Sally, leave Brendan Sadler alone, for goodness' sake," Nikki calls back to her.

"I thought we were all friends now."

"It's a touch too soon to start getting quite *that* friendly."

Sally sulks for a split second, then pulls herself together and rushes to catch Nikki and Rachel up. Clearly, in their organisation, you don't disobey her any more than you disobey Thornber himself, despite the absolute gulf between their natural levels of magical prowess.

I straighten my shoulders, clench and unclench my jaw, and go to find the rest of my family. I've simply got to make this new dynamic work.

THREE
SADIE

It's two weeks since I left Mannith. It's also the autumn equinox and the night of my family's alliance ceremony with the Thornbers. Yet I'm in London. Am I making a sensible, principled stand, or just being awkward? It's a thin line sometimes.

I've made the decision not to pursue a relationship with Gabriel and not to live in Mannith, and I still believe that's the right call. It doesn't mean I can't visit from time to time, eventually. But I know that to set foot in Mannith again this soon, while my emotions are running this high... I'd never leave again. And that's not what I want. It can't be what I want.

How is the ceremony going? Are they managing not to kill one another? There's a slight risk that one or both of the families is setting the other up. It's not like any of them can be relied on to be honest with me.

At least I've got the distraction of a new case in my normal, human job as a lawyer. Janice Denworth killed her husband. There's little to no doubt about that. My job's to prove it wasn't murder. And it's going to be an uphill struggle.

You can kill abusive husbands in self-defence. And in cases such as this, where someone's been subject to emotional and physical abuse for years on end, self-defence tends to be pretty liberally defined. But probably not liberally defined enough to encompass a scenario in which a wife buys rat killer and slowly poisons her sadistic partner over a pre-meditated period of weeks.

If it were up to me, there'd be no case to answer. But sadly, I don't make the law, I just try to make it work for my clients.

In theory, it's a great case—the legal challenge, the human interest angle. A cause I believe in. But at today's conference, poor old Janice looked haggard and broken, and she cried her eyes out with a mixture of fear and guilt, while I struck a careful balance between gentle concern and hard-nosed legal advice.

By the time we finished, I'd got all the information I needed from her and very little confidence in my ability to win this case.

Afterwards, I walked to Borough Market, a huge Victorian market hall on a site that's supposedly been selling food and drink since the early Middle Ages. It's always full of cheerfully browsing people and amazing smells from the small, tightly packed stalls piled high with fancy cheese, meat, wine and all the rest of it. I bought a lavender-infused artisan gin and some single-estate coffee beans, in a frenzied attempt to convince myself there are benefits to being back in London.

Between thoughts of Mannith and thoughts of the case, it's impossible to settle tonight. I try some light yoga, some of the new gin, a core meditation—nothing helps. I'm just throwing together a carbonara when my phone rings with a strange, ethereal tone that sounds like a fairy choir.

With half an eye on the bubbling saucepan full of tagliatelle, I pick it up. "Hello?"

"Darling Sadie. So glad I managed to get hold of you. A few of us are meeting at Tower Bridge in an hour. Shall I send a car, or would you prefer to traverse?"

"Lavinia. What's the occasion? And did you do something to my phone?"

I'd wondered when she'd get in touch. The lack of contact in the two weeks since the night we met has verged on the disconcerting, considering she's meant to be persuading me to take the mark and join the coven. And the equinox is a time when magic works more easily, hence my family choosing it for their alliance ceremony. I'd thought the London Coven might have something planned, and the fact I hadn't been invited had been half a relief, half a disappointment.

"Whenever you hear it ring like that, it'll be me, though I won't call that often."

"So why are you calling now? Why Tower Bridge?"

I can almost hear Lavinia's smug grin across the phone line. "It's a little London Coven autumnal tradition that I thought you might like to join. A chance to see how much fun we have and the sort of thing you'd be missing out on if you left the city. We're protecting the Crown Jewels for another year."

A little rush of excitement hits me, despite myself. "What, really? Is the king involved?"

"That'd be ridiculous. But his private secretary oversees proceedings."

Having declined the offer of a car in favour of traversing—traffic in the City is always terrible, however nice the vehicle—I arrive perfectly on time.

There are five practitioners waiting on the bridge. I recognise all of them from the night on Hampstead Heath. Lavinia, of course, and then Katrina, Lydia, and Clarissa. The latter is hand in hand with a woman I spotted last time but didn't get a chance to speak to. She's of East Asian descent, but otherwise looks pretty similar to Clarissa—same stature, same skinny build, same sleek bob.

"My wife, Dani," Clarissa explains.

They're mostly dressed like me, like they've just come from work or the gym. I'd been slightly concerned I'd rock up in yoga gear and everyone else would be wearing the sorts of gowns Mannith's practitioners sport for the annual Dome Ritual. Admittedly, Dani is wearing a little red cocktail dress and Lydia a floor-length swirl of green silk, but that seems to just be their personal styles.

"We can't traverse in the Tower itself," Lavinia explains. "Somewhat uniquely, the wards we set even work against ourselves. The king's representative in these matters and one of the Beefeaters will open a portal shortly. They're Taught Practitioners, of course, but I personally instructed them in the narrow range of skills they possess, so they're surprisingly competent."

I really need to make sure Lavinia and Nikki never meet. The latter couldn't cope with the former's sneering views on people who practice magic despite not having been born with it.

"Good to see you again." Katrina beams.

Maybe she's genuinely pleased to see me, maybe it's her politician training kicking in. Either way, I'm willing to seize hold of friendship where I can.

"I saw you on the news the other day," I say. "That was a great point you made, about increasing support for pregnant asylum seekers."

She smiles like that's the single greatest compliment I could pay her.

"Ready for our ritual?" Clarissa asks. She's still hand in hand with Dani, and her Dalmatian is at their heels. "I hope you're up to it, after all that time you spent avoiding magic."

"What's your dog's name?" I ask, deliberately not engaging with her barbed words.

Clarissa strokes said dog. "Astrid," she replies, then turns away.

Lydia appears by my side. "At home in Cornwall, we'd purify ourselves in the sea before a spell like this."

I shiver at the thought, and she laughs. But at least she's making vaguely friendly conversation.

"Do you feel the same way as I do?" I ask her. "That London just isn't suited to magic? There are just too many people and too much history. It's impersonal. Hard to connect to."

She shrugs. "In Cornwall, the landscape, the magic, and me are all part of one whole. I never really get that vibe here. But then again, in Cornwall, I have to deal with my family. They're big on the Old Ways. Big on running the Enclave like a medieval fiefdom. Putting up with pollution, overcrowded Tube trains, and magic that's buried a bit too deeply below the surface is a fair trade off."

"In Cornwall, she also has to deal with guarding the portal to the faerie realm," Clarissa adds. "Which I gather can be a mixed blessing."

"Mixed is right. You should visit the Enclave some time. And maybe you could show me Mannith in return."

"I realise it's sometimes harder to see the magic here than it is out in the beauty of nature or in a perfectly preserved historical town," Lavinia interrupts. "But it's the most magical place in the world.

"Look at the view from this bridge. There's the Tower of London, a symbol of strength from almost a thousand years ago. And then those gleaming, hyper-modern glass towers represent one of the most important business and financial districts in the world. In between, there are monuments of power and success from every era, like the Victorian manufacturing miracle of the bridge itself.

"If we were standing in Rome, you'd see the beauty of the past, but it's a faded glory. If you stood in New York, you'd see the success of the present, but with no more than a few centuries to underpin it. And if you stood somewhere like Singapore, you'd see the promise of the future. But London has it all. For the last thousand years, there's not been a century in which it wasn't a place of success.

"There are cities with history. Cities with political power. Cities with financial clout. Cities with culture. Ones with exciting shops and restaurants. Few have it all concentrated in the same place to quite the same degree.

"And underneath all that, it's a living, breathing city, from oligarchs of unimaginable wealth enjoying all the luxuries it has to offer, to penniless refugees hoping for a better life. And between those extremes, there are people at all levels of wealth and education, pursuing a million and one different ambitions and dreams. It draws in the best of people from across the country. Across Europe. Across the world.

"And as far as magic goes, it's a virtuous circle. There's something in the air, and the earth, and above all in the river Thames that's always made it thrive and that's acted like a magnet to people and their dreams. And the success and the energy of the city as a unit and its inhabitants as individuals builds that power more and more. It grows strong off the glories of the past and uses that to fuel the wonders of the present."

Lavinia's voice takes on a hypnotic quality. I can see exactly what she means.

"All of that's wonderful," I say, "but for me, it's also what makes it difficult. The magic—or the city's aura, if you like—is spread over such a distance and over so many people. It's powerful, cold and impersonal. It doesn't care about me, and I struggle to care about it."

Lavinia smiles. "You've never really tried working magic in London. Give it a chance."

In the distance, the city's hundreds of church bells ring out for 10 PM, and as promised, a glowing purple ring appears in the middle of the bridge, right above the spot where it can be raised and lowered. In a nice touch, a representation of the royal coat of arms floats above it.

Portal magic's never been something I've played around with. It's a bit flashy for my family's taste. The main benefit portals give over good old-fashioned traversing is the ability to bring humans or large objects along with you, and—if someone on the other side facilitates it—the ability to pass straight through wards.

I step in. A second or two later, I come out the other side and gasp. We're in the heart of the Tower, right in front of the Crown Jewels. Sometimes, I can feel a little jaded, but this is definitely enough to fill me with wonder and excitement.

I visited once as a tourist. You stand on a mechanical walkway that moves you and the other gawking tourists past heavy glass cases and gives you a general impression of magnificence.

Now, the walkway is still and the cases are open. And the crowns and other pieces of jewellery are jaw-dropping.

A Beefeater guard in full ceremonial regalia and a woman in her twenties in a stylish skirt and blazer combo are watching us.

"Welcome," the woman says, in a notably posh accent. "The Crown appreciates your continued service."

Our little group is very quiet. We're all loud, confident women, but it's hard not to be a little overawed, both by the beauty and extravagance of the pieces before us and by the knowledge of the history and power they represent.

"It is our honour, Ella," Lavinia says, more sincere and solemn than I've heard her be before. I suppose she is old enough to be my grandma. Presumably, she was brought up to be pretty respectful about the monarchy.

For my part, it's kind of a guilty pleasure. I know the institution is illogical, outdated, and dripping with excessive privilege. But I can't help but like the splendour and continuity of it all, the fascinating contrast between the symbolic nature of the royal family and the real-life individuals all that symbolism and history rests on.

"What do we need to do?" I ask, trying to focus and compose myself.

"Despite the grand surroundings and special context, in essence it's just a case of setting up a ward," Ella explains. "But we need it to be utterly impenetrable. We have all the latest security technology in place, as well as highly trained guards, but stealing the Crown Jewels is such a highly ingrained cultural trope that we really do need to cover all angles."

"I've been doing this for years," Lavinia says, with evident pride. "Last year's defences should still be untouchable, but I'd never take the risk of failing to renew them annually."

"Right, clothes off," Clarissa orders.

Lavinia nods her assent.

The others strip down matter-of-factly. I hesitate. I work out a lot, and I'm comfortable with my body and confident about getting naked in sexy situations. But this sort of day-to-day, platonic nudity is a different matter. Especially with people from outside of the coven watching.

"Come on, Sadie," Katrina says, laughing. "There's no need to be shy around your future coven sisters."

Easy for her to say. Naked, she looks like an Olympic athlete. And I slightly resent the implication that I'm inevitably going to join them in the end.

"Yes, darling, do get into the spirit," Lavinia chides. She's already stripped off and her body is depressingly perfect.

Clarissa and Lydia smirk at my hesitation as they throw off their respective blouse and billowing emerald dress.

Dani takes off her glamourous red outfit a little more hesitantly and still says nothing to me.

"Fine." I turn my back to them all and hurry out of my clothes before I can lose my nerve.

Lavinia reaches into her gym bag and hands each of us a small vial. I take a sniff of mine, then drink it down. It smells and tastes different to the concoction Mum made us drink prior to the annual Ritual, but I can tell it serves the same purpose—lowering our inhibitions, dulling our conscious mind, bringing our magic and our subconscious to the fore.

I'm trying not to stare at the coven members' bodies, but I can't help but notice the lien marks on their backs. Circular designs about the size of my palm at the top of their spines, with intricate details that I can't make out without studying them with an inappropriate degree of intensity. Still, it's a relief to see they all sport them—that it's a standard aspect of joining the coven and not something Lavinia planned especially for me.

"Now, you'll be given one jewel each," Lavinia says. "Look after it like it's your first-born child. Then form a circle around the perimeter."

"I trust Lavinia's girls implicitly," the Beefeater states. "But for the sake of form, I should emphasise that there's enough of last year's spell left that if you tried to leave with your treasure, you'd be vaporised."

Delightful.

Lavinia is reverently handed St Edward's Crown, the one that's used for coronations. Despite the fact she must have held it before, her eyes are wide with awe.

Clarissa gets the Sceptre. Her hands are shaking. Amongst other things, it contains the largest diamond in the world. Up close, its size is difficult to believe or comprehend.

The Beefeater works his way along, giving each of us one of the key pieces.

I get the Orb. It's so heavy and so beautiful, and I can't quite believe it's real, still less that I'm allowed to hold it. Terrifying visions of me dropping and smashing it stampede through my mind and drive all my other thoughts and worries out of my head.

There's background magic in the air of the ancient stone room and hugely concentrated doses flowing from the jewels themselves. It's unclear whether they were infused with magic at their creation or have absorbed it over centuries of ritual and symbolism. Learnt Practitioners often use gemstones to focus their haphazard magic, and even those of my family's calibre have been known to do the same for particularly challenging spells. I can't help but wonder what miracles we could work if we channelled our powers through these.

"Sadie, you've got the exact same look on your face that all my girls get the first time I bring them here," Lavinia says. "Yes, they are real. No, do not panic and leave the room. No, you're not going to drop it. And no, do not even think about attempting to use them to work some wild magic. It's not your magic to use; it belongs to the Crown and to the nation. Now, places every-one. Form a circle at the points of the compass."

I nod, strengthened by her words and warning. I close my eyes for a second to get a sense of my position in space, then walk unerringly to the exact northern point of the room. Clarissa, Katrina, and Lydia get into place at the other cardinal points, while Lavinia goes to the middle of the room. Ella, the Beefeater, and Dani—who has seemingly only been brought along as a treat for her and a favour for Clarissa—scoot to the edges of the room.

What follows is exactly the kind of magic I tend to hate—chanting, arm waving, swaying and undulating. In this context, though, it's more fitting than in my day-to-day life. But the real heart of it is closing our eyes, tapping into the waves of magic in the room, and shaping it in our collective mind into a web of protection.

I see the web overhead—golden tendrils with the delicacy of lace and the strength of titanium, interlaced with panels in all the colours of the jewels in our hands.

Interacting with the magic is relatively easy. The tricky bit is working with the others. I'm not used to doing magic as part of a group, and whenever I have attempted it, it's been with members of my family, whose magic feels like mine. The other women forming the circle are seamless—they've obviously crafted spells in unison countless times before. My efforts to knit the web together neatly on the northern side are clumsy by comparison, but I've got enough raw power to make it work.

At the centre, Lavinia has her arms pointed to the ceiling and is turning ceaselessly in place. The spellwork she's doing is a little different to ours. It's a bit like we're the builders and she's the decorator. Her final touches—knitting the web together at the seams between the four of us, smoothing over snags, putting an overlay across it all—take less force but a lot more delicacy and precision. And while half her mind is focused on that, the other half is drawing the rest of us together, trying to keep us in time. She wasn't bluffing about the extent to which decades of consuming vampire blood have strengthened her power.

Eventually, she comes to an abrupt halt and throws down her arms. My eyes are closed, but I see it in my mind.

There's a loud clang and, for a second, the room seems to shake. Neither the sound nor the movement are quite real—it's our normal, human-style senses trying to comprehend something that's happening on frequencies and planes we can't fully process. I see the web shimmering around us, perfect and inviolate.

"That was magnificent," Ella says, audibly exhaling.

In her voice, there's the sound of all the Learnt and Taught Practitioners who ache to do magic of this kind. It makes me think of Bren. How is he coping, with his magic so diminished? Perhaps I ought to call him, but I'm not ready for forgiveness just yet and not in the mood for a confrontation.

Lavinia steps out of the web and places one hand on Ella's chest and one on the Beefeater's. The web flickers, and they shudder as she blasts magic into their bodies.

"This will allow the two of you access. If anybody else needs it, bring them to me. The king and the Prince of Wales have access naturally, of course, as a quirk of the magic of these gems."

"Thank you," Ella says, then the two of them carefully but efficiently put the crowns and everything else back where they belong.

When Lavinia beckons us, we step out beyond the web. As soon as we do, it hardens in my vision. When I reach out and touch it, my hand won't pass back through. As Lavinia promised, we've even protected the room against ourselves.

We dress, then go outside and work gentler magics around the Jewel Tower, then around the perimeter of the site. These don't prevent entry, of course—that wouldn't do much for tourism—but they do stop magic from penetrating or anyone from traversing inside. Our spells should also stop humans with ill-intent or at least warn the guards of their presence and plans.

Once we leave the site, I'm buzzing from the excitement and the sheer joy of working so much magic in quick succession. And from collaborating so closely with the others. It's a bit like being in a sports team and winning a major event. We've not exchanged many words this evening, but I already feel a hundred times closer to them than before. And this must be the longest I've gone without thinking about Gabriel and Mannith in goodness knows how long.

"See, wasn't that more fun than the sort of magic you get to do up north?" Lavinia asks.

"It was certainly different," I reply. "Do you often do things like that?"

"The State Opening of Parliament, the installation of new prime ministers, that sort of affair. Bits and pieces for some of the financial and cultural institutions, too, from time to time."

"Look, this was fun. Exhilarating. The sort of experience

money can't buy. But my position hasn't changed. I'm interested in joining. But I won't do it if you insist on a lien mark."

"I'm not going to push the issue tonight," Lavinia says. "My position hasn't changed either, but I said you had six weeks to decide, and I'll honour that. It's only been a fortnight."

I nod. What the hell am I going to do when the time's up though?

On the night of Lavinia's ceremony, I was so relieved to be given some breathing space that I told myself I'd find a way to agree a compromise. But Lavinia doesn't seem like a woman who's prepared to negotiate.

I can't get drawn back into my family's dark magic and Gabriel's schemes. Which means I can't leave London and go back to Mannith. Lavinia will only let me stay in the capital if I join the coven—which would be fine—but she'll only let me join the coven if I take the lien. To be fair to her, lien marks are traditional in the situation and the other members seemingly all sport them, but it's an absolute redline for me.

The only remaining option would be to leave for a different city, but I'd need a new job, a new home, new friends, and nowhere else really appeals...

"I'm not going to argue with you about lien marks and all the rest of it tonight," Lavinia continues. "But perhaps I could tell you a bit more about why I wanted you, specifically, to join the coven. Over and above my general principle that all London witches report to me."

"I gathered from your letter that you didn't just want a practitioner, you wanted a lawyer. You talked about revenge. What is it you're trying to do?"

Lavinia smiles. "I want vengeance on Augustine Piso, the leader of the vampires. He thinks he and his organisation are above the law. I want to show him that's not the case."

I've been aware of the existence of vampires since I was a child. It's no secret to practitioners. But you don't come across many of them up north—they tend to be terribly upper class and congregate in London and the surrounding counties.

Besides which, rather like how vampires can't enter a house without being invited in by the owner, they can't enter Mannith at all without being invited through the Dome by my family. Once or twice, my dad did invite an individual vampire in, for one business reason or another, but we generally steered well clear.

There were more of them when I was at university, where they ran this ridiculous secret society that found influential people to turn. As a fellow supernatural creature, they'd sometimes invite me to their parties. I went once, out of curiosity, but I'd generally decline on the basis that at best, we had nothing in common, and at worst, they were utterly abhorrent. I've generally taken the same approach in London.

Practitioners are fairly well-protected against them—given their powers don't work on us and our blood is poison to them—but vampires are usually bad news.

"What do you want me to do?"

She waves a hand. "We're going to implicate one of Augustine's minions in the perfect crime, then you're going to prosecute him. I'd love it if we could actually get one of those bastards sent down, but it's just as important that we have a big, public trial and lots of media coverage. They thrive on secrecy, cover-ups, public respectability combined with behind-the-scenes control. The glare of publicity would be even more lethal to them than the glare of sunlight.

"Once their activities are brought into the light, and once I've proven they can't always bend the establishment to their will, their whole corrupt, bloodthirsty edifice will start to crumble."

I frown. Lavinia presumably thinks this will help to persuade me to join, but I'm really not sure this is the sort of thing I want to get embroiled in.

"Anyone for drinks on Parliament's terrace?" Katrina asks.

Everyone nods enthusiastically, me very much included. This is a conversation for another day. Why spoil tonight?

We hold hands and let Katrina traverse us all in the right direction. It's a shame that if Lavinia really won't back down on the lien, then I'm going to have to say no to joining and deal with the consequences, because vampires aside, I could get used to this whole London Coven thing.

FOUR

The next morning, slightly hungover after one post-ritual cocktail too many, I'm desperate to call Gabriel, partly to find out how the alliance ceremony went and partly just to hear his voice. But I don't want to capitulate.

I speak to my mum instead, to get the facts. In summary, everything went smoothly, the alliance is in place, and she's furious with me for missing it.

I restrain myself for a whole week, on top of the two weeks I've already managed, distracting myself with Janice's murder case and hoping Gabriel's going to crack first. Then on Saturday afternoon, I down a strong coffee, take a second to compose myself, then grab the phone and hit X.

"I gather you're basically part of the family now," I say as soon as Gabriel picks up, before he can get a word in.

"That's one way of putting it." There's amusement in his voice.

"And have you already had your pick of the loveliest Sadler-affiliated men and women?"

It's only been a week, but I'm willing to bet he moves fast.

"They've been swarming me. I'd always assumed I wasn't

their type, but turns out it was just fear of your father's vengeance keeping them at bay."

I laugh, though it's a little forced. The thought of him with anyone else is a physical pain. "I'm not sure that answers my question."

"If you want me to be yours and yours only, just say so."

"Have your flings. I'll have mine. And maybe someday, we'll reconsider whether we want the situation to change."

He inhales, audibly. "Give me the thought of you over the reality of anyone else any day. In fact, do you want to know exactly what I've been thinking about you?"

He's not really asking a question. I can almost see his slow, seductive grin unfolding over the phone.

"Sometimes I lay in the middle of that massive four-poster that's been in my family for generations, and I just think how insane it is that we've only ever slept together in there once. I imagine you lying next to me, in some little silky ivory nightie that you've conjured out of thin air. I'm hyper aware of the sight and smell of you. You're all relaxed and content, not in the slightest bit conflicted about me or about being there. You turn to me, and plant the lightest, softest kiss on my lips, then run your hand down my chest. And I reach out and touch you, and the gown you made is soft and smooth beneath my fingers, but not as soft and smooth as your warm skin."

I sink onto the sofa, fighting to stop my increasingly rapid breathing from being heard over the phone. Maybe he's using a light hint of magic, maybe he's just got a way with words. I can almost see the scene he describes, more like a memory than a fantasy.

I take a sip of my drink and steady my nerves just enough to speak.

"Gabriel, we're not meant to be doing this. We're supposed to be making friends. Getting to know each other better. Not getting each other off."

"Are the two things that incompatible?"

I think about how he put the lien on me all those years ago. I think about the time he tried to collapse the Dome, and all the people who got hurt in the crossfire, my sweet ex-bodyguard and sometimes lover, Connor, included. About how he killed his own father—which, yes, there were good reasons for, but it's still disturbing.

There are all sorts of other crimes, large and small. And cutting across all of it, there's his utter, uncontrollable, all-consuming obsession with bending fate to his will to make me his, regardless of the consequences.

My conscious, logical brain is all too aware of all of it. That's why I won't be with him and why I won't go back to Mannith. But those horrors are drowned out by other mental images.

The night we spent at a country hotel, with the best sex and most enthralling conversation I've ever had. The time I brought him back from the brink of death. The time he did the same for me, and how safe and secure I felt coming back to life in his arms. All mixed in with an endless stream of looks and kisses and heated words.

I can't go back. I can't be his. But maybe I can give myself just a little leeway?

"You stroke my bare arms and my silk-covered stomach and thighs, and I shiver with each touch," I whisper. I don't have quite his confidence, but I also know how to use my words. "By the time you touch my breasts through the dress, I'm pressing myself against you, and I'm a shuddering wreck. You rub your palm lightly over my nipples until they're hard. Then you snap your fingers and the dress is gone. You smile at the sight of my newly naked body, then bend over me and lick each nipple in turn. And they're not usually all that sensitive, but at that moment, you might as well be going down on me with all the noise I'm making and the energy pulsating through my body."

I stop speaking to catch my breath. I'm not sure quite where the words are coming from. They're flowing out of me without much conscious thought. I only called to see how he was, and now I'm aroused beyond all measure, by both his words and my own.

"Well, the going down on you part is definitely on the agenda for about five minutes later in this scenario. But for now, I tease your nipples with my tongue for a few seconds more, then you sigh, and guide my head up so you can kiss me hard. And then you push me back down on the bed and straddle my waist. You stroke my cock with one hand and my hair with the other and you lean down and kiss my face and neck and chest."

I've been vaguely trying to control myself, but at this point, my hand slips under my skirt and into my knickers. Bloody hell, I'm wet. A damn sight wetter from his words than from most guys' actual, physical foreplay. Can he tell that I'm touching myself? Is he doing the same? Maybe we ought to do this by video-call next time, but I'd probably be a bit too self-conscious.

"I—that is to say—you... you smell so good. And you feel amazing." It's getting harder to stay coherent, to create a sensible narrative. "We're supposed to be playing a little longer. Teasing each other. Touching each other. But I can't take it anymore. I lift myself up, and I guide you inside me, and we moan in unison."

I'm rewarded by just the sort of moan I'm imagining at the other end of the line. My words trail off as my fingers move faster.

"You're moving up and down and grinding against me. I've got one hand stroking your back and the other touching you, and nothing ever felt better."

I can almost feel his hands on my skin and his toned body under mine. With my eyes closed, it's easy to pretend that my fingers are his as they push me over the edge. I make no attempt to hide the sound of my orgasm, though it's drowned out anyway by his own sounds of pleasure.

I take a few deep breaths as the aftershocks race through my body.

"So that's basically what I've been thinking about you," Gabriel says, after a few moments of mutual silence. He sounds far too self-composed.

"Good to know."

"Perhaps we could make a habit of this sort of thing, until you're ready to come home?" he adds.

The idea makes me smile, but as the mad cocktail of hormones and base instinct fades away, some semblance of rationality returns.

"That was fun. But once again, it's not really in the spirit of our arrangement, is it? We need to keep a clear head. Sex only clouds it. Let's speak soon. But let's keep it PG."

I'd thought I could get away with phone sex as a little compromise, a reward for being sensible and controlled enough to keep my distance. But I'd forgotten the intensity of emotions even a regular conversation with him can provoke. Do that again, and I'll be racing back to Mannith and into his inviting but deadly embrace before I can stop myself.

"Whatever you say, Sadie."

It's a few days later when he calls me back. I grab a glass of water and take a couple of seconds to centre myself before answering. I need to stay calm. No tears. No rows. No sex. Just chatting to a friend. I can do this.

"Hey, good to hear from you again." I almost shout out the words the moment I pick up, seizing hold of the conversation before he can. "How's working with my family going?"

"No one's killed anyone so far, which is probably a better

result than we could have hoped for. I'm drowning in paper-work right now. Learning all about your family businesses."

It's an odd mental image. He's undoubtedly intelligent and business-minded. It's just not a side of him I've ever seen much of. And it's certainly not front and centre in his public persona.

"Got any ideas for changes?"

"For a start, I thought we could open up a gin palace in your honour, with a hundred and one gin and tonic combinations. Kind of a sister project to my Prohibition Casino. A bit of old-fashioned glamour, a bit of modern style."

"Sounds fun. And what about the other side of the busi-ness? Going to start selling love spells on the dark web or something?"

He laughs, and I try not to shiver at the sound. "Actually, I do have a plan. And it requires your help."

"My help? Why?"

"Because if the Mannith Alliance is going to attempt to make a deal with vampires, we're going to need to lawyer up."

I grip my water glass hard enough to break it. "No part of that sounds good. What's the deal?"

And who are the vampires? Are they the same ones Lavinia is trying to take down? This has the potential to get very messy.

"Vampires could help us maintain the Dome without needing the annual sacrifices. And even expand it, so it'd protect more places than just Mannith. Bren's old dream, but without the deaths his version required."

What the hell? Since when was Gabriel interested in that? He tried to blow up the Dome a few months ago.

"What would the vampires want in return?"

Nothing good, surely. Nothing simple. Not mere money or a few simple spells. Ending the sacrifices but keeping the Dome intact or even expanded sounds like the best of both worlds, in theory. But it's far from clear that the price would be worth paying.

"I'd like to explain in person. Come and visit. Quite apart from any other reasons I might want you back, we need your brains, your legal skills. And your outside perspective."

I grind my teeth together. "I'm staying in London for now. We said we were going to try to just be friends for a while."

"Sadie, I'm sorry, this is ridiculous. I'm trying, I honestly am. But I'm failing. And so are you. I love you. And I want you: your body, your brain, your heart, your soul. I know I'm not supposed to say that. I'm supposed to ask you about the weather and whether you've listened to any interesting podcasts recently, but I just can't. Every anodyne question is a lie."

I swallow hard. "I can't do it either. I want to know about your day. I want to hear your book recommendations and your jokes. But I was wrong to think we could talk about that sort of stuff in a vacuum."

"So does that mean we're allowed to indulge in grand declarations and emotions and hammer out the hard stuff now?"

I shake my head so hard the reverberation is probably audible down the phone. "It means we shouldn't talk at all for a while."

"You don't need to prove a point to anyone. We can be flawed together. We can work it out as we go along."

"I'm sorry. I'm surer than ever that I don't know or trust you enough to commit to a proper relationship. And it's increasingly clear we can't manage anything lighter. I'm not saying I never want to speak to you again. We just need some space for a few months."

I hang up before I can change my mind. I consider deleting his number, but there's little point. It's burnt into my mind.

I'm so wrapped up in the emotion of it all that it's a few hours before I realise I never got to hear what he's planning with the vampires. I almost want to call back and ask, but pride's at stake.

· · ·

A few days pass, and neither Gabriel nor I crack and call the other. I really do want to give myself some space. On the other hand, in addition to my wild uncontrollable desire to speak to him, I'm also desperate to know what the hell's going on with his vampire plan.

It's hard to comprehend that a member of my family might know anything about Thornber plots, but there's supposed to be an alliance, so it seems worth a try. There's a part of me that longs to call Bren. But emotionally, that's almost as bad an idea as calling Gabriel, given that whole thing where he almost killed me. And alliance or no alliance, it's almost impossible to imagine Gabriel telling Bren anything, or vice versa. So I compromise by phoning Chrissie.

"Do you know anything about a plan involving vampires and the Dome? Gabriel mentioned it in passing, but then I hung up on him, and I've been dying to know more ever since."

I blurt out the question the second Chrissie picks up, before we get lost in small talk and gossip.

She hesitates. "I presume you gathered that Bren really was trying to enlarge the Dome prior to his arrest."

"Yeah. Just like Gabriel claimed. Bren admitted it in the end, once his powers were gone and he had nothing to lose by doing so."

"I didn't know about it until after the trial either," Chrissie says. "None of the rest of us did. I know you think I'm awful for going along with the annual Ritual. But though it's hard not to think about all the people we'd have lifted out of poverty, illness, and unhappiness, I wouldn't have been okay with the number of deaths an expansion would have required."

There's a sudden intensity in Chrissie's voice. If we were in the same room, she'd be making extremely determined eye contact. "But we could do it without anyone having to die if we made use of the vampires' powers," she continues. "We're all agreed we need to be totally honest with you this time around, so here goes: they'd get blood."

I take several deep breaths before attempting a reply. The reason they kept things from me in the summer was their concern that I wasn't a real member of the family anymore, was barely a real practitioner.

Nothing revolving around the Dome, vampires, and blood can possibly be good. But if I freak out now, they'll never confide in me again. And God help me, I want to be involved and in the loop.

"You mean we'd provide them with victims?" I say, almost levelly, while my throat constricts.

"Not from Mannith itself. Our people are sacrosanct. But from what we'd call the Outer Dome. There'd be a permanent magic in place, to allow the vampires to hunt easily and the people affected not to suffer or remember. No one would die or even be seriously harmed. The couple of people affected each night would face nothing worse the next day than a bit of light-headedness and tiredness."

"And this is Gabriel's idea? What the hell? He killed his own father and framed Bren to stop the Dome expansion plan."

Whatever else I'd thought about Gabriel's behaviour over the summer and over the years before that, I'd believed him to be on the side of the angels as far as this issue went. But it seems he only had a moral objection to the Dome when its existence didn't personally benefit him.

Bren's words echo in my head. *I was the only one who could stand against him. Now that power's split three ways, and the family's basically ready to agree to an alliance, he can do whatever he wants. And you're naïve if you believe he won't do something awful.*

"Don't get mad. Please. With us or with him. It's not hypocrisy and it's not that bad. The vampire bit isn't great, but maintenance and expansion with no deaths is definitely a win/win situation. Anyway, we're coming to London at the end of October to meet with the vampires' leader, so we can discuss it properly then."

My body goes very still, all thoughts of vampires pushed out of my mind for the moment by this revelation. "Who's 'we'?"

"Senior representatives of the Mannith Practitioner Alliance."

I can hear the teasing note in her voice as she waits expectantly for me to ask the question.

"Just me and Liam on the Sadler side," she adds, eventually, when I fail to humour her. "We need to keep the group small, so no one outside the core family, not even Ray or Shane. Mum and Dad aren't in the mood for leaving Mannith. And we don't want to expose Bren's weakness unnecessarily."

It's hard to imagine Bren with most of his magic gone. Whenever I think about it, a toxic blend of guilt and fury assails me. In the legend Dad built around his offspring, I had brains, Chrissie had beauty, Liam had physical strength—and Bren had magic. In reality, we all had some of all four of those things, but it's hard to escape your designated role in a family.

I sigh theatrically. "And on the Thornber side?"

"Gabriel and Nikki."

Inevitably. I knew exactly what she was going to say, but actually hearing it still makes my heart race. Gabriel is going to be here. In the same city. In just a few weeks' time.

"The alliance is clearly going better than I anticipated if you've dropped the 'Gabriel-fucking-Thornber' thing."

"If it helps, Bren most definitely hasn't."

"You astonish me. So how *is* it all going?"

"Bren's being Bren, and Gabriel's being Gabriel. But against the odds, the alliance is holding."

FIVE

I've spent the last few weeks focusing on my murder case to the exclusion of almost everything else. It's partly out of genuine interest—there are some fascinating legal principles at play, and I really feel for my defendant, Janice, who killed her abusive husband in what could just about be called self-defence. But it's also partly a desperate attempt to play at being human and keep my mind off my conflicted feelings about Gabriel, my discomposure about the vampire plans, and the fact that I've almost timed out on Lavinia's deadline for joining the coven, lien and all, or leaving the city.

It's a relief to think about something easily comprehensible, and in my direct control—even if it's also tragic and a bit of a lost cause.

"And for all of these reasons, I urge you to find the defendant not guilty."

I smile at the jury, give the judge a respectful nod, then bestow the most reassuring look I can manage on Janice.

With each day this murder trial has dragged on, the bags

under my client's eyes and the sallow tinge to her skin have only gotten worse. Maybe it's the stress of appearing in court. Maybe it's the horrors of confinement—in a disgraceful decision, she wasn't granted bail. And knowing her, she's no doubt suffering from an ever-growing sense of guilt over what she did to her bastard of a deceased husband.

If she's found guilty, she'll get life—the law's the law and no other sentence is allowed for murder. In practice, given all the mitigating factors, she'd probably get parole after a few years. But looking at the state of her aura, she'd be dead way before then, whether by her own hand, a vicious fellow prisoner, or simply due to her body and mind giving up the ghost.

And there's a strong chance she's going to be found guilty. I've given it my best shot. I've thrown myself into the case in a semi-successful attempt to keep my mind off other things, but based on the judge's likely instructions and the facts of the case, it probably won't be enough to sway the jury.

As I stare at poor Janice and think about all the things her husband put her through—controlling what she ate, forcing himself on her, isolating her from her friends and family, relentlessly listing her faults—a familiar tingling builds up in my body, along with an equally familiar urge in my brain.

No. Don't do this. Stick to your words and your legal knowledge. Respect the law and due process.

Ever since I became a barrister, the temptation to use my powers to sway the outcome in certain clients' favour has struck me from time to time. But in the past, it was always easy to resist. I never used my magic for anything, no matter the provocation, and every time I exercised my self-control, it grew easier. Besides, I had the best possible motivation to keep my powers in check—use them, and my sworn enemy might have found me and sought to make good on our old, twisted deal.

Since I got back to London, though, I haven't been able to stop using magic. It's fine when I'm using it to create myself a designer outfit out of thin air or give my dinner parties a Cordon Bleu edge, but I simply can't give in and pervert the course of justice, even if the cause is just. I did it once, for my brother, but never again.

My hand rises of its own volition, desperate to draw power out of the air. My eyes will be cycling through all sorts of unnatural shades. I can't wear sunglasses in court, so I just have to hope my oversized contacts are doing enough to hide them.

I grit my teeth like I always used to whenever temptation struck and clench my hands together.

I'll rely on my words. They'll have to be enough.

I can hardly believe my luck when the jury announce the not guilty verdict. It's not even some half-hearted downgrade to manslaughter, but innocent and free to go, her husband's death justified as self-defence, just like I'd argued.

I'm too much of a professional to leap up and punch the air, but I do the mental equivalent. I'm happy for Janice, obviously. And on an abstract, philosophical level, I'm happy that justice has prevailed. But I'm also just relieved that I can still do my job the proper way—both that I can both physically resist the lure of magic and that I can get the result I want without it.

It'd be nice to think that someone finding themselves free of an abusive marriage and cleared of all charges would bound out of court and dance off into the sunset. But if anything, as she trudges out into the lobby, Janice looks even more world-weary than she did while we were waiting for the verdict.

When I got my brother acquitted, family, friends, and hangers-on damn near mobbed him the second he was out of the dock. There's no one to greet Janice. Her adult children aren't on speaking terms with her, because of all the years she let their dad hurt them like he hurt her. And he kept her isolated from everyone else for long enough that the ties eventually broke.

There is no press around either, despite the sensationalist nature of the case. Not a single word has appeared about it in print or on screen. That one's on me, a little bit of magic I feel no guilt about and fully intend to use for all my clients in the future.

Janice shuffles along, head down, moving towards the exit. Hopefully, she can start to rebuild her life and her relationships now both the abuse and the court case are behind her. Perhaps I could do some sort of spell to ensure that, but I really need to maintain some boundaries.

I catch her up. I almost want to grab hold of her and give her some combination of a hug and a shake. Or at least take her arm. Instead, I force myself to maintain a professional distance.

"Congratulations." Professional demeanour or otherwise, my joy and pride must be evident in my voice.

"I wish they'd found me guilty." She makes eye contact for the first time and sounds far more definitive than she managed in any of our conferences or in the dock.

I throw up a quick bubble of silence. No one appears to be listening, but you can't be too careful. "You don't mean that. Prison would have destroyed you."

"It's what I deserved. I killed him."

I return her stare, with interest. "And that's what *he* deserved."

"I still love him, you know. I loved him while he did everything he did, I loved him as I was killing him, and I love him now. You wouldn't understand."

"I understand more than you'd think," I reply.

Do I? I understand the loving, the killing, and the regret. I experienced all of that last summer. The bit I can't identify with is the part in the middle. Staying. Forgiveness. Letting someone hurt you.

Gabriel is very different from Janice's deceased husband. And our dynamic was very different, too. I truly believe that he loves me and would do his best to treat me right. But I'm less confident that he wouldn't end up bending me to his will, whether deliberately or just through sheer force of magic and personality. And even if he were able to keep the worst of his obsession in check and be the perfect partner, that doesn't change the things he's already done. And I firmly doubt he could control all of his wider darker impulses—this vampire plot seems proof enough of that.

However much I try to keep my distance, and however much I try to rationalise it away, I still long for him. I still want him so damn much. He once said that I belonged to him— which is such an inherently unhealthy statement—but I want it to be true. I want to be his.

"You did the right thing," I say, maybe speaking to Janice, maybe thinking aloud. There are two days until Lavinia's deadline for a decision on joining the coven is up, and I'm still no closer to squaring that impossible circle.

Janice gives me the slightest smile and some of the darkness falls away. Perhaps she can see in my eyes that I'm not just offering platitudes when I claim to understand.

"Are you okay to get yourself home? Maybe I could order you a cab."

It's outside my job description, to say the least, but left to her own devices, she'll undoubtedly trek home on the bus, and it's already starting to get dark. Kevin Denworth never let her learn to drive, and, despite being wealthy from his building firm and property empire, he'd have hit her even harder than usual if she'd so much as thought about taking a taxi.

She glances around as though searching for her husband's ghost in order to ask his permission, but eventually, she murmurs her assent.

I lead her towards the car park and taxi rank.

"Nice car," she comments as I unlock my Porsche. It's the

most cheerful comment I've ever heard her say. Maybe it's a start.

Driving flashy cars is another bad habit I avoided for years, picked back up in Mannith, and haven't quite been able to shake. It's so much more efficient to take the Tube in London for most journeys, but that doesn't provide quite the same comfort or thrill. And if the traffic's too bad for the car, then with increasing frequency, I simply traverse.

A driver gets out of the nearest black cab. Even in the early evening gloom, it's obvious that he's startlingly good looking, but there's something in his manner that makes my intuition flare.

He strides over to us. "If the courts won't deliver justice, we will," he announces to Janice. "Your late husband made a deal. It was meant to protect him against business rivals, not his wife, but I'll honour it all the same."

My breath catches in my throat, but Janice doesn't look surprised or horrified, just wearily resigned. Whatever this is, she knew about it.

I expect him to pull a knife or a gun, and I'm calculating what spells I'd need to launch in order to stop him, when I realise his aura's a black hole and spot his fangs. My heartrate spikes.

In the course of the last few weeks, between Lavinia's plot to take them down, and Gabriel's plan to ally with them, vampires have been at the back of my mind. Even so, it's disconcerting to come face to face with one again without warning. They're always extremely physically attractive—and this one is no different, with his close-cropped dark hair and rugged jaw—but there's something about their sheer presence that gives me the bad kind of goosebumps.

They're no real threat to my kind. Our blood is poisonous to them, their mind control doesn't work on us, and though they could in theory use their superhuman strength against us, our magic's a pretty good defence.

My hands are shaking, but I throw one hand out towards Janice, encircling her in a protective bubble, and with the other, draw a jagged circle around the vampire. The magical structures will be invisible to Janice and any passers-by, but the vampire can probably see their opaque, pulsing forms as clearly as I can.

The whole thing only takes a few seconds and barely requires any effort. Even a couple of weeks ago, I'd have had to think it through methodically. I'm still relying on the hand gestures most of the time, but the way my magic's growing by the day is gratifying. Though perhaps not as gratifying as the stunned look on the vampire's face. I smile despite the seriousness of that situation.

"Who the hell are you?"

"I'm Ms Denworth's lawyer. And I take my clients' cases very seriously."

That shocks him into silence.

"Now are you going to explain who *you* are and what deal you made with the dear departed Mr Denworth, or am I going to tear you apart?"

"I'm Hugo Latham. The husband had some very dodgy property dealings. He was useful to our business interests. I offered him protection."

In my admittedly limited experience, most vampires sound like aristocrats. This one speaks more like some East End gangster. His pronounced muscles are pretty non-standard, too, as is his over-sized Rolex—the undead tend to err on the side of classy and understated. He looks like he's in his late twenties, but goodness knows his real age.

Reading between the lines of some of Janice's statements, I'd gathered that Kevin Denworth had had some seriously dubious clients, but I'd assumed we were talking about people traffickers and the like, not vampires.

"You must be one of Lavinia's girls?" Hugo continues.

"She's a good friend of our leader, Augustine Piso. We stay out of the coven's way, and they stay out of ours. You don't want to cause trouble over some human woman."

Augustine's the exact vampire Lavinia wants to set up in court. Clearly, she's doing a great job of hiding her true intentions.

With that, Hugo lifts his hands and slams them down towards the ground, tearing my bubble in two.

I gasp, but throw a touch of Greenfire at him. I'd have preferred something stronger, but I don't want to singlehandedly destroy practitioner-vampire relations in the capital without consulting Lavinia first. She may want to take the vampires down, but she's been clear she wants to do it via the courts and the media, not in the streets. She's obviously playing the long game.

He laughs as the spell reaches him. The distinctive jagged green light hovers just above his skin, illuminating the scene, but not quite making contact.

"Stupid girl."

My vision blurs. I've spent the last few years relying on my words and the last few months relying on my magic. It's terrifying to deal with someone who gives no regard to either.

Hugo darts forward. Janice is frozen in place, perhaps from mind control, perhaps from shock. Within seconds, his hands are on her shoulders and his fangs are in her throat. She doesn't scream, doesn't react at all. I grab hold of his arms and try to wrench him away, but it's like trying to move a mountain. The strongest telekinetic spell I can conjure up has no effect.

I start to scream myself, not from horror—though I *am* pretty horrified—but in the tactical hope that it'll attract help.

Hugo lifts his head and glares at me, like I'm doing something uncouth in a restaurant. "No one will be able to help. And if they try, I'll wipe their memories and their will."

I push down the waves of nausea that are assailing me and

raise my hands in a defensive stance. "I might not be able to work magic on you, but I bet I can win in a head-to-head mesmerism contest."

Hopefully, that's true. But more than that, I need to keep him talking and not drinking blood.

He's not stupid, though. Without any further hesitation or debate, he plunges his fangs straight back into Mrs Denworth's neck.

I scream again, but no one comes.

I'm panicking too much to develop a coherent plan, but my magic has a mind of its own. My hands curl into a succession of shapes, flinging lightning and fire balls in Hugo's direction. All of my spells bounce off his skin like he's wearing a suit of armour.

I take a deep breath and try to think. He's untouchable, clearly, however much my sub-conscious just wants to blast him with Hellfire. I grip my right wrist with my left hand in an attempt to exert some control over my shaking body. Slowly, painfully, like someone just learning magic, I make a come-hither motion and try to drag Janice towards me. She doesn't move. It seems as though anything and anyone he touches is under his influence and beyond anyone else's power.

I charge forward and try to wrench her out of his grasp. Despite all my strength workouts, my short stature and delicate build mean I'm no match for most humans in physical combat, never mind a vampire, but I'm not thinking logically. My entire mind is consumed with a desperation to get Janice to safety. I fought tooth and nail in court for her. I resisted the lure of magic and still managed to make justice prevail. I cared about Janice's case—I can't watch her die in front of me, just when I've given her the chance to rebuild her life.

Vampires have superhuman strength. It's a basic fact. If he wanted to, he could hit me hard enough to kill me. Instead, he swats me away like I'm a naughty child. Humans are fair game, but perhaps he doesn't want to mess around too much with practitioners.

"Let her go," I cry. There's no way he'll listen, but I have to try.

I launch one more blast of Hellfire, more or less on autopilot. It's like trying to demolish a house with a toothpick.

It's only when I stop fighting that I realise I'm crying. Some of it's for Janice. But a lot of it is terror. Magic makes you feel invulnerable. It's horrifying to be reminded that's not always the case.

In the few seconds it takes for me to try to compose myself, Janice slumps to the floor, quite clearly dead. Hugo straightens up, looking horribly pleased with himself.

My vision blurs. "You bastard," I shout, between sobs. "She'd suffered enough. How many more people have you done this to?"

He shakes his head. "What sort of practitioners is Lavinia employing nowadays? All this drama over a human."

I clench my fists and try to regain some semblance of self-control. I don't admit I'm not actually in the London Coven. If they've got some form of arrangement in place, it's in my best interests that he believes I'm a member.

"I'll make sure you face justice for this," I say. I sound reassuringly threatening and in control. In reality, I can still barely see or breathe.

Poor, poor Janice. And poor me, confronted with an enemy I can't simply magic away.

"We've got a very efficient cover-up operation. The police won't get involved. It'll never make it into the press. And if by some miracle the case went to court, we've got the judges sewn up."

That's exactly what Lavinia said the vampires believe. And exactly what she wanted me to disprove by using a court case to drag their activities into the light of day.

Before I can answer, he waves a hand and Janice's body disappears, presumably ready to be discovered back at her house. And he fades into the night, leaving me crying on my knees in the street.

I'm going to get justice for Janice. I'm going to make that bloodsucker pay. I'm going to show him that laws and morality apply to him, too.

It's clear that Lavinia has some sort of clever plan, and a whole coven at her disposal. Maybe, together, we can get revenge. But that means... I'm going to have to join. And Lavinia clearly isn't going to back down regarding the lien. The concept of getting another lien mark still makes me feel sick, but not as sick as what I just witnessed or the idea of Hugo cheerfully getting on with his immortal life.

I swallow hard. For Janice's sake, and the sake of all the other victims, I'll put my old trauma aside and I'll take the mark.

SIX

Back at home later that evening, I call Lavinia with shaking hands.

A wave of nausea hits me every time I think about that scene outside the courtyard. The sheer, primal terror of it—a predator devouring their prey. And me, with all my supposed power, unable to do anything to fight back. Unable to save someone I'd tried to help from dying in the sort of way that haunts the human subconscious.

I swallow hard. I've poured myself a gin, but the scent of it makes my stomach heave all over again.

"Sadie, darling, wonderful to hear from you," Lavinia trills, before I can get a word in. "I'm with a client, so I can't talk right this second. But I can tell you've got something important to tell me, and I'd love to hear it. Come to my wellness emporium."

According to my father, Lavinia was a hard-nosed, sleekly tailored yuppie in the eighties. But nowadays, she's a purveyor of health and wellness products and advice and has a cult following on Instagram. How many other lives has she lived over the decades? Presumably, she's always tried to fit into the zeitgeist.

I close my eyes, push back the gory mental images of the vampire attack as best I can, and traverse myself to Lavinia's "emporium".

The shop is on the Northcote Road, which must have the highest concentration of women with buggies and babies in London, all of them fairly wealthy and aggressively well-groomed. People call the whole area 'nappy valley', and this is its epicentre.

Even in my shaky state, Lavinia's boutique is a gorgeous place, all mirrors and pastel walls, with lighting that flatters both the merchandise and the customers. The main room sells incredibly expensive beauty products, vitamins, and a few bits and pieces of activewear and home decoration. It's all natural and organic, with a touch of mysticism and pseudo-magic. It's basically the sort of stuff you can find in "alternative" shops in Camden, but packaged in elegant monochrome boxes with subtle, stylish flashes of colour, and with an extra zero or two added to the price tags. It's squarely marketed at that demographic where hippie meets hipster, at the sort of woman who does kundalini yoga before heading off to her job at Goldman Sachs.

The two shop assistants are intimidatingly tall, blonde and thin, in tight black jeans and softly skimming white shirts. They look like cut price clones of Lavinia and are a great advert for her products. The handful of customers milling around are also working the same look, with varying degrees of success.

"Can I help you?" one of the assistants asks. Her voice implies that she almost certainly cannot. I'm well-groomed and well-paid by most people's standards, but I'm out of my league here.

I casually pick up a large, scented candle in a black glass container, which is apparently designed to stimulate the second chakra. A snip at £90. My mum would have an absolute meltdown.

"I'm here to meet Lavinia," I say, putting the candle down and inspecting a vial of facial serum that makes the candle look like good value. It's unclear whether the proprietor has actually infused all these products with some degree of magic or whether it's all one big confidence trick.

"She's in the back room with one of her private clients right now."

The assistant says this casually, but something about her pronouncement sounds vaguely ominous.

"My name's Sadie Sadler. She should be expecting me. Could you let her know I'm here?"

Despite my distress at the day's events, my voice sounds cool and authoritative. I wouldn't have lasted long as a lawyer if I couldn't keep emotion out of my tone.

The woman glances at the MacBook on the counter. "You're in the diary." It would have been nice if she could have kept the sceptical surprise out of her voice. "No one's to go in the back while she's working her magic though. It's basically the first rule of working here."

She's presumably using "working her magic" as a figure of speech, rather than being utterly blasé about her boss' practitioner status, but who knows?

"Sit down, and I'll get you a green juice," the woman adds, trying hard to be friendly now she's established I have a right to be there, despite having mid-length, almost black hair—rather than the long, blonde variety—and not being a size zero.

I'm tempted to ask for a black coffee instead, but that'd probably get me forcibly ejected. Besides, unlike the rest of the nonsense here, my mum would approve of the juice. It reminds me of doing a purification before a ritual. There's a slight risk I'll throw it straight back up, considering how sick I'm feeling, but if I can get it down and keep it down, it might actually do me some good.

I sip the juice, take some deep breaths, and let the scent of the various candles and the general calm atmosphere of the place drift into my senses. Slowly, the last remnants of shakiness and nausea fade, and I'm able to think more calmly about what happened.

There's something fundamentally disconcerting about vampires. Something in the way they look and act so human, right up to the moment they reveal their true, animalistic selves. There are those who'd argue that practitioners also tread far too uneasy a line between human and not human. But we eat normal food, we reproduce naturally, we go out in the day and die of natural causes. We just have a bit of extra power. Vampires are all kinds of wrong.

I'm not waiting long before a middle-aged woman walks out of the back room, with her hair and skin absolutely glowing. She all but floats over to the counter.

"How was the treatment?" the shop assistant asks, dutifully.

"Marvellous, as always. She literally takes ten years off me every time."

She hands over a credit card. Considering the cost of the dubious products out here, goodness knows what Lavinia charges to practice real magic on these private customers. My family's rates for genuine spells are pretty steep. Like most things in life, London prices are no doubt worse.

A moment later, Lavinia drifts into the room, and the two attractive shop assistants and the newly glamoured customer instantly fade into the background. She's operating on an entirely different level. Clearly, she keeps all the best beautification and anti-ageing magic for herself.

"Sadie! Darling. So wonderful to see you."

"Lavinia."

"Well, don't just sit there. Come into the back, and let's talk business."

I drain the last of my fluorescent juice and stand up to join her.

The back room is like the front, only more so. Even more stylish and understated, yet at the same time, even more redolent with magic.

Chris is perched on a stool, grinding herbs and stranger substances in a pestle and mortar, supervised by Lydia, who is staring hard at the bowl, presumably doing the harder task of infusing the mixture with her own magic.

"What are you doing here?" I ask Chris. "Aren't you meant to be a charity worker? Or was that just bullshit you made up on our date?"

"That's my day job. Evenings and weekends, I do whatever I can to serve Lavinia and the coven."

I shake my head then zone him out.

"And in case you're wondering, I do potions, magic-infused makeovers, and social media," Lydia explains. "All equally important to the business."

Lavinia sits down on a white leather sofa and beckons for me to join her. Lydia comes too, her long yellow dress trailing behind her, while Chris stolidly gets on with his appointed task.

"How are things?" Lavinia asks.

I swallow hard and dig my nails into the sofa. "A vampire killed my client."

Lavinia raises a perfectly groomed eyebrow. "How distressing." She sounds like I'm talking about a bad date or a lost purse.

"Vampires kill humans all the time," Lydia says. "Less than some people might think, but it's hardly a unique occurrence."

"She wasn't just some random human." I only stop my voice from trembling because I've had a lot of practice at speaking calmly in stressful and emotive moments. "She was a good woman. I protected her in court, but I failed her where it mattered. You said you had a revenge plot that needs a lawyer. I want in. And I want Hugo Latham to be the one we drag through the courts and the press."

"So, does that mean you're going to join the coven after all? I will still require you to be marked, I'm afraid."

This time my voice does shake. "I know. I'll do it."

Lavinia glances around the room. "Lydia, close down the shop for the evening and send the staff home. I'll call Clarissa and Katrina. We all need to be involved. Chris, you can go home. There's no place for humans or men in this."

Within five minutes, the two other senior coven members, plus Clarissa's dog, have traversed into place. Clarissa is in her usual smart jeans and expensive white shirt combo, Katrina in a fitted black dress. They've clearly come straight from work, despite the time of night, dropping whatever they were doing.

"I hope I'm not interrupting anything, ladies," Lavinia says.

Clarissa shrugs. "Just a meeting with some investors. Though Dani and I are going out for supper later."

"A parliamentary debate, for me," Katrina says. "And then I was meant to be doing an hour at the athletics track and an hour at the women's refuge. And then going home to collapse with a trashy romance novel. But we know where our priorities lie."

"Well, thank you for being here. I have wonderful news, ladies," Lavinia announces. "With two whole days to go before the deadline, Sadie has agreed to join us, mark and all."

"I'll take the lien. Make it quick." I hold out my arm. It's trembling, despite my best efforts to stay calm.

Lavinia smiles. "I don't go for the arms. Too visible. They raise questions and look unsightly when you want to wear a little strappy dress."

"Where then?"

"Your back. Unzip your dress to the waist and turn around."

Mannith. Gabriel. Family. Don't do this. There's still time to back out...

But what then? I'd need to leave London. I'd either have to

go back to Mannith, with all that entails, or attempt to start again somewhere entirely new. And either way, I'd lose my chance to stop the vampires.

I turn my back on her. "I'm going to need a hand."

It's hard to say whether my voice or my body is shaking more. I'm wearing a black halter neck dress—plain, fitted body with some lace detailing around the sleeves—that I'd hoped would tread a suitable balance between witchy, business-like, and fashionable. My love of yoga means I'm usually flexible enough to unzip my own outfits. But I'm panicking too much to muster the necessary coordination.

"Clarissa, come and unzip her."

I look back over my shoulder. "Lavinia, when we discussed this last time, you said you didn't *want* me to be your sex slave."

I give an exaggerated laugh to show I'm joking. Anything to break the tension, which is likely to send me running away if it's allowed to heighten much more.

Lavinia chuckles in return, sounding genuinely amused.

"I wouldn't worry," Clarissa says. "Lavi subjects herself to a strict no female lovers, no male friends policy. Much to the disappointment of all."

I flinch as she opens my dress to the waist.

"Sorted," Clarissa proclaims. "Do you need me to hold her in place, Lavi?"

"Sadie's an old hand when it comes to getting a lien mark. I'm sure she can be trusted not to run."

I'm far from certain that's true.

Clarissa takes a step back, Lavinia takes a step forward, and before I can catch my breath, she presses her spread right hand against the very centre of my back.

"Give me your hand, Sadie," she demands.

I reach behind me and grab Lavinia's left hand with my right.

As she touches Gabriel's mother's emerald and rose gold ring, there's a tremor in her aura.

"Other hand, please."

Right in left is traditional, which is how I ended up with my old lien mark right where the ring now sits, but it's just one of those funny Old Ways things that doesn't have any practical bearing on the magic. I let go and swap hands, even though it takes some contortion to take her left with my left, while she keeps her right hand pressed against my back.

My mind's throwing up images of the last time I got a lien. Since I've got to know Gabriel better and been released from his old bargain, I think about that night a lot less than I used to. There are a lot of other Gabriel memories, good and bad, to compete with it. But at the prospect of a new deal, all the old horror is springing back into life.

"Speak the words. Pledge yourself to the coven. Make the deal and take the lien."

I nod, and the right phrasing drifts into my head from hers. My voice trembles, but I get the words out.

"I swear to become a loyal and active member of the London Coven; to use my magical and legal powers on its behalf; and to be loyal to its leader."

"I swear that Sadie Sadler will be a valued member of the London Coven," Lavinia says in turn. "Who witnesses this bargain?"

"We do," the gathered practitioners call, with one voice. She's got them well-trained. A sudden wave of queasiness assails me.

Lavinia tightens her grip on my left hand and drives her right hand into my back like she's trying to push right through it. I jerk forward, away from her hand. A pure reflex action, like touching something hot.

I take a deep, shaky breath. "Sorry. Try again."

I have to dig my feet into the ground and brace my thighs to stay in position. There's an intense but short-lived burst of heat that would probably have made me cry out, were I not so determined to look strong. Then she lets go of me and steps forward to stand by my side.

"There. That wasn't so bad, was it?" She says it like I'm a five-year-old being given a vaccination.

"I guess not. Can I see it?"

"Clarissa. Katrina. Mirrors."

The two coven members take up positions, the former in front, the latter behind. They look at each other over my head, nod, then click their fingers in unison. The simple spell leaves Katrina holding a smallish circular mirror which she angles towards the lien mark, while Clarissa supports a full-length oval one. By staring into the latter, I can see the reflection of the mark in the former, like checking out the back of your hair at the hairdressers.

It takes up half my back, extending far beyond the space Lavinia's hand touched. It's way bigger than the ones I've seen on the other coven members. On either side, there's a dragon holding a sword, which I recognise as part of the coat of arms of the City of London—you see them all over the place in statues and street signs in the legal district where I spend most of my working hours. In the centre, there's a stylised leopard's head, which I can't immediately place.

"Bloody hell. I look like I've joined the Yakuza."

Lavinia laughs, and the mirrors disappear, then she zips my dress back up. "Sorry, I got carried away. But you'll get used to it. It'll be a real talking point at the beach in summer."

I sink down onto a velvet chair. "Right, that's that done," I say, matter-of-factly. As though I've not just confronted one of my deepest fears head on. As though I've not just made a binding commitment I'd hoped to avoid. "Can we talk vampires and revenge now please?"

"I was going to suggest a few celebratory drinks first,"

Lavinia replies. "But sure, let's get down to business. What do you know about them?"

"Just the basics," I reply. "Stuck-up, good-looking bastards. Drink blood. Live forever. Can only come out at night."

"Plus, superhuman strength and speed, mesmerism that's equal to our own, and some vague magical powers, depending on the individual," Lydia adds.

"They drink blood most days, from mesmerised or seduced victims," Katrina says. "But it's rare they kill. Rarer still that they turn someone into a new vampire, which involves a human drinking a vampire's blood in sufficient quantities, and then being drained."

Lavinia nods. "Their leader, Augustine, has lived for a couple of millennia. Many of his lieutenants are centuries old. Over that time, they've gathered almost incalculable wealth. Their members hold key roles in politics, the media, finance, and the judiciary—and they put on an excellent show of not only being human, but being utterly respectable and above reproach. You'll never find a sex scandal or tax evasion story about any of them, never mind a hint of what they really get up to. Many of them are household names in the human world, or at least well-known within the relevant circles. But they are so careful that no one suspects a thing.

"And through money, mesmerism, physical threats, or the promise of eternal life, they have an enormous amount of sway over many of their human counterparts. In short, they're the establishment made flesh, the old boys' network incarnate. They think they're untouchable. I want to show them that they're wrong."

I shiver. All of that makes me even more eager to take them down. But it hardly sounds easy.

"And how do you propose to do that?" Clarissa asks, stroking her dog.

"Like I said before, despite all their powers, their true

weapon is secrecy and maintaining control from the shadows, combined with a veneer of polished respectability. They are vastly stronger than any individual human, but their numbers are small. If their existence was common knowledge, most people would be horrified—and they're not so strong against an angry mob.

"So we need incontrovertible, highly publicised evidence of their ways. Essentially, we'll engineer it so one of them attacks one of my human acolytes. Nothing too bad, just a bit of blood loss, but enough to make it a pretty serious crime.

"It's the sort of thing that happens often, but normally, they are careful to avoid witnesses and to mesmerise anyone who does see something suspicious. And in the rare cases when a vampire attack makes it as far as the police, they make use of mind control, bribery, intimidation, whatever works. Their crimes never get anywhere near a court, and above all, they're kept out of the press.

"But this time, we'll create the perfect scenario. In place of their normal secrecy, there'll be witnesses whom we'll protect from mind control. Medical evidence that we'll protect. Police officers and paramedics that we'll shield from corruption."

I nod vigorously. "The case will get all the way to court. And then in place of an easily manipulated human prosecution lawyer, I'll take him down."

"It'll be a spectacular, scandalous case," Lydia says. "And even if they keep the papers at bay, I'll make sure it ends up all over social media. And hopefully a few edgier investigative journalists will get involved, too. People might struggle to believe they are literal vampires, but we should be able to prove there's a gang of twisted rich guys who get their kicks from drinking human blood. That some of these polished politicians and businessmen are sick perverts. They'll struggle to maintain their respectable façade in the wake of that."

Katrina crosses her arms. "I'm never one to doubt you,

Lavinia, but this sounds like it has the potential to go wrong. Why are you so determined to do this?"

Lavinia smiles. "I genuinely disapprove of many of the vampires' ways, from their control over elections to the way they use women as food. But at heart, I can be petty. In a long life of seduction, Augustine Piso was one of very few men ever to have rejected my advances. I want to show that self-satisfied prick the error of his ways. And the best way to do that is by dragging the sordid and secretive organisation that he's so proud of into the cold light of day."

"Why did he turn you down?" Clarissa sounds as though she can barely conceive of such a thing.

"He killed his wife, in Roman times, to complete his transformation. Some demon promised him she'd eventually be reborn. Despite being one of the hottest, richest, and most powerful men in history for twenty straight centuries, he swore to remain celibate until she was reincarnated and returned to him. I thought he could be persuaded to make an exception, but apparently not. I've never forgiven him."

I try to keep my face neutral. If he'd stayed celibate for two thousand years of being an eligible bachelor, he must have turned down hundreds of people over the centuries. It's hardly personal. The fact Lavinia took it so hard and is now going to such extremes hardly suggests the most balanced personality. But at the end of the day, we both want the same thing, even if my reasons for seeking revenge feel rather more legitimate.

Besides, I've committed myself now.

SEVEN

BRENDAN

It's been a shit week, even by the standards of the past few months.

Last night, Becca, an old school friend of Sadie's and one of the most senior of the acolytes who report directly to me, rather than to my father, all but dragged me out to a bar in town. "You never come out anymore, boss. It'll do you good. And you need to be seen. The Thornbers are getting cocky."

"We're in an alliance with the Thornbers," I'd replied. "They're entitled to be as cocky as they want."

But she had a point, on both counts. She usually does. She has a pretty impressive degree of magical firepower, but she rarely uses it—her focus tends to be more on the strategic side of things.

So I'd changed into a smart shirt, gelled my hair back, and traversed out with her. I had enough magic left to do that, at least, though it felt like driving some old banger, having got used to a Ferrari.

We went to a little bar in the centre of town. It's either owned by the family, controlled via a holding company, or pays us tribute. I lose track. A few other friends and acolytes were waiting—presumably, the evening had been carefully arranged.

After three pints, buying a few drinks for some appreciative women, and having a laugh with the group, I felt vaguely cheerful for the first time in weeks.

Becca and a couple of the others went outside to smoke while I remained at the table with a few hangers-on.

A few minutes later, she dashed back into the bar. "Bren, quick. Josh and some Thornber idiot are ripping each other apart."

I followed the visibly panicking Becca outside. A crowd had gathered, and in the centre, two local guys were throwing fireballs at each other. One of them, Josh, had been drinking with me ten minutes earlier. The other was a Thornber guy I vaguely recognised but couldn't name.

It's relatively unusual for a magical fight to break out in town, but far from unheard of. Practitioners are like anyone else: after a few drinks too many, things can get messy. While it's ideally something I leave to Liam, I've broken up a fair few fights in my time.

The crowd parted at the mere sight of me. As soon as I was at the front, I let my magic flow. The idea was to create a shield between the two fighters and knock them both out for a minute or two.

A little jolt of power shot out from my fingers, but then it died in the air. No shield materialised, and the fight went on.

A few seconds later, the two fighters froze and turned to face me, with terrified expressions. My sheer presence had done what my magic couldn't.

"What the hell are the two of you doing?" I acted like I hadn't just failed to activate a fairly straightforward spell. "We're in an alliance. We're supposed to be making it work."

"Sorry, boss," Josh says.

"Sorry," the Thornber loyalist whispered.

"Get back home, both of you."

They complied immediately, traversing out of sight.

"And everyone else, get on with your night. Don't stand here gawping."

Only a small proportion of the onlookers were formally associated with the Sadlers, but all of them, human or practitioner, inner circle, outer circle or basically a stranger, knew me by reputation. Feared me by reputation. They scattered instantly. Seemingly, no one noticed my failed spell. Seemingly, no one realised my reputation was no longer deserved.

I stood there unmoving till Becca took my arm and manoeuvred me back inside.

"Everything alright, boss? It almost looked like you attempted to break them up with magic and it didn't quite work." She laughed hysterically, half trying to show what a ridiculous sentiment that *obviously* was, half begging me not to fire her for even implying such a thing.

I laughed in turn, and somehow managed not to make it sound too forced. "It wasn't worth wasting magic on such a petty issue, when I could stop them by just standing there."

"Makes sense," Becca replied, but she couldn't quite keep the frown off her face.

It'd have made more sense if I'd not spent my entire life wasting magic on every petty issue imaginable.

Despite her consternation and the usual strength of her intuition, Becca seemed to buy my explanation. The idea that I, Brendan Sadler, might have flunked a straightforward spell was just too unlikely a concept.

But I'll mess up again and again. And gradually, reality will start to creep into people's perceptions. And then I'll be doomed. And my family with me.

. . .

Twice, I open up the contacts list on my phone, stare at her name for a solid minute, and then close it again.

The third time that I scroll down to her number, I hesitate for more like five minutes. It's ridiculous. I've never been one for uncertainty and hesitation. But I'm not the man I was. I grip the phone hard enough to shatter it, then call before I can change my mind.

Nikki picks up in seconds. "I was wondering when you were going to ring. Want to take me up on my offer?"

"What's the catch?"

"I just want to help you out. Half general good deed, half a show of faith in this new alliance."

"And you swear you won't tell him?" There's no need to clarify which "him" I mean.

"I'm the one offering you a favour. You don't get to call the shots."

"Fine then, forget it."

"I'm not going to tell Gabe. I'd never shame someone for a lack of magic. And he probably wouldn't approve of me helping you."

I can't believe I'm even considering this. At best, it's humiliating. At worst, I'm falling into some sort of trap. But what choice do I have? I can't maintain my place in the family, the business, and the town without magic. I can't live like this.

"Fine, I'll do it." I still sound like I'm doing her a favour, rather than the other way round, but I can't help the fact I was born arrogant.

Nikki sounds more amused than irritated. "Your place or mine?"

Letting her into my house would mean allowing her through my wards. Going to hers could mean walking into an ambush. Anywhere else would carry far too high a risk of someone else finding out what was going on.

"Mine. I'll get you the address. Can you traverse?"

Is that a rude question? I don't really know how Taught Practitioners work.

"I know where you live. I'll see you in a few minutes."

It really is only a few minutes later when there's a knock on the door. I guess that's a yes to being able to traverse.

I open the door a few inches. Once, I'd have thrown it wide open, and if someone was planning an attack, challenged them to bring it on. But if I'm not learning patience, I'm at least learning caution.

Nikki is wearing yoga pants with fluorescent, swirling patterns on them, and a tracksuit top. Whenever I've seen her round town, she's tended to be in a suit if she's on formal business or else wearing fitted jeans and shirts. It's odd to see her looking so casual.

"Bloody hell, this place is warded to the hilt. How paranoid are you?"

I cross my arms. "Your boss promised to kill me. And whatever other faults he has, he strikes me as someone who keeps his promises."

Nikki laughs. "Gabe's not going to kill you. He'd love to, but it'd upset your baby sister too much."

"My 'baby sister' isn't speaking to me. One more thing that's his fault."

She raises an immaculately shaped eyebrow. I notice that sort of thing, thanks to a mixture of Chrissie's obsession with beauty and my love of drawing. "Am I going to stand out here arguing with you about other people all evening, or are you going to invite me in so I can give you some magic back?"

I stare at her, looking for any sign of a weapon, magical or physical. She seems clean. I try to read her intention in her aura, but it's much harder with those who aren't Born Practitioners. The colours and patterns are opaque and unfamiliar.

Sod it.

"Come in."

She grins and bounds over the threshold. "Nice place you've got here. Sleek. Modern. Stylish. I thought it might be a bit like Thornber Manor. Ancient furniture to show your family has run the town for centuries."

I look around self-consciously. I've got a few antiques—a massive dining table, a ship's desk, a bookcase that dominates one room—but otherwise everything's glass, chrome, and leather.

She shrugs off her tracksuit top and throws it onto a chair. Underneath, she's wearing a strappy black top that shows off her toned—no, forget that, straight-up muscular—arms and shoulders, and her chest in equal measure. The yoga pants already highlighted her long, strong legs.

I'm perving on Thornber's most feared lieutenant. Someone who's aggressive, androgynous, and to the best of my knowledge, only into women. And who, despite this odd favour, would probably happily murder me. I need to get laid more than I thought.

"Which room has got the most space? I'm dying to show you how powerful learnt magic can be."

"Conservatory, I guess." I lead her through to the back of the house.

"This'll do." She moves her hands slowly and precisely, as I stare and try to follow. She's whispering incantations under her breath and looking around the room in a focused way.

I'll use the odd hand signal from time to time, either on autopilot or for a bit of extra emphasis and drama, but her approach is fundamentally so different from the "will it, and it will be so" version of magic I've always practiced. Or always used to practice.

Once she stops moving, the furniture—a glass dining table

and a wicker sofa—slide to the edges of the room and compress until they are almost two-dimensional.

"I'll put them back afterwards, don't worry. This isn't some petty Thornber trick to mess up your house."

A few additional hand movements raise the temperature of the room—a welcome development in a structure mostly comprised of glass, in October.

"Let's start with Greenfire," she declares, hands on slender hips. "You still have some residual 'natural' magic. In some respects, that complicates the issue. Try not to call on it."

I shrug. "It's barely worth calling on."

"For goodness' sake, Brendan Sadler. So you're not a god amongst gods anymore. There are still plenty of people who'd kill for half your remaining magic. I don't know why I'm helping you. Really I don't."

My fists clench against my will. Whenever I'm the slightest bit challenged or provoked, my natural reaction is to lash out harder. But Nikki really has very little incentive to help me. I can't afford to undermine whatever goodwill is driving this.

"Sorry. Just tell me what I need to do." It's hard to get the somewhat submissive words out, but I manage it.

"As I understand it, magic's all around us. In the air, the earth, the water. The main difference between Born Practitioner magic and Taught or Learnt Practitioner magic—and for the record, I hate those terms, but they're annoyingly useful for this conversation—is that for people like you, it's also literally in your blood. And as a result of the magic inside you, you've got a really solid connection to the magic outside of you."

I narrow my eyes. It's something I've thought about a lot in the past. What is magic, really? It's hard to take a step back and try to understand when it's such a fundamental part of who I am. Or who I was.

"When they want to work a small piece of magic, a Born Practitioner can just make use of what's inside them. Shape it how they wish and throw it out into the world with no intermediary. For something bigger, they can reach out through their established connection, pull the external magic into them, and make use of that.

"For some Born Practitioners, that second step takes a bit of effort. But for those as powerful as you used to be, there's barely a distinction between the magic inside and the magic outside. It all flows together, yours to command with a thought. Or at most, a deep breath and a vague wave of your hands."

She sounds matter of fact, a professor delivering a lecture on their pet subject. But there's a hint of bitterness hiding underneath her words.

"And for those who don't have magic inside them? Or don't have enough?"

"There are three main differences. Firstly, even for minor spells, we need to draw on external magic. Secondly, we have to physically forge a connection with it each time. It's like using a dial-up modem rather than ultra-fast Wi-Fi. And thirdly, once we get the connection, it's harder to pull it inside ourselves. Harder to control it once we have. More difficult to cast it back out into the world in the form we wish, rather than as unformed power. In short, it fights us every inch of the way."

"That sounds awful." I say it before I can stop myself, more a cry from the heart than a rational sentence from my brain.

"It fights us, but we can fight back, and we can win. We just need to use all the tools at our disposal. The hand signals and incantations at the very least. For day-to-day magic, I'm past the stage of needing to use the crystals and potions and all the rest of it, but for particularly complex, sustained, or dangerous spells, they can help, too."

I nod. "It's not like I've never used those things. I always jewel up for the annual Ritual, for a start. But it's mostly for show."

"Enough talk. We're going to take it in turn to produce

Greenfire and to throw up shields." She reaches into a pocket of her discarded jacket, takes out two emeralds, slips one into her bra, and hands the other to me.

I examine mine closely. "Where did you get these? They're buzzing with power. And even just as jewels they must have cost a small fortune."

"Present from Gabe. For goodness' sake, never tell him I let you play with them."

I slip mine into the pocket of my jeans. "It's not like we have regular chats."

"Right, you go first. Close your eyes. Thumb pressing little finger, ring finger, and middle finger down into your palm on both hands. Remaining finger pointing towards the earth, arms at your side and slightly turned outwards."

I do as she says, my fingers stiff and awkward.

"Now you need to take some really long, slow, deep breaths. Think about the emerald. You sort of have to imagine your consciousness flowing into it. Then out of it into the earth. Does that make sense?"

"I guess."

"I'm going to dab a couple of oils on your face and your hands, just to help things along. Just ignore me. Keep breathing, keep focusing, keep your hands in place."

Despite her warning, I shiver as her fingers stroke mine, and almost flinch when she leans in close and runs some heavily scented substance along my cheekbones and dabs it on my third eye. It smells vaguely familiar, but I couldn't say exactly what herbs and stranger plants it contains. The sale of potions accounts for a surprisingly large proportion of the family income, but I've always mostly left the production of them to Mum and Chrissie.

"To recap, you need a channel to the emerald. Another out into the earth. And then you need to reach out through your pointing fingers and touch the magic lurking there."

Deep breaths. Emerald. Earth. I stretch my arms down as far as they'll go. And then I feel it.

I don't know whether she senses something in my aura or just sees a look of excitement on my face, but the second I make the connection, Nikki gasps.

"Now, keep your fingers in position and slowly draw your hands up towards your chest. Physically pull the magic with you. And mentally imagine it flowing from the ground and into your finger and hands."

Again, I do as she says. "Ow." I relax my fingers, pull my hands against me and open my eyes. "It burns. What are you trying to do to me?"

If Nikki's at all perturbed by the rage in my eyes, she gives no sign. "You need to move your hands more slowly. Keep breathing deeply. And pull the magic in gradually and deliberately, not let it flow in unchecked. It's not your pet anymore, it's a wild animal. Start again."

Fingers in place. Arms down. Breathing. Emerald. Earth. Successful connection.

This time, I raise my hands like I'm trying to drag a two-hundred-pound weight out of the earth. And I funnel the magic in painfully slowly, channelling and filtering it through the emerald.

"Good. Don't take too much at once. Next you need to turn your hands around and press the pads of the pointing fingers into the nubs of your collarbones. Let the magic flow into the rest of your body."

It's still a little hot and uncomfortable, but no longer actually painful. And it's working. There's a useful quantity of magic in my nerves and my blood again.

"Now what?"

"You basically have to do that bit with a few subtle variations for any spell, though with a bit of practice, you can do it in advance and store the magic."

Bloody hell. I need to do all that every time? Unless my life were in danger, it barely seems worth the effort. I think about both the great spectacles I've pulled off and the hundreds of little spells I used to work in an average day, and I'm not sure whether to laugh or cry.

"Now we need to get specific. Greenfire. You must have worked that spell a thousand times. And been a victim of it, too. Give me some words to describe it."

I purse my lips. My eyes are closed still, and it's disconcerting to have a conversation with someone I can't see. Especially someone I've always thought of as an enemy. Or at least, a villain's sidekick.

"Heat. Pain. Brightness. Force. The actual colour green. And fakery. Imagination. Because it doesn't actually do any harm."

"Perfect. Now, you need to keep those concepts in your mind. Really think about what you're trying to achieve. And then, if you open your eyes just slightly so I can demonstrate, you need to put your fingers like this."

I stare at her hands. Middle fingers crossed over pointers. Little and ring fingers bent down and held in place by thumbs. Then the sides of the middle fingers on each hand and the nails of the thumbs both touching.

It takes me a couple of seconds of fumbling to get it right.

"You've probably done this exact gesture before without even realising, when casually throwing Greenfire at someone," Nikki muses. "Gabe couldn't consciously describe or demonstrate the right gesture if you held him at gunpoint, but last time I saw him inflict Greenfire on someone, I watched him really carefully, and for a fraction of a second, his hands did that of their own accord."

Have I ever made this gesture before? It's forced and unfamiliar, but who knows?

"You're ready to go. Hands outstretched. Let the magic

that's flowing around your body come back together. Focus on the idea of Greenfire. Then force it out through your fingers."

"Am I meant to be firing at you?" Whether it's because she's a woman or because she's a Taught Practitioner, the idea makes me guilty.

"I'm sure you've attacked far more defenceless people than me in your time. Debtors. Ritual sacrifices. Your own sister. And you were going to sacrifice God knows how many people to extend the Dome."

That's all technically true and all very unfair—I had good reasons for all those things. It's not like I just go around attacking people for the fun of it.

It's unclear whether she's trying to reassure me or make me angry enough to attack, but she achieves a bit of both. I narrow my eyes just enough to see her, then work my way laboriously through the steps she describes. It's a horrible way of working magic, but when a good, strong stream of genuine Greenfire cascades out of my contorted fingers, it's all worthwhile.

The spell crashes into Nikki, and she cries out in pain. There's a part of me that longs to let it flow and flow, not to hurt Nikki, but because it's so good to feel power again. But despite what she might think, I'm a decent person, deep down, and I slam my hands down against my side, breaking the connection.

Usually, if I stop a spell, the magic just settles back down inside me or slowly dissipates into the air. Now, it all disappears with a jolt, like someone's flicked a switch.

"There was no need to stop," Nikki calls, though she's breathing heavily. "The force of it caught me a little by surprise, I've got to admit, but I'd have got my shields up in seconds. And however much it hurt, it's not going to do me any harm. Do it again. Hold your nerve this time."

I shake my head. I'm buzzing with the memory of power flowing through my veins, exhausted from the experience of trying to control it, and freshly drained from its loss.

"Put the furniture back. Sit down. We're going to have a civilised glass of wine and discuss why Gabriel-fucking-Thornber's most feared lieutenant is helping his least favourite person in the world."

I watch closely as she rearranges the room. Now I know what I'm looking for, I follow her hand gestures more easily. I recognise the bit where she draws magic up from the ground and into herself, though it only takes her a second or two. The sort of scooping and twisting motion she makes to actually move the sofa and tables is unfamiliar, but already makes a slight sense.

She throws herself full-length on the sofa. "'Most feared lieutenant'. Don't make me laugh. People give me a certain degree of respect because I'm indisputably Gabe's best friend. But everyone knows my limitations."

I perch on the one remaining bit of sofa not taken up by her long legs. "Ask any of my men or women who they'd be most scared of getting in a fight with or getting on the wrong side of. The number one answer is Thornber, obviously. But you run him a respectable second.

"There are those who've got more muscle, and those who've got more magic. But you just give the impression you'd use what strength and power you do have more strategically. More ruthlessly. Everyone's a bit fascinated and a bit terrified in equal measure."

I'd assumed I was just confirming something she already knew, but her eyes widen. "I wouldn't have thought you even knew who I was. Never mind have ever given me a second thought."

"Sure. I've never noticed the six-foot-tall, stunningly attractive Taught Practitioner whose skills put most Born Practitioners to shame. The woman who can take most men in single combat. The one South Asian person in either family's inner circle. The one who's got a different pretty girl hanging off her arm every night, and has Gabriel-fucking-Thornber wrapped around her little finger."

Nikki laughs, and almost blushes before she manages to get her face under control. "About half of that is true. I'm five foot ten, for the record."

"Go on then. What was your impression of me?"

She stretches her arms out over her head. "I've always been hyper aware of your existence. But you were kind of an abstract concept. Sort of the opposite of Gabe. Sort of an exact parallel to him. His shadow or his reflection, or his doppelganger. The demon to his angel. Or the other way round, depending on who you ask.

"All I ever knew is that you were hot, and rich, and power-ful. And kind of a dick. So once we'd forged an alliance, I thought it'd be interesting to get to know you as a person, rather than a symbol. That's why I offered to help."

I raise my eyebrows in an exaggerated manner. "And what do you make of me so far?"

She jumps to her feet. "Let's try the Greenfire again. Maybe that'll help my judgement."

EIGHT

SADIE

My chambers—aka my office, because no one could ever accuse the British legal system of not being pretentious—is, like those of many other London barristers, situated in the Inner Temple.

The name makes it sound pretty mystical and sinister. In actuality, it's merely a collection of offices and meeting rooms for barristers that have grown up in the same spot over the centuries. Nevertheless, on a cool autumn day like today, as twilight starts to fall, the ambience of the centuries-old buildings *is* fairly spooky. The little workplace buildings are built around the medieval church or "temple" that gives the area its name, an Elizabethan dining hall, endless gardens and courtyards, and a large law library.

I head towards the library. It's not somewhere I visit very often. I can find most information I need online or in my own chambers' smaller and more specialised library. But though that's got everything you need to know about criminal procedure and grisly murder trials, it's somewhat lacking on anything to do with vampires.

Rumour has it that if I ask the right people the right questions, the larger communal library just might be able to help me.

The library is one of the older bits of the site, dating back to the early sixteenth century. Inside, the light wood panelling, thousands of leather-bound books, and little hidden alcoves give it a sense of age and wisdom. Some people might find it intimidating, but places like this always put me in a good mood.

I glance around. It's fairly quiet at this time in the evening. If the librarian bursts out laughing, at least there'll be no witnesses to my embarrassment. Even so, I do a couple of laps of the room, study a few bookcases, and pretend to be absolutely engrossed in the details of a defamation case from 1956, before finally summoning up the nerve to approach her.

It's unlike me to be nervous. But then again, it's unlike me to willingly give the general public any hint that I'm anything but a normal, human lawyer.

"Excuse me. I wondered if you could help me with something."

The librarian smiles. "I can certainly try my best."

She's in her early forties and looks slightly dowdy and not at all magical. Still, I have to give it my best shot.

"Would it be possible to view the Lore Library? L-O-R-E, I mean, rather than L-A-W."

I stare down at the desk, willing her to be able to help.

When I cast my gaze back up towards her, the librarian has straightened her stance and her face seems more alert and animated.

"Who told you about our more specialist service?"

Against the odds, that seems to be both an admittance that it exists and some willingness to help.

"It's something I've heard rumours about for a while, from various people."

"And what are you?"

"Excuse me?"

"Are you a witch? A vampire? An elf or something? I doubt

you're a were-anything. Not to be too stereotypical, but we don't get many of them in the library."

Blood rushes to my head, both from the casual way she says all this, and the implications that there are all sorts of not entirely human people using this place on a regular enough basis that she has some sort of classification system in place.

"A witch, I guess. Though I tend to use the term practitioner. It has less... connotations." My family and I barely ever use the "W" word though Lavinia and her associates seem happy to do so.

"Follow me."

"That's it? I don't need to show ID or do a test or something?"

I'm not sure what ID I'd show. It's not like we're issued with special witch cards at birth, but the idea that anyone could just wander into this place makes me shiver.

She strides out from behind the desk in the direction of a row of shelves towards the back of the room. "The door will take care of that."

I follow her to a shelf that contains books on obscure aspects of chancery law. The librarian ignores all the dry tomes on probate and secret trusts, and homes straight in on one specific volume. It looks just the same as the others, with its faded green leather spine and embossed title. But "Magic and the Law of England and Wales" isn't your average title.

When she slides the book off the shelf, I almost expect the bookcase to swing open or spin round, like something out of an old Scooby Doo cartoon, but nothing dramatic happens.

"There's a little lever behind it," the librarian explains. "It responds to various things. Vampires have to provide a drop of blood. But for you, holding it and focusing your power should be enough."

I stick my hand into the gap with as much caution as

someone diffusing a bomb. I'm expecting an electric shock or an invisible barrier, but face no resistance or nasty surprises. When my hand tentatively closes on the lever, I exhale in relief at the familiar sensation. The magic coming off the device is just like whatever controls the door to the Witches' Church back in Mannith. If anything, it's less complex, considering that one requires two powerful, local practitioners to operate it.

I tighten my grip and let my aura, my sense of self, and some essence of my power reach out to touch the magic implanted in the mechanism. There's a little jolt as the lock's magic recognises mine. Then, much to my delight, the entire bookcase recesses into the wall after all.

The library fundamentally doesn't disappoint. It's similar in design to the main library, but where that's been updated over the centuries—carpets, electric lighting, computers—this seems barely changed since it was built. It's lit by candlelight and heated by a fire that is magicked to burn continuously yet not put any of the documents in danger. Many of the documents are so old they aren't really books at all, but rather parchments and scrolls.

"Good luck," the librarian calls. It seems she's unable to penetrate the barrier.

The door slides back into place and my heart almost stops, but a quick check reveals a lever that's operable from this side.

I pace the shelves, collecting a few documents here and there and taking them to an oak table so old and well used it almost seems to have its own soul.

The browsing sends me into a semi-meditative state and my mind wanders back, yet again, to the night Gabriel put the lien mark on me.

Today, though, my memories settle on an unusual aspect.

Not the fear, the magic or the sexual tension, but the way Gabriel had, of all things, helped me with my homework, picking out books for me from Thornber Manor's vast collection. I smile at the thought, then instantly pay for it with a moment of unbearably intense loss and longing. But surge of emotions aside, two rational thoughts occur to me. Firstly, the manor's library, which I've never visited before or since, surely has some tomes relating to vampires, too. Secondly, Gabriel would probably be well placed to help me find the most useful documents here.

Give him a call, my mind begs. *Invite yourself up there to see his library. Or ask him to come down here.*

I sink into a green leather armchair. Either course of action would genuinely be useful. But that doesn't make it any less of an obvious excuse than any of the others I've come up with.

Right on cue, my phone rings. I grab it, expecting to see that iconic "X" that I still keep Gabriel's number saved under.

Instead, it's Chrissie. And while I generally love nothing more than a leisurely chat with my sister, I have to fight to keep the disappointment out of my voice.

"How are the cramps?" Chrissie asks, by way of a "hello".

She and I have had perfectly synced menstrual cycles for as long as I can remember. When she was pregnant with the twins, my periods stopped for the best part of a year.

"Not too bad. I've been using the jasmine oil and all that jazz."

"Good to hear you're not completely adverse to a bit of classic witchery."

"It's funny you should say that, because as far as doing witchy stuff goes, I've gone one better than that—I've joined the London Coven."

I get the words out quickly, in as flippant a tone as I can manage. It's hard to know what my sister will make of that, but for all the tensions with my family, I want to be honest with them about this. And Chrissie seems like the easiest person to have the conversation with.

There's silence for a moment. "I don't know what to say. Doesn't that tie you to London, pretty much for good? I know there were things that upset you in the summer, but we were all hoping you'd come back eventually."

"The summer was intense. For now, I need space. But I'm going to visit at some point, don't worry about that. I'm not going into full-blown exile for another six years or anything."

"A visit sounds great. But deep down I was hoping for something a bit more permanent than that one day."

"London is my home now. And I wanted to commit to it. I wanted to embrace magic again. I wanted a sense of belonging. Hence the coven."

"Well, I'm glad you're embracing magic, at least. And spending time with practitioners. The way you blocked yourself off from our heritage for years can't have been healthy. I wish you were doing it in Mannith, with us. But I guess this is the next best thing."

"Thank you."

"Anyway, I called to say we're coming to London next week for this meeting with the vampires. You might not be ready for a visit to Mannith, but will you meet us?"

"You and Liam, absolutely. Possibly even Nikki, at a pinch. I don't think I'm in the right headspace for Gabriel-perfect-alliance-partner-Thornber just yet."

He still hasn't tried to call me. I wanted to test whether or not he could respect my boundaries, and astonishingly, he seems to be doing so. Unless, of course, this business trip to London is one big excuse to see me.

"While I'm visiting, we are going to sit down in a flashy bar, drink several cocktails too many, and you are going to tell me, in gory, gratuitous detail, exactly what happened with your mortal-enemy-turned-lover-turned-soulmate-turned-person-you're-refusing-to-speak-to. I can't believe I didn't realise it was happening until you were almost ready to leave."

"I'm not sure a respectable married mother like yourself will have the stomach for all the scandalous details."

Chrissie is indeed married, and faithful, and dotes on her baby twins. But she was absolutely wild in her teens. Now that she's seemingly come to terms with the basic fact I'd been sleeping with Gabriel Thornber, I don't think there are any details of my sex life that could conceivably surprise her, however intense some of those episodes were.

"I'll prepare to be shocked." She laughs. "And on a more serious note, will you represent us at the meeting with the vamps? We could do with a lawyer there. They're bound to be represented up to the teeth."

"I'm bringing a case against the vampires. They killed a client of mine. And beyond that, they're just awful people. If you can even call them people. There's no way I'm helping you cut a deal with them. It's a conflict of interest and completely immoral."

I sound so sanctimonious. Chrissie will probably report the conversation back to Liam, and they'll all have a laugh at my expense. But surely I'm the one in the right here. I want to stop the vampires, or at least get some small-scale justice against them. Not offer up the people on the outskirts of Mannith as a tasty snack so the Thornbers and Sadlers can consolidate their power.

"Look, I'm not going to attempt to talk you round now—suffice to say I truly do believe it's the lesser of two evils. But we can talk properly when we meet. As well as the formal meeting, the vampires have also invited us to a very flashy Halloween party. At least come to that while you decide whether to do anything more. You can get dressed up. Swan about. Drink their expensive champagne. And tell Gabriel in person just how annoyed you are with his hypocrisy."

I can feel the force of her grin down the phone, as though to imply that's the last thing I'm going to do if I come face to face with him.

NINE

BRENDAN

The following Friday, I spend an embarrassing amount of time getting both myself and the house ready. If Nikki's out to judge me, I'm going to give her something worth judging.

We've agreed we'll train once a week, every week. It's odd how much I've been looking forward to session two.

At five on the dot, the bell rings, and I open the door with slightly unseemly haste.

"Can I come in?"

"Time to get to know me better."

She laughs and steps over the threshold. "Glad you've got over your concern that it's all a complex trap."

I'm not one hundred per cent sure I have. I don't trust Gabriel-fucking-Thornber an inch, and it seems mad to trust his right-hand woman. But her training is certainly useful.

Once again, she shrugs off her jacket and heads straight for the conservatory. "I thought we could stick with the attack theme this week, and move on to some Hellfire. Not directed at each other, of course. We'll set up some barriers and targets."

I follow her through the house. "Sure."

Her straight to business tone is a little disconcerting. I'd hoped for some pleasantries first. A chance to sit and chat. The opportunity to show that I'm definitely the angel and not the demon when it comes to the dynamic between Thornber and I. But it seems we're straight to work. Which is fine, I guess. Mastering Learnt Magic is what matters here.

Nikki does the same pointing at the earth and drawing power into her body routine that she made me practice last week. Then, in a dramatic swirling of arms, she puts a protective bubble around the room.

"Okay. Words to describe Hellfire?"

"Heat. Pain. Death. Enemy. Attack. Burn."

"It's a delightful spell, isn't it? The hand gesture is like the Greenfire one, but with the fingers crossed the other way."

I study my hands. "How many times has someone got them the wrong way round and killed someone they just wanted to scare?"

She laughs, then her face turns serious. "The gestures are only half the battle. You need to visualise, too."

Like last week, I close my eyes. She dabs a different oil on me, and this time, I manage not to flinch when she comes close. It's the work of seconds to make contact with the magic in the earth, and a few more seconds to pull it up.

"That's depressingly impressive." Over the hum of the magic, Nikki's voice sounds like it's coming from a long way away. "It takes most people months just to reach the magic. Months more to draw it into themselves. I guess even with your own magic depleted, you can automatically recognise it. Feel comfortable around it. Bloody Born Practitioners."

"Maybe. Now, shall we try some fireballs?"

An hour later, and I'm absolutely buzzing with elation. It took a bit of practice, but by the end, I was blasting Hellfire all around the room.

Nikki glances at her watch. "That'll do for today. We need to be careful not to burn you out."

"I could fire off spells all day."

She shakes her head. "Learnt magic takes a harder toll."

I don't want to think about that. And for now, at least, I'm just fine. Better than fine.

"Will you at least stay for a drink again?"

"I've been looking forward to it."

I pour us each a large glass of Barolo, and we settle down on the sofa.

"Are you sure Thornber hasn't put you up to these visits?" I don't want to ask the question, but I can't not.

"What possible reason would he have for getting me to teach you magic? If he knew you were weakened, I doubt he'd want to fix the issue."

"Doesn't he always have two convoluted, over-complicated reasons for everything?"

She takes a sip of her drink and puts a hand on my shoulder. For a second, I freeze, then it feels quite pleasant. "Gabriel's got better things to do than have people toy with you."

I lean back and close my eyes. "He framed me for murder, seduced my fiancée, and screwed my baby sister."

She massages my shoulder. "He framed you to stop you committing mass murder in order to enlarge the Dome. Though admittedly—while she had the odd bit of useful intel—he mostly slept with Leah to mess with you."

"She was the love of my life. It broke my heart." God knows why I'm saying this. Nikki might take it back to him, and he'd no doubt be delighted to hear it.

"She was a pretty, shallow non-entity, with barely any power or brains. I try not to say bad things about other women, but she was dismissive as hell to me. I don't know whether it was a race thing, or a Taught Practitioner thing, or she was threatened by my friendship with Gabe, but urgh. He had to force himself to go through with it. And I'm not saying she was throwing herself at him, but it was a close-run thing."

My throat constricts, and though I desperately try to fight it, a few tears fall. "We'd been together for years. We were going to get married. Have kids. I was able to relax around her. Have fun. He's ruined my life."

"She'd have made you unhappy in the long run."

I cross my arms. "You said yourself you barely know anything about me."

"I know enough to realise that."

I wipe the traitorous tears away. "And all the shit he's pulled with my sister? That's for my own good as well, is it?"

Nikki sips her drink and shakes her head. "You don't seriously think he slept with Sadie to wind you up, do you? How self-obsessed are you?"

"Not just slept with her. Put a lien on her. Drove her out of town then dragged her back."

"I'd be the last person to say their dynamic is entirely healthy. But he's had an all-encompassing obsession with her since he was about fourteen. If anything, the things he's done to you were to get her attention, rather than the other way around."

I frown, trying to get my head round the idea. It's a strange concept, being a supporting character rather than the protagonist in my own story.

"My point is, whatever his reasons, Thornber's got form. Sending you to spy on me would be the least of it."

"I understand Gabe's faults, really I do. But he wouldn't waste *my* time on something like this. Besides, if he wanted someone to weave their way into your trust and affection, he'd have made use of someone more your type."

"What's that supposed to mean?"

"Petite, pretty, blonde Born Practitioner girls, basically. It's not like we don't have plenty of Leah clones on staff."

"Before Leah, my tastes were pretty varied."

I sound weirdly defensive. It's not a crime to like pretty blonde girls. From what I've seen of Nikki on nights out, her tastes in women are not dissimilar to mine.

"I bet they were never varied enough to encompass someone like me," Nikki says.

I stand up. "What the hell does it matter? It's not like you're here to seduce me. You're teaching me learnt magic, and you're the only person on Gabriel's team who could do that."

"You're right. I'm just here to teach you magic. And we're done with that for the day. I guess I'll see you next week."

She leaves without another word.

PART 2

TEN

SADIE

When the door intercom buzzes, I throw off my apron and gloves, whack on another coat of lipstick, then slam my finger onto the button.

It's all I can do to suppress a squeal when Chrissie's face appears on the screen. Crazy to think that—like the other members of my family—she's never visited any of my succession of London flats.

Not the filthy post-university one I'd shared with several friends, where we'd squabbled about cleaning rotas and food supplies and thrown wild parties in a desperate attempt to pretend we were still students.

Not the rather tidier but significantly more soulless one I'd shared with a fellow newly qualified lawyer whom I barely knew, once the old flat's party atmosphere proved unconducive to sixty-hour weeks and keeping myself well-presented. Our combined working hours and separate social lives had meant we were barely ever in the flat, still less present at the same time. And when we were, we generally cooked separately, and stayed in our individual bedrooms, eating and working at our desks, rather than making much use of the small communal spaces.

And definitely not this place, which I finally managed to buy last year after some lucrative trials and determined saving. I revelled in having privacy and being able to decorate to my exact preferences, while pushing down the occasional pangs of loneliness when I returned after a long day's work to an empty home.

I probably could have invited some of the family down previously. It would have been significantly less risky than visiting Mannith, as far as my attempts to avoid Gabriel knowing where I was were concerned. But my risk tolerance on the matter had been decidedly low, and it had seemed easier to compartmentalise completely than to have some half-hearted family relationship.

It's still infuriating to think about the years I wasted. I ought to hate Gabriel for it. Instead, I hate myself for desperately hoping I'll get to see him tonight. My heart races at the thought, fear, guilt, lust, excitement all mingling into one.

"Come up," I shout into the entry phone.

Half a minute later, there's a knock on the door to the flat. I fling it open and all but drag Chrissie inside.

"Nice to see you, too, sis." She grins as she closes the door behind her.

I watch her intently as she looks around, trying to guess at her first impressions. I've always cared far too much about impressing my family. I've spent the entire day alternating between tidying the house and getting myself dressed and made-up, using a haphazard combination of magic and physical effort.

"It's beautifully decorated," she says.

"And smaller than your bedroom at home." I voice her obvious unspoken thought.

She flings off her coat. "I was intending to be too polite to mention it. Particularly as it no doubt cost twice as much as our four-bed. London freaks me out. The energy feels all wrong."

"You should talk to Lavinia. She'd soon put you straight." Her claims about the magic of London echo in my head. I can't quite decide if I'm gradually coming round to her point of view or moving further away from it by the day.

I steer Chrissie towards the kitchen area of the open-plan room. "Sit down and make yourself comfortable." I gesture towards the leather and chrome bar stools which surround the little breakfast bar and then make us both a coffee.

I've spent the week since Chrissie phoned and mentioned her visit debating whether or not to go to the vampires' party—and more importantly, the family's conference with them tomorrow evening.

On one side of the equation, the idea of my family making a deal with them is morally abominable and I'm worried about conflicts of interest with Lavinia's planned case.

On the other hand, I don't want the vampires screwing Mannith over. If the Practitioner Alliance insist on going ahead with their scheme, they need legal representation. And if I got involved, I could hopefully keep the terms of the arrangement towards the unpleasant rather than the unconscionable end of the spectrum. Besides which, nothing would prepare me better for my revenge case than spending some time with vampires on their own territory.

I'll do the drinks, get a sense of the vampires we're dealing with, and maybe let Gabriel explain himself. Then I'll make a decision on the meeting.

"We need to head out soon and get dresses for tonight," Chrissie proclaims, once we've finished our coffees.

"Can't you just do your usual trick and create a dress out of thin air?"

"Vampires are all loaded. They'll be wearing designer outfits, so we deserve to as well. I reckon they could tell a fake from the real thing, and it's not a risk I'm willing to take."

Thank goodness Chrissie is staying focused on the big issues.

It's testament to my sister's powers of persuasion that an hour later I find myself in a Bond Street boutique.

The sales assistant reminds me of those in Lavinia's "emporium". The same tall, skinny build, the same supposedly natural make-up look that must have taken hours to accomplish, the same slightly supercilious expression.

"Can I help you?"

Despite her naturally haughty face, she seems to be asking the question sincerely, rather than as a way to make clear we can't afford anything they sell and should leave now. Which would be perfectly true. My legal work pays well, and we both have access to the family's ill-gotten gains, but these clothes are at an oligarch price point.

"We've got a very exclusive party later," Chrissie purrs, launching into full charm and seduce mode. "My sister and I need dresses to make us look like the goddesses we are. Once you've helped us make the perfect selection, maybe you'd like to come with us?"

Chrissie has always been able to get away with saying things that would sound either cheesy or deranged on the lips of a normal person, and making them seem both perfectly reasonable and sexy as hell.

"That would be lovely." The assistant says the words quietly and nervously, staring at Chrissie, all her bravado gone.

There are two other customers in the shop. One model type in her twenties, maybe funded by Daddy's money, maybe by that of a much older lover. And one aggressively polished woman probably in her fifties, but with the face of a forty-year-old and the body of a thirty-year-old.

They both seem like people who make it a point of principle not to be impressed or fascinated by anyone or anything, but they're outright staring at Chrissie. She smiles at them both in turn, with a smile that suggests that theirs could have been a love affair for the ages, if only things had been different. Then she shakes her head sadly, and they walk out of the shop like zombies.

"You, on the other hand, can come inside, sweetheart," she says to the massive security guard on the door, who artfully combines menace and good looks.

It tickles me that the shop can afford to handpick handsome muscle. Inevitably, he walks inside without question, locking the door behind him.

The security guard reminds me a bit of poor departed Connor. I don't think about the Sadler acolyte whom I was seeing over the summer very often—my world-class ability to repress and compartmentalise things at play yet again. But now, the memory of him makes me sad. It was just a fling, but it had felt like there'd been the potential for there to be something more. He'd dumped me after he'd found out I was lying about who I really was—that I wasn't just his employers' lawyer, but rather their daughter—but then he'd talked about trying again. Only for Gabriel to kill him when Connor tried to defend and protect Mannith's Dome...

I shiver and snap back to the present. I *really* don't want to think about any of that.

Chrissie throws her arms in the air, and the security shutters that surround the building crash down, darkening the room.

"It's good to have a little privacy." She looks at the salesgirl and the security guard in turn, letting her eyes rove over each of them suggestively.

Then, without any warning or any hint of self-consciousness, she traces a line down her body, and her dress falls to the floor.

The man and the woman's eyes are both riveted on her. I

avert my gaze and stare fixedly at a mannequin on the other side of the room. Between sharing a room with her for years on end and her teenage proclivity for pulling this sort of trick, I've seen Chrissie naked more times than I can count. While I'm usually pretty happy with my own body, my self-esteem always takes days to recover from seeing the carved-marble perfection that Chrissie owes to a mixture of genetics, determination, and magic.

"What's your name, sweetheart? And what do you think would suit me?" She asks the shop assistant the question in the most innocent tone, while her magic fills the room.

"Anna. And anything. *Everything*." Goodness knows if the sales assistant is even remotely into women in the normal run of things, but she's gawping at Chrissie like she's about to propose marriage.

"Go and pick out the nicest dress you can find, Anna," Chrissie replies. "Something slinky. Sexy. Seductive."

Anna hesitates as though she can't bear to drag herself away, but then Chrissie raises her eyebrows and she springs into action. A minute or two later, she reappears with a sapphire blue gown that perfectly matches my sister's infuriatingly perfect eyes.

Chrissie takes the dress out of Anna's outstretched hands, trailing her fingers over her arms as she does so. "Perfect. I could tell you were a girl of taste."

Chrissie always has such strong views about clothes that it's unlikely she left the choice up to Anna's judgement. More likely, she had her dream outfit in mind from before she even walked into the shop, probably from a copy of Vogue carefully scoured beforehand. It would have been easy to put the idea into the shop girl's mind. Which, frankly, I could have done myself using a touch of mesmerism, without all this drama and sexual tension.

"Will you help me on with it, darling?" Chrissie turns to the security guard this time, leaving Anna pouting.

His strong hands are trembling as he lifts the delicate piece of fabric over her head. They shake still more as he fastens the little row of buttons that run up the back, Victorian style.

I grip my phone like a life aid, studying my Twitter feed as though it might contain the secrets of the universe. Anything but watch that display.

When I risk a glance a few seconds later, Chrissie's fully dressed, thank heavens. The dress already looks fantastic on her, then she runs her hands over it, drawing little sighs from her audience as she surreptitiously uses magic to tailor it to fit her toned body even more precisely.

She does a twirl, then winks at the bewitched pair. "My lovely sister needs something equally stunning."

There's a shift in the air pressure as she relaxes the spell and tones down her sex magic just enough to allow them to transfer some degree of attention to me.

I don't get quite the same rapturous reaction, but I still manage some hungry glances from the two of them. They watch me expectantly.

"Is there a problem?"

The sales assistant wordlessly looks me up and down.

"Oh, for goodness' sake. I'm going to the changing room. Bring me something nice. I'll change into it there. Alone. With the curtain closed."

"Spoilsport," Chrissie calls.

"If I was a spoilsport, I'd have walked out twenty minutes ago," I shout over my shoulder, following Anna to the opulent changing room at the back.

I settle down on the ash-coloured chaise longue and take a few breaths to try to regain some composure.

This is small-scale stuff compared to some of what my family do in Mannith, not least the annual sacrifices. But it's a stark reminder of why I need to be careful. Not just because I disapprove, although I do. But because there's a hidden bit of me that gets a thrill from all this playing around with magic.

It's fine for today. I can enjoy myself and enjoy Chrissie's company while still maintaining some degree of moral high ground. But if I were to live in Mannith full-time, I'd make compromise after compromise. I'd let the things the others did slide, and I'd start to do unacceptable things myself. Just like in the summer, when I intimidated Leah, mind-controlled a jury, and even came close to killing Gabriel.

"May I come in?" Anna sounds timid as hell.

"Just drop the dress and leave me to it. Sorry for being snappy. And sorry about my sister being my sister."

"She's beautiful," she sighs.

I shake my head, unsure what's magic and what's simple biological fact.

I cheer up a little once I slip into the dress. The long teal chiffon affair suits me perfectly. Maybe it's pathetic, but all I can think about is how I'll look through Gabriel's eyes. I'm unsure what I'll end up doing when I see him. My aim is to have a civilised conversation, but any combination of falling into his arms, fighting with him or storming away seem equally plausible. But whatever happens, I want him wowed by me. Unable to take his eyes off me. I'm going to try to be sensible and resist him, but I want all and any memories of anyone else he's ever so much as flirted with to fade away as I sashay into view. I can barely breathe from anticipation.

"Thank you," I call through the curtain.

After a moment or two, clearly unable to wait any longer, Chrissie barges in.

"That's perfect. Exactly what I had in mind. The vampires will be defenceless against your charms. And Gabriel-fucking-Thornber will be on his knees."

She says what was once a name meant for expressing

genuine, heartfelt anger like it's a cute nickname. She waves an arm idly, and the dress loosens by a fraction of a centimetre in places and tightens in the same sort of degree in others, turning a beautiful outfit into something truly spectacular.

"What's the plan now?"

"Now we blow them a kiss, wave goodbye, and walk out of here. Perhaps scooping up a pair of shoes each."

"You're going to get us arrested. Or them fired."

She laughs. "There'll be no memory of this afternoon's excitement in their minds, more's the pity for them. And no record in the store's accounts of these dresses ever existing."

"You know, you could have just moved straight to that step, without stripping off and going full succubus."

She shrugs, causing her dress to ripple beautifully. "I mean, I could have. But where would the fun have been in that? Besides, there's power in sex magic, you know there is. A bit of magically amplified flirting like this can bend people to your will. Magic worked during sex can give someone your power or drain all of theirs. Forge unbreakable deals or break otherwise binding liens. Channelled the right way, the energy released during orgasm can do things that even the strongest practitioner would otherwise find impossible."

I shake my head. I'm about as far from a prude as it's possible to be, but there's something about mixing magic and sex that's always made me a bit squeamish. Maybe it has something to do with the terms of my old deal with Gabriel.

"Have you considered forgoing this deal with the vampires and just getting laid on Summer Hill until the Dome expands?" I raise my eyebrows exaggeratedly.

"Sadly, I don't think I've personally got enough magical firepower, or I'd be tempted to give it a whirl. I half wonder if it was at the back of Bren's mind, when he slept with Leah out there, but relying on her magic would have been a total nonstarter. Maybe you and Gabriel should try it."

I can usually read my sister without conscious thought or effort, but right now, it's impossible to know whether or not she's joking.

We change back into our own clothes—I bundle Chrissie into a changing room—then the dazed shop assistant wraps the dresses, plus some perfectly matched accessories.

Once the transaction is complete, Chrissie waves her hands, the shutters rising and the spell breaking. The staff are still staring at Chrissie, but like she's a beautiful woman, rather than a literal sex goddess.

"Bye, darlings," she calls, then strides for the entrance, giving me a pointed look.

I pause, then work the more complicated but significantly less fun spell to make sure the accounts and inventory show no record of our theft. This is completely immoral, obviously. I'd never normally dream of breaking the law. But I can't let Chrissie get into trouble. I try to justify it to myself by thinking about the brand's inevitable poor labour conditions, sexist advertisements, and over-inflated prices, but it's a stretch.

Chrissie and I traverse to the hotel where she and Liam are staying. In the normal run of things, my parents would have insisted on a Travelodge, but they've gone for an opulent Belgravia affair.

"Partly to be close to the vampires' HQ," Liam explains, when I walk into the lobby and he reads my surprised expression perfectly. "Partly because we need to show the bloodsuckers that we're worth taking seriously. And partly because Thornber's taken a suite at a similarly OTT place across the square, and we didn't want to be shown up."

I laugh, give him a hug, and try not to let my mind dwell on the concept of Gabriel's hotel suite.

The three of us spend the next few hours getting as preened

and pampered as possible, making use of the facilities in the hotel's Balinese spa, as well as Chrissie's beautification spells.

Once Liam goes back to his own room to get changed, she finishes my make-up and drags every last detail of what happened between me and Gabriel over the summer out of me. All I can think about is that in the next hour or two, I'm going to see him again. And I've no idea how he or I are going to react.

"Bloody hell. I cannot believe this was going on under my nose," Chrissie says, once I finally grind to a halt.

"You don't disapprove?"

"I wouldn't say I exactly *approve*. But it's your life. And the families are meant to be in an alliance now."

That's probably the best I can hope for. "Shall we go and find Liam?" I say, determinedly changing the subject. "Grab one drink in the bar here then head on over?"

Liam's already perched on a bar stool when we make it downstairs.

"My two favourite sisters are both looking predictably fabulous," he says, adopting an exaggerated posh accent. I've barely ever seen him out of sportswear, but tonight, he's working the tuxedo and bowtie look with aplomb.

"We ought to be, the amount of time, magic, and effort we've put into getting ready," I reply. "Anyway, what's the plan of attack?"

"We'll head over there in a cab in twenty minutes or so. It's actually only a five-minute walk, but it's what they'll expect. The place is warded to high heaven against vampires, practitioners, and anything else you can think of, so traversing is out of the question."

"And when we arrive?"

"Tonight's just a party. We'll take care of business tomorrow. I still hope you'll join us."

I sit down on a stylish but uncomfortable chrome stool and frown. "There's no such thing as 'just a party' when you're trying to form an alliance or cut a deal. They'll be watching us. Judging us. And we'll need to do the same to them."

I can't help but wish Brendan were here, however much I'd have to fight the urge to punch him. For the last few years, he's been the brains behind the family's strategic operations. None of us are ideally suited for this.

Liam raises an eyebrow. "Bringing Bren would have caused more problems than it solved, in all sorts of ways. But I'm sure Gabriel-fucking-Thornber's got the scheming in hand."

He emphatically does not use the term like it's a cute nickname. Damn his telepathy. I'm so unused to being around people with the gift.

"If there were an Olympic event in scheming, he'd definitely take gold," I say. "But alliance or no alliance, I'm not convinced his interests are entirely aligned with ours."

Chrissie perks up at this. "I'm sure as hell not naïve enough to fully trust him. That's actually half the reason we need you there: he's not going to screw the family over with you watching."

"And on that note, our carriage awaits," Liam declares. He takes our arms and escorts us out into the night.

ELEVEN

The party is held in one of those white-fronted Georgian mansion blocks that generally get converted into office premises or several small but high-end apartments. Against the odds, though, all five stories of this particular building appear to form one house. I dread to think what it'd cost—tens of millions, surely—but the question's irrelevant, since it was purchased in the 1700s and hasn't changed hands since.

It's the home of Augustine Piso, leader of the so-called Cavaliers, the main group of vampires in the UK and the same vampire Lavinia has a decades-old grudge against.

I've done my research: partly in preparation for this party and tomorrow's potential meeting; partly for Lavinia's schemes. Not that I've told her about tonight's festivities. She probably wouldn't approve, and this is family business.

Thoughts of Lavinia fade as quickly as they arise. My stomach's churning at the idea of spending an evening with the vampires. My heart's pounding at the prospect of seeing Gabriel again. There's little space for other emotions.

Lord Piso lives with his third wife—or first wife, if you believe in reincarnation. He's the head of a private bank, which accounts for some of the wealth. But living for a few thousand years while investing wisely has helped, too.

The large front door, painted black like the door to Ten Downing Street, opens before we can set hands on the brass knocker shaped like a crossed horse and sword.

A woman in a sharply tailored suit looks us up and down. "The Yorkshire Sadlers, I presume. Do come in."

Despite her outwardly normal appearance, she's quite clearly a vampire. There's an unnatural perfection about her and something subtly off with her aura. You don't tend to see many female ones.

"Thank you." I step over the threshold. Vampires always make such a big deal out of inviting you into their home. It's important to be polite about it.

"You're looking at me with altogether too much respect," the woman says. "You may have mistaken me for the lady of the house. You wouldn't catch her dressed like this. She's in the main hall, wearing far too many jewels and far too few clothes. I'm Polly, Mr Piso's chief of staff. Or housekeeper, depending on whom you ask."

"Nice to meet you, Polly." Chrissie gives her most winning smile. If you want to cut a deal with someone, there's a lot to be said for getting their most trusted staff on side.

We follow Polly through into a house whose interior entirely fulfils the promise of its grand façade. It's all marble floors, sweeping staircases and old portraits, with a few modern design touches mixed in here and there.

"You're in there," she says, pushing open two huge, polished oak doors as though they're fibreglass.

The room we find ourselves in is designed for entertaining on a grand scale. It sits at the very centre of the house and has a double-height ceiling. The hundreds of candles just about compensate for the total lack of windows. A string quartet is playing beautifully but unobtrusively in one corner. At first, I assume it's generic classical music. After a moment, I realise they're playing covers of songs from the last ten years or so: Kanye scored for cello, Billie Eilish for viola, that sort of thing. The room smells expensive: fresh cut flowers, champagne, the artisan perfumes of the guests. There are several alcoves, draped with red velvet, just perfect for secret meetings of a romantic or political nature—or, knowing vampires, to charm someone out of their blood.

I'm torn between hating it for its ostentatiousness and predictability and loving it for its decadence and the way it makes me feel like I'm in a period drama. And against my better judgement, I'm breathless at the prospect of bumping into Gabriel.

The room is full of precisely the right number of people to create atmosphere without making it crowded. Someone probably carefully did the sums. About sixty per cent of the guests show all the signs of being vampires. I recognise some of the others from politics and the media. I don't read the Financial Times often enough to be able to pick top bankers and businesspeople out of a crowd, but no doubt there are plenty of them around, too.

There are also numerous human guests in their twenties, both male and female, who are universally attractive, even if they can't quite live up to the vampires' own standards. Some will be potential new recruits, others simply food and entertainment. I try to push that thought aside. It's not like there's anything I can do to help them. Not tonight, anyway. *But maybe if I can make Lavinia's plan work...*

I grab a glass of champagne for each of us from a long table covered in flutes. I'm not enough of a connoisseur to tell normal, decent champagne from the stuff that costs a few hundred pounds a bottle, but I'd put money on this falling into the latter category.

If anyone who knows me even a little were asked to guess

my favourite alcoholic drink, they'd probably say gin. But champagne runs it a close second, perhaps even edges it out. It's just that having champagne as your favourite tipple seems both boringly predictable and a little impractical and expensive. You can't exactly crack open a bottle by yourself. Or at least, not every night.

"Are we keeping ourselves to ourselves, or are there people we ought to speak to?" I generally feel a moral obligation to mingle at parties, but I don't fancy attempting to make small talk with vampires who might be on the other side of Lavinia's dispute. Or chatting to the Home Secretary. There's obviously only one person I really want to see—and the prospect of doing so sends a rush of blood to my head—but I'm determined to stay professional.

"We ought to try and find our host and say hello," Chrissie says uncertainly. Something about the surroundings seems to have dampened even her habitual confidence and bubbly nature. "Or his wife. Or one of the other senior vampires."

We wander as a little group of three, hovering close to each other for comfort. The vampiric guests are shameless, leading their dates into secluded corners, mesmerising them, then taking a few delicate sips of their blood. All of the human guests must have been lightly mesmerised on arrival to stop them noticing the way others are falling victim to the hosts.

"I'm just going to pop to the loo," I say, after ten minutes of unsuccessful searching. I brush off Chrissie's offer to accompany me.

"You look utterly enchanting," an obvious vampire drawls, stepping in front of me with a smile.

I smile back and make taunting eye contact. "Before you go any further, I should probably point out that I'm a witch. Meaning that I'm immune to your creepy mesmerism and my blood would be poison to you."

He laughs. "Sounds refreshing. It'd be fun to see if I could charm someone on my own merits. And not everything has to be about blood."

I'm almost tempted to let him lead me to one of the secluded alcoves. Channel my energies in a different direction to prevent me from doing anything stupid as far as Gabriel is concerned.

He's predictably handsome: gelled back deep black hair; delicate cheekbones matched with a rugged jaw in a way that shouldn't work but does; piercing blue eyes. And that certain indefinable something that sets vampires apart from conventionally attractive human men. He'd no doubt also be charming and up for a good time. Whatever else they might be, vampires don't tend to be dull.

But his posh accent is already grating on my nerves and putting the fact he drinks human blood to one side, I just know that I wouldn't like his views on welfare, immigration or pretty much anything. It's unclear whether there's something about becoming a vampire that makes them all so reactionary or whether men like that are more likely to be chosen for the honour. There must be some vampires who believe in the minimum wage and nuclear disarmament, but I guess seeing humans as food makes it a little hard to accept the concept of human rights.

"Maybe later," I say, winking. I don't want to burn my bridges. If things go wrong with Gabriel tonight, I might need the comfort of a rebound. And in that situation, he might seem like a good option for a one-night stand or perhaps even a meal somewhere exclusive, if he could keep his opinions to himself for the evening.

To my intense relief, he neither tries to stop me nor makes some horrific comment about girls with spirit or the like.

I make it to the Victorian-style lavatory without further incident. When I step back into the room, the vampire who spoke to me is where I left him, with his arms around a human woman and his fangs starting to show. As I watch with a lump in my throat, he leads her away.

Before I can find my family, someone else lays a hand on my shoulder.

"Good to see there are still *some* family events you're willing to attend."

I turn, readying myself to deflect a vampire's attentions once again. Before I've even completed my rotation, my brain catches up to reality: instead of the posh drawl, a northern accent, and instead of the characteristically odd aura, one that's comforting and terrifying in equal measure, not to mention burning with magic.

He's wearing full evening dress tonight, bowtie and everything, which looks amazing on his tall and toned but slender body. The wavy, dirty blond hair that he usually aggressively styles is long and loose today, almost reaching his chin and framing his elegantly sharp facial features. His distinctive eyes —diamond-shaped pupils on top of the traditional diamond-shaped practitioner irises—are on full show, no attempt to disguise them with sunglasses in this crowd.

Part of me wants to run and hide. Part of me wants to throw myself at him. Somehow, I manage to stand my ground, give a friendly little smile, and look casually into those overwhelming eyes, which are currently a sort of rose-gold colour. But there's no hiding my instantly flushed cheeks, and no denying the way the rest of the opulent room fades to grey.

"Hey, Gabriel. Nice to see you. It's been far too long."

My entire body is reverberating. It's been impossible to keep my mind off him over the last six weeks or so, but I'd still forgotten the electrifying effect he has on me.

"You asked me to give you space. And your wish is my command."

He sips his glass of champagne. He looks very at home here, amongst all this extravagance and power. We're all descended from the same otherworldly race of demons, practitioners by birth and the vampires by blood. We always tend to think we're far, far closer to humans and to life than them, but Gabriel's demon mother goes some way towards bridging the gap. He could almost pass as vampiric—which is both a compliment regarding his looks and a less complimentary reflection on his overall vibe.

"I couldn't resist coming tonight," I say. "And not just because of the fancy house and the free champagne. Not just to humour my family, either."

He takes my hand and strokes the finger that's wearing his mother's ring where I used to sport his lien mark. Despite his apparent attempts to maintain a passive expression, there's a hint of a smile in his eyes when he sees I haven't taken it off.

At his touch, all the memories of the summer come flooding back with renewed intensity, along with all sorts of desperately repressed hopes for the future. Romantic ones. Fun ones. Sexy ones. And all the worries, too. The general moral dilemma around whether I could ever justify a relationship with someone capable of the things he's done. And the more practical concern about what his obsession with me could drive him to do, especially if things didn't go according to his masterplan.

"It's going well, working with your family instead of against them," he says.

There's an unspoken plea in his words for me to come back to Mannith and see it with my own eyes, but the comment clears my mind.

"So I gather. Apparently, expanding the Dome is less of a concern when you've got a controlling stake in it."

He shrugs. No one can shrug quite as expressively as he can. "Firstly, I want to make this alliance with the Sadlers work. And the biggest stumbling block to that is the annual Ritual. I could never condone the sacrifices, but your family would never let the Dome decay. This way, that point of contention is removed, which massively increases the odds of the alliance holding. Pooling our resources and ending the fighting is of huge benefit to both families and to Mannith."

"And your second reason?" He always claims he has two reasons for everything.

"Secondly, I was willing to bring down the Dome to stop Brendan from expanding it, when that meant a massacre. I'd always objected to the sacrifices and the larger scale plan was utterly unconscionable. But I grudgingly agree with your brother that the Dome's good for Mannith and could be good for other towns, too. Not at the cost of deaths, but if we could make it happen without wasting human lives, that's quite a different proposition."

"If we could maintain and expand the Dome without anyone getting hurt, then yes, that would be objectively amazing," I reply, hands planted firmly on my hips. "No one could argue with that. But you're talking about creating a vampire feasting ground."

I'm unspeakably grateful to have a genuine, fresh, non-personal reason to be angry with him. It's by far my best hope of keeping my deeper feelings under control. I can pretend my heart's racing because I'm furious and indignant.

"Why don't we find somewhere to sit down?" he says. "I'd be happy to discuss the ethical pros and cons over a drink. And to talk about everything else we've spent weeks skirting around, too."

It's dangerous to be alone with him. Not physically. In the past, I was straightforwardly terrified of him, while now, I'm pretty sure he wouldn't do anything to hurt me. But it's dangerous mentally. Emotionally. Almost sort of psychically or spiritually or something, like he could bend my aura out of shape or send my magic careering out of me at random.

I left Mannith—again—in large part because I didn't trust

him. And just as importantly, because I didn't trust myself around him.

And yet. And yet. It's been weeks. He's on my territory, more or less. Unless I go crawling back to Mannith, there may not be another opportunity to speak to him for months. I'm not sure I could bear to miss this opportunity.

I grab two glasses of champagne from a passing waiter. "Let's go and find one of those alcoves. If we're going to talk, we should have some privacy."

I stride along, head down. Technically, it's not like the summer, where I had to keep my dalliances with Gabriel scrupulously secret or risk the family branding me a traitor. Everybody knows about us, to one degree or another. And he's meant to be an ally now, not an enemy. Even so, I don't want Liam or Chrissie to see me with him, still less to see where we're going and draw their own salacious conclusions.

Chrissie had seemed merely amused and on the hunt for gossip when she'd forced the blow-by-blow account out of me, but while Liam doesn't despise Gabriel to quite the same extent as Bren, he probably wouldn't entirely approve.

We make it behind one of the red velvet curtains without being stopped or obviously observed either by my siblings or by anyone who appears to be a host.

"Very subtle," Gabriel says, echoing my thoughts. "I don't believe we were observed."

He says it like he cares. Maybe he doesn't want to antagonise my family before the alliance has had time to get off the ground.

"If we were, most of the guests would have assumed you were a vampire, luring an unsuspecting woman away from the party so you could feast on her blood. You really could pass as one of them, dressed up in evening dress like this. You've got vampiric cheekbones."

"I'm choosing to take that as a compliment. Although, as

your next line is presumably going to be a long list of reasons why working with the vampires is utterly immoral, perhaps not."

I close my eyes for a second so I can try to think clearly, rather than be distracted by those cheekbones and all the rest of it.

I *do* want to talk vampires. I want to dig deeper into his motivations for seeking a deal with them and express my concerns. Either talk him out of it or let him talk me into attending the meeting tomorrow. Beyond that, I want to know more about the alliance and how it's going. I want to know more about him, full stop. What he's been up to over the last few weeks, and all his deepest hopes and fears...

I open my mouth to say something calm and sensible, then I take one look at him and all my resolve fails me.

I launch myself at Gabriel, one arm tight around his waist, the other at the base of his hair. I push him back against the artfully painted wall, meeting no resistance despite his greater size and strength. I raise myself up on tiptoes and kiss him fiercely.

God, I'd forgotten how good and right it feels, as though kisses with anyone else are water while those with him are wine. Normally, however attractive and technically proficient a partner, my mind keeps up a running commentary while my body vaguely enjoys the action. With him, I'm utterly consumed.

Gabriel's eyes start to widen, but he catches himself and smoothly turns his look of shock into a smirk. "No contact for weeks, and now you've dragged me off to a dark corner to do goodness knows what to my poor defenceless body," he says. "I feel used."

"I'll be gentle," I reply, laughing. "And if you play nice, maybe I'll take you out for dinner tomorrow."

He puts his arms around me, clasping my bum through the

light fabric of my free designer gown. I relish the touch and grind against him.

He presses me in even more tightly, changing the tempo of the kiss.

I step back, just for a second, and place a hand on his chest. "Nope. You're in my adopted city, and tonight, I'm in control."

His breath catches in his throat. He's not a fan of being in anyone's control. His natural reaction in any situation is to dominate it, through magic, scheming or personality.

You could generally say the same of me, albeit to a less dramatic extent. I've certainly tended to wear the trousers in most of my sexual encounters, so to speak. With him, though, there's something oddly fitting about putting myself at his mercy, and that's generally been our dynamic. It's not like I planned tonight out in advance, but from the moment I set eyes on him, I wanted to play it this way for once.

"Bloody southern women," he says, loosening his grip on me as I tighten my hold on him. "You know, however much you've been practicing your magic, I could still bend you to my will."

"I don't doubt that for a second. And it's the fact you're not even going to try that's going to make this so fun."

I kiss him once more, hard, then take his hand and drag him to the dusky pink cushioned seat built into the wall. I dread to think how many illicit encounters have taken place on it over the centuries. I can only hope this Augustine Piso has a reliable cleaner.

I lay back against the seat and subtly gather the ankle-length dress up around my waist, to reveal that I'm wearing nothing below. When I was dressing, I told myself it was to avoid the lines showing, but that's a half-truth at best.

He kneels in front of me on the strategically placed Turkish rug, without being told. Maybe deep down, he enjoys relinquishing control once in a while after all.

"Shall I throw up a bubble of silence or shall I leave that to you?"

I lower my eyelids in my best approximation of a sexy expression. "I don't think that'll be necessary."

"And if someone wanders in?"

"Maybe I'll ask them to join us. It's a good-looking crowd."

"I'm going to hold you to that," he replies.

In actuality, if anyone wandered in, I'd die of embarrassment. But it gives everything an extra frisson, and it's hardly like vampires are particularly puritanical.

I take his head and guide it down. Even through my growing excitement at both the reunion and my own naughtiness, there's a part of me that can't believe I'm doing this. However much I play dominant, it still feels a bit like giving in to him.

The second his tongue makes contact with my clit, all my worries fall away. I give a little shriek, then frantically clasp my hand over my mouth.

He speeds up, and glances up at me with a hint of a smirk in his eyes. He's no doubt trying to make me cry out again. I close my eyes, keep my mouth clamped shut, and try to breathe.

I want to scream out his name, beg him to push me over the edge, or just give in to incoherent noises. I fight to stay silent, and the repressed sounds create a physical pressure within me. When he slides a finger inside, I almost lose control, but somehow, I stay quiet, though my breathing must be loud enough to be heard by anyone who ventures too near the curtain, especially considering vampires' heightened senses.

As my orgasm builds, I dig my nails into my palm, fighting not to make an exhibition of myself. He uncurls my hands and places them on his shoulders, either not caring or perhaps even enjoying the way I claw at him as the only way of keeping myself vaguely quiet.

A little moan escapes as his finger and tongue do their work and I get closer. A louder one follows, and I struggle to make myself care. He presses down hard in just the right place, and with a few final firm licks, I go over the edge.

The unfettered scream I was about to emit is silenced as he waves his hand in the direction of my mouth. Freed of the need to restrain myself, I dig my nails in still deeper, and let myself moan and scream and call his name, confident in the knowledge that his magic is keeping everything inaudible.

He keeps going, extending the pleasure until I come again then licking more slowly as I float down to earth, until sensitivity makes things almost painful. I release my death grip on his shoulders and gently push his head away.

He gets to his feet like someone waking from a dream, then takes my hands, raises me up to stand, and kisses me, supporting my weight as my legs continue to tremble. I kiss him back, no longer playing games or thinking about which of us is in control. It's clear that neither of us is. We're both equally in thrall to the other.

"Sit down," I whisper after an eternity—or maybe ten minutes—of kisses. My voice seems to have returned in the interim. "Your turn."

He laughs. "I don't think I've got quite your exhibitionist streak. Or your self-control. But I do have a very nice hotel room two minutes down the road if you could bear to be so painfully conventional."

"I'll meet you outside in five," I promise. "I'd better let Liam and Chrissie know I'm leaving."

"And are you going to tell them who you're leaving with?" There's a sudden seriousness in his tone. Does he want my family to know? Does he want them to approve?

"I think they might draw their own conclusions."

I find my siblings deep in conversation with a striking pair of vampires, both of whom I recognise: the vampire who attempted to flirt with me earlier in the evening, and Hugo Latham, the one who murdered Janice Denworth.

I stare at the latter, eyes narrowed, hands raising in an attacking stance. Images of Janice's death flash through my mind. The room's too hot, too full of people. I'm either going to throw up or release a fireball. Maybe both.

"Hugo, Tristan, this is our sister, Sadie," Chrissie purrs. "Tristan's a lawyer, too. Has been, on and off, for several hundred years."

She's turning on the charm almost as much as she did in the dress shop. She'd never cheat on Ray, so it's unclear whether it's habit, fun, or all part of the alliance plot. It'd be fascinating to see how well her seduction magic works on vampires.

I force my clenched hands down by my sides and dredge up a smile. "Lovely to bump into you again, Tristan. I'd love to talk nineteenth-century law with you sometime. And nice to see you in slightly more relaxed surroundings, Hugo."

It really, really isn't. I'd like to kill him where he stands for what he did. But I need to stay calm. I can't imperil either my family's plans for a deal or Lavinia's more complex plan for revenge.

"Lord Piso's an old friend of mine, and his parties are always fun," Hugo says. "We got off on the wrong foot. Perhaps some champagne and small talk, alongside your lovely siblings and one of my best friends, could help smooth things over?"

"That sounds delightful." It really, really doesn't. "But I actually came over to tell my 'lovely siblings' that I'm leaving."

"Already?" Liam seems primed to launch into a stream of reasons why I should stay, then realisation lights up his face. "Ah, okay, I see. Just make sure you use protection. Don't look into his eyes. Avoid making any weird binding bargains."

Chrissie jabs his arm. "You go and enjoy yourself."

"Will we see you at the meeting tomorrow?" Liam shouts after me.

"I'll be there," I reply.

I'm still extremely dubious about the vampire deal, but having seen some hints of the alliance in action tonight, I want that to work at almost any cost.

Besides, I can at least make sure that if they do make a deal with the vampires, it will be both fair to them and as moral and humane as is possible in the circumstances. It's the lesser of two evils. Just.

I dash out before either of them can say anything more and try not to think about what gossip and speculation they'll be sharing with the vampires.

Gabriel's waiting patiently on the entrance steps, watched intently by some sort of security guard (suspicious) and Polly, the woman who let us in (interested). I take his hand before either of them can act on their emotions.

The sight of him drives away the fury that Hugo provoked in me. It's amazing to stroll hand in hand with him through one of the nicest parts of London. There's so much that would once have seemed impossible about that scenario. There's a lot that still does, in the longer term, but like that night in the summer when we drove out to a country hotel, perhaps we can enjoy one enchanted evening in a bit of a vacuum from all the complexities of real life and everything a genuine relationship would entail?

As promised, his hotel is only a few minutes' walk away. It's a discreet, red-brick building, that's going for a "timeless luxury" vibe.

He leads me up to what I can only assume is one of the larger rooms. It sports a rather over-the-top black and gold four-poster bed and heavily draped curtains.

"If any of the vampires asked to meet me in my room, I wanted them to feel at home," he says, laughing at the look on my face as I study the décor.

I sit down on said bed and stroke the heavy cotton sheets.

At the party, I'd acted in a rush of hormones and excitement. Now I've satisfied my animal lusts, I'm oddly self-conscious being alone with him. We didn't exactly leave things on the best footing, either last time we saw each other in person or when we spoke on the phone. From the way he's pacing around and running his hands through his hair, it's safe to assume he feels the same way.

"How's London treating you?" He can barely look at me. "Was it worth turning your back on your family, your home, and your birthright, again?"

And on him, of course, but he has the decency not to dwell on that aspect.

I ought to answer honestly. Tell him about how conflicted I've been feeling. It'd do me good to get it off my chest, he'd probably like to hear it, and this relationship, or whatever the hell it is, is doomed if we can't manage a bit of openness and honesty.

"It has its moments," I say instead, smiling and wriggling out of the over-priced, ethically stolen dress, so that I'm naked but for lacy black hold-ups.

"Sadie, I really think we ought to discuss everything sensibly," he says, even as his eyes widen and a pretty obvious erection blooms in his formal trousers.

"Yes, you've always taken such a sensible, healthy approach to me and to this relationship, haven't you?"

I sprawl across the bed. I've not got quite my sister's gift for seduction, but I'm not half bad when I put my mind to it. Besides, I want him and he wants me, and that's the most powerful aphrodisiac of all.

He shrugs off his jacket, but then crosses his arms over his chest, leaving the rest of his clothes frustratingly intact. "I know I have a tendency to keep things casual with most people. And that conversely, with you, I've been over-intense. I appreciate that 'we need to talk' is one of the world's biggest clichés, but we really, really do."

I close my eyes. "And we will, I promise. Just not now."

I'd wanted to be sensible tonight. I'd wanted to resist his charms, have a practical discussion, act like we were friends rather than enemies, lovers, soulmates or any combination thereof. Perhaps I can attempt that again in the morning, but for this evening, that ship's well and truly sailed. There's no way I can manage a calm conversation with him—it'd end in tears, screaming, or declarations of love, nothing in between. So, I might as well embrace the way the evening is going and stay away from talk entirely... right?

He nods, the last bits of fight leaving him as he unbuttons his dress shirt. A few moments later, he's as naked as I am, and I couldn't be happier about it.

"How do you want to play it this time?" He lays down beside me and whispers the words.

"However you'd like." I mean for the words to sound all sultry, but there's a raw vulnerability in my tone.

"Come here." He draws me towards him, rests my head in the crook of his arm, and proceeds to run his free hand up and down my body, drawing sighs from me. I do the same to him, and it feels so right. The frenetic, semi-exhibitionist sex back at the party was great fun, but I could spend hours like this, just touching him and being touched by him. Just being together. I wish I could trust him enough to make this a regular thing.

Once I'm utterly content and melted and he's seemingly in the same state, I take a firm hold of his cock and stroke it. He gasps like it's all he wants in the world and reaches out to touch me in turn.

"I do not need any more foreplay," I sigh, just as his fingers make contact and establish how wet I still am, from a combination of my earlier orgasm and the thrill of simply being with him like this.

He strokes my clit for a few seconds anyway, while I squirm, then slips on a condom and climbs on top. Against all the odds, I come almost as soon as he enters me, as though weeks of longing have been condensed into this one moment.

As I've already had my fun, I thrust up against him, grinding at the top, trying to push him over the edge while he tries to hold back on principle.

Eventually, I win.

Afterwards, we lay there, just revelling in each other.

And then I make the mistake of rolling over, so we can spoon. Staring into each other's eyes is lovely, but sometimes it's nice to just snuggle up and be held.

He runs his hand over my back, then it freezes at the top of my spine. He doesn't say a word and I can't see his face, but it's obvious something's wrong.

"What happened to your back?"

Shit. Shit shit shit shit shit.

A protective mechanism honed over all the years I kept my branded finger out of sight kicks in, and I try to roll away. He gently holds me in place and pulls down the duvet cover so that his eyes can confirm what his sixth sense saw.

"You've got a new lien mark." He speaks the words rather than shouting them, but there's the sort of edge to his voice that you'd usually associate with someone accusing you of being a serial killer.

"It's hardly something you can take the moral high ground about."

"Who the fuck put it there? How dare they? I'll kill them. What's the bargain?" His eyes are going red.

"Nothing as bad as the one I made with you." I push his arm away, instantly on the defensive, partly due to his extreme reaction, partly because Lavinia's lien still makes me uncomfortable.

"Leave the past out of this. What the hell's going on?"

I push myself up to a seated position. Somehow, I never

think about Lavinia's brand half as much as I used to think about Gabriel's.

"It means I work for the leader of the London Coven. Just as her lawyer, nothing worse than that. It's not a sexual thing or anything."

And even if it was, it would be none of his business. We've made no vows.

He touches the mark, then pulls his shaking hand away like he just can't bear to be close to it. "There's a lot of power in this mark. It's overkill for an employment contract."

"She's a pretty full-on person. It might mean I have to take the odd case I'd have preferred not to, but that's working in law for you."

"And what do you get in return?" His voice is flat now, his eyes turning grey. He stares at the far wall like he can't bear to look at me.

"Just to stay in London. And practice magic. She made it pretty clear that no one gets to do both without putting themselves in her power."

Gabriel takes an audible breath. "Look, I want you and I to have a special bond, so the idea of you forging one with someone else – sexual or otherwise – admittedly hurts. I'd actually care way less about sex with other people."

I open my mouth to object. To remind him that this sort of obsessiveness is exactly why I'm forced to keep him at arms' length.

He takes a hold of my arm and puts a finger to my lips. "But I'm not just being jealous and possessive, I swear. I'm lashing out because I don't believe for a second that a lien like that is a simple commitment to loyalty. I don't like the idea that you could be compelled to do something you disagreed with. I hate the idea I might not be able to protect you. And above all, I love your strength, your independence. I can't bear the idea of you under some random practitioner's control."

"Whilst me under your control is just the absolute dream, isn't it?" *I'm* lashing out now, half because he's right, and half because he's hypocritical.

"I broke our lien, voluntarily. I've apologised time and again. I know I have work to do, but I'm trying. You act like it was the worst thing that ever happened to you, and you've got a point, so I'm desperately trying to make amends. And then you go and do this."

"There's nothing inherently wrong with a lien," I say, echoing Lavinia's words to me. "The problem with yours wasn't the mark on my skin, it was what you asked of me. This is nothing like that."

"Sadie, we don't need to argue all the rights and wrongs of this now. This is crazy. Come home. Work out of Leeds or some other city nearby. Why would you let yourself be beholden to some nonentity when you could be a queen in Mannith?"

"I like it here. And I like her." And I daren't go back and put myself at his mercy. Lavinia may be the one who has me under a lien, but Gabriel doesn't need magic to get in my head.

He raises his hands, and for a split second, I assume a defensive position in case he's about to work some terrible spell. But he's merely smoothing his aura, forcibly calming himself down.

"Okay. Well... I'm sorry for the outburst. I'm worried about this, but if you insist it's fine, I'll trust your judgement. Please will you lie back down? We've only got this one night, I don't want to ruin it."

I do as he suggests, snuggling as close into him as I physically can. Perhaps I ought to be uncomfortable, given the strength of his reaction. Perhaps I ought to leave. But as his arm wraps around my waist and his body cradles mine, I instantly feel better about everything.

We lie there in silence, just revelling in each other, like we've not just had a row and like there are no secrets or problems between us. In the moment, everything is peaceful, everything is perfect.

And then, my phone rings with that distinctive, ethereal sound I last heard the night Lavinia invited me to the Crown Jewels ceremony.

I jump out of bed.

"Leave it," Gabriel says, reaching out an arm to draw me back towards him. "It's after midnight."

I rummage around in my bag, hunting for the phone. "When it rings like that, it's Lavinia. She doesn't call often. I'd better take this."

"Just an employment contract. *I see.*"

I want to reply, either with something sarcastic or with a heartfelt explanation of why there's no issue here. I want to flop back down into bed and fall asleep in Gabriel's arms or make love once more, while we still have the chance. It's so difficult for me to ignore him and focus on anything else. Nonetheless, I dutifully pick up the phone.

"Darling, you're needed," Lavinia drawls. "I'll send a cab."

"Can't it wait until morning?" I know what she's going to say, but I attempt a token bit of resistance, for Gabriel's benefit.

"I'm afraid not." *Of course not.*

"What's the issue?"

"I'll explain when you get here. You just focus on getting yourself dressed." There's a hint of amusement in her voice. Considering that it's after midnight, it's not unreasonable to assume I've got undressed and gone to bed, but she sounds a little too knowing for comfort.

"Don't worry about the taxi. I'll get myself there." The offer could be a politeness. But it could be an attempt to find out where I am.

I hang up and wriggle into my dress, which is going to be ridiculously over the top for a business meeting, even one at midnight. It's bound to result in amused, scandalised comment, but there's no time to change.

I stare at myself critically in a mirror, trying to smooth down my hair and de-smudge my make-up in a desperate attempt to make myself look less like I just got laid.

Gabriel gets out of bed and comes to join me by the vanity table. "You're leaving? Seriously?"

"What, you think you're so irresistible I can't drag myself away?"

"*I think* we haven't seen each other in months, might not see each other again for weeks, and were having a passionate reunion. I was sort of working on the principle of more sex, falling asleep in each other's arms, then having that long-awaited serious conversation over room service breakfast."

I lean against him, resting my forehead on his chest. "That all sounds amazing. This might not take long. I could come back afterwards. Otherwise, I'll see you tomorrow—like I just told Liam and Chrissie, I'll grudgingly represent the alliance at the big meeting."

He puts his arms around me. "Fine. Go. Do what you need to do. I know your career's important. I'll see you at the meeting. Maybe there'll be time for a drink afterwards."

I kiss him, then traverse out before I can change my mind.

TWELVE

The next evening, I lock up my office for the night, change into flat shoes, and commence the walk from Temple to Eaton Square. Traversing or even driving would be quicker, but the forty-five-minute stroll is necessary to clear my head.

It's been a long twenty-four hours: Chrissie, the party, Gabriel, Lavinia's one AM conference, and then a full day at work. And there's still this negotiation with the vampires to come—which I still can't quite believe I've agreed to, however much I want to protect my family's interests, shore up the alliance, and get the inside scoop on the bloodsuckers before Lavinia puts her plan into effect. Coffee consumption has been high this afternoon, even by my standards.

There's no way I'd admit it to Gabriel, my family, or anyone else, but I'm extremely irritated with Lavinia. I'd assumed that whatever she was calling about was at least vaguely urgent. It turned out she just wanted to go back over the plans for setting up Hugo, yet again.

Basically—as we agreed over cocktails a few evenings ago—a few of the senior coven members, myself included, are going to a club that our research suggests Hugo frequents. Cara, one of

Lavinia's human acolytes, whom I met the night I joined the coven, will be glamoured to look like his perfect woman. She'll seduce him. He'll bite her. We'll make sure every single customer sees and remembers. When the police come, we'll protect them from mesmerism.

And then I'll have my day in court. I'll prove a point to the vampires that they can't always manipulate everything and face no consequences. And, with the help of Lydia and her contacts in the press and online, we'll make their activities subject to public scrutiny, which will undermine the combination of polished public reputations and utter secrecy about their need for blood that their entire security and way of life rests upon.

Having come face to face with that murderous bastard, Hugo, once more, it was nice on one level to be reminded that if all goes to plan, we're getting him jailed and using him to undermine the vampires' secrets into the bargain.

Even so, the meeting was pointless. Lavinia had no new ideas, information or questions, and neither did I. She's got zero boundaries or sense of appropriateness.

I breathe deeply as I walk and try to focus on each step and on small details of the surrounding area, be it the natural beauty of the river, the historical magnificence of Westminster Abbey, or the modern splendour of the London Eye. Maybe there's something in Lavinia's theory about the magic of London.

By the time I hit Belgravia, I'm calmer and re-energised, thank God. The last thing I want is to be facing a panel of high-ranking vampires while I'm exhausted or over-emotional.

"Hey."

I jump as someone touches my arm, then throw my arms up ready for spells of attack or defence.

"Ready to meet the bloodsuckers?"

My arms drop back to my side as I identify Nikki, even if she's barely recognisable, dressed in an elaborate sari in place of her usual tight jeans and T-shirt or ruthlessly tailored trouser suit. Then I throw my arms back up to give her a hug.

"Chrissie said you were in London, too," I say. "But I didn't see you last night."

"Gabe talked me out of the party. I'm not usually inclined to listen to him or miss out on things, but he had a point."

"Which was?"

She gives an elaborate, exaggerated sigh. "Born Practitioners are immune to vampire mind control and your blood would poison them if they attempted to drink it. I don't really believe in magic being some genetic gift, but that protection is a purely natural phenomenon, not something I can replicate."

"But it's safe for you to come to this meeting?"

"Not really." She laughs. "But the odds of someone trying to bite me in the middle of a formal conference seem lower than them luring me into a dark corner at a drunken party."

I shiver, longing to beg her to go back to the hotel. But if she won't listen to Gabriel, there's no way she'd listen to me.

"And the outfit? If that's not a rude question."

She grins. "I just assume by default that all vampires are massive racists. So I thought I'd provoke them."

We approach the house where the party was held. The large, black gloss door looks more intimidating now we're heading for a serious meeting rather than a drinks reception.

I allow myself a few seconds of core meditation, then knock.

Polly, the female vampire from last night, opens it. She smiles at me in recognition. A good memory for faces is presumably one of her powers.

"Sadie Sadler. Your siblings are already inside. And who is this?"

She studies Nikki intently. It's unclear whether it's her humanity or her race that's causing the consternation.

"I'm the second half of the Thornber delegation," she

replies. If she's angry—and surely, she must be—she's hiding it well.

"Ah, Ms Chana. Gabriel also arrived early. He told me to expect his lieutenant."

The room Polly leads us to this time is up a sweeping staircase. It's much smaller than the ballroom, but even more opulent, with its tapestry-covered walls and huge, candle-filled chandelier. Instead of a boardroom table, the vampires are seated on throne-like silver chairs on a raised marble dais, while Gabriel, Chrissie and Liam stand facing them at ground level, like supplicants before a medieval lord. To be fair, it's basically the effect my dad aims for when he holds his family meetings, but he's a little more subtle about it.

Chrissie and Liam are standing together. Gabriel's on his own. If they're meant to be presenting a united front and demonstrating the strength of the Mannith Alliance, they're not off to the best of starts.

Nikki goes to stand by Gabriel's side.

I hesitate for a second, then choose a spot in the middle, equidistant between the two Mannith factions, and slightly further back than the others. I'm there as a lawyer for the alliance, not as a family member.

I gaze up at the stage. There's an older man, who appears to be pushing fifty but is still strikingly handsome. God knows how old he actually is. Presumably, he's the Augustine Piso we searched for in vain last night. The one who rejected Lavinia's advances once upon a time. The woman next to him, who's the same sort of apparent age, must be the wife that Polly was so scathing about. Lavinia presumably isn't her biggest fan either.

The identity of the other couple is less clear. Both the man and the woman look significantly younger—perhaps mid-twenties—but from their position on the dais and their general demeanour, they appear to be of broadly equal status to the Pisos.

All four are white—both in the sense of being Caucasian and in the near-literal sense of having the pallor that never going out in daylight gets you—with dark hair. The women wear it long and expensively blow-dried, while Augustine sports a short, slicked back style, and the other man's is chin-length and floppy. They're beautifully dressed in suits and dresses that channel "royal at a charity event". They're all equal parts stunning and disconcerting.

Tristan, the vampire lawyer I met last night, is seated a little further back, presumably fulfilling the same role as me—legal advice rather than direct involvement in negotiations. Next to humans, he's dazzling, but he fades into the background next to the four leaders.

"Please outline your proposal," Augustine says. He doesn't sound unfriendly, but there's no room for debate or disagreement in his tone.

"Lord Piso. Thank you for your time." Gabriel speaks confidently and without hesitation, but he's uncharacteristically polite, maybe even deferent. "As I explained over email, we control and protect our hometown of Mannith through a centuries-old spell we refer to as the Dome."

Thank goodness Brendan isn't here. Apart from anything else, I don't think he could physically stand there and listen to Gabriel talk about his precious Dome—the Sadler family's precious Dome—like it's his own personal plaything. Even I find it a bit disconcerting, and for better or worse, I'm literally in love with him.

"I came across Mannith centuries ago, when I was based in Yorkshire," the other male vampire says. "I don't think this Dome was in place at the time, but it was a hotbed of witches, even then. And blessed by their magic."

Liam nods. "The Dome's a more permanent, less labour intensive way of achieving something our ancestors have always done. The magical equivalent of making use of technology."

"And you want us to help you expand it?" The younger of the two vampire women frowns.

"It's that or rely on tens of sacrifices, which is a line we're not willing to cross," Chrissie explains. "It would also allow us to stop the need to make a few sacrifices each year to maintain the Dome, which we've tended to regard as a temporary evil, but which we'd all prefer to do without."

"And if we help you, you'll help us." Augustine sounds matter of fact, like someone making a business decision.

"Precisely. A mutually beneficial arrangement." Gabriel takes a step forward, clearly keen to move the conversation on.

The older woman tilts her head to one side. "We need proof of your good intentions. Proof that you'd actually be willing to allow us to come onto your land and drink the blood of your people. Witches and vampires should be aligned, but you tend to be that bit too close to humans and your own humanity."

"We'd need the bargain to be very clear that no one could be killed or seriously hurt. Or turned into a vampire without both their and our informed consent," Chrissie says. "But we have no qualms about a little blood being spilt."

I shudder at my beloved sister's tone. It's the sort of thing I'd expect from Bren or Gabriel, but in my head, Chrissie is softer and sweeter than that. In reality, I know she presides over the annual Ritual and the human sacrifices that entails each year without a second thought.

The woman stands up and points to Nikki. "I see you've brought a perfectly good human with you. May I?"

"I'm as much a practitioner as anyone else in the group." Nikki's hands clench into fists she knows how to use. She sounds like she's about to say something else. Instead, she falls silent and walks towards the dais.

"Evidently not," the woman says, with a smirk.

A wave of panic hits me as I desperately try to think of a way to help, but it's nothing compared to Gabriel's reaction.

I've certainly seen him in various moments of high emotion, but I've never seen him this primally furious. His fists are pressed against his chest like he's trying to keep a death spell at bay by sheer force of will, and his eyes are an alarming storm-grey and fiery red combo.

When he turns to look at me, I almost flinch back from him, but his voice is studiedly calm. "Sadie, would you please give Nikki your ring, just for a moment?"

Goodness knows why that would help, but I dash forward and grab her arm before she can ascend the steps that would lead her to the vampires. Up close, there's a hint of mesmerism in her eyes. Practitioners usually merely put an idea in someone's mind or compel them to act in a certain way as they get on with their lives. The way the vampires do it tends to be more absolute. Nikki seemingly has no real awareness of her surroundings, and she'll presumably have no memory of this once she wakes up.

She struggles to get away from me. I grip her arms and fight to pin her in place, but she's physically stronger than I am and driven by instinct. In desperation, I wave my free hand in a spiral and she stays still.

I'm trying to keep all my focus on her, but I'm dimly aware of all five vampires' amused attention.

Before I can think too hard about it, I pull Gabriel's mother's ring off my finger and slide it onto hers. I'd been nervous about accepting the ring when he gave it to me, but removing it is like amputating a limb.

As soon as the ring makes contact with Nikki's skin, her eyes clear and she looks around in confusion.

"Come back here, sweetie," Chrissie calls.

Nikki walks over to her unsteadily, and my sister puts an arm round her.

Thank God Nikki's alright, but what the hell is the deal with the ring? It seems to protect the wearer from mesmerism. I can't believe Gabriel neglected ever to mention that little fact. What other hidden powers—or controls—might it have?

"I think that proves our point," Augustine says. "You're all too human to have the appetite to uphold your end of the bargain."

Gabriel traverses straight onto the dais, invading the vampires' personal space. "I'm not human. Unlike you, I was never even born human. Do you know why that ring cut straight through your mesmerism? It's made of the same stuff as your little trinkets."

He reaches out and grabs hold of the distinctive emerald pendant that Mrs Piso is wearing. She flinches, which is probably not an everyday occurrence. They've no doubt killed people for less, but they're frozen in place.

"The ring belonged to my mother. The raw materials came from her family, on the other side."

I'm pretty sure he doesn't mean Ireland. We've never really discussed this infamous "Gabriel's mother was half-demon" issue in any level of detail, but it's always at the back of my mind. And now he's saying the ring he gave me is some sort of demon artefact? And that he's never felt the need to tell me?

"I've done my research," Gabriel continues. "I know that you're one of the original three vampires. That your maker was a true demon, and that you killed him with otherworldly weapons and amulets created by his jealous and equally demonic wife.

"I'm not generally in touch with the demonic side of the family, but if I need to, I can get more items with the same level of magic. That might be a threat or it might be an offer. Take it as you will. But know that if you ever lay a finger or a mind on my best friend—or imply that she's anything other than an immensely powerful practitioner—I'll organise a little family reunion. And rest assured I'm not squeamish about spilling blood, be it human or vampire."

I can't take my eyes off him. He's utterly electrifying. And dark as his words are, I love that he's so protective of his best friend. But there's still a voice at the back of my mind screaming that he can't be trusted.

It's a minor matter in the scheme of things, but these revelations about the ring are a perfect example of the way he just can't help but plot and keep things hidden. I'm not going to show weakness in front of the vampires, but the second we get outside, I have to confront him.

Gabriel takes a step back and Augustine reaches out his arm. For a moment, I think he's going to hit him, and I dread to think what's going to happen next. Instead, he shakes his hand.

"Please believe that all of that applies if you ever touch my wife again—including her jewellery. But the fact you physically *can* touch the necklace tells its own story. We'll agree to the basics of your deal. We'll work with you to enlarge the Dome on Midwinter's Eve—the longest night is a sacred time for us. We'll sign the principles in blood tonight. Our lawyers can agree on the details over the course of the week."

The anger seems to leave Gabriel's body as quickly as it arrived. He's all smiles as he shakes Augustine's hand straight back.

"Do I not get a say in this?" The other male vampire gets to his feet.

"Do you object, Richard?"

"I object to you making decisions without consulting me."

"So, no objections to the proposal then?" Gabriel says, and strides across and shakes Richard's hand with equal fervour.

"And for that matter, don't we get a say?" Chrissie's still fussing over a dazed Nikki, but she helps her to a chair and then approaches the dais.

"Of course you do," Gabriel replies. "This is an equal alliance, after all. And you're the Sadler's lead representative."

"It's our bloody Dome," she snaps.

"And do you want it enlarged and able to be maintained without ongoing sacrifices, or not?"

Chrissie glances back at me and shakes her head in a "what the hell do you see in this bastard?" gesture.

"We'd be pleased to accept your offer," she says to the vampires, ignoring Gabriel. The two men shake her hand in turn.

I'm tempted to ask whether the vampire women get a say, but there are probably already enough fault lines in the room.

"Tristan, will you do the honours?" Augustine asks.

My fellow lawyer smiles, showing far too much fang. "Call me overly modern, but I do feel like the written contract is the most relevant part of this. Even so, tradition is tradition."

He strides to a cupboard at the back of the room and retrieves a dagger and what can really only be described as a golden, jewel-encrusted chalice. I swallow hard. I emphatically do not like where this is going.

Tristan passes the chalice to Augustine, who bites down on the vein of his left wrist, opening up a deep wound and allowing his blood to flow into the cup. As soon as he's deposited a suitable amount, he elegantly licks the cut, which instantly heals.

Tristan moves along the row, until all four vampires have shown their fangs and added their blood. Then he steps down off the dais and approaches the Mannith delegation. He holds out the dagger to Gabriel, who takes it without hesitation.

"And people say I'm melodramatic," Gabriel says, slicing his wrist without flinching and adding to the growing volume of blood in the cup.

Chrissie is a little more reticent, but manages to contribute her share.

Liam has zero fear of physical pain, but he hesitates as though disgusted with the idea, until Chrissie nudges him.

Luckily, I'm just the lawyer, so I don't have to take part.

Tristan swirls the chalice around until all the blood is

mingled together. There's a sense of power emanating from the goblet that's more than just the sum of its parts.

"I'd reiterate again that signatures on a piece of paper would be my personal preference," he states. "But for now, let us seal this deal with a drink."

"Hang on a moment," I say. "Before anyone commits to this in writing or in blood, everyone needs to know what they're signing up to."

Tristan scribbles on a paper with superhuman speed then passes the note over to me. It details what the vampires will offer in terms of expansion and maintenance and what they want in terms of blood donors. It sounds horrific, and I still can't quite believe I'm contributing to this, but it also sounds fair—both in the sense that the vampires aren't trying to screw my family over and that they aren't planning to abuse the privileges we're going to grant them.

"I want to see the formal contract tomorrow," I declare.

"Naturally," Tristan replies. He passes the chalice back around, starting with Augustine and working his way to Liam. Each person takes a sip of the blood. It's not like I'm some naïve human. I'm familiar with magical practices. But there's still bile in my throat and a cold, clammy sensation all over my body.

"Isn't practitioner blood poisonous to vampires?" I ask.

"Fatal, if we drink enough of it," Richard replies. "But in these minute quantities, it'll cause nothing worse than a mild hangover. And the fact that it's given willingly, as part of a ritual, should minimise the effects still further."

The vampires all drink without compunction, hangover risk be damned. Gabriel knocks it back confidently, though whether that's due to his demon heritage or general swagger isn't clear. I'd probably be weirdly impressed, were it not for the fact I'm furious about the ring and wondering what else he's still keeping from me.

Chrissie is almost hyperventilating, but somehow manages to push through, gagging as she sips.

Liam closes his eyes, screws up his face and swigs some like a shot.

"Do you want some?" the older of the two women says to me. "You don't need to, for ritualistic purposes. But you're welcome to take a drop. It does wonders for the skin and for clarity of mind."

Lavinia's youthful appearance and extreme powers, which she puts down to vampire blood, are a perfect illustration of that, but I've never shaken my head so rapidly in my life.

"I'll send the formal contracts over tomorrow evening for your perusal," Tristan says to me. "But as far as my clients are concerned, following this exchange of blood, the deal is in place."

With that, it's over. We head across the entrance hall, and then we're through the door and out onto the exclusive street. I gulp in fresh air like I've spent the last few hours in a dank cave.

I want to fall into Gabriel's arms. Instead, I force myself to close in on him, hands on my hips and a frown on my face. I possibly ought to take him aside for this conversation, but I'm tired of secrets. Everyone needs to understand my position.

"At the end of the summer, I said I loved you and that I believed you loved me. Even so, I left Mannith, because after everything you'd done and everything I feared you might do in the future, I didn't think we could be together. And I didn't believe we could be in the same city and stay apart.

"But I wanted to give you a chance to change my mind. To show me who you really are. To show you could be friendly and calm towards me, not just driven by lust and obsession and darkness. And above all, to prove you could be trusted."

My voice trembles but I force myself to continue.

"Those fraught, heavy, steamy phone calls didn't bode well. And though last night was fun, neither did the way we jumped straight to sex nor your reaction to me joining the London Coven. But what I've really wanted to understand was whether, after so many years of lies and manipulation, you could be honest with me. And the way you neglected to tell me about the ring's powers or provenance tells its own story."

"What are you saying?"

I dig my nails into my palm. "I still don't trust you enough for a relationship. And neither of us can manage half-measures, and I'm tired of trying. Maybe we are fated to be together, but fate can go to hell."

Chrissie puts an arm round me to stop me from shaking.

Gabriel says nothing. I'm expecting either a torrent of arguments to talk me round or possibly some sort of verbal or magical attack. But my words seem to be sinking in at the molecular level.

"You're over-reacting," Liam says. "It's been a stressful evening. Too much time around vampires messes with your aura. Don't take it out on Gabriel."

I shrug off Chrissie's arm and square off against him. "Excuse me? Since when were you team Gabriel-fucking-Thornber?" My voice rises in pitch with every word. I can barely get his name out.

"I'm *team* wanting my sister to be happy."

"And he makes me bloody miserable." My eyes fill with tears, as though I'm attempting to prove it, though right now, the only person making me miserable is me.

"We should go," Nikki says, her voice flat, unable to make eye contact with me. "Do you want your ring back?"

I maintain just enough poise not to snap at her. She's been through enough tonight and she's said nothing wrong. "You keep it. You need its protection anyway."

Gabriel's eyes flare a deep red, then fade to grey like a fire that's gone out. His hands are clenched by his side like he's having to use every ounce of self-control he possesses to keep from doing magic. His face is more or less expressionless, with just a slight narrowing of his lips, as though someone's mentioned a minor inconvenience.

He's still silent. I've never heard him stay quiet this long in any situation. I wouldn't have thought it physically possible.

It's clear my words have hit home. It's as though he knows that if he lets his emotions out, he'll lose all control. That if he speaks a word, he'll say things he'll regret forevermore. That if he lets his magic surge, he'll blow up the entire street.

I feel exactly the same way. My hands are shaking as I press them into my chest to keep my powers grounded. My vision is blurring, tears streaming down my face.

Nikki nods, then grabs hold of Gabriel's arm and drags him away in the direction of his hotel.

I watch in silence as they make their way slowly down the street. Just before they turn the corner and disappear out of sight, he looks back at me. It's only for a split second, but even for that time and at that distance, I can see that the mask has slipped to reveal an expression of absolute anguish.

And then they're gone, and I'm barely able to remain standing.

THIRTEEN

The next morning I sleep in, then decide against getting dressed. It's not technically a break-up if you've never actually been in a relationship, but it damn well feels like one. And it's completely self-inflicted. Before, when I've pushed Gabriel away, it's felt like I was saying "maybe" or "not yet". Last night, I was doing my best to say "no". To say "never".

Gabriel's probably still at the hotel. I could go over there and take it all back. Beg to try again with the phone calls, the occasional meetings, and getting to know each other better. Or go all in and say yes to a relationship.

But I can't risk doing the latter. He's so scheming. He's so ruthless. He's so chillingly single-minded about me. And after giving it a try for a few weeks, it's painfully clear that the compromise approach simply doesn't work. There are too many emotions, too much history, and way too much chemistry for that sort of thing, even if I believed he'd go with the flow rather than trying to control proceedings. Which, frankly, after learning about the demonic anti-mesmerism ring, I absolutely do not.

Chocolate's not usually one of my vices, but it's a bit early for gin, and if I have any more coffee, my pent-up energy might actually explode. So I dig out a large bar that's been hiding at the back of a cupboard and relentlessly work my way through it.

By the time the intercom rings, I'm feeling about as sick as I did watching my siblings drink blood. And I'm definitely not in the mood for company.

On the first ring I ignore it. But when it rings again, it's hard to fight back my curiosity. Might it be Gabriel? If so, I should avoid seeing him at any cost. But I don't think I could stop myself.

I drag myself over and look at the video screen. Lavinia. Can't that woman leave me alone for a minute?

I consider pretending not to be at home, but she can almost certainly tell.

I press the button to speak. "I'm not really feeling well. Can we have this conversation tomorrow?"

"It won't take long," she trills, and I find myself pressing the button to let her in.

When the door opens, I see she's brought Lydia with her. Both women's eyes widen slightly at the state of me, but they both sit down on the sofa, and Lavinia wastes no time.

"I gather you were fraternising with the vampires last night. And the night before, for that matter."

I nibble my chocolate and frown. "I'd hardly say fraternising. Just helping my family out."

"Your beloved family. Of course. It's just that it's a huge conflict of interest. We're putting our plan to set one of the vampires up in place in less than two weeks' time. We're on the guest list for the club. We've done reconnaissance. Cara is all prepped for her starring role. And there they are making deals with Augustine, with your support."

I stand up. "How did you know who I was meeting? Are you spying on me?"

Lavinia remains seated and gives me her calmest smile. "I need to know what my people are up to."

"How? Scrying? I generally keep myself protected."

She reaches out and touches my back. "Via the lien mark, obviously."

I take an involuntary step back. I've never consciously heard that you can use lien marks to spy on people. To find and stop them if they try to renege on a bargain, sure. But not on a day-to-day basis. And not at this level of detail. What else can she do with the mark?

Lydia's eyes widen still further. She's far too loyal to challenge Lavinia out loud, but I get the distinct impression she's surprised and doesn't quite approve.

"Lavinia, this isn't okay," I say. "We had a straightforward deal. You'd let me stay in London and keep my day job. I'd join your coven, do a bit of legal work for you, and help with this vampire plan. I didn't sign up to be at your beck and call. I certainly didn't agree to be monitored by you."

It's satisfying to be angry with someone about something specific and tangible. It's cutting through my despondency with surgical precision.

"If you want to go back to Mannith, be my guest." She sounds calm and reasonable, with no hint of threat or anger in her voice.

I take a deep breath and another bite of chocolate. I need to be rational and reasonable. She's picked the right day for this conversation. If she'd tried this line of argument yesterday, when I was fresh from sex with Gabriel and a fun day with my siblings, despite all the good arguments against going back, I might just have called her bluff. But after last night's arguments, going home is a less enticing proposition.

"I want to stay in London. I'm happy to work for you. Just, we need to establish some boundaries."

"Absolutely, sweetheart. Sorry, I know I'm a little intense

sometimes. It's just over-enthusiasm. For my case. For my coven. For you."

Lydia manages to force her expression back into a smile. "It's true. It's like I told you the night we met. Lavinia can be totally over the top, but it all comes from a good place."

"I understand." After all, what choice do I have?

Lavinia nods with the satisfaction of someone who came to land a single message and has successfully done so. And then she looks at me properly—certainly with her eyes, but based on her unfocused gaze, with her inner sight as well.

"Darling, what's wrong?"

I look down at my rug. "Why would you care? You've got what you wanted out of this conversation."

"I want my coven members to be loyal and focused, sure. But I want them to be happy, too. And right now, you're as far from happy as it's possible to be."

I shake my head. "Just guy problems."

She hustles me back down onto the sofa, and sits beside me, closer now, one hand on my knee, staring into my eyes.

"The first rule of the London Coven is that my girls do not get their hearts broken. We do the breaking."

Lydia nods forcefully. She waves her hand, and an oversized glass vase brimming with roses, lilies, and some other blooms I couldn't begin to identify appears on the table. "Flowers always cheer me up," she says, while I stare at them.

"I was the one who called it off. But that doesn't stop it hurting."

"We need to find you someone new. Someone right for you. But first, we need to forget all about men and have some proper coven sisters' time," Lavinia proclaims. "We're going to pamper ourselves, then we're heading out for brunch."

I manage a weak smile. "It's a kind offer. But I'm really not feeling up to it."

Lydia's smile is rather more genuine. "The less up to it

you're feeling, the more important it is that you push yourself to do it."

Lavinia is already idly waving her arms around, summoning various items from the more genuinely magical end of her shop's range. Before I can raise any further objections, there are several candles burning on my table and giving off a heady but soothing scent. Lavender, most obviously, but mixed in with more obscure herbs that I'm too out of practice to identify.

Once the room is scented to her specifications, she scoops up various sachets and some muslin squares and starts boiling the kettle and pulling mugs out of the cupboard without waiting to be asked.

"How do you want to be beautified?" Lydia asks. "Magic, the personal touch, or some combination?"

It's a similar question to the one Chrissie asked me before the party, a thought that leaves me unsure whether to laugh or to cry.

"You really don't have to do this..." I reply, but by this stage, I'm essentially hoping they'll ignore my objections.

"Bit of a mix it is," Lydia says. She rummages through the various ingredients Lavinia has deposited on the table and throws a few carefully selected ones into a pestle and mortar that's also helpfully appeared.

She mixes and grinds in a carefully orchestrated pattern, murmuring a few ritualistic words as she goes. Just watching her is comforting in and of itself. It's like being sat in the kitchen back home, watching my mum work.

She appears to be making some sort of face mask. At one end of the scale, she—or indeed, I—could just wave a hand and make my skin look temporarily more radiant. At the other, she—like any human with a bit of knowledge—could just blend a few helpful herbs together and let them work some entirely natural improvements on me.

What she's doing strikes a middle ground. All the things the ingredients would do naturally—exfoliation, closing pores, softening the skin, giving me a glow—will be multiplied a hundredfold. And the effect on my face will be real, not just an illusion.

Lavinia's herbal infusion and Lydia's beauty treatment are ready around the same time. I sip the drink—I've retained enough half-buried childhood knowledge that a quick sniff reassures me it should do nothing more sinister than help me relax and cheer up—while the mask is gently applied.

Lydia works on my hair while the mask sets, curling it with her fingers as they give off the heat of curling tongs. Meanwhile, Lavinia shamelessly steps into my bedroom and rummages through my wardrobe until she finds an outfit that meets her approval—an emerald-green wrap dress which is nominally demure, but has a low enough neckline, tight enough waist and high enough hem that the overall effect is subtly sexy.

Finally, Lydia waves a hand to remove the mask—no messing about with human approaches there—applies some make-up manually, then strokes her right palm down my face to amp everything up.

I put my coloured contact lenses in and my sunglasses on. I don't trust myself to keep my eyes looking normal, the mood I'm in.

Lavinia sprays me liberally with something that treads an uneasy line between sexy perfume and low-key love potion, then the three of us hold hands and she traverses us away.

We land in a cute little café, decorated in shades of grey and green. Without waiting to be asked, Lavinia orders a black coffee for me, English Breakfast tea for Lydia, and camomile for herself. And scrambled eggs and salmon—no toast—all round.

As I take a sip of my drink, I actually manage a proper little smile. I'm heartbroken about Gabriel, obviously—it'd take more than this sort of thing to make those thoughts and feelings disappear.

But I'm seriously touched by Lavinia and Lydia's care and concern. By the way they are acting like actual friends. The effects of the potion and the pampering are helping to keep the worst of my sorrow at bay, but the simple gratitude and relief from being cared for have even more of an effect.

After we've finished the food and ordered another round of hot drinks, I get up to go to the bathroom, which is down in the basement.

"Are you okay to go by yourself?" Lavinia asks, as though I'm recovering from a life-threatening injury rather than just moping around.

"Don't worry about me. I'm feeling much better. And I'll only be a moment."

When I step away from the table, though, I fear I may have spoken too soon. My whole body feels weak and lethargic, as though misery has melted my muscles, and only the company of the others was keeping me in one piece.

I refuse to be that pathetic, though, so I take unsteady step after unsteady step. I make it down the stairs to the level below. There's extra seating in the basement level, presumably to cater to the lunch crowd, but at this time of day, there's no one else around.

And then, suddenly, I slip.

Maybe it's the overly shiny marble floor. Maybe it was Lavinia's insistence on me wearing heels way higher than I normally attempt. Maybe someone had spilt a drink. Certainly, my overall shakiness doesn't help proceedings.

Either way, I go careering down onto the floor, landing on my bum with an audible crash. I close my eyes for a second. I'm not someone who gets embarrassed easily, and on a normal day, I'd probably be able to laugh this off, especially as there's seemingly no one else in the basement. But today, even after Lavinia and Lydia's ministrations, my confidence and self-esteem are already at rock bottom.

"Are you okay?"

I reluctantly open my eyes to find a truly gorgeous man leaning over me, his finely chiselled face the perfect picture of concern. He takes my arm and lifts me gently to my feet.

I swallow hard. "Thank you. I'm fine. I'd better get back to my friends."

The last thing I need is someone like this witnessing my humiliation, even if he does seem more sympathetic than amused. He's got dark red hair, cut elegantly. Piercing green eyes. And a face that is pleasingly angular, but still manages to look honest, open, and cheerful, despite his apparent worry about me.

His complexion is probably naturally pretty pale, but he's caught the sun, giving him a bit of colour and a subtle scattering of faintly adorable freckles. He's tall, dressed in the sort of clothes that suggests he's about to go for a particularly classy run. His bare arms and close-fitting top and trousers show off his athletic figure.

His hand is still wrapped around my arm, which may well be the only thing holding me up, considering how much my legs are shaking.

"You took quite a knock," he says. "And you look like you've had a shock. Why don't you sit there for a moment and catch your breath? I'll get you a drink of water—or something stronger if you prefer—and then, if you point them out, I'll go and find your friends and tell them what happened."

I nod silently, as he leads me to a sofa tucked away in one corner.

"I'm Seb, by the way," he says. "I'm a doctor—so you're in safe hands if you are feeling a little bruised—but it's my day off today, and I was just sitting here to get a bit of writing done. I run a satirical politics blog in my spare time."

I sink down onto the sofa, wincing slightly as my bottom makes contact. In response, Seb tucks a cushion behind me.

"I'm Sadie," I manage, even though I'm feeling overwhelmed by the entire situation. "I'm a lawyer."

And a witch, of course, but this very human, very charming man doesn't need to know that. I wonder if I've ever read his blog—I love that sort of thing. Assuming his politics broadly accord with mine, which some sixth sense tells me probably is the case.

"Lovely to meet you, Sadie. Now, do you want water? Or would a shot of whisky for the shock be preferable? Either way, I'd suggest a painkiller."

He's got a nice voice. Professional and educated, but not gratingly posh like the vampires. The sort of neutral accent that suggests he's lived in London for years, but maybe originated elsewhere in the UK.

"Just water's fine, Seb, thank you."

I probably ought to tell him again that I'm alright, that he's already been too kind, that I can find my friends myself and get on with my day. But it's been an awful twenty-four hours, and it's nice to have the undivided attention of a lovely guy, even if it's just for a few minutes.

He smiles, like this is an unexpected treat rather than a bit of a chore. "Stay right here. I'll be back in one moment."

As he dashes back up the stairs, I try to take stock. Is he just a genuinely nice guy or is he into me? The falling over bit can't exactly have made a great first impression, but thanks to the efforts of my fellow coven members, I'm looking objectively good today.

It's not like I'm on the look-out for anyone, but I could certainly use the ego boost.

As promised, Seb reappears in double-quick time, brandishing not only the promised water but a coffee and a slice of chocolate cake.

"You don't have to have them," he says. "But in my medical opinion, a bit of sugar is just what you need right now."

He puts the treats down on the table in front of me. "Mind if I join you?"

I smile the sort of smile I wouldn't have believed myself capable of just a few hours ago. "Of course. Thank you. But didn't you get anything for yourself?"

He sets himself down next to me, not touching me, but close enough that it gives me a little shiver of excitement, despite everything. I can smell his classic, subtle aftershave, and a faint, pleasant scent of him beneath it.

"I've already eaten," he replies. "I'm due to meet a friend for our weekly run any minute now, and I don't think I could move if I had anything more."

"Please don't let me keep you," I say, out loud. *Please stay a little longer*, I think.

He glances at his watch. "If it weren't for the fact my friend will already be on his way, I'd have cancelled. I don't really want to leave you like this. You still look quite shook up, despite my best efforts."

I look him in the eye. "It's been a long week. The fall was just the icing on the cake."

I'd love to see his expression if I told him about the things that have happened over the last few days. Not Gabriel, that's none of his business, and no one likes hearing about strangers' love lives. But the witches. The vampires. The plots. For a wild moment, I almost want to confide in him, but even if he were a well-established human friend, he'd think I was mad. A new acquaintance would run for the hills.

"Listen, I really do have to disappear in five minutes or so. We should get you back to your friends. But I'd love to hear about your awful week—and maybe some nice things, too— some other time? I hope this doesn't come across as creepy or anything, but would you be free for dinner on Friday evening?"

I freeze. Up until this summer, I went on plenty of dates. But it was always very controlled and researched. Dating apps. Friends of friends. At a pinch, someone I'd met at a party or a work event. I'd do my due diligence, and I'd do things on my terms. Even in Mannith, I'd known Connor's family, and I'd worked with him for a while before anything romantic happened. And the less said about Gabriel the better, although despite all the other issues, I certainly knew who he was.

But this Seb is a genuine stranger. I know nothing about him bar the handful of facts he's told me about himself. I don't even know his surname. He seems nice, and I can already feel a hint of chemistry. The idea of meeting up with him again is half charming and exciting, half terrifying.

"I'm really not sure I'm looking for anything like that right now," I say. "I broke up with someone recently."

He places a firm hand on my shoulder. I relax into it. "If it's too soon, then don't worry about it. But maybe take my number in case you'd be interested in the future."

"There you are!" I'm so focused on Seb that I fail to notice Lavinia until she's right in front of me. "Who is this?"

"Lavinia, this is Seb. I fell over, and he rescued me. Seb, this is Lavinia. The friend I told you about."

"And am I imagining things, or did I just overhear you asking the lovely Sadie out for dinner?"

I blush, and so does he.

"I was just saying how it's a bit too soon."

"Oh, nonsense. Sadie would love to go out for dinner with you."

"Lavinia!"

"It'll be fun. It'll do you the world of good."

Poor Seb looks from one to the other of us, slightly mystified.

I shake my head. "Fine. You only live once and all that. Here's my number. Let's get something arranged."

It's hard to say whether Seb or Lavinia sport the bigger smile in response.

"I really do need to dash now," the former says, getting to his feet. "But I'm so glad we met like this. I'll be in touch. I can't wait until Friday."

He helps me to stand, gives me a hug that's friendly but with the promise of more, then walks away.

Lavinia, usually the queen of poise, squeals like she's about thirteen. "My goodness! You work fast. When I said we needed to find you a new man, I didn't literally mean today. But what a hottie. And so sweet, too. Well done you."

I laugh and eat a forkful of the chocolate cake Seb so thoughtfully provided. "I don't think it will go anywhere. I'm not in the right headspace at all. But maybe we'll have a fun night."

Lavinia grins. "Well, the best way to get over a man is to get under a new one. A fun night may be all you need. Either way, we'd better get back to Lydia and tell her the gossip."

As I head back up the stairs and follow in Lavinia's wake— the crowd seems to part as she strides along—I'm suddenly freshly assailed by an almost unbearable sense of loss and of longing for Gabriel. But I grit my teeth and push the feeling down.

Gabriel might be some sort of soulmate, but for my own sanity and safety, I cannot be in a relationship with him, and that's final. I need to prove to myself that I can have fun without him. That I can have romance without him. Eventually, maybe even have love without him. I need to show that whatever fate believes, Gabriel-fucking-Thornber does not have a monopoly on my heart or my body.

Today, I'll enjoy time with my new friends. Tomorrow, I'll get back to work. And on Friday... Well, I'll see where the night takes me.

. . .

I spend Friday inspecting the contract between the vampires and the Mannith Alliance, in between bouts of tears and—despite my stern words to myself—intrusive thoughts of Gabriel. The final contract looks good—legally binding, consistent with what was discussed, detailed and specific about how far they'll extend the Dome, what their rights are as far as feeding goes, and all the rest of it.

I've advised my family to sign, though that's something of a technicality. The vampires will have seen it as binding ever since the exchange of blood.

That said, the Dome expansion will take place on Midwinter's Eve. Between now and then, either side can choose to withdraw if certain conditions are met—the Mannith Alliance breaking down, weakness on either side, the two parties working against each other—though that seems fairly academic.

In the evening, it's time for the date with Seb. I'm not usually a big fan of dates, but I'm excited despite myself. He seemed nice enough in the coffee shop. And the way we met—with me more or less literally falling into his arms—seems to have rather more soul than if I'd just come across him on an app or something.

Lavinia, who's still firmly on a mission to cheer me up—and who has absolutely no boundaries—has bought me a gorgeous new dusky rose dress that clings in all the right places. Lydia's done my hair and make-up again. And Seb has suggested a rooftop restaurant, which based on its website, looks gorgeous. Whatever else happens, I'm at least going to look good and enjoy some stunning views.

On arrival at the address Seb gave me, a uniformed concierge guides me into a mirrored lift and presses the button for the top floor. I flinch as it shoots upwards. I draw a lot of my power from the earth, as well as forcing most of my negative emotions into it. Being more than a few floors off the ground always disconcerts me, and this must be about forty stories high.

The lift opens directly onto the rooftop terrace. Once I'm outside, the cramped, nervy sensation dissipates. I can draw on the air, too, and that's plentiful here and less full of emissions than at ground level. The ivy crawling up the walls, the grass covering the concrete rooftop and the multitude of trees all combine to give the sense that we're in a park, rather than up high in one of the most urban, densely populated cities on earth. It's already getting dark—I'd not noticed how the nights are closing in, but it's November already—and as luck would have it, it's a clear night with a bright moon. The light pollution is way too strong for stars, though, which slightly ruins the illusion of rural idyll. And the beauty can't quite drive away the butterflies in my stomach.

While I'm standing around awkwardly, Seb strides over. The sight of him makes me smile in an unguarded way and my heart gives a little flutter. I hadn't misremembered how attractive he was—and hot as he looked in workout gear, he looks even better in a well-tailored suit.

He takes my arm. It ought to feel unduly forward, this early in the evening, but it simultaneously steadies my nerves and gives me a fresh jolt of excitement.

"Sadie! I'm so glad you agreed to come. You're even more gorgeous than I remembered."

I grin. "How could I say no after you literally swept me off my feet?"

A waiter leads us to an alcove on the far side of the terrace, which juts out over the building and is shielded from both the elements and prying eyes by topiary hedges that form a wall on three sides and a canopy above, all of which are set with tiny fairy lights. The fourth side is entirely open and provides spectacular views of all the lights of London.

"Gin?" he asks. "They have about fifty different varieties here. There are some amazing ones."

I study the special menu. "Am I achingly predictable or have you been stalking me on social media?"

"What can I say? I just appreciate a good G&T."

Honestly, I don't mind if he has done a bit of research. At least it'd mean he was making an effort. Either way, I order a Dà Mhìle Seaweed Gin, which is something I've been meaning to try for a while, and thoroughly enjoy it. He gets something that's tinted blue but turns purple once the tonic's added, and gives me a taste from his glass.

"So, you said you were a lawyer?" he asks, once we've both started to relax. "A good lawyer or an evil lawyer?"

I laugh. "What a question. Good, I think? I mean, people are complicated. No cases are totally black and white. I just believe in people getting a fair trial. In justice being done."

I give him a brief summary of the Janice Denworth case—minus her death at the hands of a vampire. He seems impressed. Which is a relief, as I'd struggle to date anyone who thought she deserved to be locked up.

"And you're a doctor?"

"A paediatrician. Treating sick children. Which is utterly rewarding at its best, utterly draining at its worst. Though I've learnt to blank things out."

"That's so impressive," I say. What else *can* you say in response? But my heart gives another genuine little flutter.

We both order off the set menu, which is thoroughly French. I drink my second drink of the evening and brace myself for that awful feeling that falls somewhere between disdain and contempt that always plagues me on first dates and means they rarely turn into second ones. But it never comes. I look at his steady, smiling face. I catch a hint of his fresh scent. And I'm just glad to be with him.

I reach out a hand and touch his over the table. His smile widens in response.

When the starters arrive, I dive into my game terrine, taking full advantage of the bread on the side. He eats his salmon with significantly more delicacy.

For the main course, we both have steak. Mine's medium rare, with thick cut chips and béarnaise sauce. His is about as rare as you can physically get, with just an undressed salad on the side.

"Not a carbs fan?" I ask.

"I stick to a paleo diet. Eating like a caveman. You really ought to try it."

"I'll stick to eating like a pre-revolution French princess, if it's okay with you."

He laughs. "I'm sure they were much more attractive, on the whole."

The light-hearted response fills me with relief. A bit of healthy eating is a good trait in a guy, but I couldn't cope with someone who was too puritanical about it.

"So go on, tell me about your exercise routine. No one looks that good or takes that much care with their food and doesn't have one. And no one who has one doesn't want to talk about it."

Another laugh. "God, don't give me an opening, or I'll never stop. But running and cycling, basically. I'm training for the Brighton Marathon. And a fifty kilometre cycle. Raising money for the hospital where I work, but also pushing myself. After the days at work when things don't go so well, I need an outlet."

"I'm more of a weights and yoga girl, myself. But I could probably be converted."

Despite my flippant words, I'm impressed again. That sounds gruelling. And the fundraising's a nice touch.

It's interesting. Seb's not that different from a variety of guys I've been on dates with in the past. They tend to be reasonably attractive. They tend to be reasonably nice people with interesting jobs and hobbies. But the overall package here just elevates him into a different league. And beyond that almost checklist approach, there's something else at play. Chemistry, I guess. I'm enjoying listening to him. I'm enjoying being with him.

I rest a hand on his muscular thigh under the table, and he rests his on top of mine.

I devour a particularly rich crème brûlée, and just about manage not to feel too self-conscious about the contrast with his bowl of berries.

"For my next trick, I'm ordering a double espresso," I declare. "If you go for a decaf, this date is over."

"Am I allowed a mint tea?"

I lean in. "Grudgingly."

After the drinks, I pop to the bathroom and take a moment to examine my feelings. By this point in most dates, I'm either bored and irritated, or disinterested but in the mood for sex. And then there's the insane cocktail of not entirely human emotions my handful of nominal dates with Gabriel have provoked.

Right now, I'm grinning. I just feel really, really happy and content. And at the same time, extremely attracted to Seb.

I smile at him with genuine warmth when I meet him by the lift and he helps me into my coat. "That was a really nice evening."

"Do you want to get another drink somewhere? I'd invite you back to mine for coffee, but I only have decaf and I'm scared you might murder me in response."

I pause. In one of my normal dates—and goodness knows there have been enough—this is my cue to either gently give them the brush off or drag them back to mine for fun but soulless sex.

"I'm going to call it a night for now, but I'd love to grab a drink next week if you're free? I honestly mean that, it's not a polite way of getting rid of you."

I actually *do* mean it. I want to take this slow. I want to try and make it work.

"I've had a fantastic time, too. And that sounds great. How about Wednesday? There's this great new bar just round the corner from my flat in Fulham."

"I've got a better idea. How about the London Eye?"

"Sorry?"

"I put up with all of London's housing costs, pollution and over-crowding," I explain. "I've never bothered going to most of those places people travel thousands of miles to see, have you? I thought it might be fun to do something touristy."

"It's a date."

He kisses me on the cheek, like we're in a cute 1950s romance. I almost swoon in response.

FOURTEEN

BRENDAN

It's hard to believe that the thing I've dreamt about for years might actually come true. Come Midwinter's Eve, the Dome is finally going to be enlarged. And we'll be able to do it without human sacrifices—which, contrary to what some people seem to think, was always something I considered horrific but necessary, as opposed to part of the fun.

It's bittersweet that my pet project, my ten-year obsession, is going to be pulled off with little to no involvement from me. Most of the magic will come directly from the vampires, but some of my fellow practitioners will need to help. Not me, though. It's impressive how much Nikki's already managed to teach me, but learnt magic—even combined with my remaining token amount of born magic—could never be sufficient for a spell of that magnitude.

I wasn't even able to help with the negotiations. We just couldn't risk the vampires discovering my frailty and deciding in turn that the family was weak. Still, though I'd never admit it to anyone, I've got to hand it to Thornber both for coming up with the idea and for pulling it off.

On Friday afternoon, I'm alternating listlessly between

various pieces of work: checking the accounts for our legitimate businesses like The Windmill, analysing the documents the vampires have sent us, and studying maps and stats to see how far the Dome could be extended and what the effects on unemployment, health, pollution, inequality and all the rest of it might be.

The first of those is always boring, and the second is a little distasteful. But it's unusual that anything to do with the Dome fails to hold my imagination.

The truth is, I've increasingly been living for Friday evenings. Mostly, it's about having magic at my fingertips once again. But it's also revitalising to spend time with someone from whom I don't have to hide my lack of powers.

After four weeks, we've fallen into a comfortable pattern. An hour of practice, which gets easier each time. Then an hour of conversation, which also flows more smoothly every time. Maybe I'm delusional, but I'm increasingly confident Nikki's not doing this on Thornber's orders. Though outside of our weekly sessions, we have no contact.

At four, my phone rings, and I race to grab it, in case it's her.

"Hey, it's me," Chrissie says.

"Hey, sis." I fight to keep the mingled disappointment and relief out of my voice.

"Ray and I are going out for dinner tonight, while Mum babysits. Liam and Shane are probably going to come, too. Want to join?"

"I've got too much to do tonight."

"You've got to stop hiding away. Whether it's heartbreak, stress or you're embarrassed about your powers, you need to have some fun and you need to meet someone new."

I ought just to tell her about my evening plans. But for now, my sessions with Nikki exist in a private bubble, without the complications of other people's views.

"How about I come round on Saturday evening? I can play

with the twins for a bit before bedtime, then you, me, and Ray can chill out with a few drinks."

"Deal."

I know full well she's already working out what hot, single person she can casually invite round. I'll just have to make the best of it.

Once Chrissie hangs up, I work with renewed focus, and lose track of time until the doorbell rings.

"Come in," I call. "I'm in the living room. Second door on the left."

Nikki appears a few seconds later, and glances around at the blown-up maps festooning the floor.

"For goodness' sake, Brendan. Tidy up your work stuff before I get here. I'm not spying for Gabe, I swear, but if you leave your plans lying around, it's going to be hard to resist telling him about them."

I gesture for her to join me on the floor. "Look all you want. It's the Dome expansion stuff. I'm pretty sure Thornber and I are aligned on this."

"So the black line is the current outer edge of the Dome, right? And then the red line is where the vampires could help us get it to." She studies the map closely. "What's the dotted line? And the shading? And all those coloured stickers?"

"The dotted line marks the area that would be designated as the vampires' feeding ground. The shading shows the strength of protection the Dome will offer in different places—it won't be quite as powerful on the outskirts as it is in Mannith. And the stickers are different towns. You need to cross-reference them with the chart pinned up on the back wall. It shows key stats right now, and how much I think we could improve them once the Outer Dome is in place."

She traces the dotted line with her fingers. "Are you really comfortable with this whole vampire hunting ground thing?"

"I believe in expanding the Dome more than almost anything. You know what I was willing to do in the summer."

I stare hard at the map as I say that, unable to look her in the eyes. I don't really want to remind her of that. It's a miracle she doesn't seem to hate me for it.

"Having met the vampires, this is almost worse than human sacrifices," she says, after an awkward pause. "I guess neither you nor Gabe could ever really understand. Even with your power diminished, they could never drink from you or control your mind. But I'm still human enough to fear them as predators."

She twirls a ring on her finger self-consciously.

I stare at it. "Isn't that the ring your boss foisted on my sister?"

She shrugs. "It was. For now, it's the ring that protects me from bloodsuckers. And you'll be delighted to know that while we were all in London, Sadie told Gabriel to go to hell."

Tempting as it is to make a sarcastic or triumphant remark, I let that one go. Chrissie's already given me the headlines. "Shall we get on with the lesson?"

Nikki gets back to her feet. "Before we do, one question. If you care that much about expanding the Dome, would you sacrifice yourself to do it?"

"How would that work?"

"Gabe has a theory that if you killed someone seriously powerful, in the right way, their death would release enough magical energy to facilitate the expansion. That's why he was talking about killing you, not just because he's not your biggest fan. Since you lost most of your magic, it wouldn't work."

"But Thornber doesn't know I've lost my magic. So why's he changed his mind?"

"He's happy with the vampire deal. He wants to protect the alliance. And he doesn't want to burn his bridges with Sadie. But would you have been willing to go to your death voluntarily? You're always happy to sacrifice others for the greater good."

"I'd rather sacrifice him. But I've not got the strength for that either. Now can we please get on with the lesson?"

"I thought we could try some of the mind control stuff today. That's always fun."

I lead her into the conservatory. I brushed off her question, but it's still running through my mind. Would I have sacrificed myself to achieve my dream? And if not, how can I possibly justify sacrificing others?

FIFTEEN

SADIE

On Wednesday evening, I meet Seb by the river. He's in jeans and an obscure band T-shirt today. I like each look better than the last.

He wraps his arms around me then once again kisses me on the cheek. I shiver like he's done a hell of a lot more as I embrace him back. He smells so good. He feels so warm. I'm unspeakably delighted that my body and mind are actually letting me enjoy this.

I look up at the massive wheel. I've seen it from a distance, one more part of the iconic skyline, but up close, it's bigger than I would have thought, anchored to the embankment by long steel cables.

Seb points up to a cabin that's glowing pink, in contrast to the blue lights decorating most of them. "I've booked the private one. I thought that if we were going go for the cheesy romance vibe, we might as well do it properly."

I take his arm. "Perfect."

We watch as the wheel makes its slow descent and the sun sets over the Thames. When our cabin lands, he leads me inside, where a bottle of champagne is waiting. He pours me a glass as we start to ascend, and we clink glasses.

For a horrible moment, my treacherous brain reflects on how lovely it would be to do this with Gabriel and my throat constricts. I shake my head as though I could physically fling the thought aside. I'm going to enjoy this on its own terms.

"What are you working on at the moment?" Seb asks, snapping me back to the moment.

"A pretty standard immigration appeal," I reply.

There are no supernatural elements at all. And it's going sufficiently well that I've not been the slightest bit tempted to use magic. It's a refreshing change. With the start of Lavinia's "Operation Stop the Vampires" (or STV, as I've taken to calling it in my head) mere days away, I'm enjoying the normality while I can.

Over the next hour, we work our way through the champagne and admire the view. Lavinia has a point—about London and about my need to make it work with a new man. There can't be a city in the world with such a variety of landmarks from such a range of eras. From this height, the magic Lavinia talks about is hard to miss. And Seb is just a feast for the senses.

As we near the top of the wheel, I shuffle closer and closer towards Seb, until our legs are pressed together, my hand's resting casually on his thigh, and my heart's beating a little faster.

We talk and talk. A bit about politics, where we're safely within the same bubble, but have enough points of considered difference to keep things interesting. A bit about culture, where we find some shared favourites and each give the other some new recommendations.

"You really ought to give these guys a listen," he says, pointing to his T-shirt. "They're actually playing in Brixton in a few months. Maybe we could go?"

It's a sign of how well this is going that I'm delighted, rather than unnerved, that he's making joint plans for us that far out.

We talk a bit about his background—studied medicine at Bristol University, grew up in Sussex, only child, a dad who was also a doctor, a mum who did interior design.

"Oh, and I was in a band at university," he says. "Played bass and sang. Had the long floppy hair and everything. I've got some pictures somewhere, but you'd have to drag them out of me."

"I bet you still looked cute with silly hair. And now I absolutely need to hear you sing."

"Maybe I'll write you a song one day," he says, staring out at the view for a moment then turning his gaze back on me like I'm way more fascinating than the entirety of the London skyline.

When it comes to my turn to share a bit about myself, I struggle, as usual. And then break eye contact for a moment while I give the standard evasive answers that attempt to make my enchanted hometown and sprawling magical family sound vaguely normal.

He's the first human man I've attempted to date since I started using magic again. If I said anything awkward, I could make him forget. If he did or said anything I didn't like, I could change his behaviour. The possibilities are terrifying.

I dig my nails into my palm. I absolutely need to control myself. The temptation to influence the outcome of trials is bad enough. Influencing an individual for my personal benefit would be unforgivable.

"Maybe we should get something to eat," I say, as we start to descend again. I don't want the booze to go to my head, or I might lose control. "Do you know any good places around here?"

"Yeah. My hospital is just around the corner, so I know this area really well. But why don't you come back to mine and let me cook? It's a bit of a passion of mine."

"Sounds great." I actually can't wait.

We down the last dregs of our drink as our cabin reaches the bottom. As he takes my hand and leads me outside, I've got the sort of nervous excitement I've not felt on a date in years, with the one obvious exception.

We walk a little way along the river, then snuggle close in the taxi back, like over-excited teenagers. By the time we reach his house, I'm alarmingly loved up.

He takes my hand and leads me inside. It's open plan, rather like my own flat, but a bit bigger and a lot more masculine. The kitchen is all matt stainless steel, the table's glass, and the sofas are leather. He's gone for a very minimalist vibe, with no personal possessions or superfluous decorations to be seen.

"Wine? Gin?"

"Controversially, I think I'll just have a glass of water for now. Then maybe some more wine with the meal."

"Sounds sensible," he says. "Now how about a Pad Krapow for dinner? I learnt to make it on a cookery course in Thailand. It's actually super quick, but tastes amazing."

"Sounds great. Do you want a hand?"

He opens his large grey fridge and pulls out a big bag of Bird's Eye chillies, and several bulbs of garlic. "Maybe make a start on chopping these while I pop to the shop over the road and grab a bottle of wine."

I nod, pleased to have something to focus my mind. My usual policy is to jump on guys as soon as we get through the door—but that feels wrong here. I make a start using one of the alarmingly sharp knives, then, once Seb heads out, I narrow my eyes, focus on the ingredients, and chop them all perfectly with my mind.

"Wow, that was fast," he says, when he reappears.

"I'm full of hidden talents."

I perch on a stool and watch him work, eating him up with my eyes while we chat about music and books. Soon, a delicious smell fills every inch of the kitchen, though the amount of chilli in the air is enough to make my eyes water.

"I usually skip the rice, but I can cook some for you if you'd like?" he says.

I shake my head. "I'll take a leaf out of your painfully healthy book."

We decamp to the dining table and eat the gloriously flavoured food in minutes.

After we eat, I feel suddenly shy. I know how to play things when I don't give a damn, but this is tricky. Should I make a move? Will he?

I grab the empty plates and almost dash to the sink with them.

He comes up behind me and wraps his arms around my waist, pulling me in close.

"I've been trying to play it cool, but I've got to say, I really, really like you," he whispers.

I turn around in the circle of his arms and kiss him.

"I like you, too."

I help him out of the band T-shirt. He's got the chest and abs you'd expect from all that exercise and healthy eating.

I give a little sigh, then almost without meaning to, I run my hand over his torso, admiring his physique.

He catches my roaming hand in both of his, and I take the opportunity to all but drag him to the bedroom, my heart beating a thousand miles an hour.

The bedroom is fashionably plain, like the rest of the house: stripped-back wooden floors, a king-size bed on a chrome frame with heavy white sheets, a built-in wardrobe and not much else.

Inside the doorway, he kisses me with renewed intensity, and then unzips my dress and eases it over my body.

"You're so gorgeous," he says. "I mean, you're intelligent and sweet and funny, too, but it's got to be said, you're also sexy as hell."

As I stand there, naked but for my underwear, a little tipsy and very turned on, a wave of guilt hits me. *I shouldn't be doing this. It's practically cheating.*

I close my eyes and try to rally my thoughts. It's *really* not cheating. If Gabriel and I were ever actually together, we're very definitely broken up right now. Even so, for a torturous second, he's the only person I can think about. Images of him fill my mind, and the thought of anyone else touching me is abhorrent.

I take the deepest breath I can manage and press my hands to my head in an attempt to keep the thought at bay, but it isn't working. My brain's running a highlights reel of every moment I've spent with Gabriel, romantic, terrifying, and everywhere in between.

Seb pulls off his jeans. His legs and bum are, objectively, just as delightful as his upper body. I ought to be soaking in the sight, running my hands over that wonderful body, pressing myself into him.

Instead, when he steps behind me, I flinch.

"Wow, that is some tattoo," he says, seemingly unaware of my panic.

He's been super perceptive of my emotions all evening, but he's probably not thinking with his brain at this point. He runs a hand over Lavinia's lien mark. I'm poised to dart out of his reach. Instead, I relax as he touches me and thoughts of Gabriel move to the back of my mind.

"I got it when I was a student," I say, laughing in a way that's surprisingly unforced. "Probably around the same time you were in your band."

"Is that the mark of the London Assay office?" he asks, circling a finger around what I can only assume is the leopard's head I've never managed to place.

"I've no idea what half of the designs are. The tattoo artist really went to town. What is that?"

He strokes his hand up and down my back. "It's marked on gold to show that it's real and that it was made in London. My mum's really into her jewellery."

I frown. What a bizarre thing for Lavinia to put on my back. Though maybe I should take it as a compliment? I'm a genuine, twenty-four-carat practitioner.

Before I can change my mind, I turn around, grab hold of Seb's finely honed bum and press him harder against me. He leans down and kisses me again and I respond with equal passion.

In the end, the sex is great. Somehow, I even manage to come without resorting to my old trick of running Gabriel-fucking-Thornber fantasies and horrors through my mind.

When the alarm on my phone goes off the next morning—it's a weekday, after all—it takes me a moment to figure out where I am. It's an unfamiliar experience, waking up in a strange bed. It's not like I never have sex on dates, but I usually make a swift exit or encourage them to do so.

Perhaps this ought to make me feel like I'm in too deep, but it's curiously indulgent to recline in the soft, warm bed, surrounded by the scent of Seb.

The man himself is already up and about—I can hear him bustling around in the kitchen.

I drag myself out of bed, shower in the ensuite—no time for a bath today—then pull on last night's clothes, which are thankfully still clean and sufficiently professional to pass muster at work, especially as I'm in the office today rather than in court.

Then, feeling as shy as a teenager dealing with a crush, I tiptoe into the kitchen.

Seb grins at the sight of me. He's in tight-fitting exercise gear again, and has apparently already been out for a run. He's a little sweaty, but in a way that feels masculine and appealing, rather than off-putting.

"Good morning. I was just making us some blueberry protein smoothies."

I reach out my hand and take the proffered tall glass. He's made it look very pretty, with a long, striped straw and some fresh blueberries artfully sprinkled on top. I take a slightly nervous sip—it wouldn't be my normal breakfast choice—but it's utterly delicious as well as presumably being very good for me. I could get used to this.

I perch on a breakfast bar stool and Seb picks up his own smoothie and comes to join me. We sit close together, our thighs lightly touching.

"Listen," Seb says after a moment. "I know we both need to get ready for work, and it's not the best time for a heavy conversation. But I just wanted to say I really loved last night. I really enjoy spending time with you."

I look up at him. "Me too."

He doesn't reply at first, just stares at me and takes a few sips of his drink, like he's trying to find the right words. "I know we've only met a couple of times, and I don't want to seem like I'm moving too fast, but I'd like to see more of you. I'd like to make this vaguely official. What do you say?"

Once upon a time, if someone had said that to me, I'd have run a mile. And arguably, I ought to do the same now. He is moving a little fast, and while I was keen to get out there and have some fun, I'm still not sure I'm in the right place for a relationship.

But I do enjoy being with him. Against all the odds, I could see this going somewhere.

Besides, I tied myself to the London Coven to stop myself from cracking and returning to Mannith. Maybe I could tie myself to a lovely man to stop myself from cracking and returning to Gabriel?

I take a deep breath, then lean over and kiss him. "Seb, I'd love to be your girlfriend."

When it's time for our weekly chat, I videocall Chrissie rather than just ringing. I can't wait to see her face when she hears my news.

When she picks up, I smile at the sight of Ceri and Chi playing with little wooden musical instruments in the background. They already look more grown up than when I saw them last, just a few short months ago. They'll be three before too long.

Usually, I like to get Chrissie's gossip before jumping into mine. But today, I can't contain myself.

"I've started seeing someone," I say.

Instead of the massive grin or excited squeal I was hoping for, Chrissie screws up her face, like she's simultaneously eaten something that tastes different to what she was expecting and been asked to solve a complex riddle.

"You mean like a casual fling, right?"

I frown back at her. "It's early days. But we're pretty much official."

One of the twin girls—I always struggle to tell them apart—toddles over and climbs up on her mum's knee. Chrissie keeps her expression placid so as not to alarm her daughter, but I can sense the surging emotions beneath the surface as easily as if I were in the room with her.

"But what's the point?"

"What's that supposed to mean?"

She sighs. "It's crazy to try and start a proper relationship when you know full well who your soulmate is."

I force a smile onto my face for the girls' sake. "Seb's a wonderful guy, and I made my views regarding Gabriel clear that night you were all down in London."

"This Seb could be the nicest guy in the world. He's not the person you're meant to be with."

"When we caught Leah with Gabriel, you said you didn't know how she could bear to sleep with him, that you felt sick if you so much as made eye contact with him. Now you want me to forsake all others because his mum had a dream about me?"

Chrissie hesitates before answering, pulling her daughter in closer. "He's not my favourite person in the world, though I'm coming around since we've got to know him through the alliance. But that's irrelevant. I believe his mum's dream. Just like I believed Ray's sister when she dreamed about me. You just have to see the two of you together to know it's true."

"And so I can never do anything romantic with anyone else?"

"I get that it's not like when Ray and I met for the first time on a deserted sandy beach, took one look at each other, and got married the following evening. There's a lot of messy history between you and Gabriel. So, by all means, have some hot nights or some romantic weekends away with other people until he's redeemed himself and you feel ready. But trying to start a serious relationship's not fair on you, him, or the new guy."

"Don't you even want to hear about Seb before dismissing him?"

Chrissie manages a gentle smile. "I assume he's a regular human?"

"Yes, why?"

"Because any practitioner with the slightest hint of power would see in your eyes that you already had a fated romance and steer well clear."

She smirks, deliberately winding me up now.

"Connor didn't seem to notice or wasn't bothered if he did."

Chrissie flinches slightly. It's almost like we're not meant to mention Connor, my father's enforcer and my former lover, or the fact that Gabriel killed him. It's not really on message as far as the alliance goes.

"That was before you consolidated things. And you were pretending to be someone else at the time. That probably blurred the lines."

"Lavinia doesn't seem to have noticed anything either. She's got more than a hint of power, and she was there when I met Seb. She encouraged me to give it a go."

"Did she now? Interesting. Almost like she wants to keep you in London? Keep you from being distracted by true love?"

"Do you want to hear about Seb or not?"

"Fine. Go on."

"He's a doctor, and he seems to really care about helping people—he does loads of voluntary work, too. He's really kind and cheerful, but it's not like he's super earnest or dull or anything—he also writes this really hilarious, insightful blog about politics. I'll send you a few articles, they crack me up."

Once I start, I just can't stop.

"He's into running in particular and fitness stuff in general. He's really good at it actually, speed and endurance and strength and everything. He's big on healthy eating, but he's able to laugh about it. And he's a great cook as well.

"He likes music and books and theatre—loads of the same things as me, but he's introducing me to some new bands and authors and things, too, which is fun.

"Oh, and he's really hot. Did I mention that? All the exercise and health food really pay off as far as his body goes, but he's also got a super cute face. I get all tingly just looking at him."

Chrissie gives me the widest, fakest smile. "Fascinating. Definitely sounds worth giving up the love of your life for!"

"He's just a great guy, okay? We've got similar values, similar interests. We have a nice, relaxed time together. We have a laugh. We have interesting conversations. He makes me feel safe and loved. The sex is great. And unlike Gabriel, I've never felt the urge to literally murder him, which seems like a bit of a prerequisite for a long-term relationship."

Chrissie takes a breath and forces her smile into an attempt at something more genuine. "If he makes you happy, that's great. He doesn't exactly sound like my type, but then neither does you-know-who. Get him up to Mannith and introduce us all."

"I'd like that. I think he would, too."

"Do you want me to gently tell Gabriel about this new development?"

"What, you sit down for cosy chats with him now?"

"We have a business relationship, remember? We've got all sorts of things organised to prepare for the Dome expansion and the vampire deal."

Hmm... At some point, I really do need to get up to Mannith and see how it's all working with the alliance. It's too weird to imagine the Thornbers and the Sadlers working together, socialising together. But the less said about their deal with the vampires, the better, especially with Lavinia's strike against them just days away now.

"There's no need for a formal announcement. Maybe mention it if the subject comes up."

I quickly change the subject on to Chrissie's week and relax as she tells me funny stories about the twins.

SIXTEEN

We're gathered in a meeting room in Parliament. It's Katrina's doing—the perks of being friends with a politician. God knows what plots have been made in this high-ceilinged, elaborately decorated room over the years. Our plan to set up the perfect crime scene, get a vampire convicted, and whip up a media frenzy about his kind is probably the least of it.

There is oak-panelling to chest height, with stone fireplaces built in at regular intervals. Above the panels, the walls are covered in a swirling black, red, and gold design. A huge chandelier dominates the centre of the space, while an arched doorway surrounded with stained glass marks the entrance. Somewhat incongruously, enough of Lavinia's extortionately priced scented candles are burning to land an aircraft.

The room is feverish with anticipation, like something from a mass rally. My heart starts to race, half because the excitement is contagious, but half with a sense of foreboding. I want to strike against the vampires. But there's so much potential for things to go wrong.

Despite the crowds on that first night I met her, Lavinia tends to prefer small, intimate gatherings for socialising, magic, or plotting. But almost the entirety of the coven is gathered tonight, men and women, Born Practitioners and humans.

Lavinia sashays to the front of the room and everyone falls silent.

"As we all know, the vampires have their tentacles in every inch of the establishment. They rig elections and control the media. They're so confident in their public reputation and their private secrecy that they can literally get away with murder. But not this time.

"We're going to land an assault charge on one of them. We're going to cut through their mesmerism of victims, intimidation of witnesses, control of the police and judiciary, and their massive out of court settlements.

"We're going to take the case all the way to court and force their activities into the light—and into the papers. We'll give the press perfect evidence and compelling witnesses and make this a huge story.

"We're going to destroy their reputations and we're going to get people taking the idea that vampires might walk amongst us seriously enough that the public start to put protections in place.

"In short, we'll get one of them sent down. And we'll bring the rest of them down with him."

The applause explodes again, louder than ever. I find myself joining in. When Lavinia's in full flow, it's hard not to be swept away on the tidal wave of her energy.

She beckons me over to the front of the room. "Sadie, can you talk everyone through the details of the legal side of things?"

I nod. I've done a lot of thinking about this, gradually refined the plan.

"I'll be counsel for the prosecution," I explain. "The vampire we're targeting killed a vulnerable client of mine, and I doubt she was the first woman he hurt. We're trying to strike at the vampires' overall power. But I'm also looking forward to making this specific vampire pay."

"I know all the tricks the vampires' expensive legal team will employ to make the case go away. And working together, we can undermine them all and make sure the crime scene is perfect.

"And as courts sit in daylight hours, the vampires will be absolutely powerless during the actual trial. I'll get us witnesses and evidence that the press and the public won't be able to ignore. And so no one can doubt it's a real story, I'll get us that guilty verdict."

I get a round of applause almost as enthusiastic as the one bestowed on Lavinia. I try not to think about the conflict of interest with my family's alliance.

"And I'll engage the press. And great swathes of the internet, too," Lydia adds. "Lots of the media is under the vampires' control, but I'll deflect mesmerism and work with people I trust. And while Sadie makes sure the proceedings in court are sufficiently watertight that there's something meaningful to report on, I'll work on the bigger picture stuff to ensure it's a perfect story. There's the glamorous crime scene, the beautiful young victim, and the wealthy attacker. And then there's the idea of a conspiracy at the top of society. Something for everyone."

"Thank you, Sadie, Lydia. In the first instance, though, my lovely Cara will be the star of the show. As Lydia said, a key ingredient here is a beautiful young victim."

The young human wannabe-practitioner walks towards Lavinia, wide-eyed. She's clearly not been briefed in advance, and this is the bit of the plan I'm least comfortable with.

"What service can I offer?" she asks, formal and deferential.

Lavinia smiles at her. "To be the bait."

To Cara's credit, she merely bows her head. But the fear in her usually ebullient aura is unmistakable.

"The vampire is called Hugo," Lydia says. "I've looked into

his mind and got a sense of exactly the sort of woman he likes to target, whether for sex or for blood. You're the closest fit, but we can make you closer still. Make you his dream woman. Make you so impossible to resist that he drops all his defences and any sense of caution."

Cara steps still closer to Lavinia without having to be told. The coven leader pulls her into a tight embrace.

"Slightly longer hair," she mutters to herself. "Slightly bluer eyes. Significantly more right-wing politics. A much more pronounced interest in Formula 1. An infinite ability for listening to someone talk about themselves. Just the right blend of seductive and submissive, confident and demure."

Lavinia kisses Cara right in the middle of her forehead, then the younger girl steps back. She looks different in a hundred and one indefinable ways. Not objectively better or worse. Just one specific person's subjective idea of perfection. But it's the glazed look in her eyes that really scares me. The idea that Lavinia has changed her thoughts and personality just as effectively as she's increased the size of her boobs.

It's unethical. It's horrifying. But it's also undeniably impressive. It's meant to be impossible to fundamentally change how a person looks. But as I learnt in the summer, when he made Nikki look like Bren as part of his plan to frame my brother for murder, it's something Gabriel has mastered. And so, it seems, has Lavinia.

I'm a strong practitioner myself. With enough will and determination—and perhaps some jewels and a bit of overly elaborate ritual—I theoretically could manifest pretty much anything I wanted. There's an understanding, though, about how far you should push magic. Part etiquette, part health and safety. You make yourself wealthy, but not a billionaire. Powerful in your own domain, but not a world leader. Attractive, but not inhumanely beautiful.

It's kind of like the way most people would keep a five-pound note they found on the pavement, but would hand a mysterious suitcase with hundreds of thousands of pounds in at the nearest police station. In legends and in gossip, bad things happen to practitioners who take their magic too far, as though the universe fights back.

Gabriel and Bren both have a tendency to push their luck in that respect. And I'm increasingly getting the impression that Lavinia is much the same.

"Katrina, help her get ready for a night out. Lydia, Clarissa, Sadie—get yourselves prepared for a trip to the most exclusive club in town. It's our job to ensure that what happens can't simply be mesmerised away."

"And what *is* going to happen?" Katrina asks, crossing her arms. She doesn't seem to approve.

"Nothing too alarming. A little blood-letting, that's all. Vampires rarely actually kill."

It's fair to say I've heard more reassuring sentiments.

I don't make a habit of frequenting nightclubs anymore, exclusive or otherwise.

The cheaper ones seem to be filled with people who look about sixteen—though that's probably just my jaded mid-twenties perspective; in reality, they're probably university students.

The more expensive clubs tend to be populated with women who look just as young, sleazily wealthy men in their fifties, and younger men who dream of one day being old and wealthy enough to get away with being that creepy.

I had my fair share of nights out at the former type during my own student days, and I'd dipped my toes into the latter almost as a rite of passage upon moving to London and starting to command a decent salary. But the odd hen do or landmark birthday party aside, the idea of clubbing hasn't particularly crossed my mind lately.

I came straight to Lavinia's celebration party from work. My suit dress is smart and flattering enough, but definitely not right for a club of any type. As usual in this sort of situation, I ask myself what Chrissie would do. And then, though I lack her finesse for tailoring clothes out of thin air, I run my hands down my body and create myself a passably attractive off the shoulder little black dress with subtle gold threads running through it. I force my hair into big bouncy waves and make my make-up smoky-eyed. Every time I pull this kind of trick, I wonder yet again how I coped without magic for six whole years.

A few hours later, we're inside. We each have very different styles, but we've all made an effort tonight. Lavinia's in black, like me, sporting a short, tight, lace dress that ought to look trashy but actually looks predictably stunning, her hair long, straight and unadorned. Lydia's wearing something similar to what she wore the night I first met her—swirling, floor-length silk, this time in a deep blue like the sea in a storm, with her red hair piled up high on her head. Clarissa has gone for perfectly tailored pinstripe trousers and a crisp white shirt—basically the same outfit she wears day in, day out, just with slightly more flamboyance. And we've put Cara in a strappy white silk dress— half fifties pin-up girl, half virgin sacrifice. The doorman waved us through with an uncharacteristically warm smile for someone in that position.

The club is everything I dislike about this sort of establishment. The overpriced, unremarkable drinks. The generic, uninspired house music. The monochrome, metallic décor, with no hint of warmth or personality. And above all, the way barely anyone is actually dancing, preferring instead to sit around, watching and being watched.

Lavinia leads us to a table occupied by two men in expensive but slightly dishevelled suits, a gaggle of women who look like they're auditioning for a *Made in Chelsea/Love Island* mash-up, and several bottles of champagne and vodka.

Even at the age she appears to be, never mind her true age, Lavinia's probably a good few years over what men like this would consider an acceptable cut-off for a woman—but they pat the booth eagerly and gesture for the pouting girls to shuffle up to make room.

Lavinia simply smiles and spreads her arms out wide. A slight frown crosses the men's faces, then they stand up and walk away into the crowd, quickly followed by their female companions.

Lavinia sinks elegantly into the booth, pours herself a shot of £150 a bottle vodka and downs it in a way a Russian sergeant could admire.

"So nice of them to free a table up for us. And to provide drinks, too. Looks like we've got ourselves a base of operations."

The five of us sit down and each pour ourselves a drink. It's hard to hear over the dull but insistent music, until Clarissa throws up a bubble of silence. It reduces the music to a low buzz to aid our conversation, and though it doesn't make us invisible, it serves to dull onlookers' potential curiosity about a table of glammed-up women, flashing the cash with no men in sight.

"The one we're after is over there," Lydia says, touching Cara reassuringly on the shoulder with one hand while gesturing with the other. "Hugo Latham. The one who might still have a chance with the women here even if he weren't fabulously rich."

I shiver at the sight of the bastard, memories of his attack on Janice assailing my mind.

Lavinia leans over and tilts Cara's chin up towards her, almost as though she's going to take a bite out of her herself and save Hugo a job.

"Be brave, darling Cara. Have a glass of champagne for luck and courage. And then get over there and make him forget all those girls surrounding him. Indeed, any girl he's ever known before. Make him lose control."

Cara had been looking at Hugo with a smile on her face. Perhaps she'd been worried she'd have to seduce some desiccated old Nosferatu type, in which case, the reality must have come as something of a relief. But now, with the moment at hand, her eyes widen, her mouth purses, and she can barely hold the intensity of Lavinia's gaze.

"Will one of you come with me? Will I have some protection?"

Lavinia elegantly shakes her head. "We won't let things get out of our control. But you have to take this first step alone. If he sees me or Sadie, he'll be instantly on his guard. And though he doesn't know the rest of my girls, the sight of any witches might make him wary. The fact you're human is a strength rather than a weakness tonight."

Cara picks up a glass of overpriced champagne in a trembling hand and downs it in one. Afterwards, she sits there for a moment, trying and failing to psyche herself up to move. Then all at once, like someone dashing into the ocean on a cold day after ten minutes of hesitating by the shore, she jumps up and scurries across the room as fast as her vertiginous heels will carry her.

It's a shame she has to be the one to do it. Her humanity means she's at far greater risk than any of the rest of us would be. But Lavinia's right—if a practitioner tried to seduce Hugo, he'd be instantly on his guard. And even if he was vain enough to assume one of us were genuinely interested in him, he wouldn't be stupid enough to drink poisonous witch blood.

Lavinia smiles and pours us each another glass of both Bollinger and Grey Goose. "Sit back and relax, ladies. For now, all we have to do is watch and wait."

. . .

At first, I perform an amplifier spell, and we listen in on Cara and Hugo's conversation. Partly, we're making sure Cara's not in any danger—or at least, no more danger than we've deliberately set her up to be in. Partly, we're ensuring the plan works. But we're also just being nosy.

"This is a brand-new Rolex," Hugo says, waving his wrist in front of Cara's eyes. "Limited edition. I bought it in Monte Carlo, weekend of the Grand Prix. Cost a couple of hundred grand, but I had some cash sloshing around after my latest property deal."

Cara gasps. "Wow, it's beautiful. Can I touch it?"

When he smugly nods his assent, she strokes the watch like it's a baby animal. He smiles like she's giving him a blow job.

"You know, you're pretty beautiful, too," he says after a moment. "Can I touch you?"

Cara giggles, and he squeezes one of her newly over-sized boobs through her low-cut dress.

After ten minutes or so, I let my concentration fade away from their table and back to my own. Hugo has done nothing but brag about himself and throw in a few cheesy compliments and gropes. Cara's looking rapt and giving utterly asinine, flattered replies and responses but to be fair, Lavinia glamoured her to be like that.

I close my eyes for a moment. "I think I'm going to throw up. I'd be tempted to frame him for something even if he wasn't a vampire and a murderer."

"They're moving." Lydia's voice makes my eyes shoot open.

We put our glasses down and follow at a discreet distance as Hugo leads Cara towards the door. I expect her to glance back at us for reassurance, but she's seemingly entranced with him. It's unclear whether it's mesmerism, genuine desire, or a lot of training and self-control.

I stare at the door for a second and lock it closed with my mind. I psychically seal the fire exit, too, and desperately hope there isn't any sort of emergency beyond the one we're about to create.

When Hugo realises the door won't open—not even in response to his inhuman strength—he leads Cara into one of the darker reaches of the club, successfully willing other customers to leave the area and not to see what he's about to do. It works on everyone but us.

We stand a couple of metres away and watch as he extends his fangs and sinks them into poor Cara's neck.

My hand goes to my own throat and a wave of nausea rushes through me.

Cara makes no sound beyond a little sigh of delight. She must be properly mesmerised. It's surprising that Lavinia didn't protect her against vampiric mind control, but presumably, she didn't want to raise Hugo's suspicions. And perhaps it's the kindest thing.

Lavinia raises her hand to stop any of us doing more magic before she's ready. She counts out the seconds under her breath.

My nausea intensifies as Cara swoons in Hugo's arms and he closes his eyes, savouring every sip. I look around the room. No one is paying them or us any attention.

"Three, two, one, and go," Lavinia calls.

Lydia throws her arms up towards the ceiling. The music stops and all the lights turn on at once, including a spotlight that illuminates Hugo and Cara.

I'm not just flattering myself when I say I've been given the hardest task. The first aspect is to break down the magic Hugo's worked to keep him and Cara hidden from view. Next—and this is the really tricky bit—I need to lightly influence everyone in the club at once to make them turn towards the crime scene.

Some of my panic and sickness fades away as I channel my adrenaline into magic. I try my best to fix every detail in the other customers' minds and to flush some of the alcohol from their systems. As I promised Lavinia, it's an exercise in creating a hundred perfect witnesses.

It's a sign of Hugo's all-consuming bloodlust that it takes him a good few seconds to realise that the lights are up and everyone in the room is staring at him with mounting horror. He lifts his head as Cara slumps in his arms. His mouth's covered in blood, like something from a nightmare. I work on our witnesses' eyes, making sure they spot that gory detail. People start to scream.

Hugo tries to throw up a shield, a memory wipe, some mesmerism, but he's panicking too much for precision. Whatever he attempts, I wave away.

All my instincts are telling me to go and help Cara, but I push them down. Her heart's still beating, her aura is faded but strong. I need to be ruthless and focused. We'll get our witnesses, we'll get Hugo arrested, then we'll work healing magic on Cara, and she'll be back to normal in a matter of hours.

Hugo freezes, glancing around him, equal parts stunned and affronted. Lavinia points one elegant finger at him and there's a rush of unfamiliar magic. Then he bows his head and bites back down onto Cara's throat.

"This is going too far," I shout.

Cara still gives no sign of shock, fear or pain, but most of the crowd either screams and dashes away, or shouts and surges forward. Hugo lifts his head just enough to glare at them, and the first few fall to the ground.

I push my way through the ever-growing crowd separating me from Cara and Hugo. I'm going to tear that pervert in two.

Clarissa grabs my arm and pulls me back.

"Get off me," I shout. "He's going to kill her."

"Just concentrate on protecting everyone from his mesmerism," Lavinia says. She's calm and smiling.

"You've got to save her."

"It's too late," Lydia snaps. "We need to focus on making him pay."

"There was no way in hell I'd have helped if I'd known it was going to end up like this." I shake the other coven members off, and dash towards Cara.

Before I can reach her, she drops to the floor. I reach out some tendrils of magic. She's already beyond repair. The second the last trace of life leaves her, Hugo looks up again, like someone waking out of a dream. Or perhaps snapping out of mesmerism.

But that's insane. You can't mesmerise vampires. And even if it was doable, what would that imply? That Lavinia controlled Hugo and made him kill Cara? If Lavinia was willing to see her get drained for the sake of her grand plan, that'd be straight-up murder.

As Lavinia reassured us all earlier, vampires rarely kill. If they lost control every time they drank, they'd start to run out of sources of blood, and there are only so many cover-ups it's possible to put in place. But some of them must crack sometimes, and Hugo has precedent. Besides, the fact the crowd could suddenly see him and reach him would have made him panic. It all makes sense.

But then, what was that spell Lavinia released? If not quite mesmerism, then perhaps something to lower his inhibitions or self-control?

I'm squatting on the floor with contradictory thoughts zooming through my head. I take a few deep breaths, drag myself to my feet, and stagger over to the surging mass of people who are either attempting to resuscitate Cara or trying to pin Hugo down—both fairly hopeless tasks.

Lydia scoops up her floor-length dress so she can run, catches me up and grabs my arm. "I know what you're thinking, but we need to see this through."

"Lavinia either killed her or let her die. And you were either in on it or did nothing to stop her."

"*Hugo* killed her. We need to restrain him and then make sure the police and the ambulance services see what they need to see."

"I'm leaving."

Clarissa joins us. "Forget about what Lavi did or didn't do. She's gone home in case she's recognised. You can have it out with her tomorrow. For now, let's make this watertight. For Cara's sake and the sake of your client."

"What do we need to do?"

"Take his shields down so all these have-a-go-heroes can reach him," Lydia explains.

Clarissa reaches into her Mulberry handbag and pulls out a selection of crucifixes, stakes, and torches. "And then I'll make sure they are suitably armed."

I work on the shields. I'm sick with fury towards Lavinia, but I still want to make Hugo pay, too—for biting Cara in the first place, even if he didn't intend to drink to the death, and for killing Janice, which was definitely deliberate. He'd thrown the shields up in a panicky hurry, and it's the work of seconds to break them down and give the furious crowd access to him.

Clarissa and Lydia hand out their tools. They work just enough mental magic that the other clubgoers know what they need to do and don't question the logic of these strange weapons.

Within seconds, Hugo's pinned to the floor by four burly men and one tiny but furious woman. He's attempting to fight back, but with a crucifix burning his face and the pseudo-sunlight the UV torches provide limiting his powers, there's little he can do.

A few metres away, other clubbers are desperately trying to work some first aid on Cara. It's no good. Even my resurrection magic wouldn't do anything for someone so drained of blood.

We've got more junior coven members waiting outside to ensure the vampires don't get to Hugo, the police, the coroners or anyone else.

An ambulance crew appear for Cara, attempt to restart her heart and quickly establish that there's nothing to be done. They examine her wounds with mystified expressions on their faces. They'll be key witnesses. And they probably won't be able to resist telling friends and family about what they saw. Getting the story out there.

When the police arrive en masse, we study their eyes and auras, looking for any who might have been mesmerised by the vampires or be in their pay. One or two seem suspicious, so we use our magic to send them away again. Clarissa smiles at the most senior remaining officer and hands him some wooden, engraved handcuffs, exercising just enough mesmerism that he doesn't question her suggestion to use them on the accused.

His rights are read, and then he's locked in the handcuffs and might as well be human.

SEVENTEEN

It's almost five AM by the time I traverse home. As I remove my make-up, trade my elaborate dress for pyjamas, and make a camomile and valerian tea with shaky hands, two thoughts keep cascading around my mind.

Did Lavinia deliberately send Cara to her death, or did things get out of control? And to what extent is her blood on my hands, too?

I never meant for her to die. But I agreed to the plan, which even at face value was pretty horrific. And perhaps I could have moved faster to save her.

An hour passes, and the horror and restlessness only intensify. I pick up my phone. I need to talk to someone who's not involved with all of this. I scroll through my contacts. One of the family would be the obvious choice. Or perhaps Gabriel, because if ever there was a time to break a self-imposed vow of non-communication, it's now.

Instead, I find Seb's number, and press "call" before I can change my mind.

It's early days in the relationship, and there's always the

chance that, faced with a hysterical, six AM version of me, he'll bail. But that's something worth putting to the test.

He picks up on the first ring.

"Sadie?"

"Sorry to wake you." I burst into tears.

"I was up anyway. What's wrong?"

My sobs only intensify. There's a little self-critical voice at the back of my mind that's screaming at me to get control of my emotions before I scare him away. But anyone who didn't cry in this situation would have something wrong with them. As would anyone who didn't show sympathy.

"I'm coming straight over there," he says, when I fail to reply to his question. "Are you safe? Are you going to be okay for twenty minutes while I get dressed and jump in a taxi?"

"My friend was murdered." I force the words out. "Tonight. In a club. In front of me."

"Oh my god. What happened? No, wait, don't tell me now. I'm coming to you. Just breathe."

When Seb opens the door, I collapse into his arms like he's the love of my life.

He hugs me then steers me back inside towards my little two-person sofa, fixes me a cup of tea and a glass of water, before finally sitting down beside me.

"Do you want to talk about it? Or do you want to sit quietly and try to forget?"

I snuggle shakily into his shoulder. "It was awful. Just a friend of a friend, but this guy attacked her. He bit her. It's partly my fault for not stepping in. And partly my friend Lavinia's fault for setting them up in the first place."

Seb frowns as he cuddles me closer. "Take a step back. Who attacked who?"

I try to give a brief summary, without mentioning vampires

or witches. It'd make more sense if I did, but I'd rather not have Seb think I'm clinically insane.

A girls' night out. Cara hitting it off with some guy. Said guy going crazy and attacking her with his teeth while the whole club looked on. Trying and failing to help her.

"None of that sounds like your fault. Or Lavinia's. Or anyone's but that psychopath who did it."

I nod. Without the background story, the rest of us sound perfectly innocent. There's no way to give an ordinary human the incriminating details without seeming utterly delusional. All I can do is take the undeserved reassurance.

How the hell would our relationship work long-term? Would I have to hide my magic? Or would we have The Conversation, in which I attempted a dramatic revelation and showcased some of my talents?

"Did they manage to arrest him?"

"He's already been charged. There were hundreds of witnesses. I'm going to be prosecuting."

Thankfully he doesn't ask how this can possibly be moving so fast or why I'm doing prosecution for the first time since my pupillage. At least I don't have to come up with any spurious explanations.

"Are you sure you're going to be able to cope? It's not going to be too personal?"

I laugh through the tears. "I defended my own brother against murder charges a few months ago."

"There's obviously a lot we've never talked about," he replies. "Now, if I carry you up to bed, do you think you might manage a couple of hours of sleep? It'd do you a hell of a lot of good."

I seriously doubt I can sleep without the aid of a very powerful potion—which I don't have, potion-making never having been one of my fortes, even when I lived at home—or else someone working magic on me. It's impossible to work sleeping spells on yourself, as your spell fades with your consciousness. If only Seb had some powers. I hate to even think about it, but for better or worse, Gabriel would have me out cold in seconds.

He scoops me up in his strong arms and holds me close. Even through my horror at the entire situation, I can appreciate his warm scent and the comforting solidity of his body.

He lays me down gently on the bed, strips down to his boxers, gets in, and wraps his arms around me.

For a second, I can hardly breathe.

"Are you okay?" He whispers the words with fresh concern as my body tenses in his embrace.

I force air into my lungs. "Just a little on edge. Thank you for coming round."

He tightens his hold on me. "Any time. You shouldn't be alone while you're dealing with this. I know it sounds crazy, when we've only had a few dates, but why don't you move in with me?"

I frown. That *does* sound crazy. I mean, not as crazy as Gabriel branding me the first time we ever met, to be fair, but that's not a high bar to surpass.

"I think it's a bit too soon."

He runs his hands over my skin until it tingles. "No worries. If you don't want to live together yet, I'm not going to push the issue. It was just an idea."

I lay there for a moment in silence, his strong arms holding me against the warmth of his chest. Even after all the horrors of the evening, I feel safe there in his embrace.

Is it possible I'm being too hasty in rejecting his suggestion? I've always treaded carefully. I've always steered clear of commitment. I've never tried living with a partner, never really had a relationship that's got to the stage where that would seem like a remotely viable proposition.

What's the worst that could happen if I said yes? If I took

a risk for once and dived in headfirst? I feel so much happier and calmer in Seb's presence. Wouldn't it be nice to come back from a long, hard day—let's face it, if I take on this case, there are going to be a lot of long, hard days—and be pampered and taken care of? To be able to vent to someone who cares about me and then laugh away the stresses of the day?

It's a little soon, sure. But who says I have to play by the rules?

"On reflection, moving in together is actually not a bad plan, as long as you can put up with my messiness," I say, surprising myself.

He kisses the back of my head and tightens his embrace. Before we can take the conversation any further, I fall asleep in his arms.

A few hours later, I'm awoken by that fairy bell ringtone that means Lavinia wants to talk to me. After last night, I *really* don't want to talk to her, unless it's to tell her to go to hell, but I pick up out of a lingering sense of duty.

I head over to the living room. Seb doesn't need to hear this conversation.

"How are you, darling? Did you manage to get some sleep? I know last night was terrible, but you did so well. And now we need to focus on justice for Cara."

"Justice? You set her up at best, murdered her at worst."

"Sadie! How can you say that? Cara was a dear friend. She nobly volunteered to help the coven. Like everyone else, I was expecting superficial injuries, which we could quickly heal. I'm horrified that it spiralled out of control. I feel guilty, of course I do. But I certainly didn't plan for her to die."

I attempt to listen with the dispassionate, rational mindset I'd adopt for a first conference with a client, but it's a struggle.

Lavinia doesn't sound horrified or guilty. She sounds mildly regretful at best.

"You did something in the club. Hugo was going to back off, but you worked some sort of spell."

Lavinia laughs. "You know vampires can't be mesmerised."

"I really don't know about the limits of your powers. About what exactly all that vampire blood you've drunk over the years has done to you. Maybe it wasn't mesmerism, but I know you did something to provoke or encourage him."

"You're imagining things. And who could blame you? It was an awful evening."

I cast my mind back. *I saw her do it, I'm sure I did.*

"I tried to help her. You and the girls held me back."

"I was worried about you. Scared you'd either get hurt or get blamed for her death. And it was too late to help her by then anyway. I blame myself for not intervening earlier."

"This is crazy. I know what happened."

But with every second, I'm less and less sure. I'd had a few drinks. It was dark. I was panicking. If I were a witness I was cross-examining, I'd tear my testimony apart.

"I swear I didn't deliberately get Cara killed," Lavinia says, after a few moments of silence. "The very idea is ridiculous. But what's important now isn't what happened last night, it's what we do next. We need to plan for the case."

My lien mark tingles. Maybe it's psychosomatic, maybe she's reminding me of my responsibilities.

"Everything okay, Sadie?" Seb calls out from the bedroom.

"Is that Seb? From the coffee shop?" There's a note of scandalised delight in Lavinia's tone, as though all thoughts of the murder of a supposed friend have instantly disappeared.

"We've decided to move into together."

Lavinia actually squeals. "That's wonderful news. I'm so glad you're finally over that other idiot."

To my relief, she hangs up without demanding any further

reassurance on whether I'll help her with Hugo, or even believe her at all. The truth is, I've no idea on either front.

"Philip Sadler speaking." There's a distinct note of suspicion in my father's voice when he picks up the phone. Few people have his private, direct number, being required instead to contact him via intermediaries. Those who do tend to be in very regular contact.

"It's me, Dad."

"Sadie!" His voice instantly softens. "Well, this is a nice surprise. I thought you could barely bear to speak to any of us."

"Come on, Dad. It's probably fair to say I'm not speaking to Bren. As far as the rest of you go, I'm just doing my own thing."

"Chrissie told me you'd joined the London Coven. I couldn't decide whether to be relieved or horrified. At least you're embracing your heritage again. But I'd far rather you practiced magic up here with us, where you belong."

I hesitate for a moment. "That's kind of what I'm calling about. You used to talk about Lavinia quite a bit, when we were kids. You clearly knew her well, once upon a time. And unlike most people associated with her, I trust your judgement and I trust you to tell me the truth. Do you think she'd be capable of killing someone?"

My dad laughs. "Well, yes. Obviously."

Oh. That's not quite the answer I was hoping for.

"Bloody hell, Dad. No need to sound quite so blasé about it. Who's she killed, that you know of?"

"Sweetheart, she's a powerful practitioner. She controls the magical side of one of the biggest cities in the world. Over the years, she's had to see off rivals, deal with people who've broken bargains, that sort of thing. Nothing more or less than the things I've had to do from time to time."

I shiver. Even now, even after everything I learnt in the

summer, I have a mental block as far as my family are concerned. Logically, I know they do some awful things, but on a day-to-day basis, I tend to forget it.

"Let me put that another way," I say, trying to fight off the mental images. "Do you think she'd sacrifice a member of her coven, as part of a wider plan?"

My dad gives a sharp intake of breath, like I've said something shocking. As though his casual admissions of murder don't fall into that category. "No, of course not. That's a completely different issue. Lavinia may be ruthless, but she loves her girls. Nothing's more important to her than the coven and its members. Why on earth do you ask?"

I give him a quick rundown of what happened. I have to tread slightly carefully, given his business dealings with the vampires, but whatever my dad's other faults, I trust him not to use information I've given him in confidence against me.

"Good grief, that woman is nonstop," he says, when I've finished. "I can't say I like you being caught up in all this. But if the only bit that's worrying you is whether she'd have deliberately sent this Cara to her death, then that's not the actions of the woman I knew."

"Thanks, Dad."

His no-nonsense take is more reassuring than anything anyone else could have managed. It's a little alarming to hear about the people Lavinia has killed, but on some level, I suspected that must have been the case. I grew up with the idea that some things were necessary evils to protect the town, protect the family, preserve and respect magic. Sacrificing Cara would have been something quite different.

"I know you've committed yourself to London and the coven for now," Dad adds. "And I know you're a bit squeamish about some of what we do, but won't you come and visit soon? A Christmas trip would be lovely."

"Maybe. I would love to see you all. And to see Mannith in all its festive glory."

Surely a short visit couldn't hurt? I've joined the London Coven. I've broken things off with Gabriel. By Christmas, a trip to Mannith might feel almost manageable.

In the meantime, I'd better go and tell Lavinia that while I'm still furious she put Cara in that position in the first place, I believe she didn't mean for it to end the way it did. And that on that basis, I can take the case.

EIGHTEEN

The reception area of Tristan Tregasken and Charles Chadwinton's chambers seems purposefully designed to intimidate and catch you off guard. The leather armchairs are high-backed and stiff, with a seat high enough that even in heels, my feet don't properly touch the floor. There's no natural light at all, and the electrical lights give off a sickly orange glow. The leather books covering the walls are thick and slightly faded. It's utterly silent, overly warm, and there's an intangible scent of age and wealth in the air.

"Miss Sadler, please come with me." The receptionist is a polished human woman, with the slightly dazed expression of someone who's been subjected to sustained mesmerism over an extended period of time.

I follow her through darkened corridors and up a narrow flight of stairs. The meeting room she leads me into has the same sort of aesthetic and is dominated by a large round mahogany table and several oil portraits of stern Victorian men, at least some of whom are probably still working in the building.

"Miss Sadler, welcome," Tristan says. "Miss Jones, please bring tea and then ensure that we aren't disturbed."

I've got enough human instincts that the most primal part of my brain is screaming at me to run and my legs are priming themselves to obey.

Instead, I look him in the eye and smile. "I wouldn't have thought you drank tea. Though I one hundred per cent would have guessed you employed a woman to make it rather than doing so yourself."

I'd never normally be so rude to an opposing barrister, but vampires bring out the worst in me. They're just the patriarchy personified.

He smiles right back, with only the barest hint of fang. "What sort of an Englishman would I be if I didn't drink tea? I'm not sure whether you remember me from the night your family made a deal with my sworn lord, but I'm Tristan. This is Charles."

He gestures to his junior counsel, who's sitting to his right. Charles is as obviously human as Tristan is obviously vampiric, but judging by his vintage suit and lightly powdered face, desperately trying to pretend otherwise.

"Good evening, Miss Sadler," Charles says.

"Please, call me Sadie. Or if you really can't bring yourself to be so informal, then Ms Sadler, for the love of God."

Tristan shrugs in a way that would make pretty much anyone swoon, regardless of sexuality. Luckily, I did a little magic before arriving, to ensure that my natural resistance to vampires' mesmerism was matched by an equal resistance to their more honest charms. I'm quite proud of the anti-attraction spell. Maybe I should try it next time I run into the person I am absolutely refusing to think about.

Miss Jones, the receptionist, tea-lady and let's face it, probable regular blood donor, reappears with an antique tea trolley holding a bone china teapot and a set of delicate little willow pattern cups and saucers. Tea may not generally be my caffeinated beverage of choice, but there's something nice about a properly made cup once in a while. There's always a risk it's poisoned, but that doesn't seem like the vampire way of doing things, and a quick scan of my intuition reveals nothing obviously amiss.

"Shall we turn to matters of business, Ms Sadler?" Tristan says. "We have offended your mistress by killing one of her associates, albeit merely a human one. I agree that justice needs to be served, that recompense is required. But I would hope we could settle this over a drink and a discussion.

"Failing that, there's no need to be so painfully human about things. We could nominate fighters and have a strictly controlled duel. Appeal to the demons or the fae to act as independent arbitrators. Find someone we all agree has the gift of prophecy and ask them to opine on the way forward. There are all sorts of possibilities. I am sure you and your client would not want this to end up in a human court any more than we do."

"I wouldn't be so sure about that. I have the distinct advantage of actually being able to attend court hearings," I reply. "You don't get many judges willing to sit after sunset. The chances of a win would be quite high."

I don't explain the truth—that getting this case heard in a human court, and thus exposing the vampires to human scrutiny, is half the point of the exercise. Though we need the guilty verdict to make it believable, and from my perspective, bonus points if Hugo actually ends up in jail. Ideally one with windows and plenty of sunlight.

Tristan takes a long, slow sip of his tea. "You would be surprised at what can be arranged. But on a regular basis, his ability to deal with daytime proceedings is most of the point of Mr Chadwinton."

If Charles is upset at the suggestion that his only good quality is his ability not to spontaneously combust on exposure to sunlight, he doesn't show it. He doesn't seem to show much emotion full stop.

"Besides, I doubt you want to talk about vampires in a court of law," Tristan continues.

I look him straight in the eye, despite the fact that's generally inadvisable with vampires. "I'm hardly going to be stupid enough to use the V word. I'll just get the witnesses to talk about what Hugo did and let people draw their own conclusions. Which won't be great for you considering your organisation's obsession with secrecy."

"We have the courts sewn up, you must know this. Half the judges are one of us anyway."

Lavinia strides into the room and I jump in surprise. "Then I'll do everything in my power to make sure we get one of the other half. Besides, a case like this will attract a lot of publicity. You can't mesmerise the whole world. Especially not with us taking active steps to stop you," she says.

"Ms Morven, before we go any further, might I enquire as to the precise nature of your involvement in this case? Ms Sadler is the lawyer for the prosecution. But the case is brought by the Crown. You're merely a witness, which makes it odd at best that you would be attending conferences."

"You know full well what my role is," Lavinia says. "It's exactly the same role that Augustine will no doubt be playing on your side. I suggest that you think of me as the claimant, even if that doesn't entirely make sense in a criminal context."

"Duly noted. I shall work on the principle that you have the power to drop the case, even though that is officially a call for the CPS. Though as I was just saying, I do wish you and Lord Piso could have resolved your differences over a drink instead of dragging us all into a legal circus. You are hardly the only woman he turned down in the centuries he spent waiting for his wife to be reborn."

Lavinia crosses her arms. "Watch your tone. You may be immortal, but you're sure as hell not untouchable. Not with some of the spells I know. I could have sunlight cascade through the ceiling and melt the skin off your bones this very second."

Tristan looks at me and raises his eyebrows in a shared appeal to the insanity of clients. I can't help but give a wry smile back.

"I don't think anything of that nature will be necessary," he says after a moment's pause. "This is a civilised legal conversation. On behalf of Lord Piso, I'd like to make you an offer and a promise."

Lavinia gives the most cursory of nods and sits down beside me.

"I'll start with the offer: drop the case, and we'll kill Hugo ourselves. He should never have been turned in the first place. He was new money, industrialist trash in 1900, and his tastes and manners have become no more refined in the interim. We don't tolerate public losses of control or creating a scandal."

I smile to myself at that. They don't tolerate scandals because they can't afford to. They need the secrecy. Which is precisely why we've created the perfect scandal and we're going to fan the flames of it as far and high as we can.

Vampires believe in respectability. To some degree, they believe in playing by the rules, as they define them. They don't just pretend to be humans, they pretend to be professional, influential humans. They may hide their true natures, but as individuals, they are in the public eye. If we get this case to court, they'll be bound by the normal rules of society, because they can't let the façade drop in public. So, while they'll no doubt try to mesmerise witnesses and jury members, they wouldn't, say, blow up the court building, snap the judge's neck, or break Hugo out.

"You can watch his execution," Charles adds. "You can even help if you like? Show us your sunlight through the roof trick, as long as you're careful with your aim."

I shiver at his tone. It's one thing a vampire talking like this

—it's not pleasant, but it's pretty much par for the course—but how can a human man be so blasé about such horrors?

From his slightly clouded eyes, the answer seems to be partly a light hint of mesmerism, just enough to dull his primal fear reflexes and his critical thinking. But from his arrogant expression, it's just as much to do with an inner confidence, the same lack of self-awareness that makes politician after politician confident they can get away with the exact same sex scandals or financial irregularities that have brought down their predecessors. He'll win this case for the vampires. They'd never hurt him. They're bound to turn him, or at least reward him with untold riches and power. Naïve idiot.

"I want justice," Lavinia says. "Not mob rule."

Tristan smiles, showing a hint of fang. "Of course you do. Justice for dear Cara is quite obviously the only thing on your mind."

I keep my face entirely neutral. I've convinced myself that Lavinia didn't mean for Cara to die. My father's words helped to reassure me. But sometimes, like now, I look at her, and a few doubts creep back in.

I shake my head to drive the unhelpful thoughts away. Either way, all I can do now is fight the case. Hugo undoubtedly killed Cara, whatever the surrounding circumstances. And though it's not directly relevant to this case, he murdered Janice, too. I need to focus on sending him down and destroying the reputation of the vampires in the process. Everything else is irrelevant.

"What about the promise?" I ask, snapping back to the conversation.

"I'm glad you asked, Ms Sadler. Because this one is for you. If this case goes to court, we will break off the agreement with your family. They will not get their Dome extension. They'll have to rely on sacrifices for maintenance and make their own call about whether or not to go further."

"That's all you've got?" Lavinia says. "I couldn't give a damn about that agreement. And neither could Sadie. She works for me, not Philip Sadler and his northern ruffians."

I nod through my constricting throat. "I'd ask that you don't penalise my family for something that's nothing to do with them. But equally, you can't expect me to drop a case for something that's nothing to do with me."

"I'd suggest you speak to your lovely sister and brothers and whatever that quarter-demon boy is to you, and think this through," Tristan says. "It'd be a shame if their alliance imploded over this."

I smile as infuriatingly as I can manage. I've learnt from the best by studying both Bren and Gabriel when they want to annoy someone.

"We're not standing down," I say. "This is a jury trial and an open and shut case and the defence won't be able to use any powers against the judge, jury or witnesses."

"Enjoy being all over the press," Lavinia adds, then she grabs my arm and we sweep out together.

PART 3

NINETEEN

You can be waiting months for a murder trial to start, but rather like with Bren's case, both sides want this over with and have used all their power and influence to make things move quickly.

Three weeks have passed since the night of Cara's death. They've gone by in an absolute blur. Case preparation has taken up the majority of my time.

While I've worked on the legal side of things, Lydia has focused on whipping up a media frenzy. As we'd hoped, the glamorous victim, the gruesome death, the fashionable location and the wealthy, well-connected defendant make for a story that grabs journalists' attention, so there's certainly been some early coverage.

That said, reporting has been cautious so far, given both the hold the vampires have over the media and the high risk of the very wealthy Hugo bringing a libel case if they push their speculation too far. And no one's gone anywhere near the blood-drinking angle at this stage—it just seems too unfeasible.

That's why, alongside all of Lydia's networking and leaking, it's so important that I land the case. Convincing evidence and compelling witness testimony will allow journalists to report with confidence. And if we get that guilty verdict, the papers can essentially say whatever they want.

It's also crucial that I not only convince the jury—and the public—that Hugo killed Cara, but that I also bring out the fact that he bit her and drank her blood. That I put the idea of vampires in ordinary, rational people's minds in a way that can be reported on and almost believed. And that even if it doesn't quite convince people of something supernatural, might make them believe in an establishment conspiracy.

In the middle of the chaos, I've somehow found time to move in with Seb as promised. It was uncharacteristically hasty of me—especially as I've rented out my flat on the basis it's impossible to justify maintaining two London properties—but so far, it's going fantastically.

Seb does his own long day at work—he tends to do specialist, scheduled operations, rather than emergencies, which helpfully means he rarely works nights—then gives me space to work late into the evening. He slips into our home office with a cup of coffee and a reassuring word, then leaves me to it while he goes for a run, works on his blog, or listens to music.

Once I'm finally finished, there'll be a delicious meal on the table and a hot bath ready and waiting. He'll ask a few interesting and relevant questions about what I've been up to, just enough to let me vent and show he's interested. And then he'll artfully change the subject onto lighter topics. I just feel so relaxed around him. So productive and yet so at peace.

And lest that all just sounds like he's merely the world's greatest flatmate, after I'm fed, bathed, and have had a lovely chat, we have wildly intense sex then fall asleep in each other's arms and wake up there the next morning, ready for more. Things couldn't be better really.

I checked in with my family a week or two ago. They're understandably not thrilled that I'm taking the case—I still don't think they're wildly enthusiastic about me having joined the coven full stop, instead of returning to Mannith—but despite their "promise" the vampires haven't reneged on the deal.

I've not had chance to speak to my relatives again since. Indeed, I've barely thought about anything but Seb and the case. I've barely spoken to anyone but him and Lavinia. And I've never thought about Gabriel less in my adult life.

I always get a little thrill when I take a case to what we're supposed to call the Central Criminal Court, but which everyone, from judges to members of the public, inevitably calls the Old Bailey, after the ancient street it sits on.

The Royal Courts of Justice are both more magnificent and more senior, and there are older and prettier courts to be found here and there around the country. But for me—and I strongly suspect, for many criminal lawyers—it's the only court that really matters. The true home of criminal justice for centuries. The perfect place to show an arrogant, sadistic vampire that the law applies to him and his kind, too.

I'm used to working for the defence, which means the first few days or even weeks are taken up with listening to the prosecution make their case, while I prepare to pick holes in it. Today, though, on the opening day of the trial, I've got to land the killer blows upfront, with no real knowledge of what the vampire legal team is going to get out of my witnesses. At least it's a Friday. An odd day for a trial to start, but there's nothing normal about this case. I just need to get today over with. Treat it as a trial run, then relax as best I can over the weekend and regroup on Monday.

Lavinia had wanted to come to court and mesmerise the witnesses, just to be on the safe side.

"Factually and legally, the case couldn't be more straightforward," I'd said, trying to reassure her. "The defendant attacked the victim in front of numerous bystanders who got a clear view.

Cara died of her injuries at the scene. None of the usual defences apply. Procedurally, all the vampires' lawyers can do is challenge the memory and reliability of the witnesses. We've already done the hard bit in making the crime scene perfect and getting the case to court."

"But to undermine the vampires' code of secrecy, we need the case to reach its conclusion, and all the witnesses' testimony to sound believable," Lavinia had replied, sounding ruffled. "Otherwise, Cara's death will just be treated as an unfortunate accident and rumours of biting and fang marks as the rambling of drunken idiots."

"The witnesses' testimony will sound believable because they saw what you wanted them to see," I'd said. "We've protected them outside of court, and as it's daylight, the vampires can't mesmerise them during proceedings. So there's no need for us to do so either. I've got this, trust me."

"We can't mess this up," Lavinia had said, with more emotion in her voice than I've ever heard. "I can't bear the thought of Augustine Piso being all smug at the idea that I tried to land a blow on him and failed."

She'd taken a few deep breaths then muttered an incantation under her breath.

"Just do what you can," she'd continued, her voice steady again. "I'll stay away. I'll let you do your own thing. Don't let Cara's death have been in vain. Don't let that bastard get away with it all."

It's a relief, partly as I don't want the pressure of Lavinia watching me. But most importantly, I *really* don't want her attempting to mesmerise the witnesses. The case might involve vampires, but I'm still sticking to my principles.

Just walking into the courthouse gives me strength. The physical building only dates from the early twentieth century, but there's been a succession of criminal courts on the same site since at least the 1500s, and the place feels ancient as a result. I take courage from all the people who've fought cases in the same spot over the centuries. I glance up at the famous statue on the roof: Lady Justice, with her scale and her swords. A true feminist icon.

The room's dominated by a domed roof and is full of statues at ground level and murals high on the wall, both of which show dramatic historical and biblical scenes. Underneath the paintings are quotes in giant golden letters, again mixing the biblical, the historical, and the philosophical: "London shall have all its ancient rights"; "The welfare of the people is supreme"; "Moses gave unto the people the laws of God". Something for everyone, really.

When I reach the door to the court, there's a guard on duty. When I focus in on his aura, it's clear he's a practitioner. Not a very powerful one—someone more accustomed to throwing punches than casting spells—but with enough magic that he can't be touched by other practitioners' mind control, no matter how much more powerful than him they may be.

I stride forward. "Who are you? Are you working for the vampires? What are they planning? If you're intending to mess with the minds of my witnesses or the jury, forget it. Your attempts won't get past me."

Even as I ask the question, I register the little heart and star tattoo by his ear. The sign of someone high up in the Thornber organisation.

I stare at him. "Wait, are you from Mannith?"

"All the guards on duty today are. All the admin staff, too. If you ask me, you ought to be on the other side, supporting your hometown. But then, Sadlers never have been very faithful."

"That's enough, Jake." At the sound of the all too familiar voice, my heart almost stops. "We are in an alliance with the

Sadlers, and we will be respectful towards them. Especially to Sadie."

I turn to see Gabriel, standing with Charles, the vampire's human lawyer. Smart suit to blend in, sunglasses to hide his eyes. Jake the guard shrinks back into himself, mumbling apologies, despite the fact he's twice the weight of Gabriel and looks like he could fell him with a single punch. But if he tried, his fist would probably shatter before he could make contact.

My confidence evaporates. I can stop some random practitioner messing with my witnesses. The odds of me stopping Gabriel seem rather lower. Emotional issues aside, I've got to focus on both law and magic at the same time while he just relies on his powers.

It seems I need Lavinia after all. But I've locked my phone away, as the court's rules require, and there's no time to get her here, even by traversing.

Gabriel extends an arm towards me. "Shall we go inside? I'm co-counsel."

I step back, out of his reach. "What the hell? You're not a lawyer."

Right? I actually know worryingly little about Gabriel, considering how much he tends to dominate my thoughts. He has a degree in History. I *guess* he could have a Master's in Law... but it surely would have come up in conversation?

"I am as far as all the records are concerned. Rather like the stunt you pulled with the entirely imaginary Ms Elner in the summer."

"Besides, he's not going to do anything legal." Charles smirks. "He's just going to stop you undermining our efforts."

My neck is stiff and my jaw is clenched by the time I take my seat in the courtroom. I'd expected to have space to do my own thing. Instead, I've got Gabriel—messing with my emotions and poise by his sheer presence, and openly working against me.

We're in Court One, scene of numerous major trials. What it has in history, it lacks in comfort. It's barely changed since it was built, with small, cramped wooden benches that look impressive—especially combined with the marble pillars and elaborate cornicing—but become very uncomfortable after a whole day, even for someone like me who's on the smaller side. It's also extremely chilly. Still, I love it. I'd be even more nervous in a comfortable modern box of a courtroom.

All sorts of scenarios of what Gabriel might be planning are careening through my head. But as the judge commences proceedings, and as I get to my feet to deliver my opening speech, he's silent and still. No mesmerism or other, darker magic is emanating from him. Neither is he attempting to provoke me. Having had his fun in the lobby, he's paying me no attention at all, preferring to concentrate on his notes.

It's Charles, the defence's actual lawyer, who's giving me some quite unprofessional glares and sneers. His loyalty to the vampires is so absolute that the very thought of someone defying them seemingly infuriates him almost beyond reason.

Hugo is on video link, from whatever darkened room the vampires are keeping him in. It was an unorthodox request, but I didn't contest it. They absolutely can't go outside in daylight and it's a struggle for them to leave their home. Some of the older ones physically can't wake up He's seemingly young enough not to be in that situation, but he still looks rather dazed and haunted, all bloodshot eyes and dark circles.

The press gallery is full to the brim. Reporting on the case has been muted and cautious so far, but Lydia tells me that interest has been high. Today, along with convincing the jury, I need to make sure the witnesses give them something compelling to share with the public.

I take a deep breath, zone all of them out and focus my

attention on the judge. He's not obviously mesmerised, but it's harder to say for sure whether the vampires have got to him with bribery, blackmail or straightforward threats, despite our best attempts to be vigilant about that sort of thing.

Forget it. Forget all of it. Do your job. Be a lawyer for now. Be a practitioner when you need to be.

"Your Honour, the facts of this case are clear and indisputable," I pronounce. "On 10th of November, Miss Cara Hamilton was enjoying a night out at Clique with a group of friends. She entered into conversation with the defendant, who was previously unknown to her. They shared a few drinks, and, as people will do on nights out, retired to a darkened corner of the room. At which point, the defendant attacked her, ripping into her throat with his teeth, in a sustained onslaught."

I run through people raising the alarm, the music stopping and the lights turning on. Onlookers performing first aid. Clubgoers wrestling the defendant to the floor and subduing him until the police arrived and arrested him. The ambulance crew that declared her dead. A factual, honest recital.

I almost expect Gabriel to interject, but he remains silent and still, seemingly barely interested in me or the case.

"The coroner reported that she had died of blood loss from her neck wounds. And that there was a heavy dose of sedative in her blood, which explains why she was relatively passive in the face of such violence."

My voice catches a little at my own words. Poor, poor Cara.

"Your Honour, this was a clear-cut case of murder. A violent and unprovoked attack by a man on a stranger. There can be no doubt about the facts of this case and no defence is admissible. I'd now like to call my first witness."

It's one of the men who wrestled Hugo to the floor. A human, susceptible man. It's game on.

"Where were you on the evening of 10th of November?" I ask.

"At Clique, with a few friends. One of them was celebrating their thirtieth."

A sudden flare of magic from Gabriel fills the entire room. The power of it is utter overkill for mesmerising a single human. I can only assume it's for my benefit, half an exercise in showing off, half an attempt to make damn sure I can't counteract it.

There's a strange sort of mental state I sometimes slip into in court. I block out emotions, speculation, and moral judgement, and focus entirely on facts and tactics. It's what allows me to run through the facts of child abuse cases without breaking down. To ensure that my least pleasant defendants get a fair trial. To work against opposition lawyers who are friends and others who are rivals without letting things get personal or going in too easy or too hard. Some of it's probably magic, at the margins. The rest is just professionalism and experience.

I stare straight ahead and throw myself headlong into that mindset now. Gabriel is a lawyer for the other side, nothing more, nothing less. As long as I stick to that line in my head, all I have to worry about is defeating him. If I slip and allow myself the slightest hint of admiring his beauty, thinking about how much I've missed him, or feeling angry towards him, I'll spend the entire case drowning in emotion.

I dig my nails into my palm and push back. There's something oddly satisfying about testing my powers against him. It's much clearer cut than arguing with words.

With my eyes half closed, I see our respective psychic forces meeting in mid-air, merging and surging. I'm not pushing him back, but I'm holding him at bay. It's easier than when I fought him in a similar way during Bren's trial. He wanted me to reclaim my magical heritage, and I have. Like I once told him, he should be careful what he wishes for.

"And did you see the defendant?" I choke out the question to the witness. The magical test of strength is taking up most of my energy. I've not got much brainpower left for examination.

"I vaguely registered him early in the evening, just kicking back, having a few drinks. I noticed when the girl went over to his table. She was hard to miss."

I turn to face Gabriel and stare him down, pushing back with all my mental strength. It's almost painful to look at him. I simply can't beat him in a head-to-head magical fight, not with my powers still recovering from a six-year break. I'm hoping he might take pity on me and give me a little room for manoeuvre. Instead, he redoubles his efforts. I totter backwards from the force of the onslaught, and only stay standing from the balance I've learnt in yoga class.

In the second or two it takes to compose myself, Gabriel's magic sinks its claws into the witness.

Crap. Now what? I can't just abandon my questioning, but anything I ask risks being used against me. We need the witnesses to sound confident and compelling, both to help secure the guilty verdict and to help turn this into a media story.

"When did you notice something was wrong?"

"The music stopped, and the lights came on. I heard screaming. I spotted the two of them again, tucked away in a corner, but illuminated by a spotlight. She was really drunk by then. Screaming at him. Trying to hit him. Tearing at her own hair. He was attempting to restrain her."

That's not what happened! Somehow, I manage not to snap out the words. What are the defence team going for here, with these words they're putting in my own witness' mouth? Surely they're not attempting self-defence? *Yes, my client was so terrified of this tiny girl that he had to rip her throat out with his teeth.*

"None of this is in your witness statement. Why not?"

"Everyone around me was saying he bit her. Hard enough for her to bleed to death. That's not what I saw. I just got swept along in it at the time. One of those mass hysteria things."

"So what *did* you see?"

I'm dreading his answer, but I need to know. Best to get the defence's lies—Gabriel's lies—out in the open, where I can forensically tear them apart.

"She had a long, sharp knife, like a medieval assassin might have used. She was waving it about. I'm not sure if she was threatening him or threatening herself at first. But at some point, she plunged it into her own throat, twice in quick succession. There was blood everywhere."

Right, fine. Very clever, Gabriel. And Charles. And Tristan, somewhere in the background. Suicide, not murder.

After all, the puncture-mark wounds Cara succumbed to did look more like they were caused by a stiletto dagger than supposedly human teeth.

"If Ms Hamilton killed herself as you claim, and the defendant was an innocent bystander at worst, a hero who tried to stop her at best, why did you wrestle him to the ground?"

"Instinct. I followed the crowd."

Charles whispers something to Gabriel, who looks utterly serene, with no outward evidence that he's working magic or fighting the case.

Back and forth we go. I point out all the inconsistencies and impracticalities in his story, but he doesn't back down. He's physically unable to with Gabriel-fucking-Thornber in his brain.

I'm hyper aware of the jury—as usual—but also of the press. None of this is going to convince them to write the sort of story we need them to. Nothing that sounds like an establishment conspiracy, never mind something around vampires. It just makes the rumours that have already started to swirl sound like people's drunken ramblings.

When my next witness—a female clubgoer who attempted some ill-fated first aid on Cara—tells a near-identical story of a knife-based suicide, the tension in my shoulder muscles turns to proper pain.

· · ·

The second I get out of the courtroom, I all but chase Gabriel out of the exit and onto the street, subtlety be damned.

I catch up with him on a little cobbled side street, of the sort that can catch you by surprise in the middle of London's modernity and hustle and bustle. The fact he let himself be caught and didn't just traverse back to the Piso residence or whatever hotel he's staying at suggests he wants to talk.

I grab hold of his arm. "What are you playing at? You're ruining my case out of spite."

He closes what little space there is between us, backing me against the stone wall of an old pub. His wild eyes are glowing red, and his expression is furious. I spent six years being terrified of him in my dreams and imagination. In the last few months, that's all been replaced by a dizzying mixture of love and fury. But now, I remember what the fear felt like, and I can barely breathe.

"You're working for your boss," he says. "I'm working for my business partner. Don't make this personal."

My heart's pounding, and I'm painfully aware of him looming over me. The street could be on fire. A parade could come past. Fireworks could light up the sky. I wouldn't notice.

"Those psychotic vampires killed my coven sister. You're trying to help them evade justice." My voice is trembling, but I get the words out.

"Your coven sister was sent into a trap by your boss so she could settle some petty old score. And 'those psychotic vampires' are helping your family. Helping Mannith. They can stop the need for the sacrifices. They can help us expand the benefits of the Dome without any more people having to die. They can shore up the alliance. And thanks to you taking this case on, they were on the verge of calling off the deal, until I agreed to help. I'm not their biggest fan, but we need what they promised us."

"Heaven forbid anything would get in the way of your bloody Dome expansion plans!"

"You should want the same thing. Jake, the guy I had guarding the courtroom door, could have been more diplomatic, but he had a point. You're fighting for the wrong side."

"Lavinia's methods aren't great, but the side with vampires on it is never the right side. Besides, you can rationalise this all you want. You got involved in this case to punish me."

He tilts my head back. His eyes have gone through the fiery red stage and are turning black, which is never a good sign. Maybe I ought to run. Or hit him with Greenfire or something worse. But I'm frozen in place. He's never needed magic to control me. Which is precisely why I've never risked a relationship with him.

"This is business, not personal," he says. "But either way, I owe you no loyalty."

I go limp in his grasp, forcing him to tighten his grip or let me fall. Weaponising passivity has always been the best defence against him.

"So you hate me now then, do you?" I say. "Or are you merely indifferent? So much for rings, vows, and your mother's prophecies."

For a second, he looks so bleakly furious that I throw up my shields on instinct, terrified he's going to burn me alive, to get in some delayed retribution for when I did the same to him in the summer.

Instead, he traces a finger along my cheek, then takes my hand and strokes the place where his lien mark once sat. And more recently, his ring.

"Do you want to force me to say it? You tell me you hate me, tell me we can never be together, take some random human man and claim he's the one for you. But you like me obsessed and entangled. You need me to tell you I still love you and that

I'm plotting to get you back, so you can feel smug inside and throw it back in my face."

"That's... I'm..."

I want to deny it, but I can't. The idea of him being properly over me is physically painful. The thought of him in a serious relationship with someone else makes me sick. It's selfish and unfair when I've tried to move on myself, but I just can't help it. I want him to press me harder against the wall and kiss me like he's trying to steal my soul, so I can push him away.

"I'm not going to say it," he continues. "I don't need to. You fucking know."

I nod. The magical battle in court wasn't half as draining as this. I'd like him to burn me with Greenfire again. It'd hurt less.

"I'll see you in court on Monday. I'll fight to win, but it's nothing personal. If you ever want to make it personal, come and find me."

With that, he traverses away, and I crumble to the ground.

TWENTY

Once I can summon enough composure to stand, I phone Lavinia and give her a brief summary of how the day went, through gritted teeth.

She's disappointed, obviously, but not angry. Or not with me, anyway. And she has the decency not to throw my request for her to stay away from court back in my face. Instead, she just promises to be there on Monday. I'll have to remind her just to block Gabriel, not to mesmerise the witnesses herself. But that's a conversation for next week. I've got no energy for it right now.

After the call's over, I traverse home. Or rather, I traverse to a spot just down the road from Seb's flat, walk the rest of the way, and pretend I travelled by Tube.

I've been so happy to have moved in with Seb, I've not regretted it once. Tonight, though, I wish I still had my own place. After the day I've had, I just want to be alone.

Seb opens the door himself as soon as he hears me fumbling with the keys. He takes my hand, pulls me inside, then wraps me in a tight, comforting embrace. I bury my head in his chest and try to steady my breathing.

"Tough day? I thought it might be."

He's got no idea. And I've got no way of really explaining. I'm not going to talk about vampires. Or magic. Or even my sort-of ex. But I mumble some vague words of assent while he strokes my hair.

"I've run you a bath, with some of that fancy oil you like. And I was just in the process of making you a G&T. Do you want to go straight up and have a soak, or do you want to tell me all about it first?"

"You are just too good to me. A long soak sounds amazing."

He dives into the kitchen to fetch the promised drink, then leads me to the bathroom. He helps me out of my suit, kissing me as he does so, then straight up lifts me into the scented warm water.

Alone in my flat, I'd have tried to deal with the stress of it all with a few gins too many and either frenzied exercise or moping around. Or I'd have dragged myself out with friends and been exhausted the next day. This is just so nice. I've only been back ten minutes, and everything feels alright again.

By the time I'm washed, dried, and have slipped into some silky pyjamas, Seb's whipped up a tasty stir-fry.

I almost feel guilty. He must have had a difficult day, too, one way or the other. His work's no joke. But he always seems to be taking care of me.

I just need to get through this vampire case. I'm going to be tense for the duration, that's just the reality of the situation. But once it's done and I can breathe again, I'll be sure to pay him back.

After dinner, we settle down on the sofa.

"It must be hard prosecuting a case where the victim was a friend," Seb says, rubbing my shoulders in a way that only someone with a perfect understanding of human anatomy could manage. It eases the underlying tension and makes me start to feel in the mood, all at the same time. "It must be awful having been there and being reminded of it with every question you ask."

Before I can answer, my phone rings. It's a normal ringtone, not Lavinia's weird ethereal one.

"Leave it," Seb says. "Sit down and relax."

I'm tempted to do exactly what he suggests, but a quick glance at the screen shows it's Chrissie, and I could never ignore my sister.

"Hey, how are things?" I tuck the phone under my chin and flop back down on the sofa.

Instead of launching into an excited spiel about the kids, fashion and local gossip, she sobs down the phone. I'm not sure I've ever heard her cry.

"Chrissie?"

"The police found out about what happened in that clothes shop. And the staff there seemed to remember and forget exactly the wrong combination of things. They're charging me with both theft and sexual assault."

And then the tears overwhelm her words again. Tears are prickling in my own eyes in turn.

"Wait... what? Chrissie, breathe. We'll sort this out. Have you been formally interviewed yet? Have they actually charged you?"

If you'd asked me ten minutes ago, I'd have said I didn't have any energy left, that I physically wouldn't be able to think about the law. Turns out that when my family's in trouble, that's not true in the slightest.

She makes little whimpering sounds in lieu of a reply.

"Now social services are threatening to take Ceri and Chi. And there's talk of Ray being deported."

I clutch my hand to my chest, barely able to believe what I'm hearing. "What do you mean? Even if you were found guilty—which is a big if—there's no reason for child services to get involved. And Ray's a British citizen. This doesn't make sense."

"I need your help."

"None of you say anything to anyone until I get there. There's something weird going on. But you've got money. Magic. Family. And the best lawyer there is."

There's no way this is simply due to an uncharacteristic spot of bad luck on Chrissie's part. Her actions in the dress shop weren't right, but her protective magic was on point. As was mine. She's pulled that sort of stunt successfully plenty of times over the years.

You'd need someone who'd gone looking for a way to get her into trouble, who also had the magical skills to unravel the web she'd woven. And to spin an immigration and child protection case out of a fairly minor criminal charge, they'd either need corrupt connections or serious mind control abilities. Maybe the vampires are to blame—a warning shot, a little taste of their "promise" to me?

She's still crying. "My babies. My soulmate."

"Are you at home now, or at the police station? Have they granted you bail? Has this even got to that stage? What the hell is going on?" Despite the ache in my throat, I err more on the side of assertive lawyer than sympathetic sibling, and it seems to cut through.

"Home. Charged. Got bail."

That means she's already been interviewed under caution. Already appeared in court. With either no lawyer, some randomly allocated no-hoper or, in the very best-case scenario, someone competent, but lacking my specialist skills.

"Why on earth did you answer questions without waiting for me?"

"They didn't give me much choice."

"Fire whatever lawyer they gave you. Then go to bed. You're not going to jail. Ray's not going to Jamaica other than for a nice family holiday. And my little nieces are going nowhere. I'll be up there first thing."

"Thank you." Her hysterical sobs are slowly turning into sniffles.

I'd completely zoned Seb out, but when I hang up, he's pacing around the room. "What was that all about?"

"My sister's in trouble. I'm heading home to Mannith in the morning."

"But you're in court again on Monday."

"I'll be back by then."

He sinks down next to me on the sofa. "Your family will drag you into their drama. You'll be gone for weeks. Sadie, you can't just give up on this case when you care so much about it. You can't risk them trapping you up there."

"Family has to come first, always."

I'd spent six years denying that fact, but now more than ever I feel the truth of the words.

"I'm a little hazy on the details, but from what you've told me, your family have a business deal with exactly the people you're fighting in court. Surely, it's not good to have split loyalties?"

"This has nothing to do with that. My sister's facing totally unfair criminal charges. And it's having a knock-on effect on her husband and kids."

I expect his expression to soften, for him to tell me I simply must go. Instead, he crosses his arms.

"Are you sure they're 'totally unfair'? From what you've told me about your family, it seems like it might just be justice finally being done."

I stand up. "Don't you get all sanctimonious. My sister's having an awful time, and I've got to help her."

He gets to his feet, too, and pulls me in for a hug, stroking my back. "I'm not attacking you. And I'm trying my best not to attack your family either. But there are other lawyers. You can't be expected to drop everything."

There's something about his arms around me that always calms me down and makes my entire body tingle at the same time.

"I need to go." Already, I sound more doubtful.

There are indeed other lawyers. And other practitioners, other family members. I can give moral support, perhaps even some basic legal advice from a distance. What happened with Bren in the summer was a special case, but it's true—I can't rush to Mannith every time a relative needs any kind of legal assistance.

"Text her now and tell her to keep the lawyer she's got, or find a better one who isn't you. Say you'll call in the morning."

It's ironic. If he *were* a practitioner or a vampire seeking to mesmerise me, I'd be able to resist. But his calm, reasonable, oh-so-human manner has me picking up my phone and doing exactly what he says.

TWENTY-ONE

BRENDAN

"My fucking sister," I say, as soon as Nikki walks through the door. "No family loyalty. I don't know what's wrong with her."

"I'm lost."

"Long story short, Chrissie is getting screwed over by the legal system. Worst case is her in prison, the babies in care, Ray kicked out of the country. So, thank god we've got a top lawyer in the family, right? Except that bloody Sadie can't be arsed to come back and help."

Nikki looks gratifyingly stunned. "I'm honestly not sure what to say."

"Let's just get the magic flowing. Something violent."

One of the worst things about not having magic to spare is not being able to burn through it to let off steam.

"I was going to suggest we practiced channelling, tonight," she says. "Which would require you inviting over two people you trusted and working with them in a very cautious, precise manner. But shall we just blow stuff up with our minds?"

"Perfect."

But when I reach for the magic, it jerks back out of my grasp.

"You need to calm down," Nikki calls. "Deep breaths. Stillness."

"I've always been able to transform rage into power," I snap back, battling with hands and mind to subdue the surging river of magic beneath my feet.

"How many times, Bren? You're not its master anymore. You've got to work with it, not against it."

After ten minutes of trying, I give up and slam my fist into the wall.

Nikki doesn't flinch in the slightest. "Do you want me to go?"

"I'd like to try my other go-to way of getting things out of my system."

Her eyes widen. "I thought we established I wasn't your type?"

I laugh despite the stress. "I never actually said that. But I meant drawing you."

"Drawing me?"

"Have I never mentioned my art skills? It's basically the only thing I'm good at now the magic's gone."

"If I'd known I was going to sit for a portrait, I'd have made more effort with my hair and outfit."

"You look great. You look like you. Just stretch out on the sofa there and relax."

Already, some of the tension is leaving my body. I reach into a drawer, grab one of the many sketchbooks and pencils I leave lying around for just this purpose, and begin before we can change our minds. The second the pencil makes contact with the paper, I slip into a different state of being.

"Can I ask you something?" I say, sketching out an outline.

"Sure."

"Why do you care whether or not you're 'my type'? You've mentioned it several times now. And it's hardly like I'm yours, in any way, shape or form."

"Who says you're not?"

I frown as I try to capture her eyes. "Well, you can start from the fact I'm a guy, and work back from there."

"I'm not *not* into guys."

I try to focus on pencilling in her hair, but it's getting harder to concentrate.

"I must have seen you with, like, fifty different women draped over you, over the years. I don't think I've ever seen you out and about with a bloke. Other than Thornber, who I'm pretty sure you're not sleeping with."

"God, no. But there have been some. I'm interested in practically every halfway attractive or interesting woman between the ages of about twenty and fifty. And in a small and selective group of men who precisely fit my exacting tastes."

"I get what you mean. I'm the same. Or the opposite, depending on how you look at it." I hold the pencil still. I don't think I could move it without tearing a hole in the paper. "So... what precisely are these rarefied tastes?"

She pauses, then delivers her answer like a line she's rehearsed. "Broadly speaking, hyper-powerful, morally dubious pretty boys who are the heirs to Born Practitioner dynasties. And the only other person I know like that is like a brother to me."

I pass the pencil from hand to hand. Is that a joke? A cheesy chat-up line? Or is she speaking from the heart? And what do I want the answer to be?

These Friday evenings with Nikki have been the highlight of my week since they started. I've told myself it's the opportunity to learn magic again, but now she's set me on the right path, I can practice myself, making the specific spells she's taught me second nature, and putting others together from first principles.

Obviously, the pleasure of her company is part of the appeal. She's funny, and interesting, and stands up to me, challenges me, pushes back. But I'd not thought in terms of a romantic or sexual attraction.

Because people often spend hours on end patiently teaching someone who's supposed to be an enemy out of some combination of curiosity and kindness.

"I'm not hyper-powerful anymore, remember?" I say at last.

Her constantly confident, sardonic voice sounds a little strangled. "Well, I can't expect to find someone who ticks all the boxes."

"So, I should just lean into my morally dubious tendencies?"

I busy myself in the drawing again, trying to add the finishing touches and calm my racing heart. It's not like people flirting with me is a particularly unusual occurrence. I'm usually coolly aloof or just as flirty back. But I guess the secret ingredient is not giving a damn. And I've not got that advantage today.

"Your checklist. Is that a clever line or a joke or what?"

"Gabe's been my best friend since we were five. I have zero romantic or sexual feelings towards him as an individual. But I always wished I could find someone similar for myself. I always had a vague curiosity about you, but it wasn't safe to explore."

I close my eyes. "I am nothing like Gabriel-fucking-Thornber."

"Don't lie to yourself," she replies.

My heartrate's faster than ever, and my vision's starting to blur. Her declaration of interest is sending little sparks of excitement through my veins, but her explanation for why is adding fury to the mix. I scribble frantically, trying to channel all my emotion into the paper.

"It's done," I say, a few minutes later. "Do you want to come and see?"

She looks almost unsteady on her feet when she gets up and crosses the room.

She leans over to look at it so that our heads are almost touching. "Wow, it's beautiful," she says. "You're so talented."

I slip an arm around her waist. "Not as beautiful or as talented as you," I whisper, and kiss her.

TWENTY-TWO

SADIE

As soon as I fall asleep in Seb's bed on Saturday night, I start to dream. I'm wandering the grounds of the Witches' Church in Mannith, looking at the weather-beaten statues and gravestones searching for... something.

As a child, my parents taught me to control my dreams. It's a special kind of magic. With a bit of effort, you can manipulate the visions your imagination creates. With a lot of effort, you can extend that manipulation into other people's heads or out to the real world. But I've not practiced in years, even after I allowed most other forms of magic back into my life. Most of the time, my dreams are the usual nonsensical jumble of people and places, and I don't realise I'm dreaming until I wake up.

Tonight though, I force "dream me" to take a deep breath and rub my hands down my dream body. I'm dressed normally and appear to be my actual age. My subconscious is obviously phoning it in tonight.

Almost against my will, my eyes are drawn to the statue of Gabriel's poor dead half-demon mother. Just like in real life, she glows in the moonlight, magically preserved from the elements and better tended than anything else in the graveyard. Once, her spirit spoke to me. But that was before I knew about her prophecy and decree regarding me and Gabriel. I'd love to interrogate her about what exactly she'd foreseen. But that'll have to wait for my next actual trip to Mannith—I'm pretty sure that dream magic and communing with the dead don't mix.

I walk round to the church door. It's literally just a door, built into the shattered remains of the one wall that's still intact. It can only be opened by two sufficiently strong practitioners working together. Hopefully, dream logic will do its thing.

I only have to lean against the door for a few minutes before Gabriel appears. "You should help your sister," he says by way of introduction, crossing his arms.

"Are you my conscience now or something?" I take refuge in sarcasm to keep the pounding of my dream heart at bay.

He uncurls my arms. "She's really suffering. No one can understand why you won't visit. If not to take on the case as her lawyer, at least just to tell her everything will be okay, as her sister."

"And you care about my family why?"

"Because I care about you."

He takes my hand. In real life, I'm pretty sure I'd shrug it off. But I don't have to obey my self-imposed rules in a dream, and I grasp it right back.

"We keep family matters private," I say. "Alliance or no alliance, I struggle to believe Chrissie or any of the others would have confided in you about all this."

"I have my ways of keeping track of your 'family business'. Come to my place and talk?"

"Aren't you in London? Wrecking my case?"

"I'm back in Mannith for the weekend. I wouldn't willingly stay in that place a moment longer than I need to."

We traverse to the driveway of Thornber Manor together, then walk inside, still hand in hand.

As soon as we're over the threshold, he lets go of my hand and pins me lightly against the hallway wall.

"I've missed you," he whispers in my ear. "Maybe I'm not being entirely selfless by asking you to come and help your sister."

Technically, we saw each other only yesterday. But we didn't speak, other than that one charged fight. We just worked against each other from a distance. And that's way worse than having no contact at all.

Then his mouth closes on mine. In my dream I don't even think of pushing him away or doing anything but kissing him right back.

"I've missed you, too," I murmur. "However hard I try to deny it."

If this were real life, there's no way I'd be giving in. No way I'd be doing anything but telling him once again what I thought of him working against me in court and of all his older misdeeds and manipulations. This is just a dream. But I need to retain some standards.

"I shouldn't be doing this." I summon all the resolve I can muster.

He takes a step back, but the mere sensation of his eyes on my body is hotter than almost any sex I've ever had. "Why on earth not?"

"You know why not." I try to sound firm, but my voice and my body are trembling with equal force.

"You can't cheat on someone in a dream. You can't break a vow either."

I nod shakily. I've had my share of sexy dreams over the years. A large proportion of them about him, to be fair, but also plenty about all sorts of random co-workers, clients, and entirely platonic friends, in whom I'd had no interest in waking life. I've never felt guilty. It's not like you can control your subconscious.

"This is different." I slump against the wall, longing to touch him again. "It's really you on some level, isn't it?"

Dream Gabriel shrugs. "I've not worked some overly involved bit of Oneiromancy, if that's what you mean. And I'm not controlling your mind or anything sinister. I think we were just dreaming the same sort of dream."

I reach out a hand and touch his chest. It's just a dream, even if there are two of us sharing it. I'll deal with the guilt in the morning.

We kiss again, and it's so good and right. I unbutton his blue and white striped shirt and run my hands along his skin.

I'm wearing a green dress I don't own in real life—a change from when the dream started. I don't know whether it's coming from his imagination or mine, but either way, he unzips it and I wriggle out. I'm not wearing a bra underneath. He wraps one arm around my waist and presses me into him, and with the other massages my breasts, working my nipples to hard points.

His erection is pressing against me. I wriggle against him, drawing sighs from both of us, then reach down to unzip his trousers. He gasps as my hand closes around his cock. He kisses me still harder, then reaches inside my little lacy knickers and starts to stroke me.

I dig the nails of my tightly clenched free hand into his shoulder. I can only hope that dream scratches don't leave real life marks.

"Oh God, Gabriel." I open my eyes to drink him in, then screw them tightly shut and let the building pressure and pleasure fill my whole body.

Somewhere in the distance, in the real world, a door slams shut. I fight to ignore it, but my eyes flicker open. Only to be met by the sight of the geometric wallpaper of Seb's room. For a moment, I close them again and fight to fall back into the dream. But it's no good. I'm very definitely awake and more frustrated

—both emotionally and sexually—than I ever knew it was possible to be.

Trembling, I sit up in bed, pick up my glass of water from the side table and drink it down in one gulp.

"Are you okay? Trouble sleeping?" Beside me in the bed, Seb sits up too, switches on the bedside light, and puts a muscular arm over my shoulder.

For a split second, in the half-light, he looks wrong. My feelings towards him fall somewhere between revulsion and a lack of any opinion whatsoever. Then he gives me a concerned smile, I flicker into full consciousness, and instantly, the frustration and the longing to crawl back into the dream are washed away in a wave of guilt.

"I just had a bit of a nightmare. But it's over now."

I glance at my phone. Seven AM. Early for a Sunday morning, but there's no way I'm risking going back to sleep.

I wriggle out of Seb's embrace and out of the bed, shivering at the early winter chill.

"Come back to bed," Seb calls. "If you can't sleep, I'm sure we can find some way to occupy ourselves."

I shudder, and just about manage to make it look like I'm cold rather than horrified. I'm still basically where I was when the dream ended: a few seconds and the barest of touches away from orgasm. The selfish, animalistic part of my brain just wants someone, anyone to push me over the edge. But I'm sickened at the thought of my actual lover smiling at how wet and horny I am, and growing aroused in turn, when I've been brought to that state by treacherous thoughts of someone else. And frankly, "thoughts" is putting a slightly more innocent spin on it than was probably the case.

While I'm locked in the bathroom, brushing my teeth, I almost slip my fingers under the robe I've thrown on and allow myself the minute or two of sensation it would take to give me some relief. But I keep one hand firmly clasped on the toothbrush and the other balled into a fist by my side. It would hardly be the first time I'd masturbated to guilty thoughts of Gabriel-fucking-Thornber. It was a common occurrence back when I merely feared and hated him. But now, it's more complicated, it's not fair to Seb, and I need to control myself. I'd thought I was doing a good job of not thinking about him. Why can't I ever truly get him out of my head?

As I glance at my phone on autopilot, scrolling through the morning's news, I almost want to text him. *Was that really you last night? Did we share a dream? What happened to you when I woke up?*

It's possible he'd claim not to know what I was talking about, and I could convince myself it was just my subconscious running riot. But if he admitted it was true, what the hell could I say in response? Either way, reopening the lines of communication would be dangerous.

All I want is to get back to Seb and to cling to the vestiges of the wholesome, normal life I've always wanted and have finally started to carve out for myself.

TWENTY-THREE

Monday morning, and it's time for court again. Even with my most complicated or hopeless cases, I usually relish the thought of the battle ahead. But I'm dreading this week. On top of the wider issues with the trial, having to engage with Gabriel is going to be even worse after that dream.

Still, consummate professional that I am, I pull on my suit like it is medieval armour, including the highest heels I can cope with. I fix my hair with a spell, add a subtle veneer of make-up, then read back over the witness statements and my copious notes. Today, the answers the witnesses give in court might actually bear some resemblance to their original statements. Because this time, I'll have Lavinia by my side.

I traverse over to the court. I can barely comprehend that I resisted doing that for as long as I did. It really does put the Tube to shame.

Lavinia traverses into place a few moments after I arrive, dressed much the same as I am—a million miles away from her usual floaty, high-fashion style—and beaming as though Friday's train wreck never happened.

"You really need to do more meditation," she trills. "Drink more juices. Get some sleep. You look horribly on edge."

"Are you ready for this?"

"I do not know the first thing about the law. But then again, as far as I can tell, neither does that handsome bastard on the other side. I'll deal with his mesmerism attempts. You and the vampires' human lackey can focus on the legalities."

I hug her. "This is going to make my life a thousand times easier. Are you sure you can stop him though?"

She pats me on the shoulder. "Male practitioners are a joke."

From the moment we step inside, it's a whole different trial than the one I battled through on Friday. With Lavinia focusing all her attention on Gabriel, which in turn forces him to focus on her instead of me, I'm more or less able to blank him out.

When I call my first witness of the day—one of the paramedics—both Gabriel and Lavinia let their magic flare. His always has a green tone to it, like the emeralds in his ring. Lavinia's is a baby pink shade, shot through with storm grey. The colours emanate out from the two of them and meet above our heads, pressing against each other and filling the room.

My own magic surges within my body, like a child kept indoors who's spotted his friends playing outside. It's lucky that I'm a world champion at keeping it in check.

I address my witness. "Would you please tell the court about the call that brought you to Clique on 10th of November?"

The words flow smoothly. It's so much easier to be a lawyer when you're not having to be a witch at the same time.

"There'd been multiple calls made at the same time. Tens of reports of a woman who'd been attacked and was bleeding to death."

I almost grin at his dark words. No mention of knives or suicides. We're back on track.

"What did you see when you arrived at the club?"

The force of the two competing streams of magic overhead is like an oncoming storm. It's giving me a headache, but I'll happily take a little pain in return for being able to examine my witnesses properly. Lavinia and Gabriel seem pretty equally balanced. They're keeping each other at bay, and allowing this to function like a normal trial.

Neither of them would like to admit it, but the reason they're both so strong is broadly similar—the demon blood. All practitioners have it to some degree, the result of human/demon liaisons centuries ago. In most cases, it gets watered down over the generations, but my family have preserved relatively high levels through always marrying one powerful practitioner to another. The exact effect is subject to the vagaries of genetics, as the varying magical strength of my various siblings amply demonstrates, but the practice usually gives a decent baseline and can allow for some real outliers. Gabriel, though, has significantly more than most, due to his demon ancestors being much higher up the family tree.

Vampires were also created by demons, so have something similar inside them. And whatever that indefinable quality is, Lavinia has taken it into herself by playing her vampire lovers at their own game and drinking their blood.

"The victim was unconscious. She was pale as anything. Barely any blood left."

"Did you see the wounds on her neck?"

"From the state she was in, I'd expected her arteries to have been torn to shreds and there to be blood everywhere. Instead, it was almost like she'd been bitten by a snake. Two small, neat puncture wounds, with the merest hint of blood around them."

I take a breath. This is important testimony, but I need to strike a careful balance.

"Could the wounds have been self-inflicted?"

"There was no sign of a weapon. Everyone was screaming

at me that she'd been bitten. And there was blood all over the defendant's mouth."

The psychic battle above me rages on. Gabriel's desperate to shut this plausible witness up before he gives any further credence to the prosecution case. Or worse, starts making the jury think of vampires. He intensifies the pressure. Lavinia pushes back in turn. My head is going to crack in two.

I can feel the jury sitting up and paying attention. And I can hear the gathered press scribbling furiously. Hopefully, this is starting to sound like a genuinely interesting story.

"You've mentioned a little blood on the defendant's mouth. A little on the victim's neck. But almost none remaining in her body. Where was the rest of it?"

The paramedic looks around before answering. He glances at his notes. Considers each jury member in turn. "I think he drank it."

"Please refrain from speculation," the judge says.

"Sorry, Your Honour. But in my professional opinion, there was no other explanation. There were pressure marks around the wounds. He had to have sucked it out."

I smile. "Are you suggesting the defendant is some sort of vampire?"

"I'm suggesting he's a seriously disturbed individual who gets his kicks out of pretending to be. I'm pretty sure he'd sharpened his teeth."

A few follow-up questions to clarify some points of detail, and I sit down with a smile on my face.

Charles jumps to his feet like he's going to punch the poor witness instead of cross-examining him. Allowing anyone to use the v-word in court is surely pretty high on his list of things to be avoided at all costs.

Behind me, Gabriel ramps up his magical onslaught, trying to help Charles get the answers he needs. Lavinia counters efficiently, and they're once again locked in a perfectly balanced struggle. We've got hours to go yet. They're both going to be broken by the end of the day if they keep this up. For now, though, they both look calm and composed, as though the industrial quantities of magic they are unleashing are no big deal.

I glance at Lavinia, silently asking whether she needs a hand. Ideally, I'd listen carefully to the cross-examination, rather than diverting half my attention to a magical duel, though now I don't actually have to think and speak, I've got a bit more psychic energy to spare. Lavinia shakes her head. It's not clear whether she wants me focusing on the case or her pride can't bear the idea of needing help to overcome someone else's magic. And a male practitioner's magic at that.

"That went well," Lavinia says, once court's over for the day.

We've traversed straight back to her house. She's perched on a blue and copper stool by her white granite breakfast bar, trembling and trying to pretend she isn't. She lights a few of her special candles like an addict lighting up a cigarette and within seconds, the scent of cedarwood and clary sage fills the room.

"Shall I make you one of your hideous teas?" I ask. "Or a juice? If I'd just burnt through weeks' worth of magic in a few hours, I'd have a double espresso followed by a gin. But I'm trying not to inflict my tastes on you."

She nods. "That'd be sweet of you. Astralgus root, please. A touch of ginseng, a bit of gingko."

I rummage in her well-stocked and perfectly ordered hardwood cupboards. Thanks to my mum's intensive tuition, I pick out and prepare the ingredients with ease, even though I'd never normally subject myself to anything that foul nowadays. Though in the end, I throw enough for two into the baby blue Le Creuset pan that's perched on her matching pastel Rangemaster stove. My headache faded as soon as we got out of court, but a bit of a nerve tonic's still a good idea after exposure to that much magical pressure. And as she doesn't seem to have any *actual* tonic, never mind any gin, I'll settle for what I can get.

"Thanks for the support today," I say, while the concoction boils and bubbles. "Prosecuting the case was a million times easier with you bringing the magical firepower. You must realise I'd been uncomfortable about this case and your role in it. But honestly, I loved it today. We felt like a real team."

"You're more than welcome," she replies, lighting yet another candle. "All I did was some straightforward blocking magic. And even then, I exerted all the energy I could summon and only managed a stalemate. How the hell you didn't pass out last week when you were combining that with actually doing your day job, I do not know."

"I wasn't a patch on you. I totally failed to keep his magic at bay."

Lavinia closes her eyes for a moment and gives me a strange, beatific smile, like she's recalling a particularly erotic memory. "He's very good, isn't he? You know my thoughts on men and magic. The only male witch I've ever rated is your father. But I've got to hand it to this Gabriel Thornber. Maybe I'll have to invite him for a drink once the case is over."

God knows what expression shows on my face or what disturbance flares in my aura, but it's enough to make Lavinia's eyes widen as soon as she opens them. Her sexy smile stretches into an amused grin.

"For goodness' sake, Sadie. You don't still have a thing for *him*, do you? You've found a much better man."

I sieve the infused water from the pan into two tall glass mugs so I don't have to make eye contact. "Seb's great." Seb *is* great. That stupid dream aside, I've barely thought about Gabriel in weeks. I certainly don't want to try again with him.

Lavinia takes her tea and takes a delicate sip. "It's not like you have to be entirely faithful to Seb. Have your nice, stable relationship, and have a few sexy flings on the side. But do not get dragged into the orbit of any man who can get his claws into your heart."

I swig my drink, wincing at the taste, though it quickly restores my composure. "Don't worry. I'm not going there again. It's just that he messes with my head, which makes the case that bit harder."

"On the positive side, it'll make it so much sweeter when you win."

I laugh. Luckily, she doesn't bring the idea of asking Gabriel out for a drink back up. It's unfair when I've pushed him away and met someone new, and it's irrational when I know he has flings with all sorts of people. But I could imagine something with Lavinia going deeper than that, and I couldn't bear it.

TWENTY-FOUR

BRENDAN

I spend hours the next Friday making the house as romantic and beautiful as I can in advance of Nikki's visit. Candles everywhere. Roses lining the walls. The scent of jasmine in the air. Tiny lights like stars hovering up by the ceiling. Champagne and smoked salmon in the fridge. Soft silk sheets and flower petals on the bed.

It's all a little clichéd, but that's the mood I'm in. I've no time for anything ironic or understated. I want the house to be a clear declaration of how I feel, with no room for misinterpretation.

I achieve most of it through slow, painstaking magic. The usual adage amongst practitioners is that it's more heartfelt to make gestures of love by hand, because it takes so much more effort and time. But the opposite is true for me right now. Besides, I want to show her just how much she's taught me.

Last week, we started with a hot, heavy, lingering kiss, with our bodies pressed together, our arms tightly wrapped around each other, and our breathing heavy. But just a kiss all the same.

I don't think I've let things get that far and then not gone any further since I was a teenager. But when she started unbuttoning my shirt, I gently clasped her hands and broke the kiss.

"I don't want to rush this," I said, like some sort of prim, virginal teenage girl. Even though my body was longing to rush it.

She freed her hands, placed them on my chest, and stared defiantly into my eyes. "I'm not some princess who needs careful handling. I'm sure we've both found ourselves in this situation plenty of times before."

"I'm not saying we need to wait for weeks or make this all very serious and formal. Let me take you on a date. When we do fall into bed, let me make it sweet and romantic."

She laughed. "Those really aren't two words I associate with you. But I'm intrigued to watch you try. Romantic meal in, though. I'm not quite ready for the drama of people seeing us together."

That had stung, but she had a point. "Deal."

"And in the meantime, you're just going to let me leave here all horny and frustrated?"

When I shook my head, she took my hand and guided it beneath the waistband of her skin-tight yoga pants and under the surprisingly lacy and delicate knickers below. She gasped when my fingers made contact with her clit and I gasped in turn, aroused by both her forwardness and her wetness.

She kissed me again while I stroked her, and stoked her little moans and cries. She came after a few short minutes, then slumped against me.

"I'd better go," she said, once she'd composed herself. "I'll see you next week, to do this properly."

I spent the rest of that evening almost feverish with desire, frustration, and anticipation. I mean, I took care of myself within moments of her having left, obviously, but while that dealt with the erection and the immediate lust, it did nothing to abate the slow burning sexual tension that had filled my body.

Just thinking about it now is setting me off again, those memories of last week and my imaginings of how it might go tonight working in unison to torment me in the most pleasant way.

It's odd. Nikki's scathing summary of my taste in women revolving around "petite, pretty, blonde Born Practitioner girls" is a little over-simplistic and unfair, but it's not that wide of the mark. And yet, while Nikki's personality is a major part of the appeal—her strength and control, her no-nonsense attitude, the way she refuses to accept the supposed limitations of biology when it comes to magic—there's something about her tall, toned body and her angular face that's sending me crazy.

At six, the doorbell rings. I glance at my watch. It's way too early for Nikki, I've no appointments, and I've asked not to be disturbed. My family aren't always great at respecting boundaries, but they're all out tonight anyway for another of Liam's boxing matches.

I inspect the room. I'd been planning to do a little more decorating, but that'd basically be an exercise in dispelling nervous energy. If it is her at the door, I'm ready to go.

I run another bit of product through my hair, squirt on some aftershave, then open the door.

It's Becca, my senior acolyte, who generally puts her significant magical lineage to one side and uses her head for figures to deal with the more prosaic aspects of my family business. She takes in my appearance—way over-dressed for a night in alone—and the elaborate decorations beyond, and her eyes widen in a question.

I'm expecting a sarcastic or probing comment, but any surprise or amusement in her expression immediately gives way to a solemn stare.

"You need to come to the hospital, boss." She can't make eye contact.

I frown. "Why? Has there been another skirmish?"

It's been a bit of a pattern recently. Punch-ups large and small between those traditionally loyal to my family and Thornber's men. Some of it is just drunken machismo—or whatever the female version is called. But some have been more political. Not everyone approves of the alliance. We've ordered people not to do it. We've broken up rows. And to be fair, the Thornber hierarchy seems to have done the same. But after a few drinks or an unguarded comment, tensions rise to the surface and end in brawls.

Becca shakes her head. And then she drops her usual veneer of professional composure and starts to cry. "It's your brother. His fight went wrong."

By nine, I'm back at the house. I'd wanted to stay and do the whole bedside vigil thing, but once the doctors had confirmed Liam was going to pull through, Mum had insisted I went home. Apparently, my constant threats of vengeance were putting her on edge.

Slowly and methodically, I pull each magically created flower off the walls and tear it into pieces.

When the doorbell rings again, I almost throw myself at it, desperate for news. It's Nikki, uncharacteristically dressed up in a pretty little dress.

"I can't believe you've got the nerve to show up." I only just manage not to slam the door in her face.

"I've heard the news. I knew you wouldn't be in the mood for a sexy, flirty evening anymore. But I thought you might appreciate the company."

"Not from any of you Thornber-affiliated bastards."

She slumps in the doorframe. "Let me in, Brendan, please."

"My baby brother is in a coma. One of you nearly beat him to death." My voice almost cracks. I swallow hard.

"Jake is in our custody. He'll be punished, and your father

will have a say in how. Not everyone likes the new alliance, but anyone working against it is a traitor."

I extend a shaky arm. "Come in. But this sure as hell isn't a date anymore. I want to talk business."

Somewhere at the back of my mind, I'm dimly aware she looks absolutely stunning. Some part of me is mourning the night we could have had and the future it might have been the start of. But most of my brain and body is too consumed by rage to allow for any subtlety or sentimentality.

Nikki sits herself on the sofa. Her eyes alight on the candles, the starlight, and the flowers—both the beauty of the ones still embracing the walls, and the frenzy of the ones on the floor.

"I've brought champagne," she says. "But I think a large whisky each would help this conversation along."

I pour both of us something a bar would probably describe as a quadruple.

"Jake, or whatever your henchman's called, is irrelevant to this," I say, once I'm seated and have had a large swig. "Liam's a brilliant fighter. And though he doesn't use magic for boxing, he has a bubble of protection under his skin. I put it there myself, back in the day.

"Apparently, his shields were torn away, he was immobilised by magic, and his opponent beat him as if he were possessed, with fists and spells. This Jake's presumably a decent enough boxer, but would he be able to break down my old magic, mid-fight?"

Nikki shakes her head and sips her drink. She's sitting opposite me. I wish she were curled up next to me. I wish she'd leave.

"He's much more about brawn than magical firepower. I doubt he could have defeated Liam's own protective magic. He certainly couldn't have overcome yours."

I slam my glass down on the table. "There are about three people who could rip my old shields down. Dad would never hurt Liam. And she might not be the closest family member anymore, but there's no way Sadie would either. So what exactly is your beloved boss, best friend, and blueprint for relationships playing at?"

Nikki drops her glass like she's been stunned. "Gabe would never do that."

"He straight up threatened to kill me."

She shakes her head. "But you're so much less likeable than Liam. To most people, anyway."

I don't reply, just stare at the wall. I'm longing to burn something. There's no way in hell I could defeat Thornber in a magical battle anymore. But between the remnant of my innate power and all the things Nikki's taught me, I could probably destroy a few of his acolytes before he had a chance to take me down.

"Bren, look at me, for heavens' sake. I don't need telepathy to know what you're thinking. If you want to strike at the Thornbers, just hit me where I'm sitting."

"Don't be ridiculous." The thought of attacking her is like a physical pain.

"What, you don't think I'm a credible opponent? Or you don't think you could take me?"

"Literally the only thing that could make this horror show of an evening any worse is hurting you. Or being hurt by you."

She stands up and crosses over to where I'm sitting. "I know Gabe's capable of awful things, because he always runs ideas past me. If attacking Liam was part of some plan, I'd be in on it."

I don't want to be naïve enough to believe her. I don't want her to be naïve enough to believe him. "Then who did this?"

"Someone who wants to destroy the alliance between the Thornbers and Sadlers. Or the deal between Mannith and the vampires. Someone who wants us to be at each other's throats."

"Then we need to find them and stop them. And in the meantime, if your 'Gabe' honestly has nothing to do with this, he needs to get the hell over to the hospital and put all that demonic power to good use."

"I'll ask him."

"I wanted it to be nice tonight," I say. "And now, my head's about as far from sex and romance as it's possible to be. But there's plenty of salmon and champagne if you'd like some."

She sits down next to me. "You look like you could shatter into a million pieces. I know how much you love your family. I'm here for you."

It's hard to believe the Thornbers are entirely innocent in this, even if blowing up the alliance would hardly be in their interest. But I'm past caring. I lay my head on Nikki's lap, and as she strokes my hair, some of the horror fades away.

<h1 style="text-align:center">TWENTY-FIVE</h1>

SADIE

It's weird to be alone in the house for a whole evening. Seb tends to leave for work before me in the morning, but be home by the time I get in. His hours are surprisingly regular and manageable for someone with such an important job.

He'll head out for an hour or two of running or cycling most evenings, sometimes alone and sometimes with a friend, and I'll meet up with the coven once or twice a week. Other than that, we're still very much in that honeymoon phase of wanting to spend all our time together, whether that's cosy nights in or trips out as a couple.

Tonight, though, he's at a fundraising event at the hospital that's strictly no partners. And against all the odds, when I tried Lavinia, she declared herself to be having a much-needed quiet night in by herself—judging by her usual whirl of social activity, probably her first in about five years.

I considered messaging Katrina or Lydia, but we're at that awkward stage where we'll happily chat on a pre-arranged night out, but meeting up one to one for the first time feels like a big step forward. Honestly, friendships sometimes seem more diffi-cult than relationships.

I've been letting the home exercise routine slide a little recently. When I lived alone, it was the perfect way to work off the stresses of the day. Living with Seb, it's more likely to be a meal together, a bottle of wine, and maybe sex. Which seems like a fair trade.

Tonight is the perfect opportunity to reforge some good habits.

In central London, having a spare room that you've turned into a gym is up there with a swimming pool and some stables in the rest of the country.

Seb's got a state of the art running machine, so I give it a go for a change of pace. I really do need to work on my cardio.

As is always the case when I force myself to run, the first five or ten minutes are utter torture. But I push through, focus on my music, and quickly sink into a focused but distant state not unlike the one I achieve through core meditations.

When my phone rings though my headphones, cutting off the music, I nearly fall off the machine. I press the button to slow my pace a couple of times, then reluctantly pick up. I'd never normally do so in the middle of a workout, but something tells me this could be important.

"It's Nikki. Can you talk?"

"Nikki! It's great to hear from you."

Nikki's someone I'd love to be friends with in her own right. But she's not my friend, she's Gabriel's friend. His absolute best friend. And apart from that one time in the summer when we spent a delightful evening drinking in the garden of a pub on the outskirts of Mannith, I've never dared to suggest we meet up, still less phoned her for a chat.

"Babe, I'd love to have a cheery catch-up. I wish I'd called you before now. But I'm ringing to say that Liam's in the hospital."

I have to grab the bar of the treadmill to keep from falling.

"And not with a broken arm or black eye or something, I take it?"

"He's in a coma. A boxing match that went wrong. Or if you ask me, went right for someone."

I slow the machine down to a walk. I can't run and keep up with the conversation, but if I stand still, I might collapse from the horror. Movement keeps my thoughts circulating.

"And why are you calling? Why not one of the family?" I regret the tone of my voice as soon as the words leave my mouth, but I'm not entirely in control of myself.

"Your parents are too upset. As is that Shane guy. Your sister's left her house for the first time in days to attempt some healing magic. And you're not speaking to Bren, but even if you were, he's way too angry to hold a conversation. So, he asked me to speak to you. The alliance and all that."

The concept of Bren having a civil conversation with Gabriel's lieutenant briefly pushes all other concerns out of my head. Then the mental image of Liam lying unconscious, with God knows what injuries, hits me anew.

"How did it happen? He knows what he's doing. And if someone was fighting dirty, his magical protection would kick in."

"They broke through it. And then they attacked with magic."

"Who the hell was his opponent?"

Nikki hesitates. "One of ours. But it wasn't planned, I swear."

I slam the emergency stop button on the treadmill. "How can I possibly believe that?"

"We want the alliance. And everyone likes Liam."

"So it was just some renegade Thornber acolyte?"

"It was Jake. You might have met him when he was on guard duty at the court. We've got him in our own custody right now. But he's just not strong enough to do what he did, and he's got no reason to. Someone lent him power at best, controlled him and channelled magic through him at worst."

"I see. I can't even *begin* to think of anyone who's got enough power to pull that off, enough cunning to come up with the idea, and enough hatred of my family to bother."

It's the sort of remark I'd sometimes make flippantly, but right now, my vision's blurring with rage.

"Please don't, Sadie. I've spent the last hour having this argument with your older brother. Gabe did not do this."

"So, who did? And why?"

"I intend to find out. But that's not important right now. You need to get up here."

"I know I'm not always the best family member I could be, but I don't need prompting to visit my own brother when he's in that condition."

"I'm going to be gone for a few days," I tell Seb the next morning. "My brother's in hospital. It sounds pretty serious."

I'd stayed up for hours, pacing and panicking, but by the time I finally passed out from exhaustion, Seb still wasn't back. In normal circumstances, I'd probably want to know why, whether out of concern or suspicion. But today, it seems unimportant in the scheme of things.

Seb looks gratifyingly shocked. "What happened?"

"A boxing match gone wrong."

He frowns. "I've always said it's a barbaric sport."

"This isn't the time for your opinions," I snap.

If I'd had a slightly different upbringing, I'd probably agree with him. Most of my London acquaintances are either disinterested and a bit uncomfortable with boxing, or else actively appalled. And I can entirely see the logic of their position. But it was an integral part of my life growing up. And hardly the most violent thing my family were involved in.

"Sorry. It's just that the horrors of brain injuries were drilled into me in medical school. Do you want me to come with you?"

I hadn't expected him to offer. It'd be nice to have a bit of emotional support. And in theory, nice to introduce him to my family and show him the sights. But for some reason I'm not sure he'd like Mannith, or that my parents would like him.

On the one hand, anyone ought to be an improvement on Gabriel Thornber, what with him being the family's former sworn enemy and all that. But at least he's got something in common with them, in terms of class, upbringing, and cultural background.

My relationship with Gabriel, if you can even call it that, never really reached the "dinner with parents" stage, but if it had, and if Gabriel and my dad hadn't attacked each other on sight, you could almost imagine them bonding over a cheery discussion of the best way to bend your acolytes to your will or something. I'm less sure what Dad and Seb would talk about. I struggle to imagine him existing outside of London.

"I'll do this trip by myself. Everyone's going to be emotional. It's not the best time for introductions."

"You do what you have to do."

Thank God he's not trying to talk me out of it, after the way he acted about Chrissie. But maybe the idea of a serious injury is easier for him to comprehend than messy legal dramas. Or maybe he just likes Liam more than Chrissie, based on the stories I've told. Most people do, even before you throw Bren into the mix.

"I'm going to pack a few things."

"I'll make breakfast while you get organised. Then you'd better call Lavinia and let her know."

The idea chafes. I should be able to go and visit an injured relative without having to run it past anyone. But then again, I guess she's sort of my boss now, and in a normal working relationship, you'd have to book sick leave. I won't waste time now, but I'll call her once I'm back in Mannith.

In the bedroom, I pull out a suitcase. I'm longing to lightly wave my hand and have my clothes neatly fold and stack themselves inside. The sadness and worry is building up again, and it'd be wonderful to channel it into some simple, focused magic. But I can't risk Seb catching me in the act. Instead, I pack painfully slowly and ineffectively, grabbing random outfits out of the wardrobe and stuffing them into the case.

I pull on some jeans and an old workout top, roughly wash my face, and drag a brush through my hair, so I'm vaguely presentable and ready to leave as soon as breakfast is over.

When I get downstairs, there's a wonderful smell of freshly brewing coffee and some huge, flaky croissants on the table. Seb is busying himself securing mugs and plates. And my breath catches at the sight of Lavinia perched on a stool, queen of all she surveys, Clarissa looming at her side, Astrid the dog curled up at her feet.

"Sadie, darling. I brought pastries."

"Hi, Lavinia. I'm heading to Mannith once I've eaten."

Lavinia tips her head to the side. "Come and sit down, sweetie. Get a drink and some food."

You'd think I were a guest in her house, rather than the other way round, but I do as she suggests. Coffee and a croissant is never the wrong answer.

"As soon as I heard what happened—and don't ask me *how* I heard, I make it my job to hear about everything—I knew you'd want to head north. So we came to plead with you to stay put."

I take a deep swig of coffee. "I know the case is important to you. It is to me, too. And I get that my family's current agreement with the vampires makes things a little awkward. But my brother's in hospital."

I didn't mean to say the v-word out loud. Hopefully Seb's

either not paying much attention or will assume it's some sort of nickname or metaphor.

Lavinia sips her own drink delicately. She takes cream and brown sugar, which I'd never have imagined in a thousand years. "Sometimes, you've got to be ruthless. Your brother is going to live. Phone him, once he wakes up. Send an extravagant present. You can visit him once the case is out of the way and he's on the mend."

Seb is hovering awkwardly by the oven, despite the fact he doesn't appear to be cooking anything.

"I don't want to be the sort of person who puts my family last," I say.

"You managed it for the best part of six years," Clarissa drawls.

"That's completely unfair. I didn't dare to go back to Mannith then."

I glance at Seb, standing there looking handsome. Looking human. Looking at me with worry and love in his eyes. He's had the edited highlights of my past at best. I don't want to go into any of this with him listening.

Lavinia takes the tiniest bite of croissant. "Clarissa's point is that during those six years, there'd have been any number of family crises and triumphs. You missed your sister's marriage and the birth of her babies, for a start. A few months of avoiding them now when things are so politically sensitive is nothing in the scheme of things."

My heart constricts with guilt and my lien mark tingles from Lavinia's sheer presence.

Seb walks back into the room and pours himself a black coffee, heedless of his usual attempts to avoid caffeine. "She's right, Sadie, you know she is. Maybe you could visit once the case is over. Christmas is only a few weeks away and you've told me how beautiful the town is then. We could go together."

The thought is almost enough to make me smile. My first

Christmas in Mannith in years would be worth waiting for. The family's spells make the town old fashioned and perfectly attuned to the changing seasons—two attributes that really come into their own at Christmas. My mum's cooking and the family's close-knit nature doesn't hurt either.

Over the last few months, I've ricocheted back and forth from being terrified to ever return to Mannith, lest I never leave, to wanting to scurry back there for good. And in between, I've considered making impromptu, one-off visits to deal with a crisis or a family event.

But the right answer is clearly to stay away entirely for another couple of weeks, then go for a week or two over Christmas, with Seb by my side. It'll be calm. It'll be festive and lovely. I'll make amends to my family for neglecting them, and we'll have a fun time together without me getting dragged back into their world of ruthless magic. In the new year, Seb and I will return to London. And after that, if all goes to plan, I'll have broken the cycle, and I'll be able to make casual visits whenever I wish.

Lavinia takes one more small nibble of croissant and sip of coffee, then gets to her feet and beckons to Clarissa. "I'll leave the two of you to it. It's so nice to meet you again, Seb. I'm so glad things are going well."

"So you're going to stay put?" Seb asks, as soon as she's gone.

I nod and down my coffee like it's tequila. "I'm staying put."

Christmas is a lovely idea in theory, but between now and then, my family are going to hate me.

TWENTY-SIX

It's a relief to be back in court on Monday. Every minute I haven't been working, I've worried about Liam—and about Chrissie, too. It's not like her legal problems have gone away. I barely slept last night. Every time I tossed and turned, Seb reached out and put a comforting arm around me, but it almost felt like a restraint.

When I finally drifted off, I almost hoped for another Gabriel dream, even though it would inevitably have made me guilty and he'd probably have given me a lecture about neglecting my family. A lecture, frankly, that would have been well-deserved. But the dream never came—only weird, disjointed nightmares in which my entire family suffered, sometimes at my hands.

Lavinia's already seated when I arrive in court. She smiles at me like I'm her long-lost daughter. She must have been concerned I might abscond to Mannith to support my family, despite her warnings and my promises.

When Gabriel strides in, on the other hand, he scowls, and then proceeds to ignore me. *Don't judge me for a lack of loyalty,*

I want to scream. *You murdered your own father. And you spent years working against mine.*

I can just about cope with some combination of his love, lust, obsession, rivalry, hate, and vengeance. But this judgemental disdain really hurts.

Before my rapidly fraying emotions have a chance to get out of control, the judge opens the day's proceedings. I tuck a stray strand of hair back under my wig, get to my feet, and consciously zone everyone and everything out so that the only reality is my words and the listening judge.

Over the course of the week, I'm able to lose myself in my work. Come Friday, it's time for my closing speech, which is my favourite part of any trial.

The weird circumstances of the case combined with the competing magic the defence and prosecution have worked on various witnesses means that the testimony to date is an incoherent, inconsistent mess. This is my chance to fix that. Both to win the case and, just as importantly, to make sure everyone believes the witnesses are telling the truth. To put the possibility of vampires firmly on the radar of everyone present and give the gathered press something equal parts salacious and believable to report.

"Your Honour, the facts of this case are ultimately very simple, despite their unusual and somewhat gruesome nature. The victim—a well-liked and respected student with no history of violence or mental health problems—attended a club with friends. She innocently agreed to join the defendant—a man unknown to her, but who would have given off no obvious red flags—for a drink and a chat."

My mind is flashing up images of that night. Then the pictures change. Instead of Clique and the coven, I'm seeing the Prohibition Casino and my siblings. Then the picture shifts again. Liam unconscious, his face a bloody mess. Chrissie's mascara running down her face as she sobs for her children, her husband and her liberty. I don't even know what's happening with her case. Not representing her is one thing, but I've not even checked in on her by phone. What the hell is wrong with me?

"It's at this point that eyewitness accounts in court have varied. But witness statements taken that night, when memories were fresher, are far more consistent. And the evidence of our expert witnesses has also been clear. Shocking as it may be, the defendant used teeth that he had filed to a point to bite the victim, hard enough to do serious damage. He then sucked her blood out of the wound."

I hope my family are okay. I've done the hard work of getting most of what we need out of the witnesses. I could leave tonight. Someone else could take over tomorrow, when the defence case starts.

There's less magical tension in the air than I've grown used to over the last few sessions. Gabriel's barely trying. Admittedly, there are no witnesses to influence and no point in him trying to mesmerise me, but he could go for the judge or jury. Or indeed, go for the journalists, who've not quite been brave enough to publish anything that hints at vampires, but who have definitely been printing an ever-less-flattering portrayal of Hugo and who are starting to ask questions about his associates. And who may well go further tomorrow if I do a good job today.

He's throwing out vague attacks, and Lavinia's batting them back, but it's all background music rather than a pounding baseline.

And then, for a second, Lavinia turns her attention away from Gabriel and focuses on me intently enough for me to sense it through the back of my head. It's like she wants to drag me outside and give me either a pep talk or a stern talking to.

Presumably, she can sense my hesitation and distraction, or is perhaps even picking up traces of my actual thoughts.

It's obvious what she'd say if she could speak to me directly. *You're doing great. Focus on the case. Your family will be fine. You can see them at Christmas when this is done. It's okay to put your work first, put yourself first.*

I nod as though she's really spoken the words. Then her defensive shields are back up, too quickly for Gabriel to take advantage of their brief absence.

"The report of the paramedic at the scene is clear. The autopsy is unambiguous. The victim died of blood loss. Some witnesses—ordinary clubgoers, not medical experts—have tried to claim the wounds were self-inflicted. It is the prosecution's case that this is trauma speaking. An attempt to replace an unimaginably horrific murder with something more explicable. But this version is not compatible with the medical evidence, including the suction marks on the victim's neck. Neither is it compatible with the blood around the defendant's mouth or the lack of any other blood at the scene, despite the victim having lost pints of it. Nor was any knife ever found. The defendant bit the victim and sucked enough blood out of her neck to result in her death."

For a split second, all that talk of blood once again throws a picture of Liam into my mind. But this time, I push it away with ease. Lavinia's right. I can't let family distract me.

I get through the rest of my speech without any interruptions from my conscience, my sub-conscious, or any combination of Gabriel and Lavinia.

"There is no reasonable explanation for what happened that night other than the case the prosecution has put forward. The facts may be unusual, but this is a clear-cut case of murder. There can be no alternative but to find the defendant guilty."

I stride out of court. The speech seemed to land well with judge and jury. It puts enough hints about vampires into the minds of those present, without making me sound insane. It should be enough to give the press the confidence to print something rather more speculative and sensational than their own lawyers have allowed them to do so far. And, on a personal level, it's done a good job of pushing my other worries and doubts out of my head.

"Well done, darling," Lavinia trills, once we're outside. "I know it's a difficult time for you at the moment, but no one listening to that would have suspected. You're such a professional. Celebratory drink?"

Before I can answer in the affirmative, I spot Gabriel and can't help turning to look at him. He pays me no attention, just walks to his beloved Jag and slips inside. For a second, the urge to talk to him is almost overwhelming, both for its own sake and for news of my family. But Lavinia takes my arm and draws me away, and the thought instantly fades.

TWENTY-SEVEN
BRENDAN

Usually, when the whole family is gathered in my parents' main room to receive visitors, we're the ones in control. Supplicants beg for our favour or desperately try to explain why they can't pay their debts or have broken the terms of a binding lien.

Tonight, though, we're the ones pleading for a little more time to pay. Vampires tend to have that effect on people.

They were perfectly polite, when they asked for the meeting. And Tristan, their legal representative, is just as polite now. Vampires believe in old-fashioned etiquette. They don't really do rude. They tend to jump straight from civilised small talk and compliments to ripping your throat out.

Normally, we could put on a good show, even in the face of the powerful and unnaturally polished creature before us. But the last few months have been hard on us. My magic's depleted, obviously. And though Nikki's lessons have gone a long way to helping me be able to deal magically with most day-to-day situations, the lack of natural power makes it harder to project an aura of commanding confidence.

Chrissie, who's barely left her house in weeks, has made an

effort with her looks and her composure tonight. But there are dark circles under her eyes and a slightly limp quality to her hair. It's not that noticeable—she could still walk into a modelling agency and get her pick of shoots—but for anyone familiar with the way she normally presents herself, it's the equivalent of her wearing stained clothes and not having showered in a week. Beyond her physical appearance, she's quiet and subdued, turned inwards instead of blasting her energy out to the room. Ray's not around. Presumably, he's looking after the girls, but with the utterly unfair prospect of both immigration and child proceedings hanging over his head, he's not in a great state either.

Liam's out of the hospital, thank God. Between his underlying physical fitness, excellent medical care, and the combined healing magic of half the town—including Thornber, to be fair—he went from near death to up and about in a matter of days. But he's still physically weak and emotionally frail, with no sign of his usual swagger. He's sitting bolt upright, every muscle tensed.

Nominally, Mum and Dad are fine. No particular tragedy has befallen them this autumn, but the disasters that have hit their children recently have been like an extra twenty years have settled on them overnight.

And for completeness, Sadie is absent as always. From what I can gather, things are going well for her in London. She might have been able to add a bit of spark to the proceedings, show that the family have still got some power and zest. But after neither the alliance ceremony nor either of Chrissie or Liam's disasters were enough to tempt her up, no one even bothered inviting her for this.

"I'll keep this brief," Tristan says. "My seniors made this deal on the basis of working with two strong practitioner families, united as one. Now, your alliance seems to be fracturing, and you're continuously showing signs of weakness and misfortune. Moreover, one of your members persists in working against us in court.

"If you turn things around before Midwinter's Eve, we might reconsider. But for now, I'm afraid we have to consider the deal off."

I jump to my feet. "There's no need for this. It's internal squabbles and a bit of bad luck, that's all. We can still give you your feeding ground. Please give us our Dome expansion."

My heart's pounding. I'm begging, but I don't care. We can't have come this close to success, only for the dream to die at the last moment. The last six months have been a living hell on every front. This should have been the thing to turn it all around.

Liam gets up, too, fists raised. He almost looks like his old self. "You can't pull this shit. We've got a binding contract."

I grab his arm. A physical fight with a vampire is only ever going to have one outcome, but Liam's never been great at weighing up the odds.

"There are break clauses. The deal was never intended to be final until the expansion was complete. Ask your lawyer. If she'll deign to speak to you."

The other family members and I glance at each other. There has to be something we can say, something we can do. But before we can argue further, Tristan disappears.

The fight's gone out of us. Besides, the bloodsucker's got a point. The alliance and the family are both falling apart.

"Did the vampires visit you in person to give the bad news, too?" I ask Nikki the following evening.

It's Friday again. The only evening we spend together. More or less the only time we speak. A little magical, self-contained interlude in the rhythm of the week. I wouldn't have thought anything could make me feel better about the Dome expansion plans being cancelled, but somehow, this takes the edge off.

We didn't do anything more than hold each other, last week. There was too much emotion at play. This week, I've not bothered with the decorations. I've no idea quite where today's meeting is on the spectrum from a magic lesson, to a friendly hang-out, to a date. I'd still like something to happen, and surely she would, too. But it's hard to get into the mood for love.

"They visited Gabe and his Uncle Jim. I was kept in a different room in case the vampires decided to drain me. The ring ought to protect me, but he gets very tense about these things."

"And what do you think about it all? Might we be able to salvage the deal?"

Somehow, I keep the conversation casual, but even thinking about it makes my chest constrict.

"I can't stand vampires," Nikki replies. "But everything they say is true. Something's going very wrong—and this is the town where everything's supposed to go right."

"Do you think we're being sabotaged?"

We're sprawled on the sofa, her legs slung over mine. It's like we've skipped the first few stages of a relationship and jumped straight to some easy intimacy.

"The thing that strikes me as really strange is the way Sadie just will not visit, however bad things get and however much any of us plead with her," Nikki replies. "I wonder if the two things are connected somehow."

I clench my fist. "She didn't visit for six years."

"She had good reason to stay away then. Or thought she did."

Which is probably as close as Nikki's ever going to come to admitting that her darling "Gabe" wrecked my sister's life.

"I always sort of hated your sister," Nikki says. "She had everything I'd ever wanted and fought for. Natural magic by the absolute ton. A devoted family. A hallowed place in the hier-archy of the town. A guy who was all-consumingly in love with her.

"I despised the way she had all that and threw it away. The way she chose to leave her family and Mannith behind. To stop using magic. And to hide away from Gabe like he was some cartoon villain, instead of trying to engage with him."

I open my mouth to give a suitably indignant reply, but she raises a hand.

"I realise now that the whole lien thing was messed up. At the time, I was barely out of my teens, tormented by my lack of power, and utterly loyal to my one real friend. And so somehow, it seemed more romantic than horrifying. Either way, I was worried about Gabe and his obsession, and utterly resentful of Sadie."

"Where are you going with all this?" I can't quite keep the anger out of my voice. I hate even thinking about Sadie's old lien. I hate that Thornber did it to her. And I hate that it was partly my fault. I absolutely will not be made to hear the other side of the story, not even from Nikki.

"When Sadie finally did come back, I made an effort to get to know her, just like I've tried to do more recently with you. And I realised she'd hated being in exile. That her family were more important to her than just about anything.

"When we met with the vampires in London, she was so excited to see Chrissie and Liam again. She was nervous about coming back to Mannith, but with all the things that have happened, she'd still have visited unless she was physically unable."

"So you think someone's preventing her from visiting?"

"Perhaps it's the same person who's behind everything else that's been happening. Surely the London Coven have got some members powerful enough to pull all this off?"

"But they're our allies. Dad's been friends with their leader for decades."

Nikki shrugs. "Maybe they don't like you having an alliance with us. Or maybe they hate the idea of practitioners working with vampires—they've certainly got a court case against them. I might be dead wrong, but it seems worth investigating. Besides, if we could get Sadie to drop the case, that might win us some credit with the vamps."

"So, what do you suggest we do?"

"If you went to London, do you think Sadie would talk to you?"

"Maybe a quick conversation, but probably not the sort of heartfelt one this would require. Besides, if the London Coven are deliberately keeping her away from us, then brilliant as your lessons have been, I've still not got enough magical firepower to overcome their resistance."

Nikki takes a hold of my arm and an audible breath. "Then you need to persuade Gabe to do it."

I laugh bitterly. "Hard no. I do not want to speak to him. Particularly not to tell him to go and bother Sadie. If he's finally leaving her alone, that's the one bit of good news I've heard in weeks."

She snuggles in close, overcoming my defences. "It cost him a lot to take a step back. He wouldn't listen to me if I told him to see her. He wouldn't listen to any of his friends or any of the rest of her family either. But he'd listen to you."

"I'm the last person he'd listen to, about anything."

"It'd be like you were giving him your blessing for the relationship. He likes all the Old Ways stuff. It'd mean a lot."

"Why the hell would I give my blessing?"

"To save her and get to the bottom of whatever's happening to your family and the town. And because it'd help shore up the alliance—whether or not we're being sabotaged, it's hardly a surprise that underlings are fighting when you two can barely look at each other. But also because, deep down, you know they're right for each other."

She holds out her hand, slides off her ring and gives it to me. "Give him this. Tell him to give it to her. It'll show you mean what you say. And if I get mesmerised by vampires as a result, I'm holding you personally responsible."

I examine the ring, its emeralds glowing, its intricate twisted rose-gold engravings shiny despite its evident age. It'd be beautiful if it wasn't his.

"I'll protect you from them," I reply.

She smiles. "I'll wait here. Any revelations about us might derail the conversation. Then when you get back, maybe we can finally pick up where we left off two weeks ago."

I drive out towards Thornber Manor, unable to believe I'm actually doing this. It's what I was supposed to have done the night Thornber Senior died, according to all the lies told at my murder trial. And it's what Sadie did, apparently, the night she decided to cash in the old lien. Chrissie gave me the edited highlights of what transpired between my mortal enemy and my baby sister last summer, having first made me promise not to get mad. I almost managed to keep my word.

Once, I'd have driven into the driveway at one hundred miles per hour, tyres churning up pebbles, brakes slamming to a halt, horn and music blaring. But I've lost some of my showmanship along with my magic. Or maybe I've just mellowed in my old age. I park slowly and carefully, barely making a sound.

The second I step out of the car, Gabriel materialises on the driveway. From the gratifying hint of panic in his weird eyes to the less welcome flare of defensive magic shimmering around his hands, it seems he's mistaken my subtlety for an attempt to enter his house by stealth.

"I just want to talk, Thornber," I say. "We're in an alliance, aren't we?"

Some generic Thornber-affiliated pretty boy walks out of the house, then freezes at the sight of me, as though I'm about to burn the skin off his bones. I'm half tempted to do just that. Even in my diminished state, I reckon I could take him.

"Go home, Patrick," Gabriel says. "This is either going to get very dangerous or very dull." He tosses him some car keys. Presumably not for his beloved Jag.

"Missing my sister so very much, I see."

Gabriel crosses his arms. "What do you want?"

I force down a variety of angry and sarcastic responses. "The alliance is falling apart. People are at each other's throats. We've all been hit by what appears to be a run of bad luck, but I don't believe in such a thing."

"And you blame me for all of that, I suppose. Always the villain in all of your stories."

I take a few steps closer to him. "I want to make the alliance work, get the vampires back on our side and expand the Dome. And I think we're being sabotaged."

"Considering there's nothing you care about more than your beloved Dome, that actually checks out. And as far as sabotage goes, I've been thinking the same thing. Sit down."

I follow him to an oak bench outside the grand front door. He doesn't insist on me wearing blockers, like he supposedly did Sadie. Is that meant to be a sign of trust and respect, or does he know I'm no longer a real threat?

"There was something else I wanted to talk about," I say, more hesitant this time. "The alliance stuff is business, this is personal."

Gabriel drops his semi-reasonable manner and produces one of those smirks that have always made me want to blast him, since long before he did anything specific to upset me. "I'm flattered, but you're not really my type."

"That's a lie and you know it." If he wants to be irritating, I can be irritating right back. "But what I wanted to say is that I'm worried about my sister."

"The police will let Chrissie off with a caution. And social services and immigration are not going to take their respective cases further."

"For God's sake, Thornber. My other sister. Obviously."

"Oh, her. Well, she seems fine. Legal career going well. Shooting up the ranks of the London Coven. Charming young live-in lover."

You really don't need to be an empath of Chrissie's calibre to hear the hurt and longing behind his flippant words and tone.

"Something's not right. She's refusing to talk to any of us. I blame the London Coven—and I think they might be behind all the rest of our misfortune, too. Go and see her. Please."

His eyes are turning fiery red, with some combination of emotion and magic. "Am I hearing this right? You actively want me to spend time with Sadie? I thought you were of the view that I was corrupting and defiling her."

I stand up. "You put a lien on her that obliged her to screw you, when she'd barely turned eighteen. I don't think objecting to that was particularly overprotective. She had to leave Mannith. Leave us all behind. She was terrified of you."

What little magic I still have is rising in time with my fury. I fight to push my powers and my emotions down. This isn't the vibe I'm going for.

Gabriel stands up to join me. "The things I did six years ago were wrong. As were some of the things I did two months ago. I know that."

I grind my heels into the stony driveway to ground myself. "My point is she's a grown woman now, she knows her own mind, and for reasons best known to herself, she genuinely loves you. I don't know who this other bloke is. Probably someone much nicer than you. But he's not the one for her."

I press the ring into his hand. It's redolent with power. "Nikki said to give you this back. The next time you ask Sadie to marry you, tell her you have my blessing. She probably won't care, but I want her to know."

Gabriel takes the ring and studies it intently. "Now would be an awful time to bring up the whole 'you nearly killed her' thing again, wouldn't it? Not to mention all the Dome stuff."

"The things I did six years ago and two months ago were wrong, too."

"Poor Sadie. Always caught in the crossfire of our mistakes." He sounds unusually reflective.

"So you'll see her?"

Gabriel strides towards the Jag. "I'll need to extract her from the claws of Lavinia Morven first. Time to kill two birds with one stone."

I drive back home. I'm going to tell Nikki I've done my best to work with Gabriel. And then we're going to make love. And then we're going to make things official.

TWENTY-EIGHT

SADIE

It's late on Friday evening, and after a hard week of work, Seb and I have settled in for a cosy evening. I've had a long, indulgent bath and am currently wafting around the flat in a silk nightie and matching robe, hair pinned up, make-up lightly re-applied and glass of Gavi in hand.

Following a run and a shower, Seb has changed into fresh tracksuit bottoms, and, for now at least, nothing on top. His hair's still damp and smells adorably of the Molton Brown shampoo I bought him. He's set up a new Spotify playlist, which is an enjoyable combination of some of my old favourites and a few songs that are new to me but are exactly to my taste. I can never get over the way we have so much in common and he understands me so well.

"It's so nice just to relax together like this." I smile at the sight of him as I pick up a slice of Iberico ham from the little charcuterie plate we compiled together.

I'm saying a lot with that bland pleasantry. I never expected to be able to enjoy a gentle, romantic night in with a boyfriend. It's always been fancy dates, meaningless sex, and then nights in alone. Or, on a few very memorable occasions that I'm mostly managing not to think about, something passionate, intense and shot through with emotion.

He walks over, wraps an arm around me and presses me into his bare chest. "Agreed. Now, shall we check on the massaman curry?"

It's bubbling away on the hob. It's a new recipe we found online, and we've had fun carefully sourcing authentic ingredients and then working together to prep them. It smells amazing.

We'll carry on cooking together for a little while, while we sip our wine, nibble on our charcuterie and talk about our weeks. Then we'll settle down to eat and move on to other topics: the news, politics, perhaps a hint of higher end celebrity gossip. We'll put the world to rights, agreeing on the fundamentals while enjoying just a touch of debate on some points of detail. Creating our own private echo chamber where we are right and we are good.

Later still, we'll snuggle up on the sofa and watch some Netflix drama or other. And then we'll go to bed. First sex, sometimes hot and wild, sometimes tender and sweet. And then laying there, talking and cuddling and gradually falling asleep, relaxed in each other's arms.

How do I know? Not clairvoyance, but because that's been the shape of the last few weekends. A different recipe, a different wine, a different show, but the same rhythm of wholesome indulgence.

"It's ready," Seb declares, kissing me on the head. "It smells amazing."

It's a little odd, his tendency to speak my exact thoughts out loud, but I guess it's one more sign that he's right for me.

"Shall I set the table and you can serve, or the other way round?" I'm always asking the important questions.

A few minutes later, we're seated and taking our first mouthfuls.

"It tastes even better than it smells," he says, stroking my leg with his foot under the table.

I take another large forkful and entwine my free hand in his. "Probably our best effort yet."

We relax into comfortable silence for a few minutes as we devour the perfectly tender beef and the rich, spiced sauce. I've piled my plate with jasmine rice, he's staying carb-free.

"Have you read that article about what's happening in Yemen?" My voice takes on that familiar tone of indignation that, depending on a combination of a person's political views and their opinion of me, they might call passionate or might call self-righteous.

Seb looks at me and smiles like I'm talking about fluffy puppies. "I love you."

"I—" I stop myself, halfway through saying it back to him on autopilot. I'm not the sort of person to just throw the phrase around. In fact, family members aside, I've only said it to one person in my entire life. And that came with major caveats.

Do I love him? I certainly enjoy his company. I'm certainly attracted to him. And love *could* be lurking there, somewhere in the background, ready to grow and solidify as the relationship progresses. But I still don't think I'm ready to say the words.

To my intense relief, the doorbell rings.

"I'll get it." I jump to my feet.

"You're not dressed. Sit down and finish your food."

But I'm already in the hallway. I don't know who it could be. No one visits unannounced—this is London, after all. Presumably it's an Amazon delivery or something, though I don't remember ordering anything, and it's on the late side for a driver to be out.

Seb's got a point about my state of undress, but I've collected parcels in various combinations of towels, pyjamas and sweaty workout gear. And he's not wearing a shirt either. I open the door.

"Can I come in?"

The streetlights illuminate Gabriel, reflecting off his wavy blond hair and making it look like he's glowing with some internal light. Maybe he is. God only knows the depths of his powers.

I grip the radiator by the door to keep myself from falling.

"I don't think that's a good idea."

Even as I try to dismiss him, I'm staring at him, drinking him in. And he's making determined eye contact, though whether he's trying to mesmerise me or just prove he's enough of a gentleman not to ogle my silk-clad body isn't totally clear.

Could I stop him, if he tried to force his way inside? Would he do that?

"The house is warded up to the hilt," he says, presumably reading my thoughts to some degree or another.

I frown. "Not by me." Though really, now that I think about it, that's an oversight. Even when I'd forsaken magic, I kept some token protections on my flat.

"Obviously. I'm sure Ms Morven wouldn't leave something like that in your control. Still, it counts as your house since you agreed to move in. Invite me in. Please."

"Sadie? Is everything okay?" Seb appears behind me, hands up, ready to put a defensive shield in place.

But that doesn't make sense. He knows nothing of magic. Does he?

"Nothing useful," Gabriel replies, in answer to my silent question. He casts a lazy glance in Seb's direction and literally freezes him in place.

I scream. "I don't know what possessive, jealous shit you've got going on, but you cannot come into my home and attack my boyfriend."

I manage to imbue my voice with the right amount of anger and authority. But I'm oddly dazed... and suddenly my heart's not in it. I feel bad for Seb, frozen like a statue, but the sight doesn't fill me with the sort of horror you ought to feel when something bad is happening to the person you're meant to love.

As I look from a petrified Seb to a determined Gabriel, the mist clears and the veil parts to leave me with the cold, hard certainty that I don't love Seb—and as I remember the way he's kept me away from my family for the past few weeks, I'm not sure I actually even like him. The revelation is like a punch to the stomach. What's going on?

"Someone had to come and intervene. I'd rather it was your sister or little brother—but they're indisposed. God help me, I'd rather it had been Brendan, but he didn't think you'd listen to him."

"Wait... Bren knew you were coming? He approved?"

"Again, can I come in?"

"Five minutes. And you try anything on me, Seb or the house, I'll kill you. And I won't put you back together again this time."

He steps over the threshold and closes the door behind him.

"Are you going to unfreeze him?"

I'm not entirely sure I want Seb listening in to whatever Gabriel has to say. It'd mean him learning about our relationship. About my magic. About my crazy family. But I can't just leave him there.

"I'm going to do better than that."

He strides past me and takes the motionless Seb by the shoulders.

"Gabriel, no." I grab his arm and try to pull him away. I don't want him to hurt Seb. I don't want anyone to hurt anyone.

Touching Gabriel's skin is like taking hold of an electric fence—and not in a nice, metaphorical "my feelings for him are sending shivers up my spine" way. More like the force of it almost throws me backwards. I tighten my grip, letting my own magic rise to neutralise the shock and the pain.

"Get back. Stripping down that bitch's spell is going to release a ton of magic. Don't get caught in the aftershock."

I close my eyes, try my best to breathe, and funnel my power into my hands. Gabriel's failed to shake me off, but with all my efforts consumed by trying not to be electrocuted, I've no magical or physical capacity spare to get him away from Seb.

"What are you talking about? Just let go. We can sit down and chat."

The electric force emanating from Gabriel fades just enough to turn the sensation from pain into mere discomfort. I'm about to seize control of the moment by prying his arms free, but something makes me pause.

There's a weird pulsing sensation running through Gabriel's aura and his eyes are beyond red and turning a cold, dead grey. There's a spell building deep within his body and his mind. This is the sort of magic he tapped into when he tried to bring down the Dome and when he and Bren fought. It's the kind I summoned when I brought him back from near-death. It's not the type of magic a practitioner of his calibre would use to take down a random human, or even a fairly strong fellow practitioner.

Confronted by this scenario a few years ago, I'd have assumed he was either acting utterly without reason or simply showing off. Now, I know there's always method to his madness. Against my better judgement, I release my grip and take a step back, watching to see what on earth he's going to do.

Energy flies out of Gabriel and flows all over Seb's body, soaking into his skin and illuminating him from within. I'm as frozen as he is, shock, horror and fascination pinning me in place as surely as any magic.

And then, Seb's skin starts to melt. Once again, I scream. Gabriel doesn't release his grip or the pulse of his magic. Something indefinable floats away from Seb—his soul, his consciousness, his personality?—and his body dissolves into nothingness.

I'm sobbing now. I was wrong to think there was a reason for this. It's psychotic jealousy, pure and simple. Something that Mr Denworth could understand, not something magical, mystical and beautiful. Gabriel went in a thousand times harder than he needed to because he could. Because he wanted to make a point. I may have come to the realisation that I didn't love Seb, but despite his faults, he was a decent guy. He saved kids. He fundraised. He took care of me. And now, much like Connor, he's dead, just because he had the temerity to fall for me. And everyone knows who I belong to.

I collapse to the ground. I ought to go to Seb, but there's nothing left, no body to pay my respects to, no lingering spirit to wish on its way to the next world. He's utterly gone, like he never existed.

I'm too horrified to move. And truth be told, after that performance, I'm scared. Perhaps more genuinely scared than I've ever been of Gabriel, and there's some tough competition on that front.

Gabriel doesn't move, and he keeps the magic flowing, though it's unclear what more he's trying to achieve at this point.

I close my eyes and try to block everything out.

"What did you think you were playing at?" Gabriel's angry tones cut through my catatonic state.

"She made me. She told me it'd be good for both of us."

I frown at the sound of a second voice and try to place it. It's not Seb, that's for sure. No miraculous reprieve on that score.

I force my eyes open just enough to see.

Gabriel's still standing exactly where he was five minutes or five hours ago, whenever it was that Seb died. His tsunami of magic has subsided to a gentle breeze just sufficient to keep his companion—cowering on the floor exactly where Seb had been before he was vaporised—fixed in place and suitably terrified.

I stand back up like I'm in a dream. "Chris?"

Lavinia's most infuriating indentured servant and wannabe practitioner looks at me with pleading eyes, and I start to understand.

"It was *you* all along? There was no Seb?"

He starts to cry, then grabs hold of my leg with a trembling hand. "Sadie! I'm so sorry. Lavinia took over my mind, brain, and body, and she created Seb. I wasn't acting, I was being. It's just that the person I was for these last few weeks wasn't exactly the person I normally am. It's basically the same thing she did to Cara, just a bit more thorough and long-term."

I open my mouth, preparing to scream abuse at him. "That must have been awful for you," I say instead, surprising myself. "Trapped somewhere between a zombie and an AI. Being forced into a sham relationship. I can't believe she made you do it."

He swallows hard. "It's hardly the worst thing she's ever had her human acolytes do. Besides, who wouldn't want an attractive and powerful practitioner girlfriend? Who wouldn't want *you*? She admitted that she'd never teach me magic, but that once we were married, you just might."

"Once we were married?"

His voice cracks and he tightens his grip on my leg. "It's what I wanted. I've liked you since that first date. And you'd have wanted it, too, given time, I know you would. We worked well together."

"You were living a total lie."

"Seb's not a million miles away from Chris. There's a reason she chose me both times. She just dialled up some of my natural qualities and dialled others down. Added a few other bits and pieces. Everything I said, everything I did, I might have been using Seb's voice, but the sentiments were all true."

He presses his face against my leg. I can feel how much he's trembling, feel the free-flowing tears. I can sense the desperation—not just for me not to hurt him, but for me to understand.

No wonder the way we met was so sweetly perfect. The way I literally fell into his arms in a cute coffee shop, like something from the cheesiest of rom coms. It was all painstakingly choreographed by Lavinia.

I prise Chris's fingers free and take a few steps back. He's on his knees, sobbing and pleading incoherently. I close my eyes and try to block him out. Whatever platitudes he sprouts, there's no getting away from the fact that the last few weeks have been some of the most contented of my life. And yet they amount to little more than a teenager scribbling fantasies of imaginary adventures with her dream man in her secret diary.

"I'm seriously troubled by what you class as your dream man," Gabriel says.

"Dream man *on paper*." I glare at him. I've been tricked. I've spent weeks giving my body and heart to someone who didn't exist. This is no time for either his possessiveness or his smartarse remarks.

Gabriel holds out an all too familiar ring. "Will you put this back on?"

"My latest relationship ended literally seconds ago."

"You know I'd like you to wear this as a symbol of something between us. But right now, I just need you to wear something that protects the wearer from mesmerism."

I take hold of the ring, shivering slightly as his fingers brush mine. I turn it back and forth, running my finger over the intricately engraved pattern, but stopping short of actually putting it on. "I can't be mesmerised. Not by vampires or by other practitioners."

"Not in the normal way, but you can via your lien mark." Chris is still in a crumpled heap on the floor, but when he manages to lift his head up, he has an expression like a keen student answering his favourite teacher's tricky question. "By Lavinia. And by me, since she granted me special access."

I touch my back reflectively, then look at Gabriel. "Is that a thing?"

"It's part of the reason I gave you some of my magic and made you totally immune to my mind control back when we shared a lien. Hand on heart, I didn't one hundred per cent trust myself not to take advantage of the fact otherwise."

"Remind me to give you a decency medal."

My sarcastic words hide both my alarm and my confusion. My family impose lien marks like traffic wardens giving out parking tickets. They can be used to compel the recipient to uphold their end of whatever deal has been made, but not to mesmerise them at random.

"Some liens go deeper than others," Gabriel explains. "You clearly attract them."

"That decency medal is going to be revoked if you don't stop reading my thoughts without permission," I reply. But I'm convinced enough to slide the ring on.

The moment it's in place, my head clears like I've drunk a triple espresso after one gin too many.

"That controlling, manipulative bitch!" I snap, as the realisations come thick and fast.

"Seb", even if he'd been real, was never really the right person for me, and I was never remotely in love with him. I love my family, and it's appalling that I've not been in touch when they've faced so much misfortune. And Gabriel... well, that's complicated. Perhaps Lavinia influenced me to be slightly more ruthless than I might otherwise have been in avoiding him. She almost certainly artificially kept thoughts of him at bay. But my conflicted feelings there aren't caused by mesmerism and slipping on the ring hasn't cleared them up.

"And you!" I grab Chris by his upper arms and drag him to his feet. "Tricking me. Lying to me. Working with her against me while pretending to love me. You know that getting someone to sleep with you by pretending to be someone else is legally rape according to the Sexual Offences Act, right?"

The statute wasn't designed to cover quite this scenario, but the point remains. Even after Gabriel had torn away Lavinia's specific glamour on Chris/Seb, my immediate reaction was to feel bad for him. But now the ring's dissolved her deeper and wider mind control, all that's left is fury.

Chris is limp in my grasp, unable to formulate a reply.

"Do you want me to kill him for you?" Gabriel sounds entirely casual and matter of fact.

I guess this is where I'm supposed to take a moral stand and be the bigger person. To flinch at Gabriel's ruthlessness and brutality.

"He's pulled this sort of shit twice now. He'll do it again, given half the chance," Gabriel adds, crossing his arms and staring at me. "He's entirely Lavinia's creature, and you've got to start thinking of Lavinia as the enemy. You can't let him report back to her on what you know. And all those practicalities aside, he deserves to be punished."

I relish the look in Gabriel's glowing red eyes. Jealousy is an ugly trait, but that's not what he's showing. He's genuinely furious on my behalf.

Chris looks at me, fully sobbing now, fighting to get out a response. "Sadie, please. I only volunteered for this because I've liked you since the first time we met, and the real me wasn't enough for you."

Gabriel raises his hands. "Just say the word, Sadie."

Honestly, it's tempting to say yes. I try so hard to be a good person nowadays, to always do the right thing. But I almost feel angry enough to kill him myself.

I take a deep breath. That's not who I am.

"I'll fix this," I say.

I touch my free hand to Chris' forehead. He falls away from me and flies halfway across the room before crumpling to the ground. For a moment, his eyes and mouth are equally wide then they both slam shut as he crashes into unconsciousness.

I hold my hands out in his direction and wave them experimentally. Knocking him out was a crude, straightforward piece of magic. But now, I want to remove his memories of the last few weeks and, in particular, his memories of the last hour. Messing with people's minds, beyond a quick blast of temporary mesmerism, is significantly more complicated.

I reach out with my right hand and employ a sort of clawing motion, pulling the thoughts and memories towards me, creating an opaque, glistening ball in the air. His body twitches as I do so, and there's a pressure in the air, his aura and energy fighting me and trying to keep everything intact. I can hardly make myself keep going, but somehow, I persevere. It's grim stuff, but I won't do him any lasting harm.

When I'm confident I've got what I need, I flick my left hand towards the orb I've created, and it explodes into nothingness, the force of the destruction almost knocking me off my feet.

I glance back at Gabriel for a moment. I'm not sure what I'm looking for. Validation? Reassurance? Practical support?

"It really would have been way easier just to kill him, you know. More effective, too."

I glare at him. "Apologies for making a little bit of effort rather than jumping straight to stone cold murder."

He sighs. "You do you. It's an impressive bit of magic at least. It's always fun to watch you push yourself."

I turn away before I lose focus on Chris and end up aiming a spell at Gabriel instead. I swirl the right hand back towards Chris, forcing in some other, anodyne memories of his day-to-day life to fill the gap I've created. Once again, he jerks about. Despite his unconsciousness, his hands fly to his head in some subconscious desperation to protect himself. I feel sick. It's way better than all the alternatives, but it's still a grim bit of magic.

And it's usually something you'd do with rather more preparation than this—the person you're working on made as receptive as possible, a clearer idea of exactly what memories you're planning to remove and what you're planning to replace them with drawn up in advance, that sort of thing.

Finally, I wave my left hand towards him to seal his mind and his energetic field back up. Pressure builds in the air, races towards him, then dissipates with a bang. For a split second, he sparks back to consciousness and sits bolt upright, and I almost scream. Then he slumps back down, into a deeper, stiller level of unconsciousness, and I sink to the floor in exhaustion and horror.

I'm far from certain I've performed the spell perfectly. Gabriel would probably have done a neater job, but some combination of my pride, my need for some token revenge, and my suspicion that Gabriel might still kill him given half a chance made it necessary to do it myself.

Even if it's a bit rough and ready, the spell should be enough that Chris doesn't try anything against me. And that he can't immediately tell Lavinia what happened, until I've had time to consider how to handle the situation.

And though I say no harm will be done, as an unavoidable side effect, he'll wake up with a banging headache and some sore muscles, which I can't help but feel pleased about.

Gabriel strides over to me and helps me to my feet. "We should leave," he says. "I'm sure your boss has some sort of early warning signal set up. And this is her house. She just lent it to him for the purposes of this charade."

"I live here. I have nowhere to go."

What the hell was I thinking, moving in so soon? Even if Seb had been legit, it would have been a risky commitment, compounded by immediately renting out my old place.

"I've booked a room in that ridiculous hotel again. And call me paranoid, but I've warded it to the nth degree. Stay with me tonight. Tomorrow, we'll fix this."

My first response is a dispassionate nod. I stick to that for all of five seconds before falling into his arms.

"I've been so stupid. And so awful towards my family."

He holds me as tightly as it's possible to hold another person without doing them physical harm. "You've not been stupid, you've been bewitched."

"It's so embarrassing. I like to act like I'm a great practitioner and an intelligent, modern woman. And then I let someone whack a lien mark on me for no good reason. I don't realise I'm mesmerised or my so-called boyfriend is glamoured. I get completely controlled and don't even try to break free until some Prince Charming rides to my rescue."

He strokes my hair, using the other arm to keep me pressed against him. "You're one of the most powerful practitioners and strongest women I know. You made one small error of judgement and it spiralled, that's all."

I glance behind me at Chris's unconscious form and at the remnant of what had promised to be a lovely evening: the scent of my home cooking attempts, the softly glowing candles, the chillout music that's been playing unobtrusively in the background all this time. Not to mention my silk negligee and robe, which have never felt so inappropriate.

"Get me out of here," I plead.

"Have you got the strength for a bit of traversing?"

"I'm one of the most powerful practitioners you know, remember?" I whisper the exaggeratedly cheery words into his chest as I close my eyes.

A few seconds later, we're standing by that over-the-top black bed that I remember so well from the night we met with the vampires. I sink down onto its silk sheets and curl up into a little ball, trembling slightly.

Despite my flippant remark to Gabriel, I'm feeling utterly awful. It's a bit like a break-up—one involving cheating, lies, and betrayal. It's a bit like someone has died—certainly, "Seb" has ceased to exist. I'm mourning the end of the relationship, the loss of Seb, the way the pleasant ease of the last few weeks is gone forever.

But beyond all that, I've been played. Chris may have been living a lie, but so was I—and at least he knew the truth, at least he had some sort of a say.

As the full magnitude hits me, the tears start to fall. All those lovely moments together were fake. All the nice things he said about me were like lines in a play. And in turn, every compliment I tried to bestow on him or sweet gesture I attempted to make were aimed at a man who wasn't real. I'm furious with Lavinia, furious with Chris—but still more furious with myself for being such a gullible idiot.

The worst thing of all, though—the thing that's got me hugging my arms around myself as my sobs get ever more hysterical—is that the relationship with Seb was the longest and most satisfying one I'd ever managed.

For years, I'd believed I was essentially incapable of making a relationship work, thanks to my deal with Gabriel. And then, after I cashed in the lien, and actually spent time with him, I'd realised I was capable of love—but seemingly with Gabriel and Gabriel only.

So the whole thing with Seb was such a relief. Even if that specific relationship had ended up not lasting forever, it would have proved I could have feelings for other people, they could have feelings for me, and we could make it work. Turns out, that isn't true.

Gabriel stands nearby. "Should I run you a bath? Fix you a gin? Order a coffee?"

I manage a weak smile. "That's a perfect list of my go-to stress relievers. But all I really want is to be held."

"By me?"

"Who else?"

I shrug off the silky robe, leaving only the matching negligee. Part of me wishes I was wearing something more sensible. Part of me—even through the panic and the horror—can't help but be satisfied by the admiring gleam in his eyes.

Gabriel hesitates for a moment, then takes off his shoes and jacket and joins me. I rest my head on his shoulder, feeling his body heat through his heavy cotton shirt, and the trembling in my muscles stops and the full-throated sobs reduce to little whimpers. I'm hardly fully relaxed and content, of course—how could anyone be, under the circumstances?—but it's a hell of an improvement.

"What do you want to do?" He asks the question softly, stroking my arm.

"Right now? This and only this. Nothing more and nothing less. And then in the morning, I'll go and see Lavinia."

"Do you want me to come with you?"

"I've got the ring. I'll be fine. I need to show her I'm strong."

"Just come straight back here afterwards, please. I don't trust her an inch. We're all starting to think she's behind the things that have happened to your family."

"What, Liam's injuries? Chrissie's legal issues? Why would she do that?"

"Honestly, I'm not sure. Either she's got an unspeakably complex plan or is a narcissistic sociopath."

The last of my tears fade away and my breathing starts to stabilise. Even in the midst of my stress about the evening I've just had and my anxiety about tomorrow's confrontation, it's unbelievably pleasant to just lie there pressed against Gabriel. I'd enjoyed similar moments with "Seb", but now I see it's like the difference between visiting a beautiful place and seeing a photograph of it.

So much of my relationship with Gabriel—if that's even the right term—has always been based on a frenzied lust. Even now, there's a faint but unmistakable hint of arousal hovering at the back of my mind, but somewhat unusually for me, sex is the last thing I want. I guess he can sense that, because he holds me gloriously close but makes no attempt to do anything more.

I'm not ready to launch straight back into another relationship after everything that's just happened. Not even with Gabriel, even if tonight has demonstrated that for better or worse, he'll always be the only one for me.

What I am ready for, though, is to reopen our lines of communication. To get back on track with the whole understanding him better thing. And that means letting myself enjoy his company. But it also means asking the hard questions.

"You really would have killed Chris without a second thought, wouldn't you?" I whisper after a prolonged, peaceful silence.

"He'd done so much to hurt you. He deserved to die. I killed my father, remember? Dealing with that bastard would have barely registered by comparison."

"Don't you feel bad about your dad?" It's something I wonder about a lot, and I'm almost scared to ask the question now, afraid of what he'll say.

"I fulfilled a deathbed promise to my mum. And then I made the most of the circumstances, as far as blaming Brendan went. But it was hard. I hated the way he forced Mum to wear those blocking bracelets, repressed her magic, and let her waste away and die for want of power. I couldn't stand the way he treated Nikki. I was appalled by his plans to marry me off. And there was no way I could risk letting him send assassins after you.

"But despite it all, he loved me and deep down, I loved him.

It'd have been easier if he'd beaten me or tried to keep my powers in check in the same way. But I was his golden child and he always treated me like a beloved little prince."

This is just as awful as the first time I heard about it. But now, I know more about both his good side and his bad side. I'm past waiting for him to change completely or to prove himself to me. If I want to pursue things with him, I need to accept that the dark side is always going to be there to some degree. I guess the question is whether the good stuff could ever balance it out.

If nothing else, there's his love for me, and for Mannith. I told him to go to hell, but he still came to save me, and he's doing everything he can to help the town and work with my family. But there's no getting away from the fact that there's murder set against all of that—and a whole host of lesser sins.

Where does the tipping point lie? Could my goodness provide a counterbalance? Could I hold onto my boundaries? Would I lift him up, or would he drag me down? Or could we just exist in perfect sync?

Perhaps I should stop trying to rationalise all of this and trust fate, trust my emotions. But that's a scary thought for someone who believes in research and carefully honed arguments.

"It was a lot for your mother to ask of you," I say eventually, snapping back to the conversation we're actually having, rather than the wider issues.

I'm thinking of the other things she asked of him, too. Not least, the one about marrying me. I wonder if he's ever felt as conflicted about that, ever wished he had the freedom to choose someone else. The question has crossed my mind before, but after the whole Seb thing, I'm feeling especially vulnerable, especially unsure of whether I actually have any appeal to anyone.

"You know how I always say I have at least two reasons for everything? She had about a hundred. The perils of both demon blood and really strong clairvoyance. She was permanently playing chess against the universe. I really believe she knew what was right for me."

We lapse into silence. I lay there, listening to his breathing and wondering what's going through his mind. Mine's a swirling mass of regrets about Seb, Lavinia, and the last few weeks. And on top of that, I still don't know what to do about Gabriel longer term, and the conversation has made me feel the opposite of reassured. But the one thing I know for sure is that there's no one I'd rather be with right now.

Despite all the conflicting emotions, plus knowing I've got to face Lavinia in the morning, I fall asleep. Gabriel's effect on me is stronger than any magic I know.

TWENTY-NINE

Lavinia is all smiles when I burst into her kitchen without warning or invitation, my face fixed in a scowl, my aura like a lightning storm.

"Sadie! Darling! What a lovely surprise. Shall I pour you a drink?"

She must have some suspicions about what happened last night, be it through the lien, through telepathy, or from the echo of her spell on Chris breaking, but she gives no sign of consternation.

I glare at her, and my hands raise into an attacking stance without much conscious thought. Goodness knows what terrifying colour my eyes have turned. "Don't 'darling' me. Seb wasn't real. You've been using the lien to control me and keep me away from my family. And you've been slowly destroying their lives."

I'd hoped I'd catch her unawares and off-guard. That I'd see unwashed dishes in the sink and her hair piled up in a messy bun above an un-made-up face. Perhaps she'd be in a faded tracksuit. But no. Whether she suspected I'd appear or she truly is always this perfect, there are fresh-cut flowers elegantly displayed and a couple of her handmade candles burning away, with a fresh lemon and vanilla scent. She's perched on one of her fancy stools, wearing white silk pyjamas, with her hair neatly pinned up and her skin glowing. Bitch.

She sighs. "If you've come to apologise for the fact I've had to kill Chris for being so useless, then don't worry about it. It's always a shame to lose such a blindly loyal acolyte, but you're far more valuable to me than he was. I've already had my girls start work on the cover-up. It's no crime for a witch to kill a man."

I grip her granite breakfast bar for support. *She's killed Chris?* I feel sick at the thought. For all his manifest faults, he was insanely loyal to her. If she's capable of that, she really is capable of anything. Besides, Chris was also Seb. And while it was all a cruel con, my brain hasn't quite come to terms with the idea that the man I spent hour after wonderful hour with over the last few months never really existed. On an irrational level, it still feels like she's murdered someone I had feelings for.

I touch my head and physically force all thoughts of that to the back of my mind. I can't get sidetracked by that revelation.

"We both know I've not come to apologise, Lavinia. Lift the lien, then I'll leave London."

I came to the conclusion overnight. I can't risk staying in her orbit, being at the mercy of her and her coven. I'm still conflicted about returning to Mannith long term, but right now, it seems like the right call. Head back. Help my family, despite our differences. Shore up the alliance and the vampire deal, despite my disquiet. And yes, maybe even—eventually—give it a go with Gabriel.

Lavinia laughs and pats the stool next to her. "Do sit down, my dear. I've absolutely no intention of lifting the lien or of letting you leave. You were quite the find."

I remain standing, even though something in her voice

makes me want to obey. I'm not sure whether it's magic or force of personality.

"You wanted someone who was both a talented lawyer and a powerful practitioner. That makes sense. But why the control? The lies? Creating me an imaginary boyfriend. Keeping me away from my family."

"I need absolute loyalty. And for that, I have to keep my closest people under my command. Family. Friends. Lovers. They'd all just get in your way."

Her matter-of-fact tone chills me. "But why did you hurt my family? Even if you didn't want me in touch with them, you didn't need to ruin their lives."

"Sit down, Sadie. Please."

This time, I oblige.

"Do you remember what I told you when you started the case against Augustine?"

"What, the whole 'hell has no fury like a woman scorned' spiel?"

My heart's pounding. Perhaps it's just my nerves and the stress of the whole situation, but she sounds like she's going to tell me something I don't want to hear.

"Precisely. Very few people have ever rejected me. And those that do, I make them pay."

"So, you're not just trying to control me, you're trying to punish me for something? Being reluctant to take a lien mark? Wanting to visit my family occasionally? Trying to have some semblance of a life outside the coven?"

She laughs. "Not *you*. Your darling daddy. So faithful to his precious wife, Teresa, and little baby Brendan, thirty years ago. So impervious to my charms."

I grimace at the thought of her attempting to seduce my dad, even if it's gratifying on several counts that she failed.

"But... I thought you didn't approve of male practitioners."

"I was willing to make an exception and forge an equal partnership and that still wasn't enough for him."

"But you stayed friends. Or business allies at the very least. Like when my parents used you to get a message to me at the start of the summer."

"I was biding my time. And that little favour gave me the perfect opening to investigate the brilliant practitioner and lawyer who'd been hiding out on my patch for years."

She laughs again, then her expression turns serious once more. "The fact I get to hurt your father by keeping you down here was a major motivation. But you're also genuinely useful to me. And I like you. I can imagine you taking over my role one day. I set you up with 'Seb' because it was the only way to get Gabriel Thornber out of your head. And that was an attempt to *help* you, not isolate you further."

I stand up. It's difficult, like I'm lightly glued to the chair, but I manage it. "Well, that spell's broken. And you can't mesmerise me anymore."

"Don't be so naïve. I can't mesmerise you or make you believe my glamours while you're protected by that demon stone you have on your finger. But I can still control you directly through the lien. The difference will be that you'll know you're doing things against your will. It was kinder the other way, really."

I close my eyes, drag all the energy I can muster into myself, then launch Hellfire straight at her. For a second, it looks like I'm going to score a direct hit, then she smoothly shields. One glimpse of the fury in her eyes has me fixing my own shields in place.

The spell she launches back at me is something we call Iceburn. It sits somewhere between Greenfire and Hellfire on the spectrum of straightforward magical assault weapons. Unlike the former, it actually does some lasting damage and pain. Unlike the latter, it shouldn't kill or maim.

It's a ferocious, concentrated attack, but her choice of spell suggests she doesn't want me dead, presumably because she still needs her precious mind-controlled lawyer. But for all my usual moral qualms, I'm perfectly willing to kill this woman who's actively trying to ruin my life and destroy my family. And that surely gives me an advantage.

I manage to block, though the force of her magic reverberates through my shield.

My natural instinct is to rain fireball after fireball down on her, but it's clear she could block them all day. I fire one more towards her on the off chance, because it's so bloody satisfying, then duck behind the kitchen island to consider my next step.

For a change of pace, I try a touch of telekinesis, throwing some heavy saucepans and sharp knives—all of which look very stylish and horrifically expensive—into the air and guiding them towards her. As I'd hoped would be the case, her shields are less well attuned to this kind of attack, and though she wards off the pans, one of the knives slashes her arm. Nowhere near deeply enough to incapacitate her, but enough to make her eyes turn red with fury and gathering power. I punch the air.

I look around for more makeshift weapons, even though she's now going to be on guard against that trick. Then I think of the stunt I pulled in the casino in the summer. Putting a bubble in place. Taking oxygen out of the air. It's not something you can shield against, per se. And it's such an obscure bit of magic, she might not realise what's happening until it's too late.

I run my hands down my body to help focus my mind as I tighten my shields. The spell will take a minute or two, during which time I'll be horribly exposed.

Lavinia throws another bolt of Iceburn at me, but my shields hold firm. Then she tries to simply throw me back against the wall. My heart's racing from a combination of exertion and stress, but I imagine roots growing down from my feet into the floor and stay in place. All the time, my oxygen-depletion spell builds.

At the exact moment I'm ready to unleash it, Lavinia casually waves her hand. I gasp as my shield and my emerging spells fall away. I try to regroup and reach for more magic, but I might as well be wearing blockers. I try to move, but I'm fixed in place.

When she casually throws another blast of Iceburn at me, there's nothing I can do to prevent it.

I cry out when it hits me, and crumble to the floor, though it's gentler than I might have anticipated, like being punched by a well-trained fist rather than attacked with a weapon.

Lavinia mentally drags me back to the barstool.

"Did you really think you could fight me? Even if you weren't weaker than me to begin with, I can cut your magic off through the lien. I just thought it'd be fun to see what you've got."

I'm breathing heavily from both pain and shock. I'm not sure I believe her, though. Sure, she can stop me via the lien, which isn't great. But until she resorted to that nuclear measure, we were pretty equally matched. And lien or no lien, that fact's no doubt rattled her.

"Now, tomorrow morning, I want you fresh and bright for court. But in the meantime, you are going to go and find Mr Thornber and tell him you want nothing more to do with him."

I drag my feet all the way back to Gabriel's hotel, but somehow, step by painful step, I keep walking. Lavinia has left me little choice in the matter.

When I arrive, he's up and dressed, working on his laptop. He stands up as soon as he sees me, eyes golden.

"How did it go? Want to curl up in bed and tell me about it, or shall we go out for brunch? There are things I need to tell you about the vampires and what's happening in Mannith."

Despite the seriousness of the situation and the slightly ominous implications of his words, I almost giggle. Somehow, the idea of Gabriel and brunch doesn't quite compute. But the sound doesn't make it from my mind to my mouth.

It was a nightmare. She can still control me. She's trying to hurt my family. Help me.

"It went fine," I say instead. "I'm going back to my flat. I suggest you head back to Mannith. Please don't try to contact me again."

The words feel robotic but sound natural. I try to think of a way to signal that I'm acting under duress, but nothing comes to mind.

"Sadie? What happened with Lavinia?" His eyes are wide with shock.

I grab a piece of headed notepaper from the desk and attempt to write a message.

Lavinia's still controlling me through the lien. The ring stops her clouding my mind, but she can still direct my actions. We need to get the lien removed.

It comes out as

I hate you. Just leave me alone.

I'd almost rather my mind were still clouded than knowingly have no control over my words. They're the key to my job, apart from anything else. It's like being a surgeon who's lost a hand.

Gabriel picks up the note then drops it like it's burnt him. He grabs hold of my left hand and strokes the ring, seemingly satisfying himself that it's authentic, in place, and untampered with. I let him confirm this, then snatch my hand away.

Maybe Lavinia can't make me remove the ring, the two

powers in stalemate. Maybe she wants to convince Gabriel that I'm acting under my own volition. Or perhaps, after my little show of defiance, she finds it amusing to have me know I'm being controlled and be unable to do anything about it.

"Sadie, talk to me. What's going on?" There's a note of desperation in his voice.

I take a deep breath. "I just utterly despise you. Nearly as much as I hate black coffee, strong gin, and long soaks in the bath."

I'm a little surprised that Lavinia lets me get the ridiculous sentence out, but I guess her control's focused on what she considers to be the important things. Besides, she's that self-absorbed, she's probably never paid enough attention to my preferences to notice that's actually a list of some of my favourite things.

I'd hoped Gabriel would laugh at my obvious lie, that it'd be enough to make him realise everything else I've said is just as untrue, that my words are not my own.

Instead, his frown deepens. I can't quite tell whether he's hurt or merely confused, and I can't think of any way to clarify the situation further.

Gabriel takes a hold of my arm with one hand and uses the other to tilt back my head and look into my eyes. "No mesmerism." He sounds disappointed.

"Get your hands off me." I raise my free arm, ready to throw God knows what spell at him.

He complies immediately, though this time, there's definitely a hint of hurt in his eyes. "Will you lift your top enough to show me the mark?" He sounds like he's calming a startled animal.

"No, you pervert, I will not. I've spent enough time naked around you for one lifetime."

I'm itching to do as he says, but my hands won't cooperate.

"I'm leaving," I add, with an air of finality.

He raises his hands like a reflex action, then freezes. You can see instinct fighting reason as he debates whether or not to seal the door or bind me in place or something.

I raise my own hands in turn. It's funny. He has absolutely no need for the traditional hand signals, and I barely do either nowadays. But in times of high pressure and emotion, everyone seems to revert to them.

"Try to stop me, try to do anything, and you'll be sorry."

He lowers his arms a little, keeping them primed for defence. "Go. I'm not going to waste time trying to reason with you. I'm heading back to Mannith."

For a second, my urge to throw myself at him and beg him to stay almost cuts through Lavinia's conditioning. But her powers kick in quickly enough to ensure I leave without another word.

I think back to all of last night's internal debate. All of that weighing up of the rights and wrongs of letting myself be with Gabriel. It's only now that Lavinia's taken the option off the table that I can see the truth of the matter—of course I want him. Of course we could have made it work, despite everything. Darkness to my light, the universe in balance.

The question is, is there any way I can get out of Lavinia's control? And did Gabriel understand I was speaking under duress, or does he believe that I was pushing him away for good?

THIRTY

When my usual alarm rings on Monday morning, I almost smash my iPhone into a million pieces. I set it as usual on Friday. It feels like a million years ago. I was a different person back then. I had a boyfriend I could almost love. A mind I believed to be under my own control. A friend in Lavinia.

Now, I've got nothing and no one. Lavinia and "Seb" already did what they could to isolate me from my family. Even if they reached out to me, the moment I opened my mouth, Lavinia would make me send them away. I'd hoped Gabriel might realise something was wrong from the weird way I acted in his hotel room, but there's been no word from him since.

Lavinia can make me do whatever she wants. For now, that's simply prosecuting a case I want to win anyway. But goodness only knows what degrading or immoral thing it could be in the future. And even if it's just more legal work, there's no way she'll let me visit Mannith. Little chance she'll even let me have nights out with old friends.

On Lavinia's orders, I'm still in what was supposedly Seb's flat. What would happen if I tried to stay in bed and skip court?

I could do with the sleep. The moment I so much as have the thought, I sit up and then drag myself to my feet.

"There's no need to compel me," I shout out loud. "I'm doing this case for Cara and Janice's sake. And because I want to teach those bloodsuckers a lesson."

It's unclear whether she can hear me. I thought I knew everything there was to know about liens, but I don't understand how this pseudo-mesmerism works. As soon as court finishes for the day, I'm going to try my best to get back to the Lore Library and find out what I can. If she'll let me.

I shower quickly then pull on my suit, fix my hair and make-up, and traverse to the court. The faster I do these things, the less chance she's going to force me to do them. And I couldn't bear to be dragged halfway across London like some sort of zombie.

Lavinia's already there when I arrive. I can't stand to look at her, but either she makes me or her general magnetic pull is too strong to resist. There's a stern expression on her face, no sign of her usual smiles and "darlings".

"Don't even think about trying to sabotage proceedings today." She all but snarls the words. "You wouldn't be able to get the words out anyway. But I'll know if you try."

I cross my arms. "Like I said, I'm going to do this for Cara. Who I'm now entirely sure you killed on purpose. You did something, didn't you? Not exactly mesmerism, that wouldn't work on a vampire. But some sort of spell to make him lose control and drain her instead of just having a taste."

"None of your business. Just concentrate on doing your job."

"Once again, I still want to see Hugo go down and the vampires be exposed for all sorts of reasons. Just know that even if everything else wasn't enough to make me hate you, I'd never forgive what you did to that poor girl."

It's interesting that I can say whatever I want when I talk to *her*. Maybe she gets a kick out of my impotent rage.

"She was a disposable human. If you're worried I'm going to do something like that to you, don't be. You're useful to me, and I like you. Prove you can be trusted and maybe I'll loosen the bonds a little in time."

I've heard more believable statements.

"So, how's it going to work today? Are you going to be putting words in my head or what?"

Lavinia almost manages one of her trademark sunny smiles. "I don't know the first thing about how to cross-examine a defence witness. My magic will only extend to stopping you walking away, crying out for help, or trying to undermine the case."

I walk to my seat and try to ignore her. Mercifully, she lets me.

Charles struts in a few minutes later, but there's no sign of Gabriel. If he ran in, declared he had a solution, and set me free, that would obviously be extremely welcome. Anything short of that, and maybe it's better he stays away. Not being able to say anything truthful to him and being forced to lash out is like torture.

Still, it's weird that the vampires are letting him take a day off. They can't compel him the way Lavinia can me, but the threat of pulling their Dome deal has always seemed to be enough to keep him in check.

Charles gets up for his opening statement. Between that controlling bitch, the awful defendant, and the unseen vampire masters, he's technically one of the nicest people associated with the case. But right now, his smug, pasty face is a symbol of everything wrong with my life.

"Your Honour, the prosecution's case is like something out of a bad horror film," Charles says. "They claim that the defendant killed Ms Hamilton. But they have no explanation for the 'why'. Their supposed 'how' is so outlandish as to be unbelievable. And their own witnesses' testimonies are riddled with inconsistencies at best, outright denials of the prosecution's version of events at worst."

While I scribble down notes, Lavinia unleashes a gentle stream of magic in Charles's direction, aiming to take control of his testimony, free to do what she likes with her powers without Gabriel's competing influence or any interest in my moral scruples.

"Even the prosecution's strongest and clearest witnesses report no unusual behaviour on the part of the defendant, right up to the moment of the alleged attack."

I frown. That really doesn't sound like Lavinia's taken control of his words. Consternation emanates from Lavinia, quickly followed by an intensification of her magic. But Charles carries on unabated.

"Put simply, there is no motive for the alleged attack. It would have been out of character and utterly inexplicable. And then we come to the supposed way in which the murder was carried out. According to the prosecution, the defendant bit Ms Hamilton, and then drank her blood. Let that sink in for a moment."

I stare at Charles. He's definitely not a Born Practitioner, and I've never seen any hint of him having any learnt magic. Presumably, the vampires know some tricks for how to avoid mesmerism that they could teach to a keen student. But surely not to the extent that he could protect himself from a focused onslaught from someone as powerful as Lavinia.

I can't afford to let my concentration waver too much while he's outlining the defence case, but I take a moment to close my eyes, reach out with my own magic, and inspect both his physical and energetic body. Sure enough, there's a small oval-shaped black hole in his aura in the vicinity of his upper chest. Under his close-fitting tailored shirt, he's wearing some sort of amulet with similar properties to my ring. A near-perfect defence against magic or at least mind control. Presumably a gift from his vampire masters, though it's a risk on their part, considering it would also stop them exerting any control over him. They must have real faith in his loyalty, or at least, in the strength of his desire to be turned.

I turn and catch Lavinia's eye. She starts slightly, as though I'm about to try to break free. I pointedly glance at Charles' chest. A few seconds later, her narrowed eyes switch to something approaching a frown. She lets her magic fall away with the petulant force of a teenager slamming their bedroom door shut.

Charles' protection merely means we can't influence what he says. He still won't be able to influence his witnesses or stop Lavinia from doing so if she chooses to. Which does rather beg the question of why the hell the defence aren't still making use of Gabriel's powers.

Charles finishes his opening speech. It's a solid attempt, but I'm not too concerned. He's emphasised the somewhat hard to believe aspects of our narrative, but he's not come up with a compelling alternative explanation. He's sticking with the claim that Cara's wounds were self-inflicted, but has no real answer for what happened to the weapon, how she lost so much blood from such small wounds, or where all that blood went. The jury are still likely to think that Hugo did it. And even the most rational observers—including the gathered press—arc going to start thinking about vampires. Or at least, vampire-related conspiracy theories and scandals.

There's a brief break before we make a start on the defence witnesses. Lavinia follows me to the bathroom.

"Those sneaky bastards!" she exclaims, as though we're entirely on the same side with no bad blood between us. "There can't be more than ten of those pieces of jewellery in the world. Maybe twenty at an absolute stretch. It's demon craftsmanship.

No one in their right minds would let a human wear something like that in the usual run of things. It has to have been Augustine's idea. It shows how desperate he and his little gang are."

"Then why aren't they still using Gabriel?"

"Vampires and male practitioners are both a little unstable. A working relationship between the two was always a disaster waiting to happen. Anyway, I don't want you so much as thinking about him. Ever. Concentrate on the case."

I shake my head. As if she could ever stop me thinking about Gabriel. Though if she can manage to keep us apart, I almost wish she *could* shut down my thoughts of him.

"I don't think the defence witnesses will be much of a problem," I reply, trying to stick to relatively safe topics. "What they saw is entirely consistent with our story. And enough to make the idea of vampires start to go mainstream. We've watched everyone too closely for any mesmerism to have occurred in advance and Charles can't work any magic in court. I suggest we leave off the magic today, and I focus on the law."

Lavinia leans against the sink, crosses her arms, and stares at me. "What's your game here?"

"I want to break free of your control, obviously. But I also want to win this case. I just don't believe in using proactive magic—as opposed to the defensive, protective kind—in court, unless we're left with no other choice. I believe in the rule of law and free trials. It was a principle I stuck to even when I was trying to get my own brother off a murder charge, right up until the last minute."

"I trust your skills and judgement, even if I don't trust your loyalty. We'll do this your way. But at the first sign of trouble, I'm breaking those witnesses' brains down into their component parts. Or having you do it, I haven't decided yet."

Why did I ever think I could trust or like this woman? How could I have agreed to her terms? Still, at least she's giving me a little leeway.

. . .

The first witness for the defence is a medical expert.

"In your professional opinion, could the marks on Cara Hamilton's neck have been made by human teeth?" Charles asks.

The doctor shakes his head. "From the police images and the coroner's report, it looks more like she was bitten by a snake. Though of course, that would make little sense in a London club."

"And could she have sustained such serious blood loss from a bite?"

"A bite from an animal, maybe. Again, it's unlikely a human could cause such damage with only their teeth."

I don't need to look at Charles to sense his discomfiture. He presumably wants to spin the "Cara attacked herself with a knife" story. But for anyone who's starting to pick up on the unspoken vampire angle, talk of what humans can and can't do with their teeth—or to put it another way, whether or not Hugo is actually human— is treading onto dangerous ground.

"There's been some suggestion that the defendant may have sucked out her blood. Is that even physiologically possible?"

He shakes his head again. "A few drops, maybe. And the swelling round the wounds would be consistent with that. But drinking enough of her blood to kill her? That's something from a horror film, not real life. The required force and pressure. It just doesn't stack up."

"Could the wounds have been made with a knife?" Charles's voice is full of nervous anticipation.

The doctor turns over his hands. "It would have been a strangely shaped knife and have required force and precision in equal measure. It really does seem more like she was attacked by an animal."

Once it's my turn, I launch into my cross-examination with

gusto. Seizing on his "unlikelys" and emphasising how that's different from "impossible". Demonstrating how the witness has cast as much doubt on the central defence case as the prosecution version. Showing how his best guess explanation requires a wild animal in a London club, which no witnesses have even hinted at.

I glance at the jury. It might just be enough. Technically, the onus is on me, as the prosecution counsel, to prove beyond reasonable doubt that the defendant is guilty. But juries have a tendency to think of it as a fifty-fifty shot. And either way, this is all killer stuff as far as the news is concerned.

"I'm leaving for the day," Lavinia says, when we break again. "I've got better things to do than sit here, now we've not got the man-witch to deal with. You just stay on message and keep doing a good job. Bear in mind I can control you perfectly well from a distance."

I walk away without a reply.

Charles is stood outside, smoking frantically. He crosses his arms when he sees me, leaving the cigarette dangling in his mouth.

"What do you want?"

"Don't look so nervous," I reply. "You've got your little trinket to protect you. And I must be less scary than your boss. Or indeed your supposed co-counsel. Where is Gabriel Thornber today, by the way?"

Charles takes the cigarette and grinds it out on the wall. "Don't you speak to your family at all?"

"What's that supposed to mean?"

I step closer to him. Just how much protection does his amulet offer? If Lavinia can't penetrate it, it must offer a near total defence against mesmerism. But that's not to say it'd necessarily stop something more violent.

"The Mannith Practitioner Alliance is collapsing at the seams, so my bosses withdrew from the deal to extend the Dome. The last thing they want is to be dragged into inter-familial warfare."

I lean back against the stone wall of the court building to keep from falling. What on earth...?

When I saw Gabriel at the weekend, he said the alliance was struggling. He said there were things he needed to tell me about the vampires. But then everything went wrong and the conversation never got any further. This must have been the news he wanted to impart. I'm almost surprised he found time to come to London and attempt to save me from Seb and Lavinia's clutches while all that was going down.

I need to get to Mannith. I need to talk to my family. Talk to Gabriel. Make them talk to each other and see reason. But that's a lost cause while Lavinia has me in her grasp.

"We asked Mr Thornber to stay on the case regardless, in return for a good salary and anything else we could offer," Charles continues, either heedless of my concern or deliberately ignoring it. "He politely declined. Which to my mind suggests we should give up right now. And, well... my bosses don't tolerate human failings."

He sounds almost flippant, but there's a haunted look in his eyes.

"How did you even end up working for the vampires?"

"An old school friend of mine was turned and let the secret slip. My parents both died of cancer in my early twenties. Immortality appealed. But now, I doubt I'll survive the month."

"If and when I win, I'll ask them to spare you," I say. "I've no idea if they'll listen. But I promise I'll try."

Charles glances around. "It may not need to come to that. Tristan wants to meet you. Just you. Not your boss."

"I've got even less to say to him than I have to you."

"He wants to discuss a settlement. He's got some interesting terms. And if nothing else, he'd like to take you out for a spectacular meal."

I think carefully before answering. Goodness knows what words Lavinia will let out of my mouth.

"When? Where? And is this purely business, or is he trying to seduce me?"

"Next Friday. Nine PM, to make absolutely sure it's dark. Wilton's champagne and oyster bar. And I don't think you're his type. He prefers his women slightly more mesmerisable and edible, for a start."

"I'll think about it," I reply, eventually, and manage to get the words out through Lavinia's control.

THIRTY-ONE

Monday night, I'm too drained to do anything after work but go straight to bed, and the same's true for the next couple of nights. But on Thursday, Lavinia stays away from court, the defence witnesses are easy to deal with, and Charles does nothing to provoke me. At the end of the day, I've got enough residual energy for a little trip back to the Lore Library.

The librarian nods at me when I walk past her desk and head straight for the hidden door. Inside, I search for books on how liens operate. And more importantly, how to destroy them.

Liens were a popular topic for eighteenth century magical writers. I build a little pile of books around me and give thanks that I've always been a fast reader.

The first few books all tell me the same thing. There are only three ways to break a lien. Either the terms are completed, the parties mutually agree to remove it or the bestower dies.

On the surface, the last one sounds like the best bet. I'd like to see Lavinia dead after what she's done to me and my family.

Unfortunately, as I had to remind my father and Bren on several occasions after Gabriel first branded me, there's a twist: if you try to kill someone in order to break a valid lien, you turn your power on yourself. It's an integral part of the Old Ways, a bit of folklore passed down over the generations. But these books confirm it with quasi-scientific studies and historical anecdotes. Anyone powerful enough to kill Lavinia would kill themselves in the attempt. Anyone without magic would have no chance of harming her. I can cross my fingers that she randomly dies in a tragic accident, but otherwise, that's a dead end.

Then there's fulfilling the terms. And thinking about this makes me so angry with myself. I'm a lawyer. Precise language is my speciality, but I allowed the terms of the lien to be left open-ended. I was so desperate for revenge on Hugo that my emotions clouded my judgement.

That just leaves annulment by mutual agreement. It's hard to believe Lavinia would ever set me free. But if you'd asked me last year, I'd never have dreamt that Gabriel would release me from the old lien either. Realistically, she probably won't agree to it out of the goodness of her heart. But maybe I could make use of bribery. Blackmail. Threats. Or just a fair trade. It's the start of a plan, but I've no idea what I could offer her or use against her.

"I've got the most marvellous piece of gossip," Lavinia trills, appearing from nowhere and perching herself on my desk.

I slam the book closed and open up my laptop. It's unclear whether I was so absorbed in reading I didn't notice her approach or whether she subtly traversed into place.

"I'm getting on with your case, just like you asked." I stare at my computer screen to avoid her gaze. "If you want me to be your indentured lawyer, leave me alone to get on with it."

If she knows I'm plotting my freedom, her delighted expression gives no sign of it.

"I'll give you the peace and quiet you need to crush those bloodsuckers; I just need five minutes of your time first. You'll be amused."

Despite myself, I almost want to hear what she's got to say. Her stories are usually pretty entertaining, and there's something about her that makes her oddly compelling to listen to. At least, I think that's my real view, and not just the lien talking.

"I'm going to keep going over this witness statement. If you want to talk at me, I guess I can't stop you."

"Indeed you can't," she replies, with a cheeky little smile.

Against my will, I close the lid of my laptop again and turn to look at her. I retain just enough control over my body to grumpily cross my arms.

"Fine. What's so fascinating?"

"Your little friend from back home's awfully good in bed, isn't he? I wondered why you were stupid enough to stay so besotted. I suppose that at least starts to explain it."

She's watching me like a Newsnight interviewer who's just found a politician's weak spot.

I might actually be sick over my reference books. There's no question as to what she's implying. Any possible ambiguity has been wiped away by the smirk on her face.

"I thought you didn't approve of male practitioners." I aim for nonchalant and miss the mark by several hundred miles, but at least I manage not to actually burst into tears.

"There are exceptions to every rule." She sighs beatifically, as though thinking back to some particularly delightful moment of their encounter.

I stand up. "Why are you doing this to me? Keeping me in your control makes practical sense. This is just pathetic. Teenage mean-girl nonsense is ridiculous coming from a ninety-year-old woman, however good she looks for her age."

Her delighted expression only deepens. "Sweetie, don't flatter yourself. As if I'd sleep with someone just to get a rise out of you. He's gorgeous. He's powerful. And he approached me. Thinking about your reaction was merely an added bonus."

"*He* approached *you*? When? Why? What happened?" I

shouldn't give her the satisfaction, but I can't help myself. I'm gripping the table to stay standing.

She runs her hands over her body, then waves one languidly, bathing herself in an unnatural, pink-tinged light. "Why do you think?"

It's true that she's beautiful and powerful, just like him. It's also true that we're not officially together—hell, have never officially been together—and that Gabriel can be somewhat indiscriminate with his affections.

And yet somehow, that's not enough explanation. Sure, Gabriel has flings, but given his obsession with me and my hatred of Lavinia, this tryst can't have been a casual bit of fun. Gabriel either carefully calibrated the encounter to hit me where it hurts—if he didn't realise that Lavinia was controlling my words, the things I said to him at the hotel might have left him wanting revenge—or else he had some good, complex reason for it. Or knowing him, two good reasons.

My thoughts are coming as fast as my breaths.

"Tempting as it is to give you all the juicy details, I'd better leave you to it. That case isn't going to prosecute itself. But I'm seeing him again at the weekend. Perhaps you could join us for dinner? That is, as long as you leave before things get fun."

I simply glare at her. She blows me a kiss in response, then disappears.

I abandon any pretence of working on the case and pace the room. The thought of it makes me cry. My mind won't stop flashing up images of the two most beautiful and powerful people I know, in all sorts of interesting positions. I force myself into an unsteady core meditation, breathing slowly and deeply and counting rhythmically under my breath.

My gut instinct is to assume the worst and either phone him up and scream or cut him out of my life once and for all. Lavinia would probably let me get those words out. Instead, I decide to do something radical.

I open my eyes, pick up my phone, and with shaking hands attempt to type out a text.

I love you. I trust you. I believe you've got a plan.

Inevitably, the lien won't let me write the words. But the sentiment remains.

In any normal week, dinner with Tristan the vampire lawyer would be the worst possible social occasion. But the knowledge that I've got to be third wheel on Lavinia and Gabriel's dinner date tomorrow night makes this seem almost jolly by comparison.

And this oyster and champagne bar in the city is pleasantly opulent, even if it's also predictably old fashioned—all marble counters, low lighting, and starched tablecloths, with hunting scenes and still life paintings on the walls. It's been going since 1742, according to my internet research. Maybe my companion was there on the opening night.

Tristan was the one who wanted to see me, goodness knows why. But having been offered the opportunity, it seemed short-sighted not to take advantage of it. I could try to influence the case or get the inside track on what he and Charles are planning. I could seek to persuade him to reconsider the Dome deal. Or maybe I could ask for his help in breaking the lien. Vampires aren't subject to the same rules as practitioners. Maybe he could kill Lavinia for me. It's unlikely I'll be able to get out a single constructive word, but I can try.

My mind is still utterly besieged by images of Gabriel and Lavinia. I'm clinging to my belief that it's all a complicated plot on Gabriel's part, but it's hard to keep that idea in my head from one minute to the next. I generally pride myself on being in control of my emotions, but I've burst into random, unexpected tears on several occasions over the last few days, including while doing my make-up for this meeting. But I'm determined to put on a good show for the vampire. It's never a great idea to show them weakness.

"Thank you for agreeing to meet me," Tristan says, when I walk over to the corner table where he's waiting for me.

"My pleasure," I reply. "When an attractive man offers you free champagne, it's hard to be too churlish about it."

It's surprisingly easy to slip into a flirtatious, light-hearted tone, like I'm an actor on stage.

Should I sleep with him, if the opportunity arises? He's undoubtedly physically attractive and it might even cheer me up. A little bit of getting your own back always does wonders for the mood.

And before things go that far, would it be rude to ask exactly what decade or century he was born in? My guess would be Victorian times, but who knows?

He smiles, showing the most subtle hint of fang. "I will cut straight to the point. The sooner we have dealt with business, the sooner we can get on with enjoying the evening."

"As far as 'enjoying the evening' goes, I'd like to point out for the third time that I'm immune to your mesmerism and my blood would make you very sick. But I'm also extremely open-minded."

His eyes widen, in what must be a relatively familiar experience of the strictures and inhibitions of his youth fighting against the excess and debauchery of his life as a vampire. Or maybe I'm projecting—starting from my theory that he's a Victorian and working forward. For all I know, he could have grown up in a particular orgy-prone corner of ancient Rome.

"Late eighteenth-century. Younger son of a minor aristocrat," he says, with a smile. "You could have just asked. Anyway, business first. We want you to drop the case."

I laugh, gesturing with my half-empty champagne flute. "Of course you do. That's a fairly common standpoint for a defendant and their friends, family, and legal team."

"We tend to want things rather more strongly than the average person. And we tend to get what we want."

Damn vampires. Melodramatic and entitled to their absolute core. I gesture to the waiter to bring another bottle, even though we've barely started on the first one. If I've got to listen to this, I consider it a matter of principle to utterly abuse his hospitality.

The waiter can't move fast enough. He's staring at Tristan like the staff in the dress shop stared at Chrissie.

"Even if I inexplicably wanted to drop it, I couldn't. It's not like Lavinia is suing your client. It's a criminal matter. It's out of mine and her hands now."

"I understand how the law works. I have been a high court judge three times over the course of three hundred years of reinvention. My point is that you could throw the case. You could remove yourself from it and leave it to someone less legally and magically gifted. You could use your powers to make it go away, or simply put up no resistance when we do just that.

"There are already news stories out there, but if the case collapses, the press will lose interest. The evidence will be dismissed as fabricated. You can help us clean things up with a touch of mesmerism, and all can be forgiven and forgotten."

What are the odds he's recording me? Probably low—most vampires tend to be a few decades behind the curve when it comes to technology. Besides, he'd be damning himself with all of this. Still, I need to be careful. No references to Lavinia having set the whole thing up. Oblique references to magic at most.

"Whatever the circumstances of the case, your client killed someone in cold blood. For want of a better term. And as a group, you've always relied on your carefully curated reputations, your control, and your secrecy. You've had it all your own way for far too long."

He takes a long sip of his drink. Is he capable of enjoying it in any meaningful way, or is every physical indulgence ultimately a poor substitute for blood?

"I really am looking forward to getting to the pleasanter part of the evening. The salmon here is exquisite. So let me quickly get this out of the way: if you work with us to make the case go away, we will re-honour our deal with the Mannith Alliance and help them maintain and expand their precious Dome without the need for sacrifices. If you refuse, then win or lose, that deal is dead forever."

"I'm not a part of the Mannith Alliance. I'm not in touch with my family anymore."

"We have communicated our terms to them. Whatever petty disagreements exist between you, I imagine they will be in touch."

Right on cue, my phone rings. I did the polite thing and set it to silent before sitting down to eat. Presumably either my dinner companion or the caller has over-ridden that.

"Take it. Please. I shall order some starters while you do."

I step away from the table and into the red and black lobby, glancing at the screen as I go. It's Bren. Despite the fact that I've blocked his number. Messing with someone's phone settings from afar is a relatively straightforward trick—hell, it's one the whole family played on each other in our teens. I can't decide whether it's heartening or alarming that he's seemingly retained enough power to pull it off.

"Hello?"

"Sadie, please do what the vampires are asking. We need to expand the Dome. And we need them in order to do it."

"Yes, hello my beloved sister," I reply. "Sorry again I tried to kill you. Thanks for letting me keep some magic. How have you been for these last three months?"

"You know I'm sorry. And I know you don't want to talk to me, so I'm not going to waste time on pleasantries. When you do want to chat or reconcile, reach out. For now, just give them what they want. If not for me, then for the rest of the family. Or hell, for your damn soulmate if you prefer."

He hangs up before I can get another word in. I'm dying to call him back. I hadn't realised just how much I missed him.

I resist and head back to my seat. But as I walk, I have a disconcerting sense that I'm resisting of my own volition, rather than Lavinia enforcing it.

"I'll do it," I say as soon as I sit down. "I'll drop the case."

"I knew you would see sense. We can talk practical details in the office tomorrow evening. For now, let us see where the night takes us."

I shake my head and grin. "I'm not actually going to drop it. I just wanted to see whether I could tell you that I would."

"Excuse me?"

I'd felt capable of calling my brother back. Only pride had stood in my way, not someone else's control. And just then, I'd outright been able to say something that went entirely against Lavinia's interests. Could the lien possibly be slipping?

"Never mind. The point is, I'm not going to do it. There's nothing you can say that would convince me otherwise. Whatever did or didn't happen with Cara, and whatever the other rights and wrongs, Hugo killed a human client of mine. So, shall I leave now, or shall we move on to a bit of gossip and flirtation and a lot more champagne?"

"Well, Augustine cannot claim I failed to try," he says, making the waiter appear to take our orders through either very subtle mesmerism or intense force of personality.

I'm not going to drop the case. But that doesn't mean I can't try to rebel in other ways. Tomorrow night's horror show just got a little more interesting.

Over the next few hours, Tristan and I work our way through an inordinate amount of wine and some delicate morsels of seafood.

I try to tell him about the lien, on the off-chance he can help

—I probably wouldn't like his price, but it'd be interesting to hear it—but though it may somehow have become less absolute, Lavinia maintains enough control that it's impossible to say anything about that.

Having established that neither of us are going to get anything practical out of the other, we're able to relax and enjoy a mix of small talk and meaningless flirtation. I've zero actual interest in Tristan, but I'm having a surprising amount of fun.

"You have got to move with the times," he says. "It is not always easy. I know you think we are all terribly regressive, but I do try. Supposedly, everyone has grandparents who mean no harm but occasionally make some sort of terribly offensive remark because things were different when they were young. Imagine just how different things were when I was first developing a sense of right and wrong regarding cultural norms."

I nod. He seems almost sweet. And despite his apparent concern, he's managed to get through two hours without saying anything strikingly problematic.

"It's the same with culture as with morality," he says later. "I loved the music of Handel when I was genuinely the sort of age I appear to be. I watched and listened as his orchestra played and fireworks lit up the sky. I've still got a soft spot for that sort of thing, but I got a thrill watching *Hamilton* recently. Not to mention a blast of nostalgia. I half considered wearing my old regimental uniform to the show."

When it's time to go, I let him settle the bill. I'm a big believer in going halves, as a rule, but he's presumably putting this on Augustine Piso's expense account, where it won't make the slightest of dents.

"Would it be terribly unprofessional to invite you back to my home?" he says, helping me to my feet.

I try not to be too flattered. As vampires need to use seduction to get blood, they have a tendency to default to hitting on anyone who remotely fits the definition of their type.

I shake my head. "Not while the case is ongoing."

I'm going to regret doing the sensible thing later, when I'm lying alone in bed with images of Gabriel and Lavinia keeping me awake.

Our waiter comes over to take payment from Tristan's black card. He's still looking at the vampire with a mixture of awe and lust, just like he has all night. Tristan turns his gaze full on him and the man's eyes cloud over.

Tristan takes his arm, leads him outside, and beckons for me to follow. We all trek to a secluded corner behind the restaurant.

"What are you planning to do?" My stomach constricts.

"Not kill him. I'm not some uncouth, out of control idiot like Hugo. Just a few sips of the blood I need to survive. Like your family promised us in Mannith."

I drop my head into my hands. I may be resistant to his mesmerism, but I've made the classic mistake everyone does with vampires—paying attention to their charm and forgetting the predator that lurks beneath.

Should I try to protect the waiter? I'm not sure I'm physically capable of it, and if I did, Tristan would only find someone else.

While I'm deliberating, he pushes him against the wall, tilts his head back and bites down. The man is conscious, but makes no sound, clearly deeply mesmerised.

I hold my breath, but as promised, after only twenty seconds or so, Tristan lifts his head, licks the wound closed, then waves his hand in front of the man's face.

"Shall we go back to mine for a nightcap?" Tristan says smoothly to the waiter, before the poor man has a chance to ask what's going on.

His victim nods eagerly, as though they're at the end of a delightful date.

I cross my arms and give Tristan a pointed look.

"No mesmerism at this point, I promise," he says. "We do what we need to do for blood. For sex or anything else, our more honest charms generally suffice."

I walk away without answering. I still hate Lavinia even more than the vampires, but if I had any doubts about continuing with the case, they've disappeared after that little scene.

THIRTY-TWO

The next evening, I spend hours debating what to wear for the dinner-cum-emotional torture session. The basic decision is between a casual and unmade up "couldn't give a damn" look, versus an utterly sexy and polished "see what you're missing out on" vibe, with a million points on the spectrum in between.

Am I channelling all my panic, rage, and uncertainty into a fairly inconsequential decision? I most certainly am, but in the end, I put my pride to one side and decide to live by my sister's motto that you can't control how an evening is going to go, but you can control looking fabulous.

After all the deliberation, actually getting ready takes no more than five minutes—the joy of magic. I'm never going to beat Lavinia in a straight-up beauty contest, but I'm pleased with the end result.

I'm to meet Lavinia and her date at the restaurant. Because she's an absolute psychopath, it's a gloriously romantic little spot in Covent Garden, which, based on its website, seems to be all dim lighting, flowers, and candles, with piano music playing softly in the background. We're surely going to be the first table for three they've seen in some time. The other patrons will probably presume a polyamorous set up if they're on the younger and more open-minded side, or else that I'm a servant of some kind if they're older and stuffier. I'm not sure which conclusion would be closer to the truth.

I traverse right outside the venue, but do three circuits of the street before I can bring myself to go inside.

Once I finally summon up my courage—or push down any remnants of self-respect—I spot the two of them immediately, despite the fact they're tucked away in a particularly shaded spot towards the back of the room. Lavinia and Gabriel both tend to dominate any room they're in. Together, they're like a lighthouse beacon. Especially for me.

"Sadie, darling. Do sit down. You remember Gabriel, don't you?"

She knows full well that I more than remember him, but her first attempt to get a rise out of me falls flat. I'm entirely focused on Gabriel. Like me, he's made an effort, sporting a suit that's aggressively well-tailored, even by his standards. He's removed his sunglasses in the darkened room, showing his glowing eyes. He greets me with a slight sneer. I pray that my belief this is all part of some grand plan is cleverness and not pathetic naivety.

I give each of them a brief nod, then sit down in silence with all of my nerves on high alert.

"Waiter, bring Bellinis," Lavinia calls. "I want to drink to my brilliant new lawyer and my beautiful new man."

She smiles at us both in turn. I scowl. Gabriel slips an arm around her waist.

"I remember now," Lavinia continues, while the waiter dashes to fetch her order. "Of course you know each other. You had a little dalliance over the summer, didn't you?"

"That's putting it a bit strongly," Gabriel replies. "We screwed, like, six times in total."

I do the maths in my head. It sounds unbelievably low, but he's right. Granted, that entirely ignores a whole range of other activities from almost killing each other to declarations of love, but for all the headspace our relationship takes up, that is indeed the sum total of the sexual side of things. Even the number of times we've met up and talked in person is probably still in single figures. I swallow hard and fight to keep my breathing steady.

"Goodness, really? I had something more involved in my head," Lavinia replies. "We've made love more times than that in the past week."

"And I'm sure we'll do the same again next week. But then, what you and I have is nothing like what happened between me and her."

He accompanies this with a gentle stroke of Lavinia's arm and a sultry smile in her direction. She preens at his words. I cling desperately to the scope they leave for ambiguity.

Even so, my vision's blurring and the room seems to spin. My attempts to maintain a neutral expression are rapidly failing.

"I don't think I've ever had anything like what we have," Lavinia says, with a contented sigh.

There's no ambiguity in *her* words, just a surprisingly genuine tone. I'd assumed this was mostly about tormenting me, combined with a touch of lust for an attractive man. But she sounds like she honestly adores him.

The waiter brings our drinks. I look Lavinia straight in the eye and down mine in one. She laughs indulgently.

"Why is she here?" Gabriel asks. "A reunion with an old flame is always amusing, but I want some time alone with you."

"She has something I want, and I gather it belongs to you."

I frown for a second, and then all of our eyes alight on Gabriel's ring on my finger, emeralds sparkling in the candlelight.

I couldn't physically bear for him to take the ring and all it symbolises and give it to that bitch.

Gabriel lets go of Lavinia for a moment and takes a firm hold of my hand, causing my heart rate to spike. I long to grip so hard that he can't let go and traverse us out of here.

"I'd happily give you anything else you wanted, but that's not mine to give. It was my mother's gift to her. I was just the delivery boy."

Lavinia had been leaning over the table staring at my ring, but at his words, she abruptly sits up straight. I've never seen Lavinia back off from an argument so quickly.

"I wouldn't want to cut across anything Maeve Thornber wanted," she says. "I pick my battles, and I don't pick them with demon women. Not even ones who have been dead for fifteen years."

Heedless of the tension at the table, the waiter reappears with our starters. Lavinia picks up a forkful of duck breast and delicately slips it into Gabriel's perfect mouth.

I take a deep breath. I'd like to say something clever, but there's no time. Based on the things I managed to say to Tristan last night, there's more wriggle room in the lien than there once was. I just need to get the words out.

"You're using our lien to make me do and say things against my will. I don't want to work for you. I want to see my family. I want to be with him."

Lavinia's pale face goes a few shades lighter still.

"Gabriel, help me, please," I continue. "Or if that's impossible, tell my family. They probably can't do anything either, but I want them to know I still love them."

It's against all my principles to beg him like this, especially in front of Lavinia, but I have to scream out the truth while I have the chance.

I'm rewarded with nothing more than a scathing, slightly bored expression from the man I love a thousand times more than Lavinia ever could.

"Stop talking," Lavinia snaps.

Abruptly, my words grind to a halt. The lien clearly has weakened somehow, but not enough for me to resist a clear and direct order.

"It's all nonsense," she says, turning to Gabriel and grabbing his shoulders, her eyes pleading with him to believe her lies. "I don't know why she'd say something like that."

Gabriel's hand closes over one of hers. "She's clearly just jealous. Besides, I don't care if you are controlling her. I can hardly take the moral high ground on liens and dodgy magic. And she means nothing to me."

I visibly flinch. Surely this is all an act, it has to be, but it'd be nice if he could make slightly less of an effort to get into character.

"Let's just skip the main courses and go back to my place," Lavinia replies. "I was stupid to invite her. I just want to be alone with you."

"There's nothing I'd like more," Gabriel says, bestowing upon her the suggestive smile I recognise all too well.

Without hesitation, Lavinia sweeps away from the table towards the exit.

Gabriel pauses just for a moment. It's long enough for me to abandon my last shreds of self-respect and grab his hand.

"I love you," I say. "I can't help it. Even if you really are with her now, I don't think I'll ever get it out of my system. But if this is some game, some act, please just give me a sign."

He stares at my hand on his, making no immediate attempt to get away, and my hope rises.

"Lavinia, come back. I've changed my mind."

"About what?" She can't traverse inside the restaurant, but I've never seen someone cross a room so fast.

"You can have the ring after all." He slips it off my finger before I can protest, and my whole body goes cold. "I'm sure my mother wouldn't object to you having it if she knew how I felt about you."

"Thank you." She kisses him full on the lips, as he slides the ring onto her hand. She seems lost in her ostentatious display of affection, but not so lost that she can't spare me a triumphant sneer over his shoulder.

"Let's go," he whispers. "I can't wait to get you home. And if you like the ring, there's plenty more of my mother's old jewellery I'd love to see you wear."

And then they're both gone, and I'm more alone than I've ever been.

Lavinia's mesmerism hasn't kicked back in yet, though no doubt it's just a matter of time before I once again start to lose all sense that there's a problem. She'll probably get right to it once that treacherous bastard's made her come a few times. Maybe he'll even help her out with the spell.

I wanted so much to believe I could trust him. But I asked for a sign, and it's hard to imagine one clearer than that. I desperately try to think of any positive spin that could be put on him taking away something that both protects me and that's meant to be a symbol of our connection, but I know I'm lying to myself.

At least I make it as far as the bathroom before the tears start to cascade.

THIRTY-THREE

On Monday morning, against all the odds, my professional pride kicks in, and despite my headache and shakiness, I drag myself to court. Even if it's Lavinia's case, I still believe in making Hugo pay for Janice Denworth and for Cara. And in humiliating the vampires more generally, particularly now they've screwed my family over. Besides, there's something to be said for attempting to channel my emotions into something constructive.

That said, success today entirely depends on Lavinia having the basic sense not to talk to me in person. According to the Old Ways, your own power will be turned back on you if you kill someone in order to break a lien, but if I have to look at her wearing my ring and probably smelling faintly of Gabriel, I might just take that chance.

Unless she tightens the lien back up, now she knows her control is slipping. Or even takes advantage of my ring-less status to make me forget there's anything wrong. Maybe she'll rock up hand in hand with Gabriel, and I'll smile and wish them all the best, believing that I mean it.

It's 21st December today. The longest night, a time when magic is especially powerful. Had the deal not collapsed, it was the night the vampires were going to help my family expand the Dome.

For weeks, I'd told myself I'd go to Mannith for Christmas, perhaps even with Seb, and everything would be alright again. But now I know Seb never really existed. And worse, that Gabriel, the person I really ought to have been spending Christmas with, would rather be with my worst enemy, no matter how much it hurts me.

I'd still travel to Mannith by myself, if I could. But there's no way Lavinia will let me leave London or contact my family. At best, I'll spend Christmas alone in my flat. At worst, she could have all sorts of humiliations in store for me.

By the time proceedings start, however, there's no sign of her, and my thoughts, memories and emotions are seemingly intact. I do a light core meditation, slip out of the emotional wreck of Sadie the person, and become Ms Sadler, the cold, hard lawyer.

I listen to Charles's examination of the barman at Clique, scribbling furiously. Charles is still wearing his protective amulet, but the witness is neither mesmerised nor protected. I could compel him to say whatever I needed him to, but there's little need even if I were willing to go down that route—he may be a defence witness, but his answers broadly correspond with our prosecution case.

By the time we break for lunch, Charles has failed to land any killer blows. In the afternoon, it'll be time for my cross-examination. We've almost come to the end of the witnesses. Victory is in my grasp. I might be ground down and broken, but I'm still exhilarated at that prospect.

I'm starving, having left after the starters on Saturday night and barely managed to consume a single mouthful since. I couldn't even finish my coffee this morning.

I still can't really face the thought of food, but a girl's got to eat, so I make it to a sandwich shop on autopilot, grab a little pot of mango cubes, and force them down. Then I slam in my earphones, put my musical choices in the hands of Spotify, and walk as fast as I can, fighting to turn my sadness into physical exertion. There's still no evidence of Lavinia seeking to re-control my thoughts, but there's a part of me that almost wishes she'd put me out of my misery.

This part of the City of London is beautiful, at least, and the magnificence and sense of history that surround St Paul's Cathedral and London Bridge gives me a hint of comfort. I double back along the river, then allow myself the luxury of sitting down on the stone steps of the great domed cathedral, surrounded by tourists, city workers getting some lunchtime fresh air despite the December chill, and hundreds of pigeons. As soon as I do, all the fight seeps out of me. I'm not sure how I'm going to stand up again, let alone make it back to the court and start delivering.

I close my eyes. I can give myself a minute. There's no need to be strong all the time. But however much I try to breathe deeply, think about nice things, or think about nothing at all, all I can see is a horrible montage of real memories of every word that was said in the restaurant, cut with lurid imaginings of what probably happened afterwards between Gabriel and Lavinia.

When I finally open my eyes and get to my feet in one determined motion, Gabriel's standing in front of me, watching me intently.

I scream and grab his arm to keep from falling. Some of the pigeons fly away, some of the tourists look at me oddly, but no one intervenes. For a moment, I almost wonder if I'm halluci-nating, letting my imagination become flesh.

"Can I talk to you?" he asks.

I let go of him and sink back down onto the stairs by way of reply. I long to do a spell and drive him away, but I can't even muster up the energy to tell him to get lost.

He sits down beside me. I shuffle along to increase the distance between us, then sit very still and stare intently at the pigeons.

"Here. Take this back, please."

He holds out the emerald ring.

I simply stare at it, keeping my arms folded. "You really do have a problem with commitment, don't you?" I say. And then I stretch out my hand.

Goodness knows what he's playing at. I don't want any of the ring's romantic or symbolic connotations, but I'm not stupid enough to turn down its protective power, right when I need it the most.

"I gave Lavinia a different present," he says, as he slips the ring back on my finger where it belongs.

As soon as it's safely in place, I draw my arms back around myself, resisting the urge to feel his touch a few seconds longer. "I can't imagine there's anything you could have given her that she'd have preferred to this."

"Like I said last night, I wanted her to have some other pieces of my mother's jewellery."

I frown, trying to think what could possibly be a worthy substitute. Presumably, Maeve, being beautiful, wealthy, and half demonic, had plenty of jewellery, most of which was probably magical to some degree or another. But it was the ring that he always wore, on a chain around his neck. I've never heard him mention anything else in particular.

Except for the obvious.

I look him straight in his eyes. "You don't mean the bracelets?"

"It doesn't matter how powerful someone is. They can't maintain control over someone if all their magic's blocked."

I slump back against the stone steps. "I wish I'd thought of doing that to you, years ago."

He laughs, and it's the best sound in the world.

I force myself back into a seated position and look at him properly. "So I was right first time? This was all a trick? You just wanted to get the blocking bracelets on her to cut the connection?"

"The bracelets were a last-minute stroke of inspiration. I didn't think she'd let me, but I can be very persuasive. And the ring helped to earn her trust. The original plan was to drain her magic during sex. It's your sister's trick. And it was your big brother's idea."

Is he actually trying to tell me he had some sort of sit down, in-depth, heart to heart conversation with Bren? This might actually be the most surprising element of all.

And then slowly, like the waves going out to reveal treasure on the shore, it all sinks in. The lien's broken. I'm free. I can go back home or do whatever the hell I want. And Gabriel was faking. Just like I'd thought and hoped at first, he still loves me. He was on my side all along. Doing bad things for good reasons, in a way few other people could bring themselves to.

I close my eyes and let the revelations percolate through my brain. I touch my back. "Is the mark gone?"

Gabriel shakes his head. "I don't think so. We didn't remove the lien, exactly, just nullified it. So the physical image is probably still there. But it's essentially just a lifeless tattoo."

I shrug off my suit jacket and pull my collar back so he can take a look.

"Still there," he confirms. "I suspect that means you can't personally kill her, more's the pity. But other than that, I wouldn't worry about it."

"You were an absolute bastard on Saturday night," I say eventually. "I'm sure you didn't have to be that convincing."

He squeezes my hand. "I'm sorry. I couldn't tell you my real intentions when Lavinia basically had a hotline into your mind, and I couldn't risk half measures. It killed me to watch the hope and trust in your eyes dim. It sickened me to be with her afterwards. I was so scared that by the time I came clean, I'd have pushed you away forever."

I lean into him. "I don't think there's anything you could do that would achieve that. That fact terrifies me. It'll be a while until I get some of the things you said or the thought of you with Lavinia out of my head. But right now, all I care about is your hand on mine and that look of love in your eyes. Sickening, I know."

"My car's five minutes away. Let's get home and have a proper reunion."

I cross my arms. "I want nothing more than to get home. I want to apologise to my family, then go back to your place and let you show me just how sorry you are. After which, I can show you just how thoroughly I trust and forgive you. But first, I need to finish the case. I might even be able to pull it off today."

Gabriel stands and holds out his hand to help me up. "That's absolutely insane. We need to get back to Mannith, fast. Worst case, Lavinia finds someone who knows how to remove the bracelets—which wouldn't reactivate her control over you, but would make her very dangerous. Best case, she gets someone else to do her dirty work. Inside the Dome, we'll be safe."

"I want to see Hugo Latham go down. Those vampires have been total dicks for centuries, and now I've got them on the ropes. If Lavinia tries to start anything, we'll finish it."

Gabriel starts to walk, and I follow. Despite his objections, he seems to be heading in the direction of the court. "It's crazy not to get a home advantage. And though I've broken the connection, on some level, she does have a valid lien. If you or anyone else kills her in an attempt to subvert that..."

"It's like turning your power on yourself," I finish. "I made that point repeatedly to my parents and siblings over the last six years. It's why you're still standing."

He laughs again. For a moment, I'm unsure whether to laugh along or slap him. I compromise by turning around, throwing my arms around his neck and pulling him in for the sort of kiss that seems guaranteed to make tourists turn and stare.

For a split second, he seems either caught off guard or determined to press his case about fleeing to Mannith, then he takes a firm hold of me, and gives as good as he's getting.

Eventually, we let go of each other. Or at least, settle for merely standing close and keeping our hands firmly clasped.

"I'll come with you and watch admiringly from the spectators' gallery," Gabriel says. "But at the first sign of a vengeful Lavinia, promise me you'll traverse out of there, and then we'll drive?"

"Thank you for understanding." I kiss him again, just a sweet little peck this time, but with the promise of more to come. "I just need one afternoon to take down the establishment, and then I'm all yours."

I glance at my watch as we enter the court building arm in arm. It feels like hours have passed. It's actually only been about fifty minutes, but that's still long enough for me to be verging on late.

I dash through the entrance hall, my shoes clattering on the marble floor. But before I can either reach the robing room or subtly attempt some meaningful hand gestures to smarten myself up, Charles waves me over, sporting a quite uncharacteristic beam. I slow my steps, then join him at the back of the room, where he's waiting underneath another grand biblical scene and an inscription reading "*The law of the wise is the fountain of life*".

Charles smiles at Gabriel, then grabs my hand and gives it a hearty shake. "My client is happy to accept your client's settlement proposal. I've drawn up a very rough draft over lunch. We'll need a bit of back and forth to hammer out the details before we've got something watertight, but the substance is pretty straightforward."

I extract myself from his grip and hold out a suddenly shaking hand. "May I see?"

"Of course." Charles sits down at a table, pulls out a laptop, and gestures for me to join him.

Gabriel hovers in the background. Magical energy is radiating off him. He's ready to attack at the first sign of a trick from either the vampires or Lavinia.

There's no trick. The agreement is elegantly drafted and has the complexity of someone trying to justify their exorbitant fee. But the basics are simple. The vampires will pay Lavinia a large sum, including transferring some land into her name. Her coven will mesmerise the judge and jury in order to get a not guilty verdict and then take their usual measures to make everyone forget this ever happened.

There's been press coverage, of course, but so far, it's been relatively tentative. Hugo comes off badly, but the papers have been waiting for a guilty verdict before going all in on talk of blood drinking and the like. Once the case is withdrawn, at best, the story will fall away, and worst, the papers will print stories about how it was clearly all a hoax. And as part of the deal on the table, we'll help the vampires make sure that's the case.

"I was highly surprised when your client suggested these terms. She hardly needs the money. I always got the impression this was extremely personal for her. And that Hugo aside, exposing us was half the point."

Professional pride keeps my expression blank and my tone neutral, as I desperately avoid giving any hint that I didn't know about this in advance, that it wasn't done on my advice.

"Did my client bring the proposal to you herself?"

"It was somewhat unorthodox, but then nothing about this case has exactly been normal."

I merely sigh, though rage is threatening to send my magic spewing out in all directions. "I'll have to go over the detail and get instruction from my client."

Lavinia seemed so passionate about her plan, to the point of sacrificing a promising young woman. Even if she was about to lose, she'd surely fight it to the bitter end. And somewhat against the odds, we were on course to win. To make the witnesses and evidence sound utterly compelling. To get the story out there and expose the vampires. Why would she throw it away?

"Ask me yourself, darling. I'm right here."

I stand and turn to face her, heart pounding. She's wearing a characteristically stunning sapphire dress, the blocking bracelets on her arms, and a superficially sweet expression that does nothing to hide the utter fury in her eyes.

Gabriel makes a frantic waving gesture. Not a magical hand-signal, just a silent plea for me to get the hell out of there. But the bracelets are in place and she's alone. I raise my hands on autopilot, ready to strike.

"I really wouldn't do that if I were you," Lavinia says, in a saccharine tone.

"You've done your utmost to ruin my life. Give me one good reason not to unleash Hellfire while you can't fight back."

Not attacking a defenceless opponent is up there with supporting democracy as far as universal civilised norms go, but considering she's kept me powerless for months, it's hard to feel too guilty.

"How about the small matter of attacking someone you've got a binding lien with being like turning your power on yourself?"

I'm well aware of that infuriating aspect of the Old Ways. I was discussing it with Gabriel not ten minutes ago. But confronted with her smiling face and her uncharacteristic vulnerability, it's hard to resist the violent power that's rising inside me.

Gabriel grabs my right arm and presses my hand to my chest. "She's right, you know she is. You don't need a conversation, and you can't risk a confrontation."

Lavinia glares at our intertwined hands. "As for you, Gabriel, the first order of business once this minor inconvenience is out of the way is tearing you apart. You've seen how I react to men who merely deny me. You don't want to know what I'll do to someone who uses my feelings for them against me."

Gabriel sighs. "I'm not engaging. It was enough of a struggle trying to keep up a conversation when I was pretending to like you."

She lifts her left hand as though she's about to kill him where he stands. I wince as she shudders and her hand slams back to her side. I remember the drowning sensation of accidentally attempting magic while wearing blockers. If it were almost anyone else, I'd have a hint of sympathy.

"Second order of business will be bending you thoroughly back to my will, Sadie. I'll do it properly this time. No more muddying the water with attempts at friendship on the side."

My heart pounds at her words, despite her inability to act on them right now. She smiles when she notices, while Gabriel maintains an air of perfect calmness and strokes my fingers, trying to force relaxation into me like I'm hooked up to a drip.

"You've presumably heard by now that I've dropped the case and abandoned the plan," she adds.

I resist the temptation to point out that she has no official standing in the proceedings other than being one of the witnesses and that only the CPS could drop it. It's a technicality. Her inexplicable decision to stop preventing the vampires from perverting the course of justice and to help them make everyone forget the things they saw amounts to the same thing as settling.

"Yes. Why?"

Gabriel tightens his grip. "Sadie, for God's sake. This is irrelevant."

Lavinia laughs, oh so sweetly. "To spite you, of course. It was obvious how strongly you cared about it from the way you kept working after my control started to slip. And you were so close to getting justice for Cara and your human and smashing a hole in the establishment in the process. But I'm afraid it's not to be."

"But you cared about it, too."

"I can't deny I'd have gotten a certain kick out of weakening the vampires' influence. But this was mostly about personal revenge on Augustine. And my revenge priorities have changed."

I shake my head. "You really are an awful human being. My mistake wasn't just agreeing to the lien. It was ever associating with you in any way, shape, or form."

The fury is rising again, and with it, my magic. Attacking her would hurt me as bad if not worse than it hurt her. But the logical part of my brain is not controlling proceedings right now.

"Sadie!"

I drop my head on Gabriel's chest, half for comfort, half to avoid looking at Lavinia.

"Enjoy snuggling up together. I'll have the bracelets off by tonight, I promise."

This time, I keep my mouth shut and allow Gabriel to lead me outside and over to his car.

"Mannith?" he asks.

"Mannith, as fast as you can. I do not want to be on enemy territory when she regains control of her powers."

PART 4

THIRTY-FOUR

For most of the last few weeks—or at least, for those in which I was vaguely in control of my own mind—I'd been looking forward to coming back to Mannith for Christmas for the first time in six years. But I'd imagined rocking up on Christmas Eve, the car full of presents, ready to relax and celebrate. I hadn't counted on fleeing London.

For the last three hours, Gabriel's been driving his beloved Jag with utter disregard for speed limits, keeping us safe—from both accidents and the traffic police—through a combination of reflexes and magic.

Traversing would have been quicker, but you can't pass through the Dome using magic, and we'd have been defenceless against pursuers for the minute or so it took us to get across the barrier. As well as travelling extraordinarily fast, the car is fully warded. While we're inside it, we're basically invulnerable.

We've presumably got an hour or two on Lavinia, as she would surely have wanted to get the blockers removed before leaving London. The vampires wouldn't be able to help until the sun went down, and if any of her girls could do it, it'd take them a couple of hours.

We're both a bit unclear on what will happen if she gets them off while we're outside the safety of the Dome. The temporary blockage and whatever horrific lien-weakening magic Gabriel worked during sex should mean that despite a remnant of the lien still remaining, she won't be able to control me. But if nothing else, she'll have her powers back and be able to attack. And as I'm acting in defiance of a magic bargain, I'll be powerless to fight back.

Perhaps in deference to my mood, Gabriel's been uncharacteristically quiet and let the music on the car stereo do the talking. I alternate between gazing at him and staring out of the window. The motorway signs say "The North" and count down the number of miles to the big Yorkshire cities.

If this was the start of the Christmas of my dreams, we'd probably have taken a more scenic route and stopped for lunch halfway. Or at least stopped at some services to use the loos. But the risk's too great.

Eventually, we pass a sign welcoming us to South Yorkshire, and I sense Gabriel relax by a few degrees, though his speed doesn't slow. Twenty minutes later, we turn off the motorway just outside Sheffield, and his mood improves still further.

"Home ground," he murmurs. "It's not Mannith and the Dome, but it's a start if she does pursue us."

"Now you can breathe again, tell me five facts about yourself," I say, the first words I've spoken in hours.

"Sorry, what?"

"I left Mannith and said we couldn't be in a relationship just yet because we needed to get to know each other better. Instead, we've spent the past few months fighting, or not speaking, or screwing, or plotting with or against each other. I still barely know you as a person."

He grins, as though we're on a leisurely drive and not fleeing a vengeful, powerful practitioner.

"I love food, in an embarrassingly pretentious way," he says.

"Eating out, cooking, reading restaurant reviews, and foodie blogs. It's probably the one thing I tick off on your 'dream man on paper' list."

I smile. "I guessed that from the restaurant you took me to in the summer. Anyway, my first fact is that when I was at university, I was in the drama society. I think my best part was Blanche in Streetcar. You'd love my Louisiana accent. Very convincing."

"You've got to put the accent on for your next fact," Gabriel says. "But while we're on the subject of university, I wrote my undergraduate thesis on monks in late medieval France."

We drive through one nondescript small town, then out into the countryside. This close to the shortest day, it's already dark, though it's barely evening, and my eyes take a while to adjust to the lack of streetlights.

I pause before answering and try to remember all those hours of rehearsal. "For as long as I can remember, I wanted to be a lawyer, but it never seemed a realistic proposition. It's not exactly the sort of thing practitioners tend to do."

I'm not convinced I sound *exactly* like I'm from New Orleans, but it's not the worst attempt ever.

Gabriel looks like he's trying not to laugh. "I'll keep it simple for the next one. My favourite toy as a child was a cuddly purple frog called Felix."

"Do you still have him? Can I see him?" I let my voice return to normal, but some hint of a fake southern twang remains, just like it always did when I was doing the play.

"If we make it back to Mannith in one piece, absolutely. I've saved him for our future offspring to play with."

I shake my head. He really can't get the hang of dialling down the intensity. But I don't say anything angry or sarcastic in response, because the truth is that the idea of someday having a child with him makes me smile inside.

"I was absolutely awful at sport at school," I say quickly, before I can dwell on my reaction to his baby comment or he can pick up on it. "I still got picked for teams, because given my family name, not even the meanest kids dared to reject me. But I hated it anyway. It took me until well into my twenties to realise that exercise could be fun. More than fun—a real passion."

"I can't say sport or solo exercise has ever particularly appealed," Gabriel replies. "I like to walk in the countryside, but other than that, I'm afraid I rely on my powers to stay in shape.

"Next fact. I speak some Irish. But way, way less than I'd like to or my mum would have liked me to. It would be cheating to use magic to help me. All of that goes triple for the ancient language of the demons. Maybe we could practice together."

My heart beats a little faster—and between the threat of pursuit and the extended proximity to Gabriel, it was already pretty pacey. I'm used to practitioners, obviously. And increasingly, to vampires, much as I dislike them. But actual demons are something else again. I remember the threat he made to Augustine Piso. At some point, we need to discuss that side of his family properly. But it seems somewhat outside of the scope of this determinedly light-hearted conversation.

"Can you say something in the demon language?" I ask, as a compromise.

"Not without risking all sorts of trouble. Let's save that for when I'm not driving for our lives."

Before I can give my final fact (it was going to be a very straightforward one, about my favourite childhood book) we reach Rivley, the town next to Mannith, which for centuries has served as the best argument for the Dome and the meddling of practitioners.

The local council has made a bit of an effort for Christmas, but the LED lights glistening in the rain and the straggly tree highlight rather than hide its general rundown, under-invested air. For a crazy moment, I want to go and visit Leah, Bren's ex, who's living out her exile here after she betrayed him and the rest of the family. But we've got nothing to say to each other.

"It's a horrible night." I give an exaggerated shiver.

"That's Rivley for you. Give it ten minutes, and you'll have a crisp winter's evening to enjoy."

Suddenly, the car stops dead, with a force that throws us both back against our seats.

"What the hell?" I glance in the rearview mirror. There's another car behind us, on the otherwise deserted road. It wasn't there a moment ago.

"Lavinia. It has to be," Gabriel replies.

I reach out with my mind, and sure enough, her familiar, oppressive aura is emanating from the other car. There's wild, unchecked magic in it—the bracelets must have been removed. And though she drowns out everyone around her, I can tell she has company. Presumably several of her inner circle.

"How did she catch up? We've got a head start of hours."

"I guess they must have traversed the car along with them."

Before I can respond, a fireball hits our Jag. The car is well protected enough that it bounces off relatively harmlessly, but the impact shakes the vehicle.

"Can we do the same?"

Gabriel stares at the wheel, his eyes turning red. "We're ten minutes from the Mannith border. I'm just going to drive for our lives. Help me undo whatever she's done to the car, then I need you to focus on slowing her down while I concentrate on speeding us up."

He puts one hand on the steering wheel—a human formality he rarely bothers with—and clasps mine with the other. Together, we reach out our senses. The car's too well-protected for her to burn out the engine or even burst the tyres, but she's locked ethereal clamps onto each of the wheels.

While we try to work out what to do about that, another fireball hits. And with each second that passes, Lavinia's car is getting closer.

"There's no time for anything subtle," Gabriel says. "Just imagine those clamps blowing apart. You take the left, I'll take the right."

It'd be an easy spell if they were real clamps, imposed by a human traffic warden, but unpicking Lavinia's magic is an altogether more delicate procedure. Still, I focus, I grip Gabriel's hand, and then all four blow apart and the car shoots away down the road.

Gabriel has pushed the car to its limits for the whole journey, but now he goes beyond, powering the engine with magic rather than petrol. We must be moving at about three hundred miles per hour. Sadly, Lavinia's car is keeping pace.

I don't dare to open a window, but I twist in my seat and try to exert my will on her vehicle. Unsurprisingly, she's warded it as strongly as we have ours and nothing I do makes it stop or slow down.

I'm tempted to try their trick of a fireball, but the car is probably protected against that, too, and it'd be pushing my luck as far as the rules around not attacking Lavinia are concerned.

When they fire another one at us, I deflect it with my mind.

We're heading into a wooded area near the border. If I can't affect the car, I can at least affect the surroundings. Most of the trees are pretty scraggly and unimpressive, but I look upwards at a large oak and bring it crashing down in the middle of the road.

Lavinia's car brakes hard to avoid it. It's the work of seconds for her or her acolytes to vaporise it and be on their way again, but at these speeds and this short distance from the border, a few seconds here and there count for a lot.

Unfortunately, I seem to have given our pursuers an idea: leave the car alone, focus on the road. There's a sound like thunder, and a crater opens up in front of us.

"We'd better stop!" I shout. "Facing a murderous Lavinia's better than crashing and dying."

"Screw that. Turn round. Close your eyes. We're going over."

He puts his foot down again, or whatever the magical equivalent is, and the car speeds up still further. Even with all the magic he must have worked into it over the years, I'm not sure the seventy-year-old body of it is up to the strain.

I scream again as the car leaves the ground. We're above the crater. It's unclear whether the car is flying or just being propelled forward by sheer momentum. I hold my breath, close my eyes, and dig my nails into the seat. Then we hit the ground on the other side. The impact sends shudders through my body, but the car holds together, and Gabriel doesn't slow down.

I look behind me. Lavinia's car hesitates at the crater, then it, too, lifts off the ground. But that hesitation has bought us a few more precious seconds. By the time it lands on the other side, we've pulled away.

"Brace yourself," Gabriel whispers, as the strange and familiar shimmering outline of the Dome rears up in front of us.

"Let us through," I whisper. "And keep our enemies out."

The Dome probably knows this without needing to be told, but it can't hurt to give it a bit of encouragement.

Gabriel has to slow down to cross the barrier and Lavinia's car pulls closer again, but the chill of the crossing hits me, and then we're through, safe in a perfect winter evening in Mannith.

I watch in the mirror as Lavinia's car collides with the invisible barrier. It does it no harm, but it might as well be made of lead. They stop their engine and pour out. Lavinia, plus Lydia, Clarissa, and Katrina. They fire spell after spell at it, but nothing can take down the Dome or even force it to open against its will.

Gabriel slows still further, down to normal driving speeds. We pull away from the border until the furious London witches are out of sight.

THIRTY-FIVE

Just as Gabriel promised and just as I'd hoped, it's frosty but bright in Mannith, with the sky bursting with stars and a perfect crescent moon overhead. There are candles in every window and beautifully decorated trees everywhere.

"No snow yet," I say, trying to play it cool.

"Not till Christmas Eve, remember?"

Of course. The things you forget over time. Today's 21st December. The flakes start to fall at midnight on 24th as the bells ring out, and by the time the sun rises on Christmas morning, it's as deep, crisp and even as anyone could hope for. The official line is that earlier snow would interfere with people's shopping and partying, but I suspect that the Dome—or rather, the ancestor who created it—has a sense of drama and occasion.

Gabriel parks the car on a quiet backstreet in the old town. It's solid Sadler territory. Even he probably wouldn't have risked lingering there a few months ago. Or if he had, he'd have made a big, provocative scene. Things have genuinely changed.

He audibly exhales. "We should be safe for the moment. The Dome protects its own."

"We need to do something more permanent though," I

reply. "She can't physically hurt us when we're on this side and she's on the other, but I don't want to live under siege. And she can work against us in more subtle ways."

"Agreed. And it's Midwinter's Eve. The night the vampires would have helped us enlarge the Dome if the deal hadn't fallen over. It's the perfect time to strike."

"Strike how?"

"We need to draw up a plan. Do you want to go to the manor or your parents' house?"

He asks the question oh so casually, as though it's a simple matter of establishing which direction to drive in. But I can hear the unspoken issues: why I'm back, what our status is, what life I intend to lead.

"My parents' place, for now. I think a family conference is in order. Later, we'll see."

He turns on the engine. "Should you call ahead and make sure they're all gathered?"

"In a minute. Don't drive just yet. Let's get out and catch our breath."

He obliges. As soon as we're both standing in the crisp, clean air, I take his hand.

"Let's walk."

"We should probably either be resting or plotting."

"Humour me."

I lead him through the backstreets and out of town. The cold's intense, but it doesn't bother me. There's something wholesome and hearty about it.

I keep walking until we reach the town square, dominated by a massive Christmas tree that puts all the others to shame. There's a mini Christmas market, and I grab us both a mulled wine. A few people glance in our direction. Hardly surprising, considering that we're two of the town's most recognisable citizens, and not ones that you'd expect to see together, especially not hand in hand. But everyone's got enough sense of self-preservation not to approach us or make a comment.

"Did you just want to be festive, or is there a purpose to this?"

I sip the delightfully warming drink. Some mulled wines are sickly sweet, others almost bitter. It goes without saying that Mannith gets it right.

"There are things I've wanted to say all day," I begin. "But London seemed like the wrong place for the conversation. My words mean more here."

He's holding his own cup tightly, but making no move to drink. "Go on."

"I love you. I've said that before. I meant it then, and I mean it even more now. All the ups and downs of the past few months have given me time to reflect, and I know it's true. Deep down that's never really wavered."

He glances at the tree for a moment, as though trying to absorb its strength, then turns those unnatural eyes on me.

"I love you, too. I'm not sure you need me to confirm that yet again. But whenever you've claimed my feelings are recipro-cated, there's been a condition or a 'but'."

I gulp down the drink. "What I said before was that I felt love and lust, but nothing in between. So what I want to say, despite it making me sound like a six-year-old, is that now I also like you. A lot.

"You don't always go about things in the right way, and some of your attempts to prove you're a nice person and the one for me would make any sensible woman run a mile. But I don't care anymore. You've worked with my family. You've helped me fight my enemies. You've tried to protect this town. I like you. I think we could be good together—balance each other out, be greater than the sum of our parts.

"And so, once we've spoken to my family and worked out what to do about Lavinia, I want to go back to Thornber

Manor with you. And then, if you'll let me, I want to stay there."

"Come here." He puts his drink down, then pulls me into a tight embrace, pressing me against the soft wool of his coat. He tilts my head back and kisses me. Half the town are probably staring, but all I'm aware of is him.

"I like you, too," he says after a moment. "Just in case you were wondering."

An hour or so later, we arrive at my parents' house, on foot. We could have traversed, and we probably should have rescued the car, but we were united in our desire to walk there, hand in hand, admiring each other and the festive delights of our shared hometown.

By the time I ring the doorbell, my cheeks are flushed from the cold and the love.

I never did manage to call ahead, so my unrufflable father jumps when he opens the door and sees me there, then his eyes widen when he sees who I'm with, alliance or no alliance. It's probably a good job I'd already let go of Gabriel's hand. I don't want to keep this a secret, but we should probably tackle one issue at a time.

"Sadie! Come in, love, before you freeze. You too, Thornber. My house is your house, and all that."

I cross the threshold. It's odd to see Gabriel calmly do the same, odder still to watch him make his way to the sitting room and settle down on a sofa. Once, my family and their acolytes would have tried to kill him if he'd come anywhere near.

Before I can fully reflect on this, the whole family stream into the room. Even my little twin nieces are there, solemnly holding Ray's hands and already looking far older than they did four months ago when I last saw them in person.

It's unclear whether my siblings and the extended family

had already gathered—perhaps for a relaxing meal, perhaps for something more nefarious—or whether my father got a near-instant telepathic message to them and they traversed. No one but Liam still lives with my parents, but everyone still basically treats the converted row of terraced houses as their home.

Despite the tense circumstances, just stepping inside the family house is enough to relax me. It's gloriously warm, there are brightly coloured Christmas decorations everywhere, and a smell of baking gingerbread is emanating from the kitchen. Eighties songs are blasting from one room, a football game's playing loudly on the TV in another, and some toys belonging to the twins are scattered all over the floor. It's total chaos. But it's my own, personal, comforting chaos.

After my experiences over the last few weeks, my feelings about my family are broadly the same as my feelings about Gabriel. They have their flaws. But I love them and they love me. And right now, that's all that matters.

"Back in control of your own mind, then?" Liam says, flicking a finger to cut the music and the sport.

To my intense relief, he looks fully healed.

"Shut up, Liam," Chrissie snaps, even though she has every reason to be pissed off at me. She looks a little gaunt, a little pale. Still naturally beautiful, but as though she's got bigger things on her mind than keeping her enchanted beauty regime up. "Sadie, sit down. Get a drink. Tell us what's been going on and who we need to kill to make this right."

I sink into the seat next to her, pressed up against Gabriel. I'm hyperaware of his presence beside me, but am almost as conscious of Bren, seated at right angles to us and saying nothing.

Mum fixes me a gin. It's a straightforward Gordon's and Schweppes, but tastes better than the most artisan, hipster creations I've had in London. I drink it in one gulp, take a deep breath, then start to speak.

"Firstly, Liam, Chrissie, I'm so sorry I didn't come and help when you needed me. Like you say, I wasn't in control of my own mind, but that doesn't make it any less awful. I'm going to make all this right."

They both nod.

"I'm not going to claim I've never had a bad word to say about you over the last few weeks," Chrissie says. "But I knew something weird was going on. Even when you were in full blown exile, you cared about the family more than that."

"You're totally forgiven," Liam adds. "Not that there's really anything to forgive; it wasn't you making the decisions. Lavinia, on the other hand, is in no way, shape or form forgiven. What's going on with her?"

"Good news, the lien that she has been using to control me has been neutralised," I explain. "Bad news, she's out for blood, and she's got the power and connections to get it. She's waiting on the other side of the Dome."

There's silence for a long, drawn-out moment after I get that off my chest. And it takes a lot to make the entirety of my family, plus Gabriel, keep their mouths shut.

"Lavinia was always an ally. I'd even say a friend," Dad muses, eventually.

"She wanted more," I reply. "At some point, she er... offered more, right?"

Dad frowns. "There was a drunken evening, years ago, where she got very flirty. Your mum had just had Bren. I told her I was flattered but not interested. We maintained a business alliance for decades afterwards. I'd basically forgotten the conversation ever happened."

"Well, she hasn't. I don't know whether she saw you as the love of her life who got away, or just can't take rejection from anyone. But she's been looking for revenge ever since. And this year, she started to deliver it."

Mum shakes her head. "I never trusted her. I always thought the way she looked at you was inappropriate as hell."

"What happened thirty odd years ago doesn't matter," I say. "What matters is that she wants to hurt us all. Dad in revenge for turning her down. Mum for winning. Me for escaping her clutches. Gabriel for tricking her and blocking the lien. And all the rest of you just to maximise the hurt she can inflict. All the stuff she's done over the last few months was just a warm-up."

"So we need to kill her." Liam says what we're all thinking.

"And if we do it right, there could be another bonus," Gabriel says.

I frown. Now what's he plotting? Now what isn't he sharing?

"Killing someone that powerful would release a ton of power," he continues. "Get her in the right place and do it in the right way and we could use that power to enlarge and maintain the Dome without the vampires or the human sacrifices, especially on Midwinter's Eve. I was going to do it to Brendan, but I've been dissuaded."

Bren jumps to his feet. "Fuck you, Thornber!"

"It wasn't like I was hiding it. I told you as much at the alliance ceremony. But using Lavinia instead would be ideal."

Chrissie frowns. "But how do we get her to the right place? And if she's that powerful, how do we kill her?"

I shrug. "She's waiting at the border, near Rivley. I suggest Dad reaches out and tells her he wants to make things right."

"Surely she wouldn't buy that," Mum replies.

"She'd buy it," I say. "She's incapable of believing anyone could do anything but adore her. Besides, she'll want to seize the opportunity to get to me, and even if she suspects there could be a trap, she's arrogant enough not to feel the slightest hint of concern about the idea."

"That doesn't answer the second half of my question,"

Chrissie continues. "What do we do with her once she's in place?"

"Throw everything we've got at her, surely?" Liam replies. "However powerful she is, we've got the numbers and the home advantage."

I've got faith in my family. And in Mannith itself. The town would support us. But there's still a problem.

"You know the rules. Attacking someone over something they've done as part of a legitimate bargain means turning your power on yourself."

"Surely this doesn't fall into that category," Liam says. "The lien's broken. This is just self-defence."

If only I had access to the Lore Library. "Bargains are tricky things," I say. "And I've still got my mark, even if it's dormant now. If she directly attacks and we retaliate, then maybe. But luring her in, setting up a ritual, standing by with lethal spells at the ready—we'd all be taking a massive risk."

Bren stands up again. Other than his one moment of snapping at Gabriel, he's been so quiet I'd almost forgotten he was there. Part of me had been longing for him to join in the conversation so we could start to forge a truce. Another part wanted him to stay silent or perhaps even leave the room.

"She couldn't turn power back on someone who didn't have any," he says softly.

I stand up, too. "Bren, you don't need to go there."

He crosses the floor until he's standing in front of me. "Take what's left. That last third will only be a liability."

I hold out my right arm. It's half a gesture of pacification and reassurance, half slipping into the appropriate hand gesture to do what he's asking.

"Have I missed something?" Gabriel asks.

"This is family business," I reply. Our stock answer.

Bren shakes his head and turns towards Gabriel. "As punishment for what I did to Sadie, Dad decreed that each of my siblings would take a third of my power. Sadie refused, but Liam and Chrissie did what they were told. You were the last person in the world I wanted to know about this, but I guess I'm going to have to trust you for once."

I've never seen Gabriel look quite so stunned. Mouth open, weird eyes wide and flashing silver. Even coming from a place of love, it's quite satisfying.

"How the hell did I miss that? And how did Nikki fail to notice, given the amount of time she's been spending with you?"

Bren smirks like he's delivering a killer blow, despite having just revealed his weakness. "She promised she wouldn't tell you, but it was a struggle to believe her. So, it's nice to see you looking genuinely shocked."

Gabriel clenches a fist. "Why wouldn't she say anything? She was only spending time with you at my request. Keeping an eye on you. Looking for your weaknesses. Now you're telling me you were *all* weakness and she didn't pass that information on?"

It's only because I know my brother so well that I sense his sudden deflation at Gabriel's words. A slight hunching of his shoulders. A subtle dimming of the glow in his eyes and the colour in his cheeks. What the hell passed between him and Nikki?

When he speaks, though, there's no sign of what, to me, is his evident distress. "The point is, she's been teaching me how to do magic without relying on inherent power. So, I'm perfectly placed to take on Lavinia with impunity."

"A few half-hearted Learnt Practitioner tricks won't work against someone like her," Gabriel says. "You'd have struggled at your full power."

"I'd love to hear you say that to Nikki," Bren replies. "But I know my limitations. The key is that everyone else prepares the ritual, weakens and traps her, and strengthens me. Then I strike the killing blow."

"It's too risky," Mum says.

I shake my head. "It's the only way."

I'm not just thinking about how to stop Ms Morven. I'm thinking about how to save Bren's soul, restore his self-respect, restart our relationship.

Before anyone can argue further, I stretch out my hand until it's touching his chest and drag the last of his magic into me. He tenses, like he's about to change his mind, but I hold firm. I leave just the tiniest slither, enough for him to see the patterns we'll be putting into place. If Lavinia turned that back on him, it'd basically just give him a bad cold.

"Right, Dad, get on the phone," I say. "Grovel as sincerely as you can manage. Get her up here. Everyone else, let's get out to Summer Hill."

Going there, of all places, on Midwinter, seems perverse, but we are where we are.

"I'm calling Nikki," Gabriel announces. "Maybe she'll want to take advantage of having no tangible power that can be turned against her to join the front line, too."

He walks out of the room for the conversation. No doubt he'll also be having words about her keeping Bren's diminished state a secret. Much as I love Gabriel, I dread to think what he might have done to my brother if he'd known. Hopefully our relationship is now strong enough that I can keep him in check. But maybe I'm just being naïve.

"Thanks for doing that, sis," Bren says.

I shake my head. "When this is over, I'll give your magic back to you."

He smiles, and I almost dare to hope we could piece together a functioning sibling relationship again.

"What the hell's been going on with you and Nikki?" Chrissie comes to join us, lured by the scent of gossip like a hound following a trail. "That was not the expression of someone who thinks they've been betrayed by a platonic friend.

I didn't know she was into guys. And I certainly didn't know she was into Sadlers, or I might have hit on her myself a few years ago."

"What went on was that Thornber sent her to spy on me, and she complied." He says it with such finality that neither of us dares to ask a follow-up question.

"And you and Gabriel?" Chrissie looks determined to get something out of someone.

"I guess it's finally really happening," I reply.

But we've got to deal with Lavinia before I can start to think about what that means in practice.

THIRTY-SIX

Later that evening, I'm standing at the summit of Summer Hill, on Midwinter's Eve. It's freezing cold and the trees are bare of leaves and stark against the dark sky. You can see the lights of the town in the distance, but they might as well be on another planet.

It's hard to believe it's only a few months since I participated in my family's annual Ritual here, when the trees were full and the night was warm. And even less time since I stood in this same spot and almost killed Gabriel. Tonight, he's at my side, my hand in his.

Chrissie and Ray form another corner of the traditional triangle, with my mother and Liam completing it. The inclusion of men in the inner circle is a twist on the usual Ritual— something to do with tonight being about destruction as well as creation. Lavinia would not approve.

At the centre of the circle and the absolute peak of the hill, where my father normally holds court, Nikki and Bren are hand in hand as the ritual demands, but refusing to make eye contact with each other. A Taught Practitioner and one who's had almost all their plentiful natural power drained—the only people who could stand safely against Lavinia and against the Old Ways' zero tolerance attitude to fighting against fairly made deals.

Dad's in town, wining and dining the woman in question. A bit of an apology, a hint of a rekindling of an old flame. Then a trip out to the hill, to show his sincerity and sorrow by offering her access to our Dome and a better idea of how to create one of her own, in return for her formally renouncing her vows of revenge and her claims over me.

"Do you actually think she'll show?" Liam calls across the circle. "It's too obvious a trap."

I give him an exaggerated sigh in return. He and Chrissie have been rehearsing the same argument all day. "Her default assumption is that all men want her, all women want to be her, and anyone who strays from that path for a moment will be desperate to apologise and make amends."

Gabriel nods. "She's a smart woman. A powerful one, too. But her ego's her weak spot. It's the only reason my plan worked."

"Even if she's not arrogant enough to think Dad's whole-heartedly trying to make amends, she's definitely confident enough to think she can beat us if she is being led into a trap," I add.

"And are we sure she's wrong?" Chrissie huddles closer to Ray.

I expect a cocky response from some combination of Gabriel and Bren, who undoubtedly have more similar person-alities than either of them would like to admit. But they—and everyone else—remain uncomfortably silent.

"All we can do is give it our best shot," Nikki says eventu-ally. "And on that note, are we going to make a start?"

Bren nods, as though speaking to her in actual words would be a betrayal of everything he stands for. It's patently obvious that he's almost as hurt as he was when Leah betrayed him.

There are few people my brother really cares about, but when he does open his heart, he opens it wide.

"*Mannith is a blessed place,*" Bren intones, without further hesitation. "*It's always drawn something from the rivers and mountains that surround it, and for the last one hundred and fifty years, it's our power and our sacrifices that have protected it from the decay facing the wider country, the wider world. But that power must always be restored and maintained if we wish our beautiful town to flourish.*"

He and Nikki lift their arms as one, pointing them to the sky. Just like in the summer, I see the Dome—or at least, a physical representation of an intangible concept—glowing above me.

"*Tonight, we extend the Dome,*" Nikki proclaims, in a slight twist on the traditional wording, which focuses on maintenance rather than growth.

The two of them sink elegantly into a core meditation. Still holding tightly to Gabriel's hand, I begin to pace around the triangle, and the rest of the immediate family does the same. Beyond, more distant relatives and assorted acolytes—those loyal to the Sadlers and those allied to the Thornbers—move in concentric circles, just like those on our side do every summer. Our deadly plan is a whole-town affair. Just one more event in the festive calendar. That's how things work around here.

We continue through the steps of the Ritual. You're supposed to keep your mind blank, through a mixture of self-control, fasting, and potions. But I'm using only the most token hint of all three tonight. I need my subconscious to work the ancient, instinctive magic. But I need my conscious brain in easy reach in case everything goes horribly wrong.

At least I'm not conflicted. Last time, I was reluctant to participate at all, even when I thought we only cut the sacrifices, and I was utterly horrified when I learnt my family actually killed them. But tonight, with Lavinia as the potential sacrifice, I have no such scruples.

Power is buzzing in the air and across the earth, like it always does during the annual Ritual. It's drawn by Bren and Nikki's words and our movements, as well as by the concentration of magic in the blood of those forming the triangle.

I draw the power towards me, then clasp it to my chest and breathe. It's easier than last time. Several months of practising magic again means my control is much better and it's far less likely to tear me apart. Gabriel's hand on mine helps, too, both for moral support and for sharing the load.

We both draw a ceremonial dagger, from my garter and his belt. In the normal ritual, you cut the back of your own hand. Tonight, we need to do it to each other. The symbolic gesture is an odd mirror image of the very real damage we did to each other a few short months ago.

I fight to keep my hand steady. I love him. I trust him. I really do. But there's a bit of me, deep down, that can't entirely shake off the suspicion that he's playing us all and is going to slice open an artery instead of nicking a vein.

I gasp as our two daggers each make contact with the other's skin. Partly from the sudden hot pain in my hand, partly from the horror of cutting him. A split second later, we withdraw our weapons, clasp our hands together again, and raise them to the sky. He's done me no more harm than what the ritual demands. If he is playing us, he doesn't intend anything this crude. And I've not lost control and hurt him either.

"*We give our power to the sky and our blood to the earth.*" Nikki chants the traditional words as our blood drips down and our power surges upwards. "*We give ourselves to Mannith to secure its protection.*"

Bren opens his eyes. "*Blood and magic are worthy gifts. But our Dome must be strong and for it to grow, a truly great sacrifice is needed.*"

And in the normal run of things, this is where the participants would each stab some poor volunteer to death in order to give the Dome what it wants. But today, we wait. The Dome is ready, and the trap is set. We just need our great sacrifice to sashay into the circle. And pray she turns up tipsy, enamoured, and unawares, not on her guard and spoiling for a fight.

Waiting for what could be an ambush or could be a fight to the death wouldn't be wildly relaxing at the best of times. But it's made a thousand times worse by the fact we're having to keep the magic alive and waiting without letting it dissipate, take us over, or tear us in two. My control may be a lot better than it used to be, but is it really this good? It's only been a few minutes, but my hands are burning and my vision's blurring. We really have to hope that Dad and Lavinia aren't going to linger over the meal. It's a good job she tends to avoid desserts and coffee.

By the time Dad and Lavinia traverse into the centre of the clearing, my muscles are shaking and I can barely see, such is the strain of keeping the Dome's magic live but under control. But as soon as she appears, I take a deep breath and strengthen both my resolve and my spell. The other five people who form the inner triangle do the same, while Nikki and Bren slip into fighting stances.

"What a beautiful spot," Lavinia drawls, her eyes on my father in a way that'd be pretty sickening even if I wasn't his daughter and she wasn't my worst enemy.

Instead of replying, he immediately traverses away again, like we all agreed in advance. The circle of strong practitioners just beyond our triangle throw up their arms and form a cage of power to stop her doing the same once she realises something's wrong. There's not a single person in that outer circle who could hope to stand against Lavinia alone, but if they hold their nerve, then sheer force of numbers should achieve the desired effect.

"Philip?" Lavinia whispers my father's name, then looks around.

Even from several metres' distance, I can see in her eyes the exact moment she realises we've tricked her. To her credit, she doesn't try to flee. Nor does she rant and rave or launch an attack. She gives me a respectful nod, one powerful woman to another. She gives Gabriel the dismissive scowl you'd bestow on an ex from years ago that you've long since regretted ever having dated. And then she ignores the rest of us and strides towards Bren, for all the world as though she isn't caught in a trap.

"Brendan Sadler. You're everything your father was thirty years ago, only more so. More handsome. More powerful. More cunning. I made a mistake trying to rake over the past when I could be focusing on the future."

She's beautiful in the moonlight as she sashays into Bren's personal space. I've been so consumed with hate for her these last few weeks that I'd forgotten just how attractive and charming she naturally is, and how she can enhance those quali-ties still further when she puts her mind to it.

"I'm not powerful anymore," Bren whispers.

I don't know whether he's baring his soul or attempting to lull her into a false sense of security. I'm praying it's the latter. Bren's always tended to be the seducer rather than the seduced. But after Leah betrayed him and after whatever has or hasn't happened between him and Nikki recently, he seems oddly vulnerable to her charms.

Lavinia shrugs then runs a slender finger down his arm. "I know all about your family's silly punishment. But a temporary lack of magical firepower doesn't change anything. Power is your birthright. You've got the tank. I can help you fill it up again."

At my side, Gabriel tenses. Which is pretty impressive, considering we were both already about as tense as it seemed physically possible to be. "Please tell me this entire plan isn't now hinging on Brendan-fucking-Sadler choosing to do the right thing."

I don't reply. I'm far too consumed by the spell to utter a single word. God knows how he's holding a conversation while keeping the magic flowing, but that's Gabriel for you.

He's being a bit unfair to my brother. I'd be the first to admit he's done some awful things, but I still believe he's a decent guy at heart. Though if Lavinia really does have a way to restore his power, I wouldn't want to stake my life on him resisting temptation. So it's unfortunate we're doing exactly that.

Bren throws up a bubble of protection. It's a laborious process compared to the way he'd once have done it, relying on incantations and pronounced hand gestures, rather than simply willing it into being. But he does it quickly and it looks solid. He really can do magic in the Taught Practitioner style, and he's not stupid enough to simply stand there listening to Lavinia's spiel and risk her blowing him apart.

"How would you restore my powers?"

My momentary confidence fades again as soon as Bren asks the question. There's hope in his eyes. He doesn't appear to just be stalling for time.

"In much the usual way," Lavinia replies. "By taking it from someone else. The trouble is that no one's up for giving you the amount you need as a gift, and you don't have the strength to take it by force."

"But you do." He sounds contemplative, working it out as he goes, running both the logistics and the pros and cons through his mind. "So you'd overpower someone for me. Then open a channel between us."

Lavinia's smile is predatory as hell. "Precisely. And I suggest we make use of Mr Thornber. No one else has quite the firepower you deserve. Besides, I think we'd both rather enjoy that."

"Does she really think she can take me in a fair fight?" Gabriel muses. "Has she got some backhanded plan? Or is she just toying with him?"

It's painful to speak, but I force out a warning. "You can't leave your spot in the circle or let the spell drop. If you did, best case is that the magic would tear you and probably the rest of us apart. Worst case, the Dome would implode."

Which was precisely what he wanted just a few short months ago, but I'm reasonably confident that his thinking's moved on since.

"And even I'm going to struggle to fight her off with one hand while keeping all this force in check with the other," he says.

"Exactly. If she attacks you, she also risks destabilising everything. But I suspect she's past caring."

Before anyone can say another word, Nikki shoots a fireball at Lavinia.

Lavinia screams, spins around, and blocks the attack.

"I've always thought there was something rather pathetic about Learnt Practitioners. But then again, most of the ones I've come across have been men, and they're pretty pathetic at the best of times. You, on the other hand, have got magic and you've got guts."

Nikki's moving her hands and muttering under her breath as quickly as she can, readying another fireball.

"Please don't do that, sweetheart," Lavinia continues. "Just then, you had the element of surprise. You did a great job, but I stopped you easily. If you carry on, you're going to get yourself hurt. Leave. And tomorrow, when all this is over, come and join my coven."

Nikki shakes her head violently as fresh fire blooms between her palms. "I've heard about what happens to my sort of practitioner in your coven. And even if I believed you'd welcome me as an equal, I'm loyal to this town and this alliance. And so is Brendan."

Lavinia laughs, seemingly unperturbed by either her magic or her conviction. "Brendan, what do you say? Do you care about the family that's ground you down and the old enemy who's taken your place, or do you want power and position back?"

Bren looks between the two women. "If you helped me get my power back, what would happen next? Would you just drift off back to London while I took control of Mannith? Would you take over the town? Or something in between?"

"We can work out the exact arrangements over a drink. I'd want some control over the Dome and some information on how to create my own, like your father promised, but I wouldn't want to cheat you out of anything that was rightfully yours."

"Bren, for goodness' sake," Nikki snaps. "Stop even discussing this. Think about what she's done to your family. Think about what she might do to the town. Help me fight her."

Bren drops his head in his hands. "You don't understand. Losing my powers makes me feel like I've lost a leg and lost my soul all at the same time."

"How can you say that, to me of all people? Sure, I don't know what it's like to *lose* powers, but I know what it's like to long for them. I grew up surrounded by powerful practitioners. I was often the only person in the room who couldn't remodel the universe to their whim. Do you know how many times Gabe and I experimented in our early teens with ways to give me true magic?"

"But it was impossible," Bren says. "That must have hurt, but you never had to make the choice. Can you honestly tell me that if there'd been a way, you wouldn't have taken it, whatever the cost?"

Nikki raises her arms, ready to fire. "Sure I can. Because in the end, we found a way. But it involved the less salubrious branch of Gabriel's family. Demonic possession, basically. Grim as it sounds, I was tempted. But I said no."

Bren closes his eyes. "I'm sorry I don't have your strength."

Nikki screams in frustration and fury, then releases her fireball. Lavinia gets her shields up in time, but it's close, and Nikki's already reloading.

"We need to help," Gabriel says, with way more panic in his voice than I'd usually expect. "Nikki's a brilliant practitioner, full stop. But she's not equipped for dealing with someone on Lavinia's scale alone."

"We can't leave the circle. We can't fight." I'm aching to help my friend and to strike at the woman who came close to ruining my life, but we simply can't.

"I was really hoping for a bit of female solidarity with you," Lavinia says, dodging another attack. "Perhaps even the start of a beautiful friendship. But I'm afraid you just don't know when to stop."

She casually raises her arm, more for effect than necessity, and Nikki is thrown across the clearing by an unseen wind. She hits the ground, spasms, and goes still.

I scream, and it's echoed by her friends up and down the hill in the various concentric circles. Gabriel doesn't scream. He goes deathly still beside me and the magic we're trying to keep under control starts to flare.

I grip his hand. "I'm pretty sure she's still breathing. We'll get her the help she needs."

"Lavinia's going to kill her," he whispers. "And even if she decides to leave Nikki alone, we're stuck here until either she's killed, she kills us, or the Dome and this enhancement spell destroys us all. And the only one who can kill her is your nightmare of a brother."

"He'll do it. He might have been wavering, but he won't leave Nikki to die."

"He's taking that bitch's hand. I should have destroyed him when I had the chance."

It's true. And now they're walking towards us, hand in hand.

Lavinia smiles when she reaches me and Gabriel, though Bren's expression is carefully blank.

"I can't say I'm wildly happy with your sister, but I assume you'd prefer that I let her live, with her powers, her mind, and her freedom intact?"

"God, yes," Bren says, as though the concept that Lavinia might harm me has only just crossed his stupid mind.

"Then we'll focus on this bastard." She runs a finger down Gabriel's chest. He doesn't flinch. "Let go of his hand, Sadie, darling. Or you'll be caught in the crossfire, and your lovely brother will be terribly upset."

I grip Gabriel's hand harder and glare at her.

"I'll try my best not to hurt her, Brendan, I promise. But if she will be stubborn, there's only so much I can do."

"Let go, sis, please. I don't want you to get hurt."

"It didn't bother you in the summer. I can't believe I thought you might actually have changed."

Gabriel turns to me and pries my hand free. "You won't be any use as a human shield. He doesn't give a damn about anyone."

I squeeze his hand once, then let it drop. "I love you."

"I love you, too."

With that, Gabriel seems to zone me out. "Brendan, I know there's no point asking you not to hurt me. And probably not much point appealing to your better nature in general. Just promise me you won't let Lavinia hurt Sadie and that you'll get Nikki help."

Before Bren can respond, Lavinia touches her palm to Gabriel's chest and taps her fingers three times, opening a channel. Only a sharp intake of breath hints at the combination of fear and pain that must be afflicting him.

There's no one who can touch him for sheer level of power and he's honed his natural skills to their limit. Lavinia's one of the few people who's in the same sort of league, but even she would have no chance of pulling this off in normal circumstances—all that vampire blood she's ingested over the years is no match for his demon heritage. But right now, we're stuck in a web of our own making, and so is anyone who might be willing and able to help.

Lavinia places her other hand on Bren's chest. I'd assumed she was going to literally or metaphorically stab him in the back, but she appears to be honouring her side of the deal. "Kneel and take what's yours," she intones.

Magic flows out of Gabriel, through Lavinia, and into my brother. Lavinia is serene, obviously delighted with the turn the evening's taken. Bren is shuddering as the unfamiliar magic is pumped into him. Gabriel's still just about managing to put a brave face on things, but the pain in his eyes hurts me in turn. And with the best will in the world, he's going to lose control at some point. First of the magic, then of himself.

My blood is pounding, and my vision is clouding over. I twist my head from side to side, glancing around the clearing, hoping someone's coming to save us. Our best bet seems to be Nikki waking up, but that's looking less and less likely by the second. And even if she snapped back to consciousness, she'd be in no fit state to fight, even if she were capable of standing against Lavinia in the first place.

When Dad traverses back into the clearing, it's like the answer to all my prayers. He looks around, seeming to take the measure of the situation immediately.

"Dad, you've got to stop her!" I shout.

Lavinia closes her eyes and sighs. "Once upon a time he may well have been able to. But unlike me, he made the mistake of letting himself grow old. He'll have to content himself with the success of his son and heir."

Gabriel lets out a little gasp that appears to be his equivalent of an agonised scream. His hands shake and the magic around us starts to waver.

"If you break him any further, you'll blow us all to pieces. Stop, please," I beg. "Maybe we could all give a bit of magic to Bren."

"That'd be far less fun," Lavinia replies, but she glances up at the swirling magic in the sky with some concern.

"Gabriel, have you got the spell under control for now?" Bren asks the question through gritted teeth.

Gabriel gives him a "not going to dignify that with an answer" scowl of affirmation.

"Dad, do you want to close the Ritual?" Bren adds.

Lavinia nods. "Good idea. Shut this down. We don't want any more deaths than are necessary. And we don't want the Dome getting ruined. Not if I'm going to be given a controlling stake in it."

"*We give our power to the sky and our blood to the earth,*" Dad intones. "*We give ourselves to Mannith to secure its protection. Blood and magic are worthy gifts. But our Dome must be strong and for it to grow, a truly great sacrifice is needed.*"

Lavinia stares at him, fascinated.

And then Bren reaches out across their connection. Suddenly, the flow of magic is different. Nothing more is leeching out of Gabriel. And Bren is using the power he's already taken and the channel Lavinia has forged to pull her own magic forcibly into himself.

She screams and tries to break free, but she forged the bond too strongly.

"I once told someone that given the choice between saving someone he loved or killing someone he hated, he'd choose love," Bren muses. "But the best scenario of all is when you can do both with one stroke."

Lavinia's glamour fades. For a second, there's a ninety-year-old woman standing there, elegant and well-preserved, but looking her age. And then she falls apart.

There's blood and unconstrained power everywhere.

"Do it," Bren screams.

It takes me a second to understand what he means and another second to get over the shock enough to move, but then I pace around the triangle again, three times in total, the traditional end to the Ritual. I have to drag Gabriel around, but we make it.

"*Blessed be this town,*" all six of us cry out in unison.

The circles of people below stop moving. The fires around the circle extinguish then ignite again. The Dome flares above us like the northern lights. And then, as we all collapse to the ground in exhaustion and exultation, it starts to grow.

For a few seconds, I just stare at the expanding Dome, too dumbfounded to move or even think. Everyone else seems to be taking the same approach.

Slowly, though, reality kicks back in. Lavinia's dead, the Dome's expanded without any wider bloodshed—which presumably also means we can maintain it without further sacrifices—and best of all, Bren not only didn't betray us, he actually pulled all this off. But it doesn't change the fact that Gabriel is barely conscious. Right now, I'd throw away all our other gains if it could make him better.

"Bren, you need to pump magic back into him," I call.

At first, I'm not sure he's physically able to hear me. From his wide eyes and glazed expression, it's as though the combination of strain and success has temporarily pushed him onto another plane of existence.

"I know it must be the last thing you want to do," I add. "But I'm begging you."

Bren snaps out of his trance and stumbles over to me. "I'll do it. For your sake, because it's the right thing to do, and because I don't need his power anymore. But I'm going to deal with Nikki first."

I nod, abashed. I'd selfishly almost forgotten about her injuries, that worry drowned out by exhilaration at Bren's victory and alarm about Gabriel. But she's still collapsed where she fell.

"Wouldn't you be better leaving it to Chrissie? Healing's never been your forte."

"I'm going to do it. Then I promise I'll mend your boyfriend, too." His voice leaves no room for argument.

"Just one thing before you do," I say. "Was that your plan all along, were you making things up on the spot, or did she really almost turn you?"

He shrugs. "A bit of all three."

That's probably the most anyone's ever going to get out of him on the subject. It's hard not to suspect he almost betrayed us all to Lavinia for power, only changing his mind at the last moment. But maybe I'm being unfair. I guess all that matters is that he did the right thing in the end. Maybe it even makes up for what he did in the summer.

The rest of the family rouse themselves from their semi-stupors and watch as Bren strides over to Nikki. He scoops her up into his arms. I'm expecting more of the same effective but drawn-out manual magic he used during the fight. Instead, he waves his arm once in a leisurely fashion and Nikki instantly opens her eyes.

For a moment, I think he's going to kiss her and even through my panic about Gabriel and my shock at the events of the evening, the idea fills me with a wild joy. Instead, Bren gives her one appraising glance, then sets her down on her feet and walks away.

Nikki reaches out an arm and grabs him. "What the hell happened? Last thing I remember, I was giving a completely one-sided fight my best shot, and you were going over to the dark side."

Bren gives another of his infuriating shrugs. "I killed Lavinia and expanded the Dome in the process. You fought like an absolute star, but she knocked you out. I've healed you. I suggest you go and find your friends in one of the outer circles."

He shakes her off and strides back over to me.

"What the hell was that?" I whisper to him. "You're acting like she's a passing acquaintance you did a minor favour for."

"That's basically the truth," he replies, with yet another bloody shrug.

"*It's nice not to have to choose between killing someone I hate and saving someone I love,*" I paraphrase. "We all heard you."

"Do you want me to fix Gabriel-fucking-Thornber or not?"

I cross my arms. "Give Gabriel his power back, and I'll keep my mouth shut for now. But I am totally going to pursue this Nikki thing later."

"Can you support him in a sitting position?" Bren sounds incredibly matter of fact, a doctor dealing with a patient.

I kneel down and drag Gabriel up with me. Bren perches on the grass in front of us.

I ought to be nervous. Bren could do a variation on the trick he pulled on Lavinia—open up a channel and then drain Gabriel of the little magic and life he has left. But I trust him to do the right thing. If only because Nikki would never speak to him again if he hurt Gabriel. And we both know that would matter to him.

Bren places his hand against Gabriel's chest and touches their foreheads together. Quickly and efficiently, he taps his fingers against Gabriel's chest and opens the channel. It's usually difficult to force magic into an unresponsive person, but it's Gabriel's own, distinctive magic that was dragged out of him, and it seemingly can't wait to return to its rightful home. As a result, it's like pouring water downhill.

The colour returns to Gabriel's face almost immediately, and it's only a minute or two before he wakes up. I want to shriek, hug him, kiss him—but anything like that could be dangerous, so I content myself with a gentle squeeze.

"What the hell is going on?" Gabriel raises an arm as though he's about to blow Bren away.

"I'm giving you back the magic Lavinia drained away," Bren says, pushing his hand down. "My sister was very determined on that point. But one smart-arse remark, and I swear I'll leave you powerless."

"You could keep a little, if you like," Gabriel says. "I'm impressed you resisted Lavinia's offer. I'm not sure I could have in your position."

Bren keeps channelling the magic in. "You can have all yours back. I got all of hers for myself."

THIRTY-SEVEN

"I'm happy for Bren," I muse, curled up on a fur rug by the fireplace at Thornber Manor the following evening. It's a cold house with its stone walls and floors, but this spot is toasty warm. "Yet he was well on his way to learning that he didn't need innate power to be great. Instead, he's more powerful than ever."

Gabriel wraps his arm even tighter around me. "I think he learnt plenty. And I used to hate the idea of him having so much power, because I didn't trust him not to abuse it. I do now... more or less."

It was well into the early hours by the time I got to bed. After the exhaustion of the drive and the ritual, I took a moment to check my back in the mirror. Once I'd established the lien mark was finally entirely gone, I fell straight asleep, alone, at my parents' house. I slept for most of the morning, then I spent the afternoon making Chrissie's legal problems go away.

There wasn't actually that much for me to do. Whatever complicated web of lies Lavinia had put in place had mostly fallen away with her death. As a result, the Home Office, child protection, the Crown Prosecution Service, and anyone else she'd set against Chrissie would probably have dropped their respective cases for lack of evidence. I just helped the process along by changing their records. The look on my sister's face when I told her there was nothing more to worry about was one of the most beautiful things I'd ever seen.

An hour or so ago, I finally made it over to Thornber Manor, ready for dinner and whatever else the night might have in store.

"And do you have any clue at all on this whole Bren and Nikki thing?"

He shakes his head in frustration. "I can't get a word out of Nikki about it. And we usually tell each other everything."

"Why did you send her to spy on him?"

"Because I'm a paranoid, controlling dickhead?"

"From now on, we're doing this alliance properly. No lies. No mistrust. No factions. I thought we could seal it the medieval way."

He frowns in confusion.

I look at the floor, then stare at one of the tapestries on the far wall. Finally, I manage to force my gaze back to him and stare into his weird eyes, just like everyone used to warn the Sadler faithful not to do. I twist my hair around my fingers. It's so hard to get the words out. There's no way he'd say no, surely. But that logical certainty refuses to reach my subconscious or my body.

"I thought medieval history was your specialist subject," I say eventually, my voice shaking in a way it never does in court. "Seal it with a dynastic marriage, I mean."

Pressed this close to him, I can feel his heart rate increase and his breathing deepen. But even from the other side of the room, I'd have been able to see the wild, multi-coloured flare in his aura and in his eyes. It's hard to catch him off guard, but I appear to have managed it.

"Sorry, are *you* proposing to *me*?"

I smile and lower my eyelids. Now the words are out, all my nerves are gone. "Is there a problem with that?"

"I just assumed that if I ever managed to move things to this stage, I'd be the one doing the proposing. I've done most of the chasing."

"Did you have some incredibly elaborate plan that you've been working on since you were about seventeen?"

He laughs, sounding half amused, half genuinely stunned. "Have you ever known me not to have a plan? But that's not important. Yes. My answer is yes."

I slip his ring off my finger and onto his little finger, where it just about fits.

He looks at it there, grins, then wriggles it back off and slides it onto my finger. The ring finger of my left hand this time, where you'd expect an engagement ring to sit.

I hold my hand out and just stare at it for a moment. I've worn the ring for a while, on and off. But now, it's imbued with a totally different meaning.

Happiness suffuses my body. All I want to do is kiss him, cling to him, undress him. Instead, I make myself speak.

"Before we go any further, is there anything else I ought to know? Any secrets, any plots, any old promises? I don't think there's anything you could say that would make me change my mind or regret my decision, but I can't bear for you to be hiding anything from me."

He closes his eyes and appears to be giving the question genuine consideration. I'm starting to worry that he's taking too long and is going to come out with either an absolute litany of terrible revelations or else a total lie, when he opens his eyes again and vigorously shakes his head.

"No. There's nothing more like that, I promise. You've accepted me at my worst. It's time you got me at my best."

Then he pulls me in for a kiss and lays me down on the rug. I've never felt more content, more certain that I'm making the right decision. My heart rate and breathing are slow and steady. My aura's like a gently lapping stream. All the stress of the last few months fades into nothing.

"You probably had some incredibly well-thought-out wedding plan, too, didn't you?" I ask, once I finally come up for air. "But I don't want to waste any time or risk things going wrong. You. Me. A few friends and family on each side. The Witches' Church. Christmas Eve—which has the double benefit of being one of the most magical nights of the year and only a few days away. What do you say?"

"I told you once I'd always intended to marry in the Witches' Church. You must have known I meant to you. And believe it or not, I've always had Christmas Eve at the back of my mind. Or a winter wedding at any rate."

"Then let's get the news out. Chrissie can make me a dress. Mum can create a cake and a feast. And I'm sure between us and the rest of the congregation, we can sort out most of the other details without too much trouble."

"Let's. But first, I want to take my fiancée to bed. Six times really isn't enough."

I kiss him again then smile dreamily as he helps me to my feet. The same expression is reflected on his face.

We're halfway up the stairs when someone knocks on the door. The sound echoes through the stone walls, magically amplified.

I glance back towards the hallway. Somehow, it seems unlikely to be a casual visitor, and even less likely to be good news. I pause, close my eyes, and let my vision move down the stairs, through the hallway, and beyond the solid walls of the old manor.

"Charles? Tristan? What the hell?"

I open my eyes a split second before Gabriel opens his, having clearly pulled the same trick.

Most vampires can't come into the Dome at all. Tristan will

already have been invited into Mannith for prior negotiations. But presumably never into Thornber Manor.

"I can't think of a single good reason for the vampires to send their lawyers to Mannith," Gabriel muses.

"Are we going to let them in?"

"Not a chance. But we'll stand this side of the doorstep and hear what they have to say."

Despite his cautious tone, Gabriel is all smiles when he opens the door. "Tristan. Charles. So nice to see you both again."

They're all smiles, too. Which is particularly disconcerting in the case of Tristan, who, away from London, in the enchanted air of Mannith, is making no effort at all to hide his fangs.

"Mr Thornber. Such a shame you declined to stay on our team. Still, no hard feelings. Besides, we're here to see your... friend."

"Fiancée," I say, with an equally wide grin.

Tristan's eyes widen. If Charles feels the slightest hint of joy or shock, he does an excellent job of keeping the emotion away from his face.

"We are here half on behalf of Lord Piso, half on behalf of the estate of Lavinia Morven."

I frown. "Lavinia's estate? How the hell is that in your hands?"

"She spoke to us before travelling north," Charles replies. "With the case settled, there was no further bad blood. She suspected she might not survive the trip. She needed a watertight will in place, and she needed lawyers who understood the supernatural aspects."

"And what, I'm a beneficiary?"

Tristan waves a hand. "Let us deal with Lord Piso's matters first."

"Fine." But my mind's already rushing ahead to whatever

elaborate punishment Lavinia might have left me lurking in her will.

"Firstly, you will be glad to know we have already executed Hugo Latham in the traditional manner. Staked to the ground by his arms and legs at midnight so that he burnt to death when the sun rose. He was a disgrace to the fine reputation of our organisation."

Gabriel raises an eyebrow. "Because he killed someone, or because he got caught?"

"A little of both. Plus, he was just so uncouth. I hope Ms Sadler will consider it justice of a sort for her friend."

"Of a sort, yes. I'd still rather he'd faced a guilty verdict in court. And that your organisation's 'fine reputation' had been rather dimmed as a result."

Tristan acts like he hasn't heard me. "The second point of business was to offer a reinstatement of the previous agreement between Lord Piso and his organisation and the Mannith Alliance. It's clear now that most of the discord we were concerned about was Ms Morven's doing."

"There's no need for it anymore," Gabriel replies. "We've enlarged our Dome without your help. No strings attached."

"So I gathered on the journey here. The towns out beyond Mannith are glowing with new colour and purpose. But perhaps we could agree a friendliness going forward? A mutually beneficial, ad hoc business partnership?"

Gabriel shrugs. "Maybe. We can certainly be on broadly friendly terms. Whether we want to formalise or commit to anything beyond that is a question for my alliance partners."

Tristan slowly lowers his head. "Noted. I will take that response back to Lord Piso. If you ever want to reformalise things, the offer is on the table and you know where to find us."

"And Lavinia's will?" I can't contain myself anymore.

Charles stares at me. "She's left you her house. And control of the London Coven."

It's the most emotion I've ever seen him show, but it's nothing compared to the whirlpool of contradictory feelings that take hold of me. Gabriel's still holding my hand, and he goes painfully still.

"Why would she do that?" I ask.

"Don't ask me to second guess that crazy bitch," Charles replies. "What? I'm a lawyer who specialises in disputes involving vampires. If I refused to speak ill of the dead, I'd never get any work done."

I'd laugh, were the situation not so disquieting. I turn to Gabriel, holding out my hands as though begging him to enlighten me.

"Did she secretly always like and admire me? Is she trying to make amends? Or still trying to control me from beyond the grave? Maybe it's a trap, and if I went back, the other coven members would kill me on her instructions?"

"I have zero clue," Gabriel replies. "Despite the fact she did nothing but talk about herself on our fake dates, I never got much insight into how she actually thought."

"It cannot be the last option," Tristan says, still entirely calm and neutral. "Members of the London Coven swear an oath to its leader, not to Lavinia Morven. The protection of that oath should pass seamlessly from one leader to the next. The witch is dead, long live the witch, that sort of thing."

"And if they tried to ignore their vow? Refused to serve me at best, killed me in revenge for Lavinia at worst?"

"My understanding is that it is not quite as all-encompassing as the sort of lien she forged with you, but breaking it would be physically difficult. And if they managed, that would have repercussions for their magic, health, and sanity."

I close my eyes for a second. I could go back to London on my terms. Have power and people at my command. And at the most basic level, stop the coven from seeking revenge.

I shake my head as vigorously as I can manage to drive the

images away. "I don't want it."

"Excuse us a moment." Gabriel takes my arm, pulls me aside, and throws up a bubble of silence around us.

"I don't want it, honestly," I repeat, in answer to the question burning in his red eyes.

"It would give you the balance you always wanted. Magic and your legal career. London as a base, with the ability to leave. Friends without cutting off your family."

"That's not the life I'm looking for anymore."

"I don't want to trap you here. I don't want to make you sacrifice your career and your life."

I put a hand on his chest. "You kind of do, though, if you're honest with yourself, don't you? You literally had a years-long plan to get to this outcome."

He drops his head into his hands. "Fine. If you walked out of that door right now, there's a dark part of me that would immediately start coming up with strategies to make you come back. There's a darker part of me that would long to literally trap you. But I've got those parts under control."

"I didn't believe you in the summer, and that's why I wouldn't commit. I believe you now, and that's why I proposed. And nothing Lavinia can offer me from beyond the grave could make me change my mind."

I glance out beyond the bubble. Charles and Tristan are still there, standing still and quiet with their arms crossed, watching and waiting. Then I turn back to Gabriel, and as always, the rest of the world fades away to nothing.

"I'm not just making this choice because of you. Admittedly, you're probably the deciding factor, but I'm choosing my family, too. I'm choosing Mannith. I believe I can balance that with the things I believe in and not get sucked in too deep—especially now we've removed the need for the annual sacrifices. And you don't know me at all if you think I'm giving up my legal career—I've got a plan."

Gabriel pulls me into an embrace, and any lingering shred of doubt fades away. I click my fingers and the bubble of silence falls away.

I extract myself from his arms and turn to face the lawyers. "As I was saying, I don't want it."

Tristan shakes his head in the most languorous fashion. "It is not something you accept or turn down. Both the legal documentation and the underpinning ritual leave no room for debate. The title and everything that goes with it passed from the deceased to you at the moment of her death."

"Presumably I could ignore it. Stay here. Avoid the other members."

The head movements intensify. "London and the coven would call to you. The call would be hard to resist. And if you somehow managed, it would break you down over time."

"I presume the coven's inner circle is still lingering just outside Mannith?" I try to imbue my voice with a certainty and determination I don't really feel.

"Why don't you take a look?" Gabriel grabs a decorative dish from the windowsill in one hand and a vase of flowers in the other, tips the water from one to the other, then hands me the makeshift scrying bowl.

I don't really need to scry to find out what someone's up to —now I'm regularly practicing proper magic again, I could close my eyes and bring the visions straight into my head. But it's a type of formal magic I've always enjoyed.

I swirl my engagement ring-clad finger in the water and think about the people I want to see. At first, the water ripples in response to my movements, then the eddies and waves take on a life of their own. Once it stills again, Clarissa, Lydia, and Katrina are as clearly visible as if they were in the room with me.

They're still where I left them. I didn't pay much attention on the way in, considering we were fleeing for our lives, but I had a vague impression of scraggly trees and weeds growing on the verge. Now, the road is smooth, the trees are all magnificent oaks and pines, and the weeds are festive holly bushes, covered in blood-red berries. It looks to be a cool, crisp night, just like in Mannith. The area is under the protection of the Dome now.

"I need to see what Rivley looks like," I say, thinking of Mannith's rundown neighbouring town.

"Beautiful, I expect," Gabriel replies. "But it's not just these outlying areas. The effect gets weaker the further out you go, but we reached a good few neighbouring towns."

"This is absolutely insane," I whisper. Somehow, I completely take for granted the unutterably weird effects the Dome has on Mannith, because it's always been that way. But seeing it replicated on a larger scale feels like real magic.

"Are you going to speak to the coven members?" Tristan asks.

I take Gabriel's hand again. "If we're all inside the Dome, I guess we can traverse there now."

The three women jump when we appear before them, but to their credit, they immediately recover their composure.

"You killed her, didn't you?" Lydia sounds more stunned than angry. She's picked some of the freshly grown holly and pinned it to her dress.

"Technically, my brother did. Between the remnants of the lien and the coven vows, I'd have been torn apart."

Katrina maintains the poise and diplomacy of the consummate politician she is. "That really is a technicality. I can't believe you did it."

It's a little unclear whether she means morally or magically.

"It was kill or be killed. Or at least, kill or be dragged further into servitude and isolation, while my family suffered."

Lydia tosses her long red curls over her shoulder dismissively. "It's none of our business anymore. We serve you now. I, for one, am no breaker of binding vows."

"We'll do your bidding. And we certainly won't harm you. Just don't expect us to be your friends," Clarissa drawls. It's weird seeing her without either Dani or Astrid in tow. The little group must have left London at zero notice.

"Did any of you know what she was doing to me?" I ask, trying to regain the offensive.

Clarissa seems the most likely to have been in on it, though Lydia potentially also had a hand in the Seb/Chris thing, considering she was there when we met.

"I just can't get my head around the idea that she left you in charge," Katrina says, shamelessly skirting the question.

"Neither can I," I reply.

Lydia crosses her arms. "She just wanted her coven in good hands. And that meant two things to her: power and lineage. And let's face it, you were winning on both fronts."

I stare at an individual holly berry, letting my vision blur. Could it really be that simple?

None of them have so much as looked at Gabriel, despite the fact he's a pretty bloody difficult person to ignore. Or Tristan, who's got all that vampire magnetism in his favour. Lavinia's weird misandrist beliefs are still clearly fully in force.

"I'm staying here in Mannith," I say. "I don't want this."

"It's not something you can ignore," Lydia says, echoing Tristan's warning. "It'll call to you. Ignoring the call would destroy you."

Clarissa narrows her eyes. "Why on earth would you throw this away?"

I shrug. "I guess my priorities are different to yours. Maybe I'll be forced to change my mind in time. But for now, I want the three of you to run it, as regents. I'd hand it over, if we could find a way. But this is the best I can manage. What do you say?"

Katrina, who's standing in the middle, looks at the other

two, clearly having some kind of telepathic debate that I'm being kept out of. Then she lowers her head.

"Some of us would rather you came back with us and led us properly. Others are delighted you're stepping back. Either way, we agree to serve you, but also to your regency plan."

Clarissa scowls. "You still don't know much about the coven, do you? You'll manage a year—three, maximum—before it drags you back to us. More's the pity."

"Then in a year's time, or three years' time, or whenever, I'll make a new plan. But for now, I want to do this the easy way. So, are you all agreed?"

"We are," they say, with varying levels of enthusiasm.

"Are you going to brand us?" Lydia asks.

"Hell no," I reply. "I've had enough of those for one life-time." This one would be entirely in my control and my favour, but nothing could make me do it.

"Then how are you doing it?" Clarissa demands.

Everyone's warnings about how I'll be dragged back eventually are playing on my mind, despite my best attempts to focus on the present rather than worrying about the future.

"I'm your matriarch," I say, with more confidence than I feel. "I'm going to declare it, and it's going to be so. I declare the three of you regents of the London Coven. Protect it and let it thrive. And don't do anything I wouldn't do."

I'm actually also going to have Tristan draw up some employment contracts, that set out precisely what they can and can't do. But I don't tell them that—I don't think they'd approve.

They all kneel before me, which is exactly the sort of vibe I'm looking to avoid.

"I guess you could all head back to London now," I say. "But I'm getting married on Christmas Eve. I'd love to have you there. I can't think of a better way to show there's no hard feel-ings about the past and to look forward to the future."

Lydia's eyes widen still further. "I'd love to. But I need to get back to my family in the Cornish Enclave. We make a big deal out of Christmas. And the walls between realms are particularly sensitive from then until Twelfth Night. Perhaps I could visit in the new year, and you could show me around properly?"

I nod. "Enjoy Christmas. And that sounds great. I'd love to visit your hometown someday, too."

Clarissa simply sneers. "I don't think so. Unless you're going to order my attendance, in which case, as a loyal coven member, I guess I wouldn't have a choice."

I shake my head, letting her off the hook. To be fair to her, she probably wants to get back to Dani (though she'd have been very welcome, too) but she could have had the basic politeness to make an excuse.

"I'll come," Katrina says. "As a formal representative of the leadership of the London Coven. And as a friend."

I give her a hug. "Thank you. There's a nice pub in town called The Windmill. We'll get you a room there."

"Tris, do you want to come, too?" Gabriel asks. "We should probably celebrate the fact Mannith's relationship with the vampires is back on a positive footing."

I expect him to blanch at the very idea, but he lowers his head. "It would be an honour."

I guess politeness really, really matters to vampires. I try not to think about the impact he's going to have on my catering arrangements.

Within a few minutes, everyone's dispersed, until Gabriel and I are alone.

"That should keep the problem at bay for a while," Gabriel says. "But the others are right. Pretty soon, the coven will start to call to you. Within a year or so, you'll be physically struggling to resist. Putting yourself in danger if you try."

"I'll cross that bridge when I get to it," I say. "And in the meantime, I'll research ways to pass on the leadership position without doing myself harm."

"I'm glad to hear it. Because I've got an early wedding present for you," he says. "Or maybe an early Christmas present. One that relies pretty heavily on you not disappearing back to London."

He reaches into his pocket and pulls out an envelope.

I examine it. "What is this? A honeymoon?"

"We absolutely are going to book one for the new year. But in the meantime, no, this is something more permanent."

I open the envelope, and pull out a deed, an estate agent's brochure, and two glossy leaflets.

"I'm not sure I understand."

"You never did tell me your plan for combining your career with not going back to London, but I thought I could guess."

"Find a chambers in Leeds and persuade them to take me, basically."

"No need. I've bought you this building in the city. And I've registered the company. Liminal Chambers. Look at the leaflets."

One is what I'd expect—touting my legal defence and human rights services. The other describes me as the country's foremost expert in supernatural law.

"I've already put feelers out. There's so much demand. People wanting to get out of liens, or make sure they stick. People considering more modern contracts to formalise equally magical arrangements. People wanting advice before agreeing to faerie deals."

"This is amazing." My head is spinning as I think about the possibilities. "I'm so unbelievably touched that you thought seriously about my career. And I'm so impressed you've pulled all this off. I can't wait to get to work."

It's utterly perfect. I'll make this work. I'll drown out the siren song of London and the coven.

He wraps an arm around me. "Let's enjoy the wedding and Christmas before you get too absorbed in work. But over the holidays, we could drive over there so you can check the building out."

I reach up and kiss him. For several minutes, I'm lost in the kiss, conscious only of him and of the rightness of all this.

"Now can I take my fiancée to bed?"

I glance around. "Why wait for bed?"

If we take a few paces away from the lane and under the oaks, this spot seems perfectly secluded. A little chilly, but nothing we can't remedy with a spell or two.

I wave my hands airily, and a thick, soft tartan rug and a delightfully hot fire both burst into being a few metres away. As Gabriel watches, I stroll over, lounge on the rug and run my hands down my body until my clothes fall away. The fire keeps away most of the chill, but allows just enough of the winter air to reach me that all my sensations are heightened.

Gabriel can't stop staring.

"Join me?"

He doesn't mess around with even token hand gestures. One minute, he's standing up, fully dressed. The next, he's kneeling beside me, as naked as I am.

"Should we throw up some sort of bubble?" he asks.

I grin. "It's very unlikely anyone would spot us out here. But that tiny risk that they might is part of the fun."

He leans over and kisses me on the lips, stroking my face and hair as he does so. Then he works his way lower, kissing my chin and neck, then my upper chest. I'm breathless and sighing before he even reaches my breasts. He kisses around the nipples, which are as hard as anything thanks to both the cold and the arousal, then takes first one and then the other into his mouth, licking and sucking until I'm a squirming mess.

While I murmur his name and run my fingers through his hair, he continues his journey downwards. By rights, kisses on my stomach and hip bones should feel slightly less erotic, but I'm getting more excited by the second.

For a moment, I look around me. It's almost a full moon—the actual one will hit on Christmas Eve in time for the wedding—and the sky is full of the sort of stars you never see in London. Barely even see in the centre of Mannith. There's not a cloud to be seen. The tree branches are stark against the clear, glowing sky and the holly bushes are bright and beautiful and giving off a wild, festive scent. There's the gentlest of breezes, but otherwise, everything is silent and still, like we're the only things in the universe.

I look back down at Gabriel. He looks so utterly beautiful in the winter moonlight, his pale skin almost glowing, his hair wild. I can't believe I was ever afraid of him, ever doubted that we were meant to be together.

It's not like I was wrong about him, exactly. He does have a dark side. He has done bad things, and, honestly, there's a chance that at some point in the future he'll do more. But he has lots of good qualities, too, and perhaps I can help to bring them to the fore. Besides, we complement each other perfectly. Light and darkness and all that. I want to make this work. And I believe we can pull it off.

He adjusts his position and works his way lower still, kissing my inner thighs.

"Shush. Stay still. Don't make me fix you in place," he says, in a teasing tone, as I writhe and gasp.

I almost wish he would. Now I know it's safe, there's something unbearably hot about being overpowered and in his control, like that night at the hotel in the summer. But there'll be plenty of time for playing around with power dynamics. Tonight's not about games. It's about love, and a physical representation of the things we've declared to each other.

He slips his head between my thighs and continues with his kisses, staying maddeningly away from my clit.

When he finally gives in and lands a little kiss there, I cry out. I can almost feel him smile. Then he stops teasing me and starts licking me in earnest.

I'm close after only a minute or two. Tempting as it is to have him push me straight over the edge—or, knowing him, string it out until I'm begging him for release—I lift his head up.

"Come here," I whisper.

When he props himself up, I reach out and take hold of his erection. A few strokes, and his moans are almost putting mine to shame.

Without further ado, I guide him to my opening. "I want you, Gabriel," I say, remembering the effect those simple words had on him that first time.

He slips inside me in one smooth motion, kissing me on the lips again at the same time. I thrust my hips up beneath him, grinding into him as he pushes me down.

My first orgasm hits me in seconds, as I call his name and cling to his neck. As the waves of pleasure subside, he takes me more gently but more deeply. The sensations rise again, until we cry out in unison, like wolves in the night.

For a moment, he rests on top of me, as though we're one entity, then he rolls off, lays down beside me, and guides my head onto his shoulder.

We lounge there in silence, looking at the night sky and at each other.

"I love you," he says.

"I love you, too," I reply. "And I lust for you, and I like you, and all the rest of it. I can't wait to be your wife."

He waves a leisurely hand and covers us with a warm cashmere blanket. With my eyes half closed, I can sense that he's done something subtler, too, some sort of protective circle to keep away animals, the elements, or surprised visitors.

I snuggle into him under the soft wool, and drift into an entirely contented sleep.

THIRTY-EIGHT

"Stay still," Chrissie orders, as I slump down in my chair. "We need to find you the perfect dress."

"This dress *is* perfect. So were the last five. Every dress you've ever made me has been beautiful."

"But this is your wedding dress. I aspire to a whole different level of perfection."

It's Christmas Eve morning. We're in what used to be our shared bedroom at our parents' house. The ceremony is in just over twelve hours. We're cutting this slightly fine.

Chrissie waves her hand over my body, and the long, lacy satin sheath turns into something with a bodice and a wide skirt. She shakes her head, and the neckline lowers, waves it again, and embroidered patterns bloom. It's the most exquisite one yet.

"Still not right." Chrissie waves her other hand in the air, scrolling through holographic images of historical dresses, celebrity dresses, and random, stunning brides. It looks like a futuristic government control room in a cheesy spy film. If the spies were obsessed with subtle differences between satin and silk, lace and organza, cream and off-white.

She pulls two of the floating holograms towards her and

stares at them like she's trying to see into the model brides' souls. "Right, the skirt from this. The corset from that. And a little something all of my own."

She closes her eyes this time, like she's really having to concentrate.

"Close yours, too," she insists. "And once again, will you please sit still?"

I do as she commands, and a few seconds later, feel lace against my skin and a sensation of my waist being pulled in.

Chrissie gives a little gasp. "Now *that's* perfect. Open your eyes."

I do, and when I look into the mirror, I gasp in turn. The others may have been perfect in their own way, but this is perfect for me. Embroidered lace. A tightly fitted corset top with a heart-shaped neckline and no sleeves. A tiny waist, then a billowing, floor-length skirt with petticoats and a long train.

"Thank you so much."

She hugs me gently, careful not to disturb the delicate folds of fabric. "Nothing could make me happier. Honestly."

"Mum, come and see what Chrissie made me," I call. She's several rooms away, but we have ways of making ourselves heard.

She traverses into the room in a cloud of flour and sighs loudly. "You look beautiful, darling. And well done, Chrissabelle."

"Just wait until I've done her hair and make-up," Chrissie replies, grinning.

"How's the food coming along?" I ask.

Mum shakes her head dramatically. "It'll never be ready in time."

Chrissie laughs. "You say that about every Christmas meal ever. And they're always amazing."

"But most years, I'm not catering for half the town, our old enemies, representatives of the bloody London Coven, and a couple of vampires."

"Use magic, Mum, seriously," I say, for the fourth time in three days.

She looks at me like I've suggested poisoning the food. "I'll use the magic of my cooking skills. And perhaps a few tricks to help things along the way. But don't think for a moment that I'd whip up my own daughter's wedding feast out of thin air. And for the record, the cake's been made with no magic other than a mother's love."

For some reason, while no one has a problem with doing it with clothes and things, creating food entirely out of magic tends to be viewed as inhospitable at best, unwholesome at worst. You can use magic like a super-powered food processor or particularly fast oven, but there are only so many corners you're supposed to cut.

I smile. "Thanks, Mum. It'll be amazing. Just don't stress."

She smiles right back. "I know, love. I just want it to be perfect for you."

"Why don't we all have a glass of fizz before we send Sadie off for her bath?" Chrissie suggests.

"I really will never get the food finished if I do that," Mum replies.

"One drink," I say.

"One drink. Then I need to instantaneously smoke some salmon."

Chrissie waves a hand, and a bottle of champagne appears.

Mum puts her hands on her hips. "What have we discussed about magicking food and drink out of thin air?"

Chrissie laughs. "I just took it from the stash for tonight. A bit of magically transporting fizz from one place to another never did anyone any harm."

We've just settled down with our glasses when there's a knock at the door. "Is everyone decent?" Dad calls.

"One second," I reply, slipping out of my dress and into a furry white robe. I don't want anyone else to see it until I'm totally ready.

"Right, come in and get a drink!" Mum shouts.

"Ready to walk me down the aisle?"

Dad takes the glass of champagne that Chrissie offers him. "I distinctly remember you telling me, aged about fifteen, that being 'given away' is sexist and outdated."

"It is. But I'm marrying an old enemy of this family. I need that public demonstration that you approve. For my benefit, Gabriel's benefit, and the benefit of the entire town."

Dad pulls me into a hug. "It'll be my honour. If he makes you happy, I approve. And it'll increase the odds of the alliance lasting long term."

I hug him back. "Thank you, Daddy." He almost looks like he's about to cry. It's the sort of tenderness neither his enemies nor his officers and lieutenants would ever believe him capable of.

There's a sudden noise downstairs, as Liam, Shane, and Ray burst back into the house.

"We're upstairs," I shout. "Come on up. Get a drink."

Chrissie looks pointedly at her watch. "We need to start getting you prepared."

"There are hours to go yet. Let me say hello."

The three men pour into the increasingly cramped room. They're dressed in tracksuits and have the ruffled air of people who've done a lot of physical exertion.

"Right, that's the Witches' Church prepped for the ceremony and Mannith Town Hall prepped for the reception," Shane says. "They were both already decorated for Christmas, but we've added a few extra flourishes. And if you've ever wondered how many fir trees it's possible to fit into a chapel, we've got an answer."

Ray hands me a pack of photographs. "Do you want to take a look and check you like it, or would you prefer a surprise?"

I don't ask how he's developed them so quickly. Like Mum's cooking or Bren's drawing, Ray's photography is a strange blend of magic and natural skill. He's going to be official photographer this evening, though sadly he'll only be able to capture the surroundings and the human guests. The rest of us don't show up in photos.

"I'm going to indulge myself and look at one," I announce.

The one I draw from the pack shows the huge door to the church, ringed with holly in unnaturally vivid shades of red and green. Fairy lights, real candles, and tiny golden bows are interwoven into the foliage, and a gigantic wreath sits on the door itself.

I grin at the three of them. "Wow. If that's the door, I can't wait to see the inside."

Shane laughs. "Ray did all the artistic design. We just did the lifting and shifting. A bit of magic, a bit of old-fashioned strength."

Mum grabs the pack of photos. "Sadie may have the patience of a saint, but I sure as hell do not. Let's have a look at your handiwork."

Chrissie joins her, and they flick through. Their "oohs" and "aahs" are reassuring.

"By the way, the non-practitioner guests will actually be able to see the inside of the church, for once," Liam says. "We bumped into your fiancé and his uncle, working some sort of incredibly elaborate spell to make that temporarily possible."

"Did he seem nervous?" I ask.

"I'm not convinced he's physically capable of nerves, are you?" Liam replies.

Strangely enough, I don't feel nervous either. I tend to worry and overthink far more minor decisions, but this is utterly right.

"Okay, that's enough," Chrissie says, giving the final photo a nod of approval and draining her glass. "Everyone, get back on with what you're meant to be doing, or start getting yourself ready. Sadie needs to be bathed. Then it's hair and make-up time."

"Thank you, everyone," I say. "Both for the practical help and for supporting this wedding full stop. It means so much to have all the family around me."

Or nearly all the family, anyway.

"Does anyone know where Bren is?" I'm not sure I want to hear the answer. "Do we know if he's actually coming to the service?"

Mum crosses her arms. "He'll bloody well be there." She makes it sound like he's still a naughty five-year-old, whom she'll physically drag into church if she needs to.

"He's going to come," Liam confirms. "And he's not going to cause a scene. But it'd be optimistic to expect him to help with the preparations."

I shrug, as though it doesn't really matter. And logically, it doesn't. But it'd mean so much for him to say he approved. Or at least, didn't actively disapprove.

"Sadie, bath. Everyone else, shoo," Chrissie says, with an air of finality this time.

They all file out without a word of complaint.

Chrissie leaves me alone to go and run the bath, then reappears two minutes later to tell me it's ready and lead me into the master bathroom. The water of the oversized roll top tub is a delicate pink, with perfectly preserved rose petals floating on top, and tiny pieces of what appear to be citrine and rose quartz decorating the bottom. A complex mixture of floral and woody scents fills the air.

"Jasmine, mostly. A bit of ylang ylang. Vervain, inevitably. More rose. Some pine. A hint of lavender. A few spices. My priority was love and seduction, in the crystals and the scents.

But I'm also aiming to keep you calm and make things a bit festive. Now get in. You're to do nothing but soak up all the essences and vibrations for thirty minutes. Then I'm going to come and wash your hair."

"Thanks, sis," I say, throwing off my robe without a hint of self-consciousness and slipping into the water.

A few hours later, and somewhat against the odds, I'm ready with time to spare, entirely thanks to Chrissie's beauty skills and ruthless organisation.

I smell amazing, from a combination of the lingering effects of the ritual bath and liberal application of one of Chrissie's home-made perfumes, comprised of similar scents. My make-up is mostly subtle and delicate, but my lips and nails are a bold red for an element of drama. My hair has been fixed into loose curls, then pinned up in an elaborate cascade. The dress looks even more astonishing than it did earlier, after Chrissie spent a good thirty minutes tightening it in places, adjusting the shade in almost imperceptible degrees and adding extra detail to the lace.

I'm wearing the shoes Chrissie designed for her own wedding, which are higher and sparklier than I might have chosen, but make an excellent "something borrowed" to go with the new dress and the old pearl and rose quartz choker Mum gave me earlier.

"Right, done," Chrissie announces. "You look stunning. And I'm not saying that just because you're my sister, it's your wedding day, or it's mostly my handiwork."

I hug her wildly, while she fights to keep me slightly at arms' length in the interests of protecting the dress. "Thank you so much. Now we just need something blue."

Chrissie frowns. "Good point. I've got some sapphire earrings back at my place that you could borrow."

There's a knock at the door, and without waiting for a reply, Bren strides in. "I've got a better idea."

Chrissie puts her hands on her hips. "Oh my God, Bren, you are not supposed to be in here. No one is supposed to see her till she makes her grand entrance."

But he's wearing a tuxedo and the white rose buttonhole the men of the bridal party are meant to sport. The relief that he's actually planning to turn up is enough to push any irritation clean away.

"You can come in," I say. "Chrissie, why don't you go and get yourself and the twins ready?"

"I will be back here at ten, with Mum and your little flower girls. You'd better be ready to roll. And Brendan, if you say anything to upset the beautiful bride-to-be, I will literally murder you."

With that, she disappears into the ether.

I gesture to the chair near mine where Chrissie had been perching, and Bren sits down. "Well?"

He looks at the ground. "I just wanted to say good luck. Or congrats. Or maybe even 'you have my blessing', if that doesn't sound completely condescending."

I stare at him until he meets my eye. "That means a lot. Honestly. Coming from you more than from anyone else."

He steeples his hands over his mouth and nose and takes an audible breath in. "I do not like your fiancé. I suspect I never will. I still wish your soulmate was anyone else. But I believe you love him, he loves you, and despite your somewhat twisted dynamic, you're right for each other."

"Thank you, Bren."

"I'm going to be there tonight, if I'm welcome. I'm not sure I'm a good enough actor to spend the evening pretending I'm overcome with joy or I adore the bridegroom, but I'll stick on a smile and I'll stay polite and calm. I'm going to avoid talking to him and to his duplicative, scheming 'best woman', not to be petty, but because I don't trust myself to say the right thing."

"Maybe stop talking now."

He smiles. "Here's your something blue."

He reaches into his pocket and hands me something small and sparkling.

"Is that Nan's old brooch?"

She'd worn the silver and aquamarine ornament every day. I'd loved it and always wondered what had become of it after she died.

"She gave it to me. And made me promise to give it to you when the time was right. I considered handing it over after what happened a few months ago, as a way of saying I was sorry, but it seemed way insufficient. Now, I hope it's a way of demonstrating that I mean it when I say you have my blessing."

I study the brooch, running my hands along it. "Thank you."

As always with Bren, there are some irritating aspects mixed in with the sweet sentiments, but it's good enough for me. There's an awful moment when I wonder whether this is all a double-bluff and he's put some terrible enchantment on the piece of jewellery in order to stop the wedding in its tracks, then I shake my head and pin it on. I can't think like that.

"Now stand up and let me draw your wedding portrait. And if you like, after the ceremony, I'll grit my teeth and do one of you and him together."

I comply, and we stay there together in companionable silence while he works.

He's just putting the finishing touches to it when there's another knock on the door.

"Come in."

It's Dad, Mum, Chrissie, and Ceri and Chi, all dressed up and looking handsome, beautiful and adorable respectively, though Chrissie has had the decency to slightly dial down her natural jaw dropping looks, to avoid any risk of upstaging me.

They gasp at the sight of me, then gasp again at Bren's drawing. When he holds it up for me to see, I do likewise. It's true to life, but captures some essence of me and of my joy and anticipation that even the mirror doesn't quite show.

"Quick family portrait?" Bren asks.

Chrissie looks at her watch, as she's been doing at ten-minute intervals all day.

"If you make it super-fast."

As I pose with my family around me, I'm utterly, obscenely happy, and the ceremony hasn't even started yet.

An hour later, me, Dad, Chrissie and the twins are waiting outside the church, on the white pebble path that's been lined with hundreds of candles for the event. Mum and Bren travelled with us, but have gone inside to join the rest of the family and the other guests who've already arrived.

Chrissie is frantically doing some last-minute neatening up of the whole group—we travelled as far as we could in two specially decorated black Mercedes, but we'd forgotten to factor in the fact that half the magic of the Witches' Church is that you have to walk the last mile. The journey is uphill, through woodland, and tonight at least, freezing cold. Which isn't ideal in a billowing floor-length dress and massive heels. Between us, though, we worked enough protective magic to make it doable, and now we've made it in one piece, we're already all laughing about it.

The door to the church looks as impressive as Ray's photograph suggested, and the area around the entrance has been similarly decorated. But what's most impressive—and presumably Gabriel's handiwork—is that the church actually looks whole for once, rather than appearing to be a ruin from the outside. Its Gothic magnificence is quite something. Organ music is streaming out—played by Shane—and the multitude of candles that always illuminate the inside are glowing through the elaborate stained-glass windows, casting swirls of colour over the frosty churchyard.

"We're going to attract so many spirits," I murmur.

"I think some of them are on the guestlist," Dad replies. "Your nan was never going to content herself with just giving you the brooch. And I'd be actively astonished if Maeve Thornber didn't rouse herself to see the results of her machinations."

Before I can respond, the church bell strikes eleven and organ music blasts out from the church. Dad takes my arm, and Chrissie falls into step behind us, with a sleepy but over-excited flower girl holding onto each hand.

"Ready?" Dad asks.

I look up and smile at him. "I've never been more ready for anything in my life."

Despite my brave—and honest—words, I'm trembling as we push open the doors and step inside. Dad keeps me steady on my heels, and Chrissie's comforting but commanding presence behind me keeps me moving forward.

I attempt to take a calming breath, but it catches in my throat as I take in the sight before me. Full-size fir trees, decorated in red and green, line the aisle and appear to be growing out from the floor. They fill the church with a festive scent that no scented candle could replicate, helped along by the incense that billows in the air. Wreaths and holly adorn every pew. While the church usually boasts hundreds of candles, today there must be pushing a thousand—enough to make the usually dim space bright even though the sun set hours ago and even to provide some protection against the chill of the winter night.

Overhead, what appear to be free-floating tiny stars flicker and shine. In stark contrast to the otherwise wintry theme, roses of all shades bedeck the altar.

I take the decorations in during my first few steps, and then switch my attention to the crowd. The invitations were somewhat open, and most people associated with the Thornbers or the Sadlers have made it—practitioners, human acolytes, and affiliated businesspeople and dignitaries. For the most part, the two sides are keeping a wary distance, the former on the right, the latter on the left, but there are no obvious hostilities. I see my old friend Becca, and a few friends of Gabriel's who I vaguely met in the summer and would love to get to know better. Tristan and Charles are there on Gabriel's side, Katrina on mine. My mother and brothers are in the front row, smiling at me.

As Dad warned or promised, we've even got a few spirits. I'm not usually able to see them. When the magical gifts were handed out, that one seemed to skip me. I don't know whether someone like Liam, who's much better in that regard, has worked some special magic to help me along, or whether they are projecting to me on my special day.

I make eye contact with my beloved nan, and subtly point to the brooch, winning myself a smile which dispels any lingering doubts that Bren might have had ulterior motives in giving it to me. Gabriel's mother is right at the front on the Thornber side, staring at me with genuine warmth. What was it she once saw, that made her so certain her son belonged with me?

Gabriel's father's ghost is conspicuous by his absence, which is probably for the best on several levels. There are other, less distinct ghosts that I don't recognise. They could be distant relatives, or just residents of the church's graveyard attracted by the light, music, and joy of tonight's proceedings.

It takes me a couple more steps to absorb all of this, and then the surroundings and the crowd fade away, and all I can see is Gabriel, waiting for me at the front of the room. With his usual composure, he stares straight ahead, not turning his head even a fraction to confirm I'm there. Though to be fair, he no doubt has his own ways of seeing. His dark blond hair glows in the candlelight, and his closely tailored tailcoat and tight black trousers make me think of the body beneath. I take slow step after slow step, staring and taking him in.

Nikki is standing by his side, performing the role of what would usually be called best man. She's wearing a similar outfit to him, cut to her somewhat different shape. Lacking quite his self-control, she glances back at me, exhales, as though she'd been terrified I wouldn't show, then smiles at me.

Bren's staring at her like she's simultaneously his most hated and most adored person in the world. Like he wants to kiss her and destroy her all at the same time. Most people would struggle to understand his expression, but not only do I know my brother, I know that exact feeling all too well. I never did get to the bottom of what happened between them, but I know one thing for sure—at the reception, I'm playing matchmaker.

It seems to take forever to reach the front. There's a part of me that can't believe this is really happening. There's another part that can't believe it's going to be *allowed* to happen—our love has always felt somewhat star-crossed, and there remains a chance someone could still throw a spanner into the works. I'm marrying my family's old enemy. There are surely people from both sides who don't approve of this.

Then all of a sudden, I'm there, by Gabriel's side, and the awed look on his face pushes any lingering worries to one side.

"You look so beautiful," he whispers.

"So do you," I whisper back. It's true, from the way the light falls on his cheekbones to the copper shade of his eyes, right down to his forest-green silk waistcoat. Handsome doesn't quite cut it.

The priest is from one of the churches in Mannith town

centre. He's not mesmerised—no halfway respectable practitioner would do such a thing—but he looks somewhat confused
to find himself conducting a wedding in the infamous Witches'
Church on Christmas Eve. Still, he starts proceedings without
hesitation, half traditional wedding service, half midnight mass.

I'm in a dream as I recite my vows, say "I do" and hear
Gabriel say the same thing back.

A surge of utter contentment hits me. I'm married to a man
I adore, who adores me in turn. I'm back in my hometown at
last, which in addition to being special to me, is literally blessed.
We've extended that blessing out to cover neighbouring towns,
with no bloodshed save that of someone who wanted to hurt me.
I've got a brilliant new career to embrace and my family nearby.
Admittedly, the spirit of the London Coven is in my blood,
desperate to drag me back and make me rule it. But that's a
problem for another day. And it's one Gabriel and I can solve
together.

The whole thing takes a very precise hour. As the organ
music bursts out again, the bells ring for our marriage, and for
midnight, and for Christmas Day. We take each other's hand
and lead the procession out of the church. We step outside, kiss,
and right on cue, it starts to snow. Because it's Christmas, it's
Mannith, and we do traditions right.

EPILOGUE

NIKKI

It's two AM at Mannith's wedding reception of the decade, and against all the odds, no violence has broken out. More than that —everyone gathered in the Victorian splendour of Mannith Town Hall actually seems to be having fun. There's drinking, there's dancing, there are adorable children playing underfoot despite the late hour. People loyal to the Thornbers and those connected to the Sadlers are interacting with each other in a way I've never really seen before, despite the alliance having nominally been in place for several months. There's nothing like a dynastic marriage to shore things up.

The couple at the centre of it all are half holding court, half lost in their own little world. Gabe and Sadie both look beautiful tonight and they're radiating power. They've barely let go of each other's hands or broken eye contact all evening. They've danced and kissed like no one's watching, despite the fact the eyes of the entire town are firmly on both of them.

I once essentially told Sadie that she'd be crazy to marry Gabe. Which was pretty disloyal of me, considering that he's my best friend and there was literally nothing he cared more about in the world. I feel reassured now, mostly, watching them together like this. Sadie's powerful in her own right and she's gone in with her eyes open. And Gabe's trying to do this right, I know he is.

It's impossible to look at them together and not smile, both at the love on their faces and at everything this represents for the town. And yet I do still worry that one day the fragile equilibrium will snap. As I told both Sadie and Bren, though I tend to let Gabe's faults go, I understand them better than anyone.

Officially, I'm not on duty tonight. The trouble is that when your best friend is also both your immediate boss and the sworn leader of the organisation you're loyal to, the boundaries between work and play get pretty blurred. I'm not drinking anything but water. And I'm standing in an archway at the back of the room, keeping a careful eye on things.

Every time my eyes forensically scan the crowd, looking for trouble, they inevitably end up falling on Brendan Sadler, despite my best attempts not to gaze in his direction. I probably shouldn't be surprised that he's here—it is his sister's wedding, after all—but given his feelings regarding Gabe, I'm amazed he was physically able to sit through the ceremony.

He looks stunning tonight, all dressed up in the most elegant of formalwear, raw power blaring out from him once again. The perfect Born Practitioner heir.

He's surrounded by supplicants, well-wishers, and wannabe lovers—mostly the sort of pretty little things I kept teasing him about liking—from both the Sadler side and the Thornber side. If we're even meant to talk about sides anymore. Which of them will he go home with tonight?

It's not like I have to be stood all alone. I could seduce some pretty little thing, too, if I felt like it. Or at least have a laugh with my friends. But any time anyone comes near, I make the briefest of polite small talk, then send them away.

I'm trying to stay calm and focused, but I can't help but think of those evenings, just me and him. The way he'd listen to my teachings like I actually had something helpful to share with him.

Those days are over, though. He can bend the world to his will with a simple thought again now. Which rather negates the value of my advice on learnt magic.

I'm being unfair, I know I am. Maybe he *would* have dropped me anyway once his powers returned. That would certainly have been consistent with the Brendan Sadler the Thornber faithful traditionally believed in. But let's face it—the reason he's blanking me is because he believes I betrayed him.

And just to make things super fun, so does Gabe. When he found out I'd been keeping the truth about Bren's lack of power from him, he was more stunned than angry. He probably would have killed most other acolytes for such a staggering show of disloyalty, but I don't think his mind could quite process the fact his best friend had so spectacularly lied to him by omission.

I shut down and refused to answer any questions on the topic whatsoever. And he just shook his head and let it go. If he had any suspicions about why I'd done it—which he surely must have—he didn't raise them. He still asked me to be his "best woman" for the wedding, but he's hurt, I know he is. I tried to tread some uneasy middle ground, and now no one who matters to me entirely trusts me.

Maybe I stare at Bren for a fraction of a second too long. Or maybe his sixth sense is just that bit too good, now he's back to full strength. Either way, in the middle of laughing charmingly at some hanger-on cracking a joke, he catches my eye.

For a moment, he just stands there, staring at me with the strangest expression on his face. Not any one thing, really. Just pure emotion. Love and hate and anger and sadness and joy in one unholy mix.

The next thing I know, he's pushed through the little crowd surrounding him, and he's coming over.

I've never backed down from a challenge or a fight. I always pride myself on my confidence and poise, my ability to triumph in any situation. But as he strides towards me, I almost run for it.

"It's a beautiful wedding, isn't it?" he says when he steps under the archway into my secluded space.

I nod, unspeakably grateful for the simple, civil words. "Gorgeous. And no one's killed anyone yet, which has to be a bonus."

"They do look good together," Brendan says.

I'm amazed he can get the words out, even if it's essentially objective fact at this point.

"I'm glad you came," I say, managing to make eye contact, but only just.

"The entire family gave me very little choice on that front." He gives the barest hint of a smilc. "But I wanted to see my little sister get married, even if it's not the groom I would have chosen. And honestly, I wanted to see you."

My heart constricts. "I've been here all night."

"I've been psyching myself up for hours. I didn't know what to say. I didn't know if you'd even want to talk to me."

I reach out a tentative hand and rest it on his arm. His wild, super-sized aura flares. "Why would I possibly not want to talk to you?"

He looks down at where I'm touching him. "Did you *ever* want to talk to me? Ever want to spend time with me? Or were you just doing his bidding, as usual?"

I take a tiny step closer so our bodies are almost touching. I want to press myself into his chest and make him understand. But we're in public and we both have reputations to uphold, so I try to retain some decorum.

"Gabe didn't want to send me. He didn't think you'd be into me, and he didn't think it was a good use of my time either way. He wanted to use just the sort of generic girl we kept joking about being your type. I insisted on doing it myself. So yes, I went in as a spy. But it's true what I said before, about how I'd been curious about you for a long time."

Bren peels my hand off him. "I can't believe you played me like that. I've never opened myself up to anyone like I did you. I've never felt like that about anyone. And it was all just pretend."

"It wasn't pretend, Brendan, I swear. I might not have gone in with the best of intentions, but from that very first day, none of it was fake. Everyone I'm close to has always thought of you as the enemy and you genuinely have done some terrible things —but from that first moment I helped you draw magic out of the earth, I just wanted you with an intensity I couldn't quite explain."

He closes his increasingly fiery eyes. Are the memories running through his brain like they're running through mine?

"I bet you had such a laugh about it all with your beloved best friend, didn't you? All those sweet, private moments. Maybe they weren't entirely fake, but I bet my every action and every emotion was carefully conveyed to the person I hate most in the entire world."

I reach out a hand again. I just want to touch him. I want to somehow force the truth of all this into his blood.

"I... I gave some reports," I say, my voice trembling. "I had to. But just inconsequential things. Never ever anything about your power being diminished. And never anything about any burgeoning romance either. I played it like we were casual friends. I shared some things you told me about your family or your thoughts on the alliance and the vampire deal. And I feel bad enough about all that."

His aura surges again. He looks like he could cry. He looks like he could burn the place down.

He thinks what I did is awful, obviously. He doesn't understand what it cost me to keep the truth of his lack of magic from Gabe. I've never hidden anything of that magnitude from my best friend before. I wouldn't have thought myself capable of it. But had I let slip the fact that Brendan had no real power to call on, I really do think he'd have struggled to resist the temptation to kill him. And from the first time I had a proper conversation with Bren, for all his equally obvious faults, I wouldn't have been able to bear that.

From nowhere, Bren wraps an arm around my waist and pulls me against him. "You know the worst thing? I believe you. Maybe I even forgive you—and I'm not the forgiving sort. Worse still, there's a bit of me that would like to try again."

I nod frantically. "Bren, please. You can trust me, I swear."

He tightens his hold. "I believe you'd try to make it work. That you'd try to be honest with me. But though I know it isn't romantic or sexual with Gabriel, when push came to shove, I still think you'd choose him over me. And I can't put my heart or my body in that position."

I swallow hard. I want to deny it. But doesn't he have a point? I might have managed not to tell Gabe Bren's biggest secret, but it was hardly like I announced I was in love with Bren and ordered Gabe to leave him alone. My feelings for Bren are real. But my friendship with Gabe goes back decades. It's entirely platonic, but no weaker for that.

I glance over my shoulder and gesture lightly to where Gabe and Sadie are still slow dancing, lost in each other's gaze and embrace.

"Look at the two of them. There's a true alliance now. You'd have nothing to worry about, any more than Sadie does."

"I disagree. There's trouble still to come. I gave Sadie my blessing, but not everyone agrees with this marriage. The Colsons are some of our most loyal acolytes, and they didn't show, for a start. Hardly surprising, when the girl their dead son loved is marrying the guy who killed him. And what about this London Coven thing? A year or two, and it'll call to her. What'll he do when she tries to leave?"

I shiver. I've had similar thoughts about the future.

We study the bride and groom and the other dancing couples for a few moments, then Brendan releases me and holds out a hand. "Enough talk. Let's dance."

My eyes widen, but I allow him to lead me out of the archway and over to the black and white tiled dance floor. I feel like people are staring, but maybe I'm just being paranoid. We're far from the only couple across Sadler/Thornber lines. But other than Sadie and Gabe themselves, we're probably the most high-ranking and noticeable example.

We dance to a slow song, our bodies pressed together. It's everything I want. I wish I could freeze the moment in time.

"I meant everything I said tonight," he whispers, as the song comes to an end. "I hate what you did. I still don't trust him an inch. And I'm terrified to open myself back up to you again."

I freeze in his arms.

"I also meant everything I said before. There's trouble to come. But if you'll have me, I'll take my chances and face it with you."

With that, he leans in and kisses me. My heart races, every muscle in my body relaxes until I almost collapse in his arms. I kiss him back, heedless of who might be watching and what the future might have in store.

A LETTER FROM THE AUTHOR

Dear reader,

Huge thanks for reading *The Binding Mark*, I hope you were hooked on Sadie and Gabriel's journey. And Bren and Nikki's story this time around, too! If you want to join other readers in hearing all about my new releases and bonus content, you can sign up here:

www.stormpublishing.co/sophie-williamson

If you enjoyed this book and could spare a few moments to leave a review that would be hugely appreciated. Even a short review can make all the difference in encouraging a reader to discover my books for the first time. Thank you so much!

There's a pretty sensible piece of writing advice that suggests you shouldn't waste energy on writing a sequel until you've got a deal on the first book. But whether I'm an eternal optimist or just a big fan of the world I've created, I couldn't resist starting work on this book almost as soon as *The Twisted Mark* was completed. So I'm so happy that everything worked out and I ended up being able to release it just three months after the first book!

I've lived in London for over a decade now, and it's a place I have complicated feelings about. I loved developing Mannith last time around, but it was fun to shift the setting to a real city this time.

I've mentioned before how I love writing characters who tread a fine line between villain and love interest, and I continued to have great fun with Gabriel in this book. But I also thought it would be interesting to play with the more unusual idea of someone who's half villain, half platonic friend. Hence the complicated nightmare that is Lavinia.

On a related note, having made Bren essentially turn out to be the bad guy in Book 1, I basically had to give him a romance arc this time around. Villain romance inception! The whole Nikki/Bren thing started life as essentially a dare from one of my CPs, but it ended up making the cut and being one of my favourite parts of the book.

And then there's the vampires. Much as I adore witches, vampires were my first supernatural obsession, and it was so fun to get to include them here.

Finally, if you've worked your way through two of my books to get to this note, you'll know by now that I love twists, unconventional endings, and dark elements. But I've got to say, I also loved channelling cheesy, small-town Christmas movie vibes for this ending. As Nikki points out in the epilogue, there are undoubtably challenges ahead, but for now at least, I wanted to give Sadie and Gabriel a full-strength, no-holds-barred happy ever after.

Thanks again for being part of this amazing journey with me and I hope you'll stay in touch. Pretty much every passing reference in this book—from the Cornish Enclave to Gabriel's demonic extended family to the more obscure inhabitants of Mannith who keep popping up—come with potential future storylines attached. And in the meantime, if you visit my website and sign up to my personal mailing list, you can download a prequel short story from Gabriel's point of view...

Sophie Williamson

www.williamsonwords.net

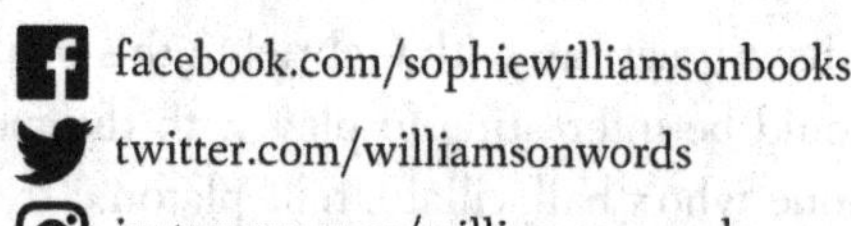
facebook.com/sophiewilliamsonbooks
twitter.com/williamsonwords
instagram.com/williamsonwords

ACKNOWLEDGMENTS

Last time around, I went wild with the acknowledgments. The thing about getting out the sequel just a few months after the first book is that I don't really have many new people to thank. If you helped me before, you probably helped me this time, too.

I do know a bit more about how Storm work by this stage in the process. So having focused all my love on my editor, Kathryn Taussig, last time around (who totally deserves thanks again, so thank you!), let's widen it out. Thanks to Alexandra Holmes for all the logistical support and helping to turn words on a page into an actual book—that's a kind of magic right there. And thanks to Anna McKerrow and Elke Desanghere for all the publicity stuff, especially my gorgeous graphics. The risk of singling people out is the odds of missing someone, so thanks in general to the whole team. And on a related note, thanks again, too, to my agent, Marlene Stringer.

I thanked my CPs last time around, and this one had essentially the same pairs of eyes on it. But special shout out to Rachel, for inadvertently inspiring the Nikki/Bren angle. Eve, I hope you're glad I cracked and went for a proper happy ending this time, after your romance writing heart was so upset by the conclusion to Book 1! Marith, thanks always for the support. Adrianne, I'm glad you got to read this one at an earlier stage— and thanks for all the social media boosting, too.

Freddie, I felt like I said everything I possibly could say last time around, but as a quick addition, on top of all the more serious and fundamental stuff, thanks for the framed prints of the covers. You've really helped make this whole experience extra-special.

And finally, thanks to everyone who's read, reviewed, or interacted with the first book. All the love for it that started pouring in while I was working on the edits of this sequel kept me motivated in a way nothing else could.